THE
FOXFIRES
TRILOGY

About the Author

E. C. Hibbs is an award-winning author and artist, often found lost in the woods or in her own imagination. She adores nature, fantasy, and anything to do with winter. She also hosts a YouTube channel, discussing writing tips and the real-world origins of fairy tales. She lives with her family in Cheshire, England.

Learn more and join the Batty Brigade at

www.echibbs.weebly.com

Also by E. C. Hibbs

THE FOXFIRES TRILOGY
The Winter Spirits
The Mist Children
The Night River

THE TRAGIC SILENCE SERIES
Tragic Silence
The Libelle Papers
Sepia and Silver

Blindsighted Wanderer
The Sailorman's Daughters
Night Journeys: Anthology
The Hollow Hills Tarot Deck

Blood and Scales (anthology co-author)
Dare to Shine (anthology co-author)
Fae Thee Well (anthology co-author)

AS CHARLOTTE E. BURGESS
Into the Woods and Far Away: A Collection of Faery Meditations
Gentle Steps: Meditations for Anxiety and Depression

The Mist Children

The Foxfires Trilogy
Book Two

E. C. Hibbs

First published June 2020

Cartography, cover design, cover artwork, book production and layout by E. C. Hibbs

Cover stock image from AdobeStock

Author photograph by Allison Page-Hibbs

www.echibbs.weebly.com

For Tara,

Amazing friend and boss.

Without you, I never would have known the frozen north.

Prologue

At the outskirts of Poro village, the sound of friendly jeering carried over the frozen surface of Lake Nordjarvi. On the banks, three children – two boys and a girl – ran about with lengths of rope in hand. They had stuck a pair of antlers into the snow and were testing how far away they could get before the lassos landed short.

The girl tossed her rope and it fell pathetically, three feet from the antlers. The boys shrieked with laughter.

"What kind of throw was that?" one of them snorted.

The girl glowered. "Shut up, Niko. Mine was better than any of yours!"

"Alright then, let's try something else, and see who's best," said Niko. "Boden, get the antlers and pretend you're a reindeer, and then Inga and me will try to catch you! Whoever lassos first wins!"

"Fine!" Inga snatched her rope with newfound vigour.

Boden dug the antlers out of the snow and held them against his head. He loped around, kicking and snorting like a calf. Inga and Niko tossed their lassos, but both missed, and they gave chase.

"Come on!" Boden shouted. "You can do better than that, can't you?"

Niko shoved his way past Inga and threw his rope. It snagged on one of the antler points, but slipped off before it could tighten.

"I'll get you!" he cried, the words broken with laughter.

Excitement overcame them and Boden soon gave up impersonating a reindeer. He sprinted towards the Nordjarvi. The others ran after him, giggling wildly, slipping as they left the bank and emerged onto the lake. There was still a layer of snow lying on top of the ice, but their shoes sank straight through it, all grip gone.

Boden lost his footing completely and went flying onto his backside. The antlers fell from his grasp and skittered across the surface. A lasso landed neatly around his torso.

"I got you!" cried Inga triumphantly. Then she turned on Niko. "I win!"

"Shut up," Niko glowered. He glanced uneasily at the antlers. "Why did you throw them?" he demanded.

"I didn't throw them. I dropped them," argued Boden as he disentangled himself from the rope.

"We've got to get them," said Niko hotly. "My Papa will be so cross if I lose them. He said he needed them later to make new knife handles."

"Well, go and get them," said Inga. "The ice is still thick enough to walk on."

Niko nodded – more to himself than the others. He had never liked being out on the water in the middle of winter. Even though he'd crossed lakes every year on the migration, and sometimes came ice fishing with his family, there was something about doing it which unsettled him.

It was a frozen purgatory; water, yet solid: a thin skin which he could crash through at any moment. Eevi, his older sister, had told him: if you fall under the ice, the cold would kill you before you could drown, before you could even shout for help.

He shuddered. He couldn't wait for summer.

But he couldn't let Inga and Boden see he was afraid, either. They were his friends, but they would still tease him. So he straightened his back and headed towards the antlers.

They were several feet away, but the distance seemed like miles as the anxiety tightened his muscles. The soles of his shoes were made from the fur of a reindeer's head, and the strands, sticking out in all directions, gave a fantastic grip. But he still moved slowly, listening for the slightest crack.

After a few tense seconds, he reached the antlers and snatched them up. He let out a small smirk of relief and turned back to his friends.

But they weren't looking at him. Their eyes carried on past him, wide with alarm. Inga's mouth had fallen open and her breath fogged in the air.

"What is it?" Niko asked.

They didn't reply. Niko slowly turned.

A boy was standing on the ice, just out of arms' length. He looked about the same age as them, or perhaps a year younger, with sandy blonde hair reaching to his shoulders. Ugly burn scars shone on his cheek. He was dressed in a baggy coat, decorated with the patterns of Poro, but Niko couldn't remember seeing him before. He was dripping wet from head to toe, clothes clinging to his skinny body. His eyes were closed.

Niko shivered just looking at him. How had he not frozen solid, soaked as he was? Where had he even come from?

"Uh… hello," he said uncertainly.

The boy didn't reply.

Niko threw a confused glance at Boden and Inga.

They were muttering between themselves, but they didn't come closer to investigate. No matter that the ice was still sturdy; they all knew that too much weight in one place was never a good idea.

Niko fidgeted, rocking back and forth on his heels. Unsure of what else he could say, he asked, "What's your name?"

The boy tilted his head slightly. The movement was strange and fitful, more like a bird than a human. He kept his eyes closed.

"I'm Aki," he said, barely above a whisper. When he opened his mouth, water spilled out and dripped down his chin.

Niko fought the urge to recoil.

Inga took a tentative step forward. "Is everything alright?"

"I think so," Niko called back.

"Do you want me to get my Mama?" she offered.

Niko refused, then addressed Aki again.

"Hey… aren't you cold? Do you know you're not supposed to go out in wet clothes?"

Aki didn't say anything. The only movement was another twitch of his head.

The silence began to get uncomfortable, and Niko went to ask something else, to break it. But then Aki murmured, so quietly, he had to lean in to hear.

"It's my birthday."

Niko hesitated.

"Happy birthday," he said. "How old are you?"

"I'm five."

"Uh… well, do you want to play with us?"

Aki nodded woodenly, but didn't take a single step. Then he opened his eyes.

Niko screamed. They were completely white and clouded over, with no hint of colour at all. It was like they belonged in a corpse.

He bolted for the shore, for his friends, but they were screaming too. Niko slipped, arms flailing frantically as he tried to stay on his feet. Dense mist spread around him, as though a giant being had let out a lungful of breath into the winter air. It enveloped him first, then Boden and Inga as they tried to run.

There was a slippery sound, like fish squirming over each other, followed by the gnashing of teeth. And then, as though the icy layer had given way beneath them, the children disappeared from view.

On the hill nearby stood the Poro mage, Enska. He had heard the commotion and arrived just in time to see Inga fall. His eyes strayed to the little boy, standing in the middle of the lake, and his blood ran cold.

There was nothing to be done for the youngsters now. He turned back and hurried towards the village.

"Lilja…" he muttered under his breath. "Lilja, what have you done?"

Chapter One

Formless. Endless. Infinite. That was what it was like.

Lumi's grasp was firm around Tuomas's wrist as she pulled him up through the air. He could still feel Elin's arms pressing into him even as he melted away, body-soul and life-soul spinning around each other in expectation.

He sensed a faint pressure, like a bubble popping around his entire body. It surrounded him, but it didn't hurt. He passed through it, into the World Above, and he opened his eyes.

A spectacle of light greeted him. It was still dark, but the night seemed to stretch on forever. The stars shone so close and so brightly, he could have reached out and touched them. In their constellations, he saw the faces of nameless Spirits, their eyes turned on him. Lumi's aurora flowed all around like a river of green and blue. It drifted in a wind he couldn't feel, swelled into waves and dipped in waterfalls.

Unlike her, he was still in his physical body. It wasn't the same as when he had travelled here in trance, but he didn't care. He was aware of his skin and bones encasing his souls in a peculiar fleshy cage, yet every fibre of him felt unbound. He was cold and warm all at once; he breathed without needing his lungs; he saw with a depth beyond mere human vision. Up here, he was not only Tuomas, the boy from Akerfjorden, but something else: something older and more powerful. He was a mote of dust suspended in the starlight. He was a Spirit in human form, and he was free.

Lumi hovered in front of him. She still had the face of a girl, but it was clearer than he remembered, as though her skin had disappeared and left only an impression of light. It shifted around itself, fusing perfectly with the aurora's trails. She was solid and yet not, pure energy even as she held him. Then he blinked, and she was a fox; then a simple orb. But more than seeing her, he *felt* her: the part of her which could have taken any form in any space in time, and he would have always known it to be her.

Welcome home, she said inside his head. There was no need to move her lips; no need to vocalise anything.

Tuomas glanced back at the World Between. It was so far away. He could see the curvature of the land, covered with snow and ice. The largest trees were the size of twigs; entire forests seemed no denser than the hairs on his arm; reindeer herds several hundred strong could have been blotted out with his thumb. Even the mountains and the islands were like mere pebbles, forcing their way upwards through an unmarked sheet of whiteness.

So small. So distant. So perfect.

I can't stay forever, he said to Lumi. *I promised Elin I'd be back for the migration.*

And you will, she replied. *I shall take you back there myself.*

When?

Whenever you want. You are not a prisoner here. But first…

She reached towards him and grasped his hand.

Come with me, she said. *There is somebody who you need to see.*

Who? Tuomas asked.

The Sun Spirit.

He froze. He didn't know what he had been expecting when he chose to come to the World Above, but meeting his Spirit mother took him by surprise.

How? he asked. *You can't go near her... can you?*

He remembered walking the forests with Lumi during the Long Dark and how she had recoiled at the faintest stretch of daylight. Even the blue dusk was almost too much for her. But Lumi sensed the concern as it flowed through his mind, and though he couldn't see her smile, he felt it.

You forget that she raised me, she replied. *She and I cannot shine onto the World Between at the same time. But we are above such physicality here. I can take you to her.*

Before he could say anything else, she pulled him through the sky. Something warm and powerful spread over the back of his neck and an overwhelmingly bright light engulfed him. He spun away, but Lumi kept hold of him.

Do not be afraid to look at me, a voice said. It was barely above a whisper, yet soft and gentle, like the clear sweetness of a summer's day.

He turned back to the light, but wasn't blinded again. There was no fiery white glow which the people of the Northlands saw, but something as formless and flowing as Lumi. He couldn't make out a face, yet in his mind he sensed a radiant beauty cloaked in gold, hair like flames, eyes brighter than the stars. She twisted into shades of red, yellow and white. He smelled honey and pollen, and the dryness of baking soil under a blazing sky. Heat was everywhere; more heat than he'd ever felt in his life, yet it wasn't unbearable. It didn't burn him, but soaked into him, spreading through his entire being.

He sensed himself in that warmth. He was a part of it. A part of her.

Lumi let go of him and drew back to a respectful distance. The Sun Spirit reached out and swept him close. Inside his chest, Tuomas felt his life-soul pulse with happiness. He had never known his human mother, but in an instant, he knew what it would have been like to be held by her.

My dear son, the Sun Spirit said lovingly. *My dear Red Fox One.*

He melted into the sound of her voice. He recognised it. He had known her for so long; longer than the boy called Tuomas could ever imagine.

I love you so much, my sweet son, she whispered in his mind.

I don't understand, Tuomas said. *Wasn't I here before I came into this body? I was with you after the time of the Great Mage, I know I was.*

True, the Sun Spirit said, *but it does not matter. No matter how endless we are, no matter whether it is by a day or an age, I will always miss you. Every day in your human life, I have gazed down upon you, as your sister has every night. Every day, I longed for you and loved you.*

She moved away from him a little so Lumi could approach. The aurora bloomed around them, filled with souls. He regarded them: lives once lived now frozen, frolicking here with Lumi until they chose to leave the World Above and be reborn. There were thousands of them – millions – more than he could have counted even if he had tried until the end of time.

Tuomas, Lumi said so only he could hear, *I want you to remember this moment. This is your mother. Not the Silver One. She is mine, though she would rather have you over me.*

Tuomas nodded. How could have ever been a fool enough to think that any Spirit besides this one was his parent?

Lumi heard his thoughts, and so did the Sun Spirit, and he sensed a red flare deep within her.

I will keep you from my sister while you are here, she promised. *She will never steal you away again, my son. Beware her. No matter what she says to you, do not allow her to ensnare you again.*

Tuomas felt the gravity in her words, but he didn't worry. He was too happy and contended to be concerned about anything. No amount of dreaming could compare with the beauty; no days spent floating in summer lakes could come close to the weightlessness. Time had no meaning and could have stretched on forever. He could spend an eternity up here trying to touch every star and swim every inch of the sky.

Lumi and the Sun Spirit let it lie. They swirled around him: a perfect fusion of warm and cool; then Lumi swept him into her grasp and floated away. She pulled him close to the skin of the World Between, flicked her tail and sent out a fresh wave of Lights. They were freezing cold – colder than even ice could possibly be. A shiver passed through Tuomas but he ignored it. It was too wonderful. *She* was too wonderful.

He eyed the tiny huts below; the snow extending to the horizon.

Can they see us down there? he asked.

Lumi smiled. In response, she took his wrists and wheeled him in a circle. With every movement, the Lights grew stronger until they filled the entire sky.

Dance with me, she said.

The Sun Spirit rose and fell. With each passing day, she regained her strength. At first, she was barely a line of golden light above the horizon, but slowly she grew, rising a little higher and shining a little further. It was so gradual, Tuomas didn't even notice it. He was too busy frolicking in her glow, spinning through the World Above with Lumi, soaring and diving in ways no bird could ever match. He ran and floated, swam and danced. There was movement everywhere and nowhere at the same time. He felt the heartbeat of all living things pulsing through him, like the most perfect drum had struck up the rhythm of truth.

It would be so easy to stay here. If the events of this winter had taught him anything, it was that things were so much larger than he ever could have imagined. Sometimes he thought they were *too* large. How could so much have happened in such a short space of time?

How long has it been? he asked Lumi one night. *How long have I been here?*

Does it matter? she replied.

He smiled at her. No, it didn't. Not at all.

You will have to go back soon, she added. *The reindeer are becoming restless. It is almost time for the people to move on to the summer islands.*

Tuomas's heart jumped. *It's almost migration?*

He turned to the World Between and looked at the herds. She was right. Many of the animals were already corralled outside the villages. Tuomas imagined himself standing in the middle of them as he had so many times before, a lasso in his hand, eyes darting over the ring of stampeding deer to find one with his mark cut into its ear. In his memory, he caught the musky smell of them; the sound of the tendons clicking in their knees.

Lumi's hand appeared on his shoulder, so faint, he barely felt it. He glanced at her.

You want to dance again? he asked.

In a moment, she said.

Tuomas noticed why. A faint light was coming towards her, like a cloud which had somehow formed arms and trailed stars in its wake.

He recognised it at once. He was the Spirit of Passage: the one who attended all things as they died and delivered them away from the World Between. Practically every day, this entity had approached Lumi with human souls. Tuomas watched as he passed three to her, then disappeared into the night.

She cradled the shining souls like infants. Tuomas drew close to see, and instantly realised they had come from three children. They were older than that – as old as the first lives which they had lived; yet they rang with youth, still moulded to their last existence.

Is that all I get? one asked.

I am afraid so, Lumi replied tenderly. *But now you can dance with me, with your ancestors. They are all waiting for you in the Lights.*

As she spoke, she flicked her tail and a faint green glow appeared behind her. In it, Tuomas felt other body-souls drawing close: ones who had been generations of mothers and fathers. Their happiness and love flowed through him as though he had sunk into a cool lake in summer.

Lumi stroked them and began to separate body-soul from life-soul. The first would stay with her up here, and the second sent back, to give its power to a new-born thing. It could be a tree, or a reindeer, or another person. Nothing was for certain.

Then she paused in alarm.

What is it? asked Tuomas, but he felt it as much as she did. The souls were pushing against her. They seemed to be repelling her… no, *dragging* away from her. Something was trying to rip them out of her grasp.

The ancestors bristled with fright. Lumi raised her voice.

Carrying One! Why do you bring me these? The Horse-Riding One calls for them!

Tuomas frowned at her. *The who?*

Lumi didn't answer. She was too concerned with holding onto the souls. The Spirit of Passage drew himself out of the darkness so he was facing her. He inspected the souls, and Tuomas felt a spark of horror flash between him and Lumi.

He is not what calls, White Fox One, he said. *I am so sorry… I thought you might be able to fight it this time.*

Lumi's tail stilled for a moment, as though she had been struck. Then she swept it again, more furiously, and behind her, the Lights flared bright red.

No… she snarled. *I will not let them be taken! They stay with me, or they go to the Deathlands… to no place else!*

One of the souls almost escaped her arms. Tuomas flew forward and tried to help her hold onto them. Their glow dazzled him, but then he noticed the brilliant light was marred by patches of black, like soot from a filthy hearth, or water that had lain stagnant and turned into a bog.

What is that? What's wrong with it? he cried.

The Spirit of Passage drew close. *They are strong. You cannot fight, White Fox One!*

I will not let go! Lumi shouted.

A cry suddenly surrounded them. It wasn't coming from the soul; it wasn't from anything in the World Above. It echoed from beneath them, deep in the lakes and rivers and the frothing sea… like a little boy, screaming and howling.

The intensity of it shook Tuomas the most. It was warped by *taika* into something shockingly powerful.

21

Give me my friends! Give them to me!

Tuomas's heart beat so fast, it hurt. His own *taika* twisted inside him like a blade. The tug intensified. Lumi held on firmly, refusing to let go of the souls even as they slipped further away from her.

Release them, White Fox One! begged the Spirit of Passage. *It is too late!*

The Lights raged like wildfire. The ancestors cried out in sorrow.

Lumi screamed with distress and loosened her grip.

She turned away, unable to watch the souls disappear. Tuomas spun on the spot, hands to his chest as he struggled to keep control. The shrieks grew gradually quieter, and then vanished, as though they hadn't been there at all.

Beside him, Lumi lay shaking in the weightless dark. The Lights slowed to a faint watery dance, but their edges still glowed a fierce red.

Tuomas trembled. It felt like time had slowed to a complete standstill. The air was dense and dark, with a murkiness he had never sensed before.

Lumi? What just happened? he asked, quietly, in case his own stream of thoughts could somehow tempt the thing to come back.

Something I always wish I will never see again, she replied, not looking at him.

Her tone sent a shiver through him. It was like splinters working into his muscles.

He glanced between her and the Spirit of Passage, but both appeared just as upset as the other, so he turned to look at the World Between. There was no sign of the souls anywhere. They had completely disappeared.

But then he noticed something which hadn't been there before. A thick white mist had spread across one of the lakes near Poro. Some of the other lakes and streams were covered with it too, and it was slowly snaking down the frozen Mustafjord towards Akerfjorden.

Lumi! he cried. *What is that?*

The fright in his voice got her attention. She shot to his side and peered over his shoulder. Her tail froze in mid-air.

She grabbed his wrists. Her thin fingers clutched him so tightly, he thought she might break his bones.

What is it? he asked again. *Is it dangerous?*

Yes! Stay here! she pleaded. *You cannot risk it!*

I need to go and warn them! Tuomas insisted, trying to pull his hands free. *Lumi, let go of me! You're hurting me!*

Lumi tightened her grip. Her eyes were fierce. It wasn't a girl who was holding him anymore; it was a mountain.

I forbid it! she snapped. *Stay here! Please! Listen to me!*

He hesitated. In a heartbeat, he was on the ice again at the start of his quest, terrified of her, protected only by a magical circle as thin as her own patience. In the face before him now, he saw the danger; felt the power of thousands of years in the hands crushing his wrists. Back when he had first met her, she could have ripped his soul out if she'd wanted.

She still could.

But he was just as powerful as her, just as old. He had stopped her Lights in the past; he was the only one able to counter her.

He tasted lingonberries. The aromas of flowers lingered in his nose; summer warmth on his skin, spreading like fire, burning…

He pushed back. The *taika* bloomed out from his chest so violently, he lost control of it. Lumi's eyes flashed with panic. For the smallest moment, her grip loosened.

Stop it! she cried. *You have forgotten... You do not understand! Stay here! Tuomas, no!*

Before she could say another word, Tuomas wrenched himself out of her grasp.

She tried to pull at him, but he forced her away, and then he was spinning and cartwheeling through the air. Stars whirled, falling and rising as he plummeted downwards. There was a faint tug as he slipped through the invisible barrier between the Worlds.

Something tore, like fabric wrenched in two directions.

He became heavier. He drew icy breath into his lungs. Then he slammed down on his back and gasped, all the wind knocked out of him. Gravity pressed on him; his muscles ached as though he had run for miles. It was so strange to be held to the earth, unable to spin and twist like before. The ground was hard and cold – had he landed on a rock? No, it was too smooth for that. Ice.

He opened his eyes. The crisp air stung them; it was denser here than in the sky. It felt like he was underwater, with pressure on him from all angles, trying to push his skin in on itself. Tiny icicles formed on his lashes as he blinked.

He wiggled his fingers and rolled his ankles, then looked around. He was in the middle of a huge expanse of frozen water. Two steep cliffs stood on either side; their rocky flanks rendered white by a thick blanket of snow.

He was on the Mustafjord, just outside Akerfjorden. Exactly the same place as where he'd stood to leave the World Between.

Then he glanced over his shoulder and gasped with fright. The mist was still billowing down the fjord like an avalanche, coming straight towards the village – and straight towards him.

Chapter Two

Tuomas struggled to his feet but immediately slipped. The ice grazed his chin. Feeling for blood and finding none, he started to crawl towards the bank. He took a deep breath and forced it out in a shout.

"Hello? Paavo! Henrik!"

His voice cracked as he used it. He stood up again and staggered forward. His legs flew in all directions like a newborn deer. The cold bit at him; the wind channelled through the fjord and sliced down his neck. He had never felt so relieved to be fully clothed.

He looked over his shoulder. The mist was getting closer. On the surface, it looked no different than any sea mist which might have swept in, but the way it moved unnerved him. It was coming fast – too fast.

"Hello!" he cried again, stronger this time. "Anybody?"

He noticed a stirring among the huts. Doors opened and the silhouettes of curious people poked outside.

Then the mist caught up with him and swallowed him whole. He coughed as he breathed it in and he stumbled onto all fours. The village faded to a faint outline, then disappeared altogether.

"Henrik!" Tuomas yelled again. The echo surrounded him; everywhere he looked, he saw only a thick grey wall. When he extended his hand, he could barely make out his own fingers. It was denser than any fog he had encountered before. He felt as though he were underwater; the tendrils curled around his legs and wormed down to his lungs. His heart fluttered; his *taika* quivered, like something was plucking at it.

There was a sudden slithering noise somewhere behind him, as though an entire shoal of fish had somehow found itself on the surface of the ice. It cut through him and for a horrible moment, his vision failed and was encased in darkness. It pulled and sucked at him, right down to his souls.

He panicked and sprinted as fast as he could, hoping it was in the right direction.

"Henrik!" he cried.

"Tuomas!"

He skidded to a halt. "Paavo? Is that you?"

"Yes, where are you?"

"I'm here!"

"Follow my voice! This way!"

Tuomas focused on it and ran. A silhouette emerged from the cloud. They saw each other at the same time and bolted forwards. Paavo flung his arms out and caught Tuomas as he stumbled, almost toppling both of them.

"Are you alright?" Paavo asked.

"I'm fine!" Tuomas replied. "Come on, we need to go!"

The slithering grew louder. Paavo snatched Tuomas by the front of his coat and began bundling him across the ice. After several awfully slow moments, the village swam back into view. A sizeable crowd had formed on the bank, many people coughing and sputtering as the mist swept between the huts. Henrik, the old mage, was standing in front of them all, a drum in his hands.

As soon as Tuomas and Paavo were past him, he drew his arm in a line across the entire width of the fjord and hit the drum with an antler hammer.

A protective line flew up and the topmost layer of snow shot into the air. Tuomas felt the energy rise until it formed a great invisible wall, hugging the ground and all it touched. It wasn't a complete circle; there wasn't enough time to spin one of those, but it still held. The mist on the other side pooled against it and formed a thick grey block. The vapour which had reached the village slowly broke off from it, hanging in the air like a low cloud.

Paavo immediately pulled Tuomas into a crushing hug. Tuomas gasped for breath as his brother showered his head with kisses.

"I'm so glad to see you!" Paavo cried. "You have no idea… Are you sure you're not hurt? Are you cold?"

"I'm fine," Tuomas insisted. "I'm happy to see you too. Paavo, let go, I'm alright!"

He squirmed free and squinted through the barrier. He could still hear the slithering.

"What is that?" he asked in an undertone. "Can you hear that?"

"Hear what?" Paavo frowned.

Tuomas stared at him, then at Henrik, but nobody else seemed aware of it. He held his breath, not daring to tear his eyes from the mist. But then the strange sound receded as if it had never been there.

The village leaders hurried forward. Maiken was only wearing a single layer and hadn't even tied her shoes closed. Anssi walked close to the barrier and went to touch it, but Henrik quickly shouted a warning.

"Leave it be! Shields and circles are always weaker on the inside."

Anssi lowered his hand. "Will it hold?"

"Not forever," Henrik admitted, "but it will do for now."

Sisu turned to look at Tuomas. "Did you bring that mist with you?"

"No," Tuomas replied quietly so nobody would overhear. "I saw it coming, that's why I came back."

He glanced around at the crowd to make sure they weren't listening. The children were spluttering; parents gathered them in their arms and slapped their backs. They seemed happy to see him, but there was a dark wariness in their eyes which took him by surprise. Several were whispering to their neighbours. Even with the distance between them, Tuomas caught some of their words.

"He's back…"

"He fell out of the sky…"

"Son of the Sun…"

Tuomas took a deep breath to quash a wave of unease. He could forgive their alarm at the mist, but people he had grown up with were now regarding him as though he were a complete stranger.

Mihka watched from the side. His hair was still a shock of white – Tuomas supposed that if it was going to turn back to its original colour, it would have done it by now. Considering what had happened to him, it was a small price to pay for insulting Lumi.

Then he realised someone was missing. There was no sign of Lilja.

Before he could say anything, a figure burst from the throng and flew at him, almost knocking him to the ground. He looked down at a head of shiny black hair.

"Elin? What are you still doing here?"

"I stayed to wait for you," she said, her voice muffled by his shoulder. "I had to – I was the only one who knew where you'd gone!"

"Luckily," Paavo added. The relief on his face slowly transformed into anger.

Henrik struck the drum a second time to strengthen the barrier.

"It should be fine until we leave," he said to the leaders. "But I don't think we should take any chances. We should set out as soon as possible. We were going to go in a few days anyway. And now we don't have to wait any longer," he added, throwing a pointed glance at Tuomas.

"Alright," said Maiken, then raised her voice to address everyone. "Go put some layers on and meet us at the central fire pit."

"What is that?" a man called, pointing at the mist.

"The barrier is just a precaution, Jukka," Henrik replied. "If all that streamed into the village, we wouldn't be able to see a thing."

His voice was quiet, but deep, and carried a respect and assurance that settled even Tuomas's mind. Slowly, the crowd dispersed and returned to their huts. The vapour clung to them as they moved, but their footsteps were sound from years of walking the same paths between the shelters.

When they were alone, Henrik hobbled to Tuomas and began checking him over.

"I'm fine," Tuomas insisted.

"I'll be the judge of that," Henrik snapped. He rolled back his eyelids and held two fingers to his wrist to check his heart rate. Finally, he let go and nodded.

"I'm sorry for waking everyone," Tuomas said.

"Oh, you'll be sorrier than that by the time I'm done with you," Paavo snarled. He grabbed a handful of Tuomas's coat and hauled him up the bank. Elin hurried behind them, her eyes wide.

When they reached one of the outer huts, Paavo elbowed the door open and pushed Tuomas inside. He tripped over a reindeer skin on the floor and fell.

"What were you thinking?" Paavo hissed. "How was I to know what had happened or when you were coming back, huh? You just disappeared! I woke up one morning and you were gone!"

Tuomas held up his hands. "I'm sorry! I didn't know… how long was I up there?"

"Nearly a month," Elin said quietly from the corner.

He stared at her. "*What?*"

"Exactly!" Paavo continued. He knelt in front of Tuomas. "Listen, do you remember how upset you were when you thought you'd lost me? Well, how do you think I felt when you vanished with no warning? My first thought was that a wolf had gotten to you, just like Father! If it hadn't been for Elin, I wouldn't have known where you were! And even she couldn't tell me how long you'd be up there! You'd already been away for the entire Long Dark… I was worried sick!"

His eyes blazed with angry tears. "Don't you ever do anything like that again, do you hear me, Tuomas? I don't care that you're a mage or the Son of the Sun or anything at all, except the fact that you're my brother! No matter how old you get, *I am your brother*. Your *family*. Do you understand?"

Tuomas bit his lip and nodded. "I'm sorry. Really, I'm so sorry."

Paavo ground his teeth in frustration and strode across the hearth. His shoe knocked a log as he passed and it tumbled into the embers with a flurry of sparks. Elin scrambled out of the way as he snatched his coat off one of the roof beams and stormed outside.

Tuomas and Elin sat still for a moment. Paavo wasn't the type to lose his patience, so when he did, it set Tuomas's teeth on edge.

He glanced around the hut in an effort to distract himself. The beams were made from single limbs of wood, bound to their neighbours with reindeer tendons spun into twine. Various tools and handicrafts hung from knots on the walls. There was nothing frivolous here; everything had a use, but it was intricately decorated with carvings and beads, or dyed with earth pigments. Even the hearthstones were arranged so lines of smaller rock wove between the large ones, creating the image of a tree.

"He's really mad," Tuomas said quietly. "I've never seen him that mad."

"Can you blame him?" Elin replied as she started wrapping up in her layers. "He's got a point."

"I know."

"Are you going to talk to him?"

"When he's calmed down. He won't listen if I try now."

Elin finished tying her coat closed and headed for the door. "Are you coming?"

"Hold on," Tuomas muttered. He tore open a nearby food sack and grabbed the first thing he found: a parcel of flat salmon cakes. The sight and smell reminded him how ravenous he was. He stuffed them into his mouth, barely chewing before he swallowed.

Elin stared at him. "Hungry?"

"Starving," he said, holding a hand over his lips so nothing would fall out. He snatched a wooden cup, dipped it into the pot of water near the hearth and gulped the contents down. When he was done, he collapsed against one of the beams with a gasp.

"Didn't you eat anything up there, or something?" Elin asked in shock.

Tuomas shook his head. There was no need for any food in the higher realm. The more he thought about it, the more he wondered how he had even managed to survive.

The answer intruded into his mind as though he had pricked himself with a needle.

Red Fox One.

He screwed his eyes shut and forced the thought away.

"Are you alright?" Elin asked.

"I'm fine," Tuomas said.

"Are you sure? You look like someone walked over your grave."

"I'm fine, Elin. Really. I'm just… hungry."

She held his eyes for a moment longer before stepping outside. He knew he hadn't fooled her; she was as sharp as an arrowhead. But now was no time to dwell on Spirit matters. He decided to deal with that baggage later, when he was alone, able to truly think about what it all meant.

He took one more salmon cake from the parcel, then got to his feet and followed Elin out of the door. The two of them walked in silence towards the fire pit. A circle of logs lay around it, laid with thick reindeer hides. The fire itself was still smouldering with the ashes of the evening's gathering, and a ring of icicles had formed around it where the snow had melted and then re-frozen in the bitter night. Everyone's breath rose in clouds and they huddled together for warmth. A faint breeze was blowing from the north, and though it wasn't strong, it bit through to the bone.

The lingering mist dispersed the low light into a shadowy purgatory. Already, it was starting to lift, but Tuomas was glad to reach the other villagers. It was thinner away from the water, and it was a relief to be able to make out individual faces and bodies as they sat on the logs.

Tuomas and Elin squeezed in beside Paavo. He tried to catch his brother's attention, but Paavo didn't move. Tuomas looked down guiltily and nibbled on the salmon cake.

Sisu got to his feet and everyone immediately silenced.

"I respect you all enough to not keep secrets," he said. "We don't know what happened here tonight. I'm happy to say that Tuomas is back with us…"

He motioned to Tuomas and a multitude of eyes immediately turned on him.

"And now that he is," Sisu continued, brandishing his hands at the mist, "in light of whatever this is, I think we should leave for the migration as soon as we can. I think we can all recognise that it's not a normal fog. Too dense for that."

Tuomas watched in silence. Timing was everything when it came to the migration. They needed to travel through the mountain passes and into the north, where the summer grounds lay on the ancestral island of Anaar. If they left early, the mountains could still be clogged with snow; too late, and the reindeer cows risked dropping their babies before they reached the coast.

"Aslak," said Maiken. "how quickly do you think we can go?"

"The reindeer are ready," Aslak replied. "We've corralled them all and checked their teeth. Most of them are healthy enough. The females will start walking as soon as we open the gate."

"So, we only need to gather the supplies?" asked Anssi.

"Yes, and they're practically all ready, too. They just need loading into the sleighs."

"Can we do it now? Does everybody feel able?"

There was a faint muttering among the crowd, then a woman raised her hand.

"Wouldn't it be best to wait until this mist has gone?" she asked. "The migration route takes us down the Mustafjord and then through the little pass in the cliffs. We can't use that now."

"And even if we could," another man added, "what if there's something out there that we can't see?"

At that, Maiken turned to look at Tuomas and Paavo.

"Did either of you see anything?"

They both shook their heads.

The leaders exchanged worried glances. Several villagers made the sign of the hand to ward off evil. Even in the gloom, Tuomas felt them all looking at him, like a physical weight on his chest.

"Wait a moment," an older man said, "what about the caretakers? If there's something on the Mustafjord, we'll still be here when Henrik's shield comes down."

"There's nothing on the Mustafjord," Henrik said.

Tuomas's breath caught in his throat. He had a mind to speak up, but he hesitated – it would suit Henrik to know, but everyone else would panic. So he bit his lips together and resolved to tell them later.

"But," Henrik continued, "with such low visibility, it's dangerous to go across the ice, and we can't afford to wait on the chance the mist will burn away before we leave. It's too thick for that."

Sisu's eyes darted in all directions as he mulled over the situation.

"I agree with Henrik," he said. "As for the reindeer… it's not going to be easy for us, but we could go through the forest around the west flank of the fjord. If we harness a tame leader, the rest of the herd will follow."

Aslak nodded. "That could work. It will take all of us to manage, though."

"What about the sleighs?" another man protested. "The trees are too dense!"

"We'll just have to take our time," said Sisu. "It's not the best solution, but I'd rather take it than risk riding through that mist."

"So, you want to leave right away?" asked Paavo. "Should we go and get the reindeer ready?"

"We should be fine to catch a few more hours' sleep," Henrik said. "The barrier will hold, and I'll stay up to make sure it remains in place. Tomorrow will be a long day."

"Then it's decided," said Maiken, clasping her hands together. "Everyone, go back to bed. I'll shout when it's time to move."

The crowd immediately stood, parents sweeping sleepy children into their arms. A couple of the youngsters coughed gently, their eyes heavy and red with tiredness. Paavo got to his feet too and headed for the hut. Tuomas cagily watched him go, but his brother didn't wait or look back.

He went to follow, but then Maiken spoke up.

"Tuomas, stay here a moment, please."

Elin hesitated, but Tuomas gave her a nod to tell her to go. She offered a small smile, then walked away.

Tuomas crammed the rest of the salmon cake into his mouth. He skirted the edge of the fire pit so he was closer to the leaders and sat down again. Maiken, Anssi and Henrik remained, but Sisu ushered Mihka back to the shelter of their own hut.

The three of them looked at him steadily. The weight of their gazes was so heavy, he wanted to curl up into a ball and disappear under the snow.

"I'm sorry I went. I know what it must have looked like," he said. "I didn't mean to hurt anyone… I just didn't think."

A muscle twitched in Henrik's old face. "That's no excuse, boy. You passed your test; that makes you a mage now. You can't just *not think* when you're in my position, and you will be, one day."

"I know," Tuomas said carefully. "But I'm sorry."

"That's not why I asked you to stay," Maiken cut in before the argument could escalate. "You and Henrik can speak about this another time. For now, we're just glad you're back. But things have happened since you left, and you need to know."

"Forgive me, but there's something you need to know, too," Tuomas cut in. "I don't know what that mist is, but when I was out there, I heard something – it sounded like fish, all slithering over each other. And something was… pulling at my *taika*. Like it knew I was there."

Henrik stared at him. "Are you absolutely sure you didn't see anything?"

"If I did, I would tell you," Tuomas replied. "I just heard the sound. And… when I was in the World Above, something pulled three souls out of Lumi's grasp, just before I saw the mist on the Mustafjord. She tried to stop me; she said it was dangerous."

A small shuffle of discomfort washed through them as he spoke of Lumi. The three leaders glanced among themselves and anxiously fingered the bone beads on their clothes. Even

Henrik, who had more dealings with the Spirits than any other, wore a guarded expression.

"Interesting that the one who ripped a child's soul away speaks of danger," Anssi muttered, but Henrik shot him a stern glare and Anssi quickly lowered his head in respect. Tuomas knew it wasn't just to Henrik. The mist had blocked out the sky, but he was sure Lumi was still up there watching, and after the way he wrenched himself away from her, she wouldn't be in a forgiving mood.

"Henrik?" Maiken said quietly, "what are your thoughts?"

Henrik had pursed his lips so tightly; they had turned white.

"I... have no reason to believe the two are connected," he admitted eventually. "And if they are, it sounds like it is something to do with the dead, not the living, and nothing dead can harm the living. The souls may have just been destined for another place, boy. It happens. Sometimes, not all body-souls go to the Spirit of the Lights. As for the noise... probably just a shoal of fish, like you said. Nobody else heard anything."

He spoke assuredly, and although discomfort still writhed in Tuomas's stomach, Henrik's voice calmed him. It had been the constant sound of reason through his whole life. He was the village mage; the oldest one of all – probably the oldest that had ever lived. He would know what he was doing.

"Alright," Tuomas said. "I just wanted to make you aware."

"Thank you for that," replied Anssi. "Now, listen, Tuomas. Messages have been sent out between Akerfjorden, Poro and Einfjall. We're not going to just meet up on the route this time. All the leaders have decided to combine the herds when we reach the coast, and shelter as one large community on Anaar. It's the biggest of the islands; it will take all of us easily."

Henrik nodded. "The demon-master may be gone, but we're not taking any chances. Where one evil treads, another can certainly follow. It's better to be safe than sorry, and we have safety in numbers."

The mere mention of Kari made the hair on the back of Tuomas's neck stand up. He pressed a hand to his chest and glanced over his shoulder at the mist still hanging across the Mustafjord, confined behind the invisible wall Henrik had laid down.

He hadn't sensed any kind of evil when he heard the slippery sound, but the more he thought about it, he realised he hadn't sensed *anything*. In the sudden darkness which had seized him, it was as though whatever had made the noise had come from a place devoid of all things, and that unnerved him even more than if another demon had come charging out of the fog.

Henrik noticed his discomfort and rested a hand on his arm.

"Things will be fine, boy," he said. "We will follow the same means as the reindeer. Stay together, protect each other. We will be as one herd."

"That hasn't happened in generations," Tuomas said. "Not since…"

"The time of the Great Mage," Maiken finished.

As she spoke, a darkness came into her eyes, and everyone looked at Tuomas as though they were seeing him anew. He squirmed under the pressure of it and turned his attention back to the Mustafjord.

Underneath that frozen sheet, he had drowned, once. He wondered what it would have been like to breathe and draw in only water, choking and spasming down there in the dark…

Down there, with a Spirit for a soul, encased in a prison of flesh and bone…

Red Fox One…

He shook his head, trying to push it away.

Henrik lifted his hand and tapped him on the shoulder.

"Go and get some rest," he said. "But when we make the first camp, I want you to come and see me."

"Alright," Tuomas agreed. He bid goodnight to the three of them, then trudged his way back towards the hut. With every step, his shoes crunched in the snow, and he was painfully aware of their eyes watching until the mist swallowed him. He tried to hold his breath as he walked through it, so he wouldn't breathe it in. Whatever it was, it unnerved him.

When he ducked inside, Paavo was already asleep, snoring softly in his usual place with his face turned to the turf wall. Elin was in her sleeping sack too, but as soon as she saw Tuomas, she propped herself up on her elbow.

"What did they want?" she whispered.

Tuomas placed a new log on the fire so it would burn through the night.

"They just wanted to tell me about the villages joining together," he replied. "Elin, do you mind if we talk in the morning? I don't want to disturb Paavo – he's in a bad enough mood already."

She nodded, then shot him a friendly smile before lying down on her back. She clutched her bow close in one hand, the pale wood shining in the flickering firelight.

Tuomas fetched his own sleeping sack and unrolled it. It smelled a little musty – he supposed it had been stored at the back of the shelter ever since he'd left. But he ignored that, pulled off his shoes and coat and wriggled into it. It was made from two reindeer hides stitched together, the thick hair on the inside to hold in warmth, and he had no sooner settled before he felt tiredness sweeping through him.

The last thing he saw was Paavo turning over, waking for just long enough to cough.

Chapter Three

Tuomas barely felt as though he had closed his eyes before Maiken's voice cut through his slumber. He jolted awake and sat bolt upright, narrowly missing hitting his head on a low-hanging beam.

"Everybody up!" she called, clapping her hands. "It's time to move!"

Paavo kicked out of his sleeping sack. He glanced at Tuomas, then busied himself with pulling on layers. Tuomas tried to give him a smile, but Paavo didn't return it. He hoisted a coil of rope over his shoulder.

"I'm going to go help Aslak prepare the herd," he said stiffly. "You two help take the supply sacks to the sleighs."

Tuomas stood up. "Paavo – "

"Later," Paavo snapped. "There's too much to do. Come on, get ready and get to work."

He stepped outside before Tuomas could protest and kicked the door shut behind him. Tuomas sighed and pushed his feet into his shoes.

"I hoped he might have woken up in a better mood," he said. "I'll try again later."

"He's just pre-occupied," Elin said. She fetched her bow and slipped her head and arm between the wood and string so it sat snugly on her back.

When they emerged from the hut, Tuomas was both surprised and relieved to see the mist in the village had lifted. A thin film of it lingered here and there, but the majority of it had pooled on the Mustafjord, like a cloud had somehow dropped fully-formed from the sky. Every now and then, wafts of it would press against Henrik's barrier and rebound back on itself. Henrik himself sat on the bank, a reindeer skin and small fire all which kept him from the snow beneath.

Tuomas tried to peer through the mist to the fjord beyond. This was the first time in his life when he wouldn't be starting the migration by following its icy path.

In the forest above Akerfjorden, the air was filled with the ringing of bells as the reindeer jostled about, eager to get moving. Tuomas couldn't see Paavo anywhere, but knew he would be up there with the other strong young men. Everybody else was still in the village, lighting flaming torches so they could see what they were doing. The Sun Spirit would not rise until close to midday, but the fires threw their glow across the snow, and outside their flickering rings, the surroundings appeared even darker. The shadows held the depths of a land which had almost forgotten what daylight looked like.

As soon as the paths between the huts were lit, every man, woman and child sprang into action. Maiken spoke with the older people who were staying behind to maintain the winter camp. Mihka and Sisu set up the numerous sleighs required for the journey, scooping snow out of their bellies and lining them with hides. Anssi went into the woods to gather any moss and lichen which hadn't yet been eaten by the reindeer. There would be places on the route with no trees for the animals to forage from, and no vegetation beneath the snow which they could dig up. Taking a backup supply was essential for the two long weeks which lay ahead.

Elin and Tuomas fetched numerous pairs of skis and laid them across the back of one of the sleighs. Then they packed food and tools into sacks and carried them to the edge of the village. For Tuomas, every movement was painful – his muscles screamed in protest as they moved properly again for the first time in a month.

"I can't believe I was gone for so long," he said.

"Neither can I," said Elin. "When you said you'd be back in time for the migration, I didn't think you'd cut it so fine."

"I didn't mean to," he insisted. "That reminds me, where's Lilja? I haven't seen her anywhere."

"She left ages ago," replied Elin. "She went back to Poro with Enska. I thought she told you that was what she was planning?"

"Yes, she did. But I didn't think it would be so soon."

"It's Lilja. What did you expect?"

They each picked up a sack and hoisted it over their shoulders, then started walking. A pile was already starting to build against the wall of the furthest hut. In front of it, Mihka and Sisu pulled rows of sleighs into position, all pointing towards the western forest. The trees were heaped with snow, their branches holding all they could bear – a single flake more, and the entire load would plummet to the ground.

"Was Enska the one who took the message about the herds combining?" Tuomas asked.

"Yes. He said he'd let Einfjall know on the way back to Poro," said Elin.

"Why didn't you go with them? You could have been home by now."

"I was going to, but Paavo insisted that I stayed. I don't think he liked the idea of me leaving when I was the last person who saw you."

Tuomas winced. "I know I should have told the others…"

"You weren't even going to tell *me*," Elin pointed out. "The only reason I knew at all was because I followed you."

"I know. And I'm sorry. I feel like I'm saying that a lot."

"Because you have a lot of people who need to hear it." Elin tossed her head to flick her fringe out of her eyes. "Speaking of which, what did you do up there for a month?"

"Just spent time with Lumi," Tuomas replied.

Elin cocked an eyebrow. "Yes, but what did you *do*?"

"I... don't really know," he admitted. "Danced, mainly."

"Danced?" Elin didn't sound impressed.

"Well, we talked as well. But it's not talking like this. You don't need to speak. There's no..." he searched for the right word," *boundaries*."

They reached the pile and Tuomas threw his sack down on the top. Mihka hovered nearby, but then Sisu called him from the other end of the sleigh line and he hurried off.

"I can understand a little more, why Lumi found it so hard to be down here," Tuomas continued. "Here, you can only be in a single place at once; only do one thing at a time. And you're always *aware* of the time, of things which need to be done. It's so complicated. It's not like that up there."

Elin put her sack over his, then leaned against the wall of the hut and twirled the end of her braid in her fingers.

"You sound like you didn't want to come back," she said.

"I promised I would," Tuomas replied.

"That's not what I meant."

He approached her and laid an earnest hand on her shoulder.

"Elin, I was always going to come back. It's just different, that's all. I know what it's like up there now; I understand it a little better. I need to get used to being here again. A few days and I'll be fine."

He paused. "And thank you for waiting for me."

Elin glared at him for a moment, then her expression softened and she gave him a playful shove.

"Well, don't expect me to be dancing with you for a month," she said through a sharp-toothed grin.

Tuomas chuckled and pushed her back. She side-stepped and tripped him, sending him tumbling into the snow. He narrowly missed a torch wedged in a bank and she stuck out her tongue at him.

He laughed. For as close as he felt to Lumi, this human playfulness was something he had truly missed.

He got to his feet, brushed the snow off his clothes, and returned to the sacks. By the time they had fetched the last ones, the sky had transformed from deep darkness to a faint icy blue, and the Sun Spirit rose. Her face kissed the horizon as she struggled to peer over the Northlands. As soon as she appeared, the mist in the village finally burned away, but the cloud over the Mustafjord lingered stubbornly, like the last dregs of ice which clung to the sides of a thawing river.

Tuomas turned to watch. The light hurt his eyes and he held up a hand to shield them. She looked so far away now; further even than she had seemed when he was a child and knew nothing of the truth. But the moment her golden glow hit him, he felt it like a soft caress, and a small smile broke across his face.

"What are you grinning at?" Elin asked.

Tuomas shook his head. "Nothing."

Elin shot a glance at him, but didn't press the matter.

"I hoped the Sun Spirit would have been able to lift it," Tuomas said.

"The mist?" Elin said. "Do you think it's something more?"

"I don't know," he admitted.

Elin worked her mouth nervously. One hand went to her bowstring where it pressed against her chest.

"Lumi said it was dangerous?" she asked quietly.

Tuomas nodded. "And the way she reacted… she didn't want me to come back. She said I couldn't risk it."

"But you still did," said Elin.

Tuomas looked at her. It suddenly occurred to him that he had never seen her in the daylight before. All the previous times, she had only been lit by fires and Lumi's aurora. Now, he noticed tiny details in her face which he'd missed in the gloom: how ruddy her cheeks were; small golden flecks in her brown eyes. Dark circles had formed under them and her expression was heavy with fatigue. She looked as though she hadn't slept since the night he'd left. And her hair seemed blacker than it had during the Long Dark, as though some of the shine had drained out of it.

"Hey, you two!"

Tuomas and Elin turned around to see Sisu waving at them.

"Fetch your last-minute things! It's time to go!"

They hurried to the hut, rolled up their sleeping sacks and fetched the last supply of food. Paavo had obviously been back before them, because the reindeer skins on the floor had been hung up on the beams to keep them off the ground; the fire was extinguished and all the non-essential tools stored in their proper places. It was to keep the shelter as low-maintenance as possible for the older caretakers who always remained in the village through the warm months.

Tuomas closed the door behind him and threw the belongings into the belly of his and Paavo's sleigh. It was the same one he had taken on his journey into the north, and one of Paavo's reindeer was already hitched up to the poles at the front. Several other bulls also stood ready to pull the rest of the sleighs. They grunted indignantly as Tuomas and Elin passed, making no secret of how they would prefer to still be with the herd. The urge to migrate wasn't as strong in them. It was the females who drove the whole movement, knowing they needed to get to the summer grounds before giving birth.

Tuomas and Elin headed to the edge of Akerfjorden, where many of the villagers had formed a human wall. The reindeers' instinct would drive them down towards the Mustafjord, so it would take everyone to channel them the other way into the forest. Paavo stood several metres away with a tame reindeer in a harness. As soon as the others saw it, they would naturally follow in its footsteps.

When everyone was in place, Aslak and Anssi pulled open the corral gate. The reindeer rushed out: a surge of brown against the pearlescent snow. Powder flew in all directions as their hooves churned it up. Tuomas spread his arms to make himself appear larger. The animals quickly realised that their usual path was blocked and headed into the trees. On the other side, he heard the shouts of more herders, preventing them from moving too far away. Eventually, they settled and started to follow the lead reindeer. Only a few remained behind: the older ones, with worn teeth. They had been separated in the corral, and for those staying in the village, they would provide food through the summer.

As Paavo led the way, the rest of the herders struck up pace behind and flanked the reindeer. It was a struggle to manoeuvre the runners across the uneven ground, but everyone pulled together to help guide the sleighs through tangles of roots and hidden rocks.

By the time they were clear, the Sun Spirit had already begun to set. Everyone paused briefly to bid farewell to the caretakers, then set off through the forest. Tuomas wiped sweat from his brow and turned for one last look at the village.

He had lost count of how many times he had come and gone from it throughout his life. It would be a hard journey for them all, but they were used to it. The people had followed this route through the Northlands twice a year for generations, ever since the dawn of life.

We can survive anything, he told himself. But when he caught sight of the mist on the Mustafjord, a shiver ran down his spine. He turned his back on it and followed the herd into the woods.

They made frustratingly slow progress through the labyrinth of trees. Every few feet, a sleigh would grind to a halt as the runners struggled over the snow. It was thick from an entire winter of being undisturbed, so in places, grown men would sink up to their hips. Wading through it took every ounce of energy, and nobody dared ride in the sleighs for fear of weighing them down.

As they fought on, Tuomas had to remind himself that spring was on the way. The land was still locked in ice, but the Long Dark was over, and as the Sun Spirit regained her strength, the grip of winter would soon start to lose its hold. Until then, the hours of daylight would remain short, and every single one of them counted.

The stars were spinning overhead and the Moon Spirit high in the sky by the time the reindeer finally drew to a halt.

The herders urged them onwards until they came to a clearing large enough to support them all, then everyone busied themselves with setting up shelters. In the back of every sleigh, alongside the sacks of food, lichen and tools, were long poles and tarps made of a patchwork of hides. The poles were brought together into a conical skeleton, then the tarp draped around them and tied in place. More hides were thrown down inside to serve as carpet. Whilst they were built, other people went to the trees, gave thanks to the Spirits, and cut low-hanging branches to serve as firewood. They didn't take any more than they needed, and never enough so the tree itself would die.

Soon enough, the camp was set, and everybody huddled together around a fire in the middle of the tents. The flames turned the snow golden and threw strange shadows in all directions. The boughs overhead, plumed with ice, flickered in and out of the gloom as though they were breathing.

Paavo set to work among the other cooks whilst the crowd chatted idly. Small children in their parents' arms yawned and struggled to stay awake.

"Why don't we have a story?" Aslak volunteered. "Just until the food's ready. Jaana? What would you like?"

Jaana coughed into her sleeve. She was only young, but her eyes lit up with a peculiar light at Aslak's suggestion.

"A scary one," she said.

"Really?" her father asked through a laugh. "You're a strange girl."

"I know," Jaana said proudly. "The scariest one you know, Aslak. Please!"

"Alright," chuckled Aslak. "Do you know the Lights, dancing away up there in the sky? You know how powerful and strong she is? Well, she's not the only Spirit who oversees the dead. Deep down under the ground, so far away that nothing –

human, animal or Spirit – has ever stood there… lie the Deathlands."

A few of the parents shuffled uncomfortably. Tuomas twisted his fingers together until his knuckles hurt. He remembered this story. He'd heard it once before, when he was barely older than Jaana, but he'd reacted very differently. The tale had terrified him so much, he had refused to sleep until Paavo curled into his sack with him.

"How do we know they're there, if nothing's ever been?" asked a little boy.

"Because the mages have seen it in trances," answered Aslak. "You don't need feet in a trance, do you Henrik?"

Henrik shook his head.

"Have you ever seen it, Henrik?"

"No, Jaana," Henrik said. "And I hope I never do. Honestly, Aslak, *this* is the story you chose?"

"I like it! It's creepy!" Jaana grinned. "Go on, Aslak! What's in the Deathlands?"

Aslak laughed, then lowered his chin so the fire lit up the hollows of his cheeks.

"It's where many souls go, who don't want to dance in the Lights. Plants, moss, wolves, even some reindeer. But legend says that human body-souls are sometimes taken there, if they aren't ready to be reborn yet; or if they did terrible deeds. They are trapped by water that no living thing can drink, and watched over by a powerful Spirit. Nobody has ever laid eyes on him. He is the Spirit of Death. He is a thing of shadows and darkness, forever hidden and silent."

"Is he a fox, like the Spirit of the Lights?"

"No-one knows," Aslak said ominously.

"Yes, we do," Henrik cut in. "Not much, Jaana, but enough to know he is not a fox. There are only two fox entities in existence."

Tuomas kept his head down and stared intently into the fire.

"If it will put an end to this story," Henrik continued, with a pointed look at Aslak, "the Spirit of Death rides a black horse. Now, can we please leave this subject and move onto one more merry? Would you like to know about the time when I woke up and a wolf had come into my tent, trying to steal my food? So I sat up and smacked it on the nose! That taught it not to sneak up on me!"

"The food's ready!" Paavo called.

The coughing children immediately sat upright. Everyone got up to help themselves. It was a fine feast – the last large one they could expect. There was sautéed reindeer, smoked char, flatbread and a generous serving of jam made from last autumn's cloudberries. After this, they would be relying on their hunting and fishing skills until they reached the coast.

Mihka squeezed in beside Tuomas.

"Nice to see you again, idiot," Tuomas grinned.

In reply, Mihka, shoved him with his elbow. "Were you honestly that desperate to get away from Henrik's lessons?"

"Shut up," hissed Tuomas, very aware that the mage was only on the other side of the fire. "Haven't you learned a thing?"

"Where's the fun in that?" Mihka smiled, showing his small white teeth. But then he relaxed and held his hands towards the logs to warm them. It seemed the memory of his previous disrespect was still fresh.

Tuomas could barely contain his hunger as the familiar aromas wafted up his nose. Paavo approached with two bowls of stew in his hands. Elin followed, clutching her own helping. Mihka shot her a scornful glance as she passed him.

Paavo held out one of the bowls to Tuomas.

"Are you still mad at me?" he asked carefully.

"I'm always mad at you over something," Paavo replied. "I've said my piece, you've heard it. You've apologised, and I've accepted it."

Tuomas smiled. Paavo gave him a long look, then returned it and put his arm around him in a half-hug.

"You have no idea how much I missed you," he said.

"I missed you, too," said Tuomas.

Relieved, he drew a knife from his belt and shovelled the sautéed reindeer into his mouth. His eyes closed in ecstasy. It was better than he remembered; he was acutely aware of every herb coating the tender meat, the undertones of the lichen and moss which the animal had eaten months prior. It tasted of wildness and ruggedness: the frozen landscape captured in a single mouthful.

"You still enjoy my cooking, then?" Paavo chuckled.

"I will *never* get tired of your cooking," Tuomas said.

Paavo kicked snow at him. "Well, don't make a habit of running off in the middle of the night, and I might just carry on feeding you."

He turned away and coughed violently into his elbow. As he breathed in, his lungs rattled. Tuomas lowered the bowl in alarm and slapped his back.

"Are you alright?" he asked.

"Yes, don't worry," Paavo spluttered.

"Are you feeling ill?"

"No, it's just a tickle. It will be gone in a few days, don't worry."

Tuomas frowned. Paavo was one of the strongest men in the village – he never got sick. But now he looked at him, he noticed his brother's face bore a pallid undertone, like old leather. His eyes, usually bright and alert, were dulled; not quite focusing on his food.

Tuomas heard more faint spluttering over the crackle of the fire. It was coming from the children. He'd assumed their lethargy was just tiredness at waking so early, but now he noticed their eyes held the same heaviness as Paavo's. Some of the parents themselves looked ill too: the younger ones, in their twenties.

"Henrik?" he asked. "We should give them herbs. Angelica and nettle are good for coughing."

Henrik wiped his thin lips and narrowed his eyes.

"I've been a mage for long enough to know how to treat a cold, boy."

Tuomas worried he had stepped over a line. But Henrik didn't scold him again, so he changed the subject.

"You didn't wait too long for me to come back, did you?"

Sisu shook his head. "A few days. Nothing much."

Tuomas glanced up through the trees. The faint green glow of the aurora was starting to wave between the faraway stars.

"You could have left without me," he insisted. "I'm sure Lumi would have put me back somewhere on the route, if need be."

At mention of her, everyone drew in a gasp. Many people looked at the sky and lowered their heads when they noticed the growing Lights. Tuomas watched the reaction warily. The only people who didn't seem concerned were Elin – and, to his surprise, Mihka.

"The Spirit of the Lights aided you against that wicked mage," Henrik said in a careful tone. "But I think I speak for all of us: we don't wish to see her again. Not down here, anyway. We may meet her at some point, when it's time for our souls to move on, but until then... she should stay in the World Above where she belongs."

He gave Tuomas a sharp look as the other villagers murmured in agreement.

Tuomas did his best to speak calmly. "I brought her down here by accident. I'm not going to do it again."

"Regardless," said Anssi, "let's just leave it at that, please."

Tuomas nodded, but couldn't help shooting a glance at Elin. Her eyes were tired, as if she had also tried and failed to talk about this.

It didn't matter that they had all seen Lumi in physical form just a few weeks ago. She was still the Spirit of the Lights: a being of darkness and pride. Revered as she was for leading the ancestors in their spiralling dance, she remained one of the most feared entities of all. The knowledge the people had held for generations would take more than a single winter to change.

Tuomas looked at his wrists. He could still feel her frantic hold around them. Had she known people were getting sick, and didn't want him to catch it? Yes, that must have been it.

Beside him, Elin helped herself to some char, then she coughed into her scarf, quietly, so nobody would notice.

Chapter Four

When the last of the food was eaten, everyone headed towards their tents to bed down for the night. The Lights were still strong overhead, and even as the fire died, they cast a green glow upon the forest. All the snow-covered branches were edged with it and stood eerily still beneath the waving river in the sky. The temperature plummeted; every breath Tuomas drew stung his lungs. Tiny drops of ice froze on his eyelashes and he fought the urge to brush them off in case the hairs snapped.

He helped Paavo to clear the bowls and scour them with snow and birch branches. Then they placed them back in the sleighs and drew a reindeer-skin tarp over them. Tuomas could tell from the clear sky that no snow would fall, but it would also dissuade the animals from rummaging through the sacks for the backup lichen.

He was about to follow Paavo into the shelter when he noticed Henrik standing expectantly by the fire, eyes fixed on him.

Paavo hesitated. "What's wrong?"

"Henrik said he wanted to speak to me about something," Tuomas said. "I almost forgot. You go in, I'll be back soon."

"I'll lay out your sleeping sack for you," said Paavo, then stepped inside and closed the flap behind him.

Tuomas crossed the clearing until he was standing in front of Henrik.

"What is it?"

"Go into my tent," Henrik replied.

Tuomas did, and as soon as he ducked inside, he was greeted by the scent of herbs and outrageously strong tea. He wrinkled his nose. He had never been in Henrik's tent, only his permanent huts at Akerfjorden and Anaar, but even now he couldn't get away from the smell. It had seeped into the hide tarp from years of brewing. He took stock of how weathered the tarp was; Henrik must have used it for every single one of his migrations and simply patched it whenever it wore thin.

He sat down by the fire. It was an act of politeness upon being invited into one's shelter, but Tuomas also knew that he would probably be here for a while. A conversation with Henrik rarely ended quickly.

Henrik stepped past him and picked up something from the foot of his sleeping sack. When he turned around, Tuomas's breath stuck in his throat.

It was a drum: the one which Henrik had given to him when he set out from Akerfjorden at the beginning of the Long Dark.

"You left this behind when you went to the World Above," said Henrik. "Paavo found it in your hut and asked me to look after it for you. Now it's time for you to have it back."

Tuomas's eyes wandered over the stretched skin, tracing the markings painted on it in red alder bark juice. The Great Bear Spirit stared at him from the centre.

"Are you sure?"

"I gave it to you," Henrik replied firmly. "And I've made myself a new one, as I said I would. This is yours."

He passed it to Tuomas and sat opposite him, groaning as his old knees hit the reindeer skins on the ground. Tuomas held the drum by the back beam and ran his palm across the surface; then pulled the antler hammer from inside the frame.

Its weight felt comfortable in his hand, as though it was merely an extension of his own limb.

"Thank you," he said. "I didn't realise how much I'd missed this."

"Enska told me you didn't even need it at one point," Henrik noted. "He said you managed to enter a trance without it."

"Once," Tuomas insisted. "I still prefer using a drum, though. It gives me something to focus on."

Henrik nodded understandingly. "And with a *taika* like yours, you need all the assistance you can find."

Tuomas glanced up at him. A memory flashed in his mind: of Lilja's drum on the fire; her scream as all her magic blew out of her control. That power was in the mage themselves, not the drum, but the instrument was the focal point which allowed them to direct it. He could tell from Henrik's expression that he was thinking of the same event.

"How was she?" Tuomas asked. "Before she left?"

"Fine, as far as I could see," said Henrik. "I gave up trying to talk to her in the end. I would have had better success drawing blood from a stone."

Despite himself, Tuomas smirked. "How was Enska with her?"

"Again, fine," Henrik said, with the same gruffness. "He wanted to wait for you, but when he came here, it left Poro without a mage. He had to go back, and she went with him."

He flexed his fingers, bones and tendons sliding under liver-spotted skin.

"I was glad to see the back of her, if I'm honest. Strange woman," he said.

"She helped me," Tuomas protested.

Henrik shrugged, clearly not wanting to talk about it any longer. He shuffled to the door and swept some virgin snow off the ground. Then he came back to the hearth, laid a pot over the fire, and dropped the snow inside to melt. Tuomas watched in silence as he tossed herbs into the water, fighting not to grimace at the size of the handful. He wondered if Henrik had somehow managed to destroy his own sense of taste from always brewing his tea so strong.

Now it was on the fire, it was a courtesy to stay and drink. As Henrik stirred the pot with a bone ladle, Tuomas rested the drum across his lap and swept his hand over the skin to clean it. He traced the spirals and paintings with the stump of one frostbitten finger.

It still brought a jolt of shock to see those two digits missing their tips, suddenly ending in a blunt mass of flesh. It made his hand look somewhat unreal, like a drawing a child might have made in the snow. Luckily, he hadn't lost enough to hinder him – he could still grasp things and pick them up.

Just as with Mihka's white hair, it was a small price to pay.

"You could have had it a lot worse," said Henrik, noticing his musings.

"I know," said Tuomas. "I could have been dead."

Henrik paused, running a pale tongue over his lips. Then he dipped two wooden cups into the tea and passed one to Tuomas.

"I did my best to prepare you," he said. "I had my reasons for not telling you about the Great Mage."

Tuomas laid the drum aside and took the cup with a nod of thanks. He wanted to put off drinking it for as long as possible.

"Are you going to tell me those reasons?"

"To spare you. The knowledge was heavy on my shoulders, and I'm an old man, I've lived my life. You were just a boy."

"I'm fifteen. I'm a man now."

"That's still a boy."

Tuomas bit back a snide retort. A forty-year-old would probably still be a boy in Henrik's eyes.

"Fine. Tell me later. There will be time on the migration," he said instead. "But I have something to ask you."

"What?"

"I know I'm… well, a Spirit." Tuomas gritted his teeth together at hearing his own words. "And I know I've passed my mage test. But I know there's more I need to learn. So, I wanted to ask if I could be your apprentice again? But this time, please don't keep any secrets from me. About who I am, I mean."

Henrik chuckled, blowing on his tea before taking a noisy slurp. The steam twisted and writhed in front of his face, then mingled with the smoke from the fire.

"Fair enough," he said. "But, to be honest, you don't need tutoring. At least not in the way you think. You just need help in enhancing your *taika*, and continuing to control it. As you said, you've passed your test."

He scratched his head through his hat. His mouth worked uncomfortably, as though he was trying to swallow something sour.

"For as much as I don't want to say this, I know it's the correct advice. It may be better to ask Lilja if you can study under her, instead."

Tuomas was startled.

"Lilja?" he repeated.

Henrik grimaced. "As I said, I don't like it, either."

"No, it's not that. You really think she'll have me?"

"Well, you can but ask. The worst she can do is say no. And she probably will."

"But you don't even like Lilja. Why? She helped me; she delivered me when I was a baby."

"So did her brother," Henrik said, a dark edge to his words. "I appreciate her skill, but I don't understand her, and I don't like what I can't understand. But she's also the only mage left in this World who can come close to you in *taika*. I respect that, even if I don't respect her."

Tuomas couldn't help staring. Henrik had never made any secret of how wary he was of Lilja. She had, after all, been personally touched by the Great Bear Spirit: something unheard of among many mages, and had wandered for years without a people or even more than a couple of reindeer. She was strange and quiet, and not easily read. For Henrik to recommend her above his own tutelage was notable indeed.

"In any case, we'll probably happen across her on the migration. You can enquire then," said Henrik, and drank again.

He cleared his throat loudly and Tuomas realised he still hadn't touched his. He took a small sip, making a conscious effort not to grimace. It was as bitter as ever. Henrik didn't notice however, and stared softly into the depths of his own cup.

"You should expect this migration to be unique in more ways than one," he said eventually.

"Why?" Tuomas asked. "Because all the villages are meeting up?"

"Not just that." Henrik gave him a piercing glance from across the fire. "Word has got around about you. Everyone knows you're the Son of the Sun. Some might not say it to your face, but don't expect them all to keep quiet about that knowledge. It's likely not just here, either; if Poro and Einfjall don't know already, they will soon."

Tuomas immediately recalled the wary looks he had received by his neighbours. He had been the only one in the village who managed to pull Mihka to safety when the Lights struck him – not even Henrik had gotten close enough. Then he had returned from his journey with a Spirit at his side; and vanished into the sky after facing down the most wicked mage in recent memory.

In the heat of the moment, they had celebrated, but he should have known things would be different now. No mage should have been able to do what he did, not unless they possessed some other power.

The power of a Spirit.

He swallowed his tea too quickly and it scalded his throat. He coughed and tears rose to his eyes, but he blinked them away.

"Speaking of which," continued Henrik, "it's interesting to note that ever since you came of age, strange things began to happen. You've only been fifteen for seven months, and already we've seen a wicked demon-driving mage, and the Spirit of the Lights walking in the World Between. And now we have a strange mist descending on the fjord and not going away."

"I had no control over any of those things!" Tuomas protested.

Henrik cocked an eyebrow.

"Well, fine, I know I pulled the Spirit out of the sky," Tuomas said. "But I never would have done that if Mihka hadn't insulted her in the first place. And Kari was planning on coming for me ever since I was born. It's not my fault that this soul decided to enter me when I was a baby!"

"I'm not blaming you," said Henrik, his deep voice softening into a gentler tone. "However, it is interesting to note how quick *you* are to try to shift blame. You pulled the Spirit from the World Above, but why do you call Sisu's son into it?"

Tuomas fought the urge to roll his eyes.

"Because if it hadn't been for him acting like an idiot, I never would have needed to go out looking for Lilja. I never would have drummed against the Lights, and I never would have gone into the World Below and let Kari loose so he could try to kill me!"

"Still angry," Henrik muttered, shaking his head. "Anger will do you no good. Was it not anger which caused you to summon her in the first place?"

Tuomas's knuckles went white around his cup.

"You need to control that, as well as your *taika*. Son of the Sun or not, that's part of being a man," continued Henrik. "But my point is, if things like that could happen simply because you exist, with no prior knowledge of who you are, whatever might come now that you *do* know?"

He looked at Tuomas firmly and pointed with a gnarled finger.

"I didn't tell you that you were a Spirit because I hoped you'd never need to use that knowledge. But now, you'd best be prepared, and start acting like a man. You might not have asked for the Great Mage's life-soul, but you've got it, whether you like it or not."

Tuomas lowered his eyes as the fury faded out of him. Henrik brought up a disturbingly accurate point. For his whole life, he had been respectful of the Spirits and the stories around them, but never had he thought he might actually come into contact with the entities themselves. Or be the target of such selfish and calculated evil. And through it all, he had been reckless, with many of the times he had escaped trouble being down to pure luck. He couldn't afford to take chances like that again.

"Do you think the thing in the mist is what I need to be prepared for?" he asked.

"That's the main reason why I wanted to speak with you, in private," Henrik replied. A heaviness came into his watery eyes. "There's nothing in the mist. I told you, the sound you heard was just fish heaving under the ice."

"I've never heard a shoal make a noise like that," Tuomas insisted.

He paused when he saw the expression on Henrik's face. The old mage was staring intently at the cracks in the burning wood, as though searching their red lines for an answer.

"Henrik…" Tuomas said, "You said yourself, it's not a normal mist. Do you know what it is?"

For a long moment, Henrik didn't move. Then he heaved a sigh from so deep in his lungs, his entire body slumped when he exhaled. He took another sip of his tea and swallowed it hard.

"This isn't the first time a mist like that has swept in," he admitted. "The last time it happened, I was just a couple of years older than you. It seems to happen every generation or so."

Tuomas stared at him. "But… you said…"

"That was to keep everyone calm," Henrik cut in. "I think I'm one of the few still living who remembers the last one; even the oldest caretakers are younger than me. They're lucky."

"Why?"

"Because… when the last mist like this came down the Mustafjord, it brought a sickness with it," said Henrik.

"What kind of sickness?" Tuomas's eyes widened. "Wait, why did you let the caretakers stay behind?"

"They're immune to it," replied Henrik. "It only targets the young ones: the children and young adults. Those who you see as old men now, they weren't even born when it happened last. But I was struck down with it. Why else do you think I make my tea so strong? It's because I can still feel it on my lungs."

Tuomas was so shocked, he almost dropped his cup. He glanced at the black liquid inside it. He had choked on this brew more times than he could count, but only now did he suddenly recognise the aromas rising out of it.

"Nettle and angelica," he said. "For treating colds."

"That's all it is," said Henrik. "A very nasty cold. Like pneumonia, almost. And it comes back once every generation. We just need to ride the wave and get to the summer islands. The last time it hit, we were on the migration too, and by the time we reached Anaar, it was all over."

Something about the way he spoke chilled Tuomas's bones. He thought about the coughing which had risen on the air that evening. It had only started since the mist had swept into the village.

"All over?" he repeated slowly. "Henrik… is this going to kill people?"

Henrik gave him a steady look over the tops of the flames.

"There will be deaths. Some will manage to fight it off, like I did, and others won't. You and I must manage things as best we can."

Tuomas felt as though he was going to fall through the ground.

"But –"

"Not a word of this to anyone," Henrik warned. "Not for now, at least. People will panic, and that's the worst thing they can do. We need to keep moving forward."

He stabbed at the fire with a stick until the bottommost logs broke up.

"That's why you wanted us to leave so quickly," Tuomas realised.

Henrik nodded. "You haven't lived through a disease before, boy," he said, his voice as heavy as a stone. "I hoped it wouldn't happen again in my lifetime, but in another respect, I'm grateful, because I can teach you how to manage it before I die. But this is yet another aspect of our work as mages: the unglamorous, messy, tragic part. As I've told you, it's not all about going into trances and hitting a drum. It's cruel as much as it is beautiful."

Henrik downed the last of his tea. Tuomas quickly did the same so there would be none left, biting his tongue to keep himself from grimacing.

"We have to do something," he said quietly.

"We'll do what we can," Henrik replied. "We'll pass a shrine in the next week. You and I will go there and make an offering to the Sun Spirit. She is the one who heals the sick. We'll need her help."

He tossed the stick into the fire. It crackled angrily and for a brief moment the tent lit up with sparks.

"Now, go and get some sleep, as best you can," he said. "I'm sorry I've had to burden you with this."

Tuomas woodenly got to his feet, picked up his drum, and stepped outside. But once the flap was closed behind him, he didn't move a muscle. Anxiety raced in his blood and he peered through the trees in the east. The herders had moved too far inland to still see the Mustafjord, but he imagined the mist still clinging to its surface, filled with invisible poison.

Then he looked into the sky and almost fell over in alarm. He turned back to the tent and barked at Henrik to come outside.

Henrik grumbled.

"What in the name of all the Spirits –"

"Hurry up!" Tuomas hissed.

Henrik crawled over as fast as he could and stumbled through the flap. His mouth fell open.

The night was darker than ever. Lumi had disappeared, leaving only the stars, but while many of them remained in their places, some had broken free and cascaded towards the horizon. Glittering trails streamed behind them, the light edging the trees with silver.

Other people had also noticed and started to emerge. Some made the sign of the hand and muttered anxiously among themselves.

"What's going on?" he asked quietly.

"I don't know," Henrik whispered back.

And then, as quickly as the shower had begun, it was over. Everyone stood frozen, too shaken to do anything except continue to stare. A breeze swept snowflakes off the branches, and as they settled on the ground, Tuomas heard the faint sound of children coughing in the shelters.

Chapter Five

She watched from the World Above and she danced the formless dance. She had faded during the day, as she was bound to do, but now the Sun Spirit had retreated, it was her time to shine again and fill the sky with her aurora.

The forest looked tiny from here; the people even more so, hurrying all over the place. The pregnant reindeer walked through the trees, flanked by males and herders and sleighs. They moved with an urgency embedded into their instinct over centuries of survival. Some of them wouldn't make it. Wolves, wolverines and eagles might swoop in; or they might break a leg. It had happened before and it would happen again. For as skilled as the people were, nature was the ultimate ruler.

The herders drew to a halt and put up their tents. The hearth fires turned the walls of hide tarp a warm orange colour and threw a soft halo of light over the surrounding snow. She could see through the smoke holes to where they lay, eyes closed. Only a few remained awake, sitting close to the reindeer as they watched for wolves.

She gazed upon them in their fur-lined sleeping sacks, beheld their simple dreams, felt the Spirits wandering through the forest all around them. Spirits of trees and rocks and the nearby fjord; of winds and ice, of spring plants slumbering under the snow. The Spirit of Motherhood passed by the female reindeer and caressed the thick fur on their bulging bellies. When the unborn babies felt it, they kicked softly, as though eager to taste the crisp air and feel the grass beneath their hooves.

She rolled around, sending a new blaze of green across the sky, and looked back at Tuomas. Even he was asleep, his human urges having overtaken him. It was only when he was up here with her that he behaved like the Spirit he truly was. But now, contained in this simple single form, there was only so much he could do.

Tuomas. It was still a little strange to call him that. Up here, he had no name, as she had no name; only a title which he'd never used. In the World Between, they had called her so many things through the ages. Moon Daughter. Spirit of the Lights. Fox Fires.

But *he* had called her Lumi. Only him, her dear brother. And by doing so, he had almost destroyed her. A formless being such as her could not be anything less, and a name given in affection was like poison in the blood. After he called her Lumi, she had begun to feel. Human emotions kindled within her as a fire would spread through tinder – she could remember the water running down her skin as she melted away.

Yet it held a special significance within her, over all the other titles and semi-solid names. It was a literal description of how she appeared in the human form he had given her: pale as snow, cold as winter, perfect as her beautiful Lights.

Never mind that she was the White Fox One. If she were to be known as anything until the end of time, she would have it be that. *Lumi.*

It was still dark when the people struck their tents and carried on. They struggled through the forest, but the trees gradually thinned and the reindeer became a living cloud fanning over the snow. Tuomas and Elin were near the head of the formation, walking alongside the lead reindeer, each holding a flaming torch to cast a small reach of light.

Even though their faces were obscured by scarves and hats, she could recognise them anywhere. Especially him. She saw souls before she saw eyes or body, or indeed anything physical. And his shone brighter than any other.

Not far behind him was the ignorant boy. Mihka. His hair was so white, it was almost lost against the snow. If she had still had a mouth, she might have smirked at the sight. But she had made good on her promise to Tuomas and released him. He didn't seem too damaged by the punishment she had dealt. She would leave it at that.

Other children and young adults brought up the rear, making sure the male reindeer didn't fall behind. Many of them were lagging, and they paused often to cough or hold a hand to their heads. When they spoke, their words were heavy and gargled, as though they had water stuck in their throats.

A shadow passed over her. Why hadn't Tuomas listened to her when she had held him?

The stars around her suddenly plummeted towards the ground. They shot through the night, too many to count; too fast to catch. They tore between her Lights and sent her into a spin. For a horrible moment, she lost all sense of direction. The souls within the aurora clamoured with fright.

And then, just as quickly as it had happened, it was over.

She hung still while she regained her bearings. Deathly silence fell over the World Above as the Spirits drew close together.

Then she saw why. There was a hole in the skin which separated them from the World Between. It wasn't large, but inside, there was nothing. Not a single light glimmered. It was blacker than black; sheer oblivion.

She swam over to it. As soon as she drew close, she shuddered; the void chilled her in a way no cold could. She let a hand take shape so she could run her fingers across the edge of the hole. It folded under her like the thinnest fabric.

Proceed with care, White Fox One.

She felt something approach. There was no warmth or coolness; just pure energy drawn from all things, from the highest mountain to the tiniest clump of moss. It swirled and shimmered into the face of the Great Bear Spirit.

What is it? she asked.

Exactly what it looks like, replied the Bear. *A tear between the Worlds. Your brother caused it when he pulled away from you.*

She spun around and her Lights flared in alarm.

He tore the Worlds?

It was an accident, but a costly one.

Will it hold?

For now. It could have been much worse. And do not blame yourself, White Fox One; you could not have stopped him. He is of equal power to you, and he knows that now.

How can that matter? she snapped. *We have always been of equal power, and yet he was able to pull me out of the sky, even as I resisted. I should have been able to keep him here – I only tried to so he would not put himself at risk!*

The Bear glanced at her knowingly. *But if you had not been pulled from the sky, how would he have learned the truth?*

Do you imply that I wanted to go down there and take that human form? she asked incredulously.

Not to the World Between, said the Bear. *But to him… I do not need to imply anything. You wanted to be reunited with him ever since he was reborn. And remember, he would have learned who he is without you, but he would not have survived. You saved each other.*

The Lights twisted like the branches of a tree. She couldn't bring herself to agree, but she also knew that the Great Bear Spirit would not speak such words unless they were correct. It knew everything. It was not good or evil; male or female; past, present or future. It was the essence of existence itself, and bore the ultimate truth of all which came to pass.

She looked at the rip again, and then back at Tuomas. The Bear appeared at her side and regarded him with its penetrating black gaze, darker than the furthest reaches of the night sky.

Could you not have stopped him? she asked.

No.

But...

It does not matter what I could have done or not, the Bear replied in a voice like smooth water. *All I do in any World is maintain the balance, and that cannot happen without change in the first place.*

You intervened with the wicked demon-mage, she pointed out. *You took him to the World Below twice. You intervened with me: you turned me into a fox so I could survive.*

And on both occasions, you and the mage made a choice of your own, the Bear countered. *The mage chose to make a demon. You chose to reveal your emotions to your brother. Both times caused a change which I could correct. The balance is an ever-moving thing. Even on the coldest and darkest winter day, the Worlds are turning towards summer. Everything happens in response to the other, never at the same time, for without one, the other could not exist. That is where my power lies, White Fox One. Not in causing or preventing a thing, but facilitating its recovery.*

She flicked her tail slowly from side to side. The aurora took on a crisp turquoise glow and sent fresh tendrils swimming through the darkness.

And now Tuomas has made a choice, she said.

He needed to make it, replied the Bear. *I intend for him to put an end to the suffering once and for all. In order to learn how, he must see the effect of the draugars for himself.*

What if they take him? They know he is alive again.

She suddenly paused, her Lights hanging still in the empty air

This is all my fault, she whispered. *I should not have brought him up here; that was when they sensed him.*

They were due to return with or without your actions, the Bear replied. Its voice was both accusing and comforting, yet neither at the same time. *And when all is done, an even greater task will await him: that which he was reborn to accomplish in the first place. I shall summon him when the time is right, and you and I will remind him of what he has forgotten. And I will tell him what he must do.*

I wish you would not speak in such riddles.

It is what I am, White Fox One.

She thought she heard a flicker of a laugh in the words, but they did little to lessen her anxiety. Even as the youngsters sickened, Tuomas was in the most danger of all.

The days rolled by. Everyone awoke early and walked until their feet ached. The Sun Spirit only rose for what felt like a few heartbeats at noon. Her glow was the sole break in the monotonous blue twilight which engulfed the land. It was a stark reminder that while the Long Dark was over, the grip of winter still dug its fingers deep.

When they reached the next camping spot, the shelters went back up, once more under cover of night. The snow was thinner here, with a frosty crust on the top and a layer of ice underfoot. Tuomas joined Paavo and Elin, assembling the poles against each other, hacking notches into the ice so the ends could grip. Tuomas knelt on all fours and Paavo stood on his back to tie them together at the top.

Paavo coughed so violently, he grabbed hold of the poles and almost fell. Elin snatched his legs to steady him.

"Get down," she insisted.

Paavo coughed again. "It's alright, I can do it."

He bound the cord in a knot and jumped back into the snow. Tuomas got to his feet and went to check him, but Paavo waved him off.

"Don't worry about me. I told you, it's just a tickle," he insisted. "I must have swallowed a hair or something."

Tuomas bit his lip nervously. "Does it hurt? Is it on your lungs?"

Paavo slapped his chest hard. "A little. I'm fine, I promise. I don't feel unwell."

"You're not convincing me," said Tuomas. "Go inside, I'll be back."

He walked over to Henrik, who had just finished putting his own tent up with help from Aslak and Anssi.

"Do you have any nettle or angelica?" he asked. "I need to make some of your tea."

Henrik looked at him for a long moment, then nodded at an array of sealskin pouches in the nearest sleigh.

"Use a little, but brew it for longer than you think you need to," he instructed. "We have to save the supplies for as long as possible."

Tuomas muttered thanks and rooted through the bags until he found the herbs he needed. He pulled off a mitten, shook the contents into his open palm, then grabbed one of Henrik's tools: a pestle made from the carved end of a reindeer's femur. When he had everything, he headed back to the shelter. Elin had already started to build a fire, and a pot filled with snow sat waiting to be placed onto it. As the flames grew, Tuomas upended the utensil sack and retrieved several wooden cups, hollowed out of birch tree burrs. He used one with the pestle to grind the dried leaves together.

As he worked, he heard Henrik's voice in his head from months ago:

"Strike them hard, boy. The goodness inside them needs to come out if it's to heal."

As soon as the snow had melted and started to boil, he threw the herbs in and steeped the mixture until it formed a dark fragrant tea. He grabbed another cup, filled it to the brim, and forced it into Paavo's hands.

"Drink that," he ordered.

Paavo sipped from it and wrinkled his nose in disgust.

"By the Spirits!" he cried. "And I thought Henrik's brews were strong!"

Tuomas couldn't suppress a chuckle. "Oh, come on, it's not that bad."

Paavo raised his brows. "You're sure about that, are you?"

"Well, I'll take your word for it." He picked up the pot with a cloth. "I'm going to give this to everyone who's been coughing. And no cooking tonight, alright? You need to rest."

"Oh, I'll have to put up with your cooking as well as your awful tea?" Paavo said, but there was a gleam in his eye.

Tuomas gave him a soft kick and then ducked back into the open.

All the tents were up now; the villagers had done it for so long, it took barely any time. He walked to the nearest one and poked his head through the flap. A family looked up at him: his and Paavo's closest neighbours from the winter camp. Right on cue, the little boy spluttered in his mother's lap.

"I've got some tea, for the illness," he said, holding out the pot. "Would you like some?"

The mother's eyes darted between him and her son awkwardly. Then she nodded and handed over a cup. Tuomas filled it and she turned her attention to encouraging the youngster to drink it.

Tuomas removed himself from the shelter and went to walk away, but then he heard the mother and father's hushed voices. He didn't catch every word, but the ones he did drove dismay into his heart like needles.

"Son of the Son…"

"Great Mage…"

"Spirit in human form…"

Tuomas pressed his lips together. These were people who had helped care for him and raise him. Akerfjorden wasn't just a village, it was a family; there was nobody unconnected to all the others by blood or marriage. But as far as they could see, he had left at the beginning of the Long Dark as the boy they had always known, and now returned as a complete stranger with powers they didn't even recognise.

Could they even still see him anymore? Had he really once wanted to be a mage so he could feel special?

He sighed and walked to the next tent, dealing out the tea until he was scraping the bottom of the pot. Practically every family with children took a cup, and some of the parents too.

However, behind the grateful smiles, everyone's eyes were dark with wariness. It pressed on Tuomas's shoulders like a physical weight. When he stepped outside for the final time, he took a deep breath, trying to shift it.

There was a faint green glow over the snow. He looked up, straight into a blazing green aurora.

Those sitting on wolf-duty immediately bowed in respect. Tuomas lowered his head too. This wasn't the first time Lumi's Lights had shone since leaving Akerfjorden, but it was certainly the brightest. She was close to the skin between the Worlds. As the ghostly colours spread new streaks across the sky, he could almost see her at their head, sweeping her tail and shooting them from her hands.

He stood still and spoke silently.

I know you can hear me. I'm sorry. I know I upset you when I pulled away. I had to help them; it's a good thing I came back. You must see that.

She didn't reply, just carried on dancing.

Lumi? he said. *What happened with the stars? Is everything alright?*

The Lights slowed, drifting like fabric in water. A tiny edge of blue crept through them, then disappeared, and he knew he would get nothing else.

He kicked out at the powdery snow in frustration, but it didn't lessen the heaviness in his heart, so he trudged back to his tent and crawled inside. Elin was already cooking sautéed reindeer in a spare pot. He was relieved to see that Paavo had almost finished the tea, and his bruised eyes looked more tired than ill.

They ate in near-silence, too exhausted from the day's walk to speak about much. Then they unrolled their sleeping sacks and settled down. Tuomas turned his face to the fire, closed his eyes and immediately slipped into slumber.

He felt the heat of the hearth permeating his dreams; then the touch of snow on his cheeks and a pressure around his wrists, as though they were bound. He smelled woodsmoke and something rotting, like carrion on a hot day.

A man's face leered before him, smeared with ash, blinded in one eye. A terrible wound lay open on his throat.

Kari.

The demon pinned Tuomas's arms behind his back and the man drove a knife into his chest. Pain tore through him. He struggled, but he couldn't move; his body had turned to stone. His own scream surrounded him and threatened to swallow him whole. The blade slid deeper; he felt blood running down his naked chest... Kari was close, too close, too real...

He woke with a start. It was dark – for a horrible moment, he forgot where he was. Something was wrapped around his legs. Was he still tied up?

Then the details of the shelter swam into view. The pressure on his legs was just his sleeping sack. He kicked free of the tangle and fumbled with his tunic until he could see the scar over his breastbone. It was still there, healed, bloodless. Beneath the flesh, he felt his heart beating.

He gasped with relief. He told himself he was safe, that Kari couldn't hurt him anymore, but a ball of anxiety grew to replace the phantom pain of the knife. It didn't matter that Kari was gone; the memory of him lingered like a burn.

Elin stirred. Tuomas turned his head to watch her, but she didn't wake; only coughed and burrowed deeper into her sack like a mouse. Then she suddenly kicked out, her face knotted with distress. She flung up her arms as though trying to fight something off and hit one of the tent poles. The entire shelter shuddered.

Tuomas hurried to her and grabbed her wrists. She struggled against him with a frightened whimper.

He threw a quick glance at Paavo. His brother was still asleep, but Tuomas knew he would wake up soon if Elin carried on.

"Elin!" he whispered, as loudly as he dared. He let go of her with one hand and tapped her cheek.

Her eyes flew open. She looked around in alarm, then into Tuomas's face.

"Where's the boy?" she cried. "There was a boy…"

"It's alright," Tuomas assured her. "There's nothing here. You just had a nightmare."

Elin peered at him for a moment longer, then he felt her relax and released her other arm. He checked Paavo again, but he hadn't moved. His gentle snores filled the tent.

"Why are you awake?" Elin asked groggily. "Did you have a one too?"

Tuomas nodded. "It's nothing. Go back to sleep."

He had barely finished speaking when Elin closed her eyes again. Within moments, she was breathing heavily – and, Tuomas was pleased to see, her face looked much calmer. She turned onto her side and flung out her hand, her fingers landing on the arch of her bow.

Before he returned to his own sleeping sack, Tuomas drew back the flap just enough to peer out at the sky. To his relief, the stars were all in their proper places. Not a single one had fallen since that first night, but unease twisted in his gut nevertheless.

He placed a fresh log on the fire so it would burn until they woke, then laced his tunic shut again and laid his head down. He took hold of his drum and pulled it close, hugging it to his chest like a shield.

Then he caught sight of his belt, draped over his brown fur coat. Alongside his knives, a number of small leather and sealskin pouches were tied onto it. He grasped one at the back, which he'd completely forgotten was there, and untied it so he could peer inside.

The contents were still there: a lock of Mihka's snowy hair, and a bone carved into the shape of a fox.

Tears prickled his eyes, but didn't fall. How could it all seem so long ago, when he had set out into the Long Dark? Back then, when he had yearned for more, without knowing truly what that wish would bring?

He stared into the flames as they licked around the wood, watched the gentle red glow emanating from the embers, and listened to their crackle until slumber swept back to claim him.

Chapter Six

The next day, the convoy finally broke free of the forest and emerged onto the tundra. No longer funnelled by packed trees, the three hundred-strong herd spread out and transformed the flat snowy plain into a heaving sea of brown. The soft blue glow spilled over everything and cast no boundary between earth and sky. Wherever Tuomas looked, it was always the same: huge, open, with only the occasional shrub bent low by fierce blasts of wind.

Despite the endless nothingness, the reindeer knew where they were going. They walked unfazed into the north, following the secret hidden instinct which drove them every year towards Anaar. Even if the weather turned bad, they would carry on. But luckily, the spring was proving mild so far, and the previous cold weather had frozen the snow solid, making it easier for the animals to walk. Their large cup-shaped hooves splayed effortlessly across the surface.

The air was filled with the clicking of thousands of tendons in the reindeers' knees. They moved as one massive being, pushing through the snow with the occasional indignant snort. When the wind picked up, they huddled close together to keep warm, and the females' antlers waved like a giant living forest. The bulls had all shed their antlers near the end of the Long Dark, but the cows would keep theirs through the winter until after they gave birth.

After the burden of wading through deep powder, many of the herders had taken the earliest opportunity to wear skis. Like the reindeers' hooves, the long thin planks spread out their weight, and they slid alongside the herd on all sides to make sure no animals wandered too far. Others rode in the sleighs beside the cargo, or balanced on the backs with their feet on the runners.

As he skied along, Tuomas looked at the bull nearest to him. A quick glance at the series of notches cut into its ear told him it was one of Mihka's. Everyone's mark was different, as distinctive as a face, and they could all recognise their own even in the middle of a hectic corral.

The bull's large black eyes shone in the low light. Tuomas could imagine all the stars existing in those eyes. It reminded him of the legend which said that the Great Bear Spirit had used its own ancient body to make the three Worlds. Its blood transformed into the rivers and seas, its fur into the trees and bushes, and its skull into the sky. It had spread itself across everything which had ever existed, and allowed a giant invisible tree to grow through its remains, connecting the realms together. And it still stood even today: branches in the World Above, roots in the World Below, and trunk here in the World Between.

He slipped a hand out his mitten and dug around in a bag tied to his belt. He had filled it with dried jerky before leaving the camp that morning, so a snack was never out of reach. He pulled a strip free and took a bite out of it, then let his eyes wander over the tundra.

Somewhere out there, Lilja would be walking with the Poro herd. How was she managing with being around people again? In this endless whiteness, she could be anywhere if she wanted. She could disappear as she always had, never to see another human for the rest of her days, and she would have been perfectly happy with that.

Or would she? For all her wanderings, she had never been truly alone.

When he met her again, would she take him on? Tuomas gnawed on his lips as he thought about it. They were dry and cracked from cold, but he ignored the pain.

Paces turned into miles; hours into days, until an entire week had fallen behind them. The pale Sun Spirit passed from the right hand-side to the left, and eventually skimmed the horizon, throwing yellow highlights and blue shadows across the unchanging land. The snow turned lilac and pink and glittered in pastel glory.

It might have been easy to forget they were making any progress at all, save for the trail of churned-up prints left in their wake. Tuomas focused on the necessary things: one foot in front of the other; left ski pole into the snow, then right ski pole.

He followed the age-old route in his mind, imagined himself soaring above it like an eagle to behold it in its entirety. It would take them over the tundra, then up into the mountains, through the snowy passes where nothing grew. Then down again, far past the mouth of the Mustafjord, towards the sea.

Mihka appeared beside him and jostled his shoulder. Tuomas jumped, caught off guard.

"Good, you're awake. For a moment there, I thought you were sleepwalking," Mihka said, his voice muffled by a scarf.

"You can't sleepwalk in skis," Tuomas countered.

Mihka shrugged. "Whatever. How are you?"

Before he could reply, Mihka turned away and coughed. He spat phlegm into the snow. Tuomas noticed a tiny line of red on his lip.

His heart raced.

"Are you alright? There's blood."

"Huh? I've probably just strained. No need to worry."

"You're not getting sick too, are you?"

"I hope not," said Mihka. "How am I supposed to keep everyone entertained if I can't speak?"

"I think we'll be glad of the silence for once," Tuomas said.

"Very funny."

They trudged onward, the crunch of snow broken only by Mihka's coughs. He wiped his lips and left a scarlet smear across the fur on his mitten.

"I haven't seen much of you," he said.

"Nobody has," said Tuomas. "I was away, remember?"

"Yes, I *remember*," Mihka drawled sarcastically. "But even since you got back, I've hardly seen you. You've only spoken to me twice since the migration started."

"Because you've been riding with your father. I've been up here all the time, or making tea for the kids," Tuomas said. "You should have some of it later, by the way. You don't want that cough to get worse. I mean it."

"I don't want to not talk to you, either," Mihka retorted. "You saved me. You did everything for me. Now you're back, I'm back…"

He threw a glance at Elin, who had skied ahead to join Paavo and Aslak at the front of the herd.

"Have you got a new best friend, or something?" he muttered, his tone hard.

Tuomas frowned at him.

"What are you talking about?"

"Don't act stupid. You've been with her all the time. Loading the sleighs, walking up here. What's so special about her?"

"Nothing," Tuomas insisted. "We're just friends."

Mihka coughed again, then scowled at him. "But she's a girl."

"So?" Tuomas exhaled sharply, trying to keep his frustration in check. "She's a good person. She saved my life. A few times."

"What, and just because I didn't, she's better than me?" Mihka said, sullenly casting his eyes down. "It's not my fault I was asleep."

Despite himself, Tuomas couldn't hold back an explosion of laughter.

"Not your fault? Come on, Mihka, you insulted the Lights! You know you're lucky to be walking right now."

Mihka's cheeks reddened. "Well… yes, alright. But it doesn't feel like you're here much. Not with me, anyway."

"I haven't been with anyone all that much. Not even Elin. All I've done is help her carry the food sacks," said Tuomas. "You know how busy everyone is at this time of year. There's no time to do anything else. And she's only sleeping in our tent because Paavo made her our guest."

He gripped his ski pole tightly and glanced down at his chest. He hadn't had the nightmare again, but it was still horribly close.

"And… I've had a lot to deal with," he added, dropping his voice so nobody else would hear. "Did Henrik and Sisu fill you in while I was gone? About the demon-mage?"

Mihka nodded. "Did he really try to kill you?"

"He tried to do more than that," Tuomas said. "And I know he's gone now, but it scared me, Mihka. I'm trying to work through it, so I just need you to be patient with me. Things will be back to normal soon enough."

Mihka was silent for a few moments.

"No, they won't," he said, notably quieter. "It's not the same. *You're* not the same."

"Don't be silly. Of course I am."

"No, you're not."

Tuomas looked at him quizzically. Mihka met his eyes, and then he instantly understood what his friend meant.

"I'm still Tuomas," he insisted. "What life-soul I have doesn't make any difference."

"It does to everyone else," said Mihka. "You should have seen them, while you were away. You were all they talked about."

"What did they say?"

"That it's an omen. When the Great Mage was here, he led the people to Akerfjorden to get away from the Moon Spirit."

Tuomas gritted his teeth, painfully recalling the words he'd heard upon sharing out the tea.

"Well, don't worry about that. I spoke with the Great Bear Spirit when I was in Poro, and it didn't seem to have any issues about me. Things can go on as they always have," he said, but he cut his words off when he noticed Mihka's wide-eyed expression.

"This is what I mean," he said. "You're just talking about this Spirit and that Spirit, like you've known them all for ages. Henrik's been a mage for… what, centuries? And even he can't talk to them like that. And you never did, not before all this. It's not normal."

Tuomas swallowed nervously.

"Does it really matter if it's normal or not? I can do it. So what? It will help me be a good mage."

Mihka gave an uncomfortable shuffle on his skis.

"They were saying that you've been reborn with that life-soul for a reason. That it means bad things are coming, and you'll have to get us out of it again."

"Again?" Tuomas smirked. "The only one I've *gotten out* of anything so far is an idiot who had his hair turn white."

That did it. Mihka raised one of his ski poles and smacked him across the legs. Tuomas shoved him back and pulled down his scarf a little to stick out his tongue – the only part of his face which was visible from under his layers.

The two of them chuckled, and as though nothing had happened, it was like it had always been.

But then there came a sudden shout from the front of the herd. Tuomas looked up in alarm. The reindeer beside him jostled, spooked by the sound.

"*Henrik!*" somebody yelled. Elin.

Tuomas craned his neck to see, but the mass of reindeer blocked his view. Then he noticed Elin powering towards them on her skis. He reached out as she passed and snatched her arm, pulling her to a stop.

"Where's Henrik?" she asked breathlessly.

"At the back," said Tuomas. "What is it?"

She motioned behind her with one of her poles. "It's Paavo. He's collapsed!"

Tuomas's heart rose into his throat and he forgot to breathe.

"Get Henrik and meet me there," he snapped.

He pushed forward and shot past the herd. He headed in the direction Elin had come from and immediately noticed where the reindeer were walking around an obstruction in their path. Sure enough, there were a few figures on the ground; others were standing with their arms out to guide the animals away.

Tuomas hurried over and skidded to a halt, sending snow flying.

"What happened?" he asked as he kicked his shoes out of the skis.

Aslak's eyes were wide with panic and he pushed Paavo onto his back.

"He just fell," he said. "He was coughing, and then his voice slurred, and he went down."

Tuomas yanked Paavo's scarf away from his face. His skin was alarmingly pale, lips turning blue. There were specks of blood around his mouth.

Aslak hovered behind Tuomas.

"Is he alright?" he asked anxiously.

Tuomas didn't reply. He pulled off his mitten and held a finger under his brother's nose. He felt a waft of warmth followed by a cloud rising into the air – he was breathing. Then he searched Paavo's wrist. His pulse was ragged, racing one moment and skipping beats the next.

He looked up frantically. The reindeer were continuing to move past them; all he saw was a heaving mass of brown fur.

"Where's Henrik?" he snapped. "Henrik!"

"Tuomas, I've found him! We're coming!"

Elin drew to a stop at Tuomas's side and stuck her poles upright in the snow. Henrik appeared moments after, running as fast as he could. He grabbed hold of Elin to steady himself while he caught his breath, then eased himself to his knees and lifted Paavo's head into his lap.

He took some tea from a flask at his belt and held the rim to Paavo's lips. Tuomas caught a strong woody whiff of angelica. The brew wouldn't be hot, but Tuomas couldn't help but recall the times he had joked how it could probably wake a corpse.

Please let that be true, he thought, and sent out a silent prayer to all the Spirits he could think of.

Paavo spluttered, coughed up half the tea, then fell back against Henrik's chest. He let out a frantic gasp. His throat sounded horribly tight, as though an invisible rope had been tied around it.

"Are you alright?" Tuomas asked over Henrik's shoulder.

"Mmnnh," Paavo groaned. "What happened?"

"You fell," Elin said. "Are you hurt?"

Paavo shook his head and tried to stand, but Henrik and Aslak pressed him down.

"Oh no, you don't," Aslak said. "You sit and ride for a while. Tuomas, can you fetch a sleigh, please?"

Ignoring Paavo's protests, Tuomas retraced his steps until he reached the first wave of sleighs. Maiken was sitting in the nearest one, on top of a mound of sleeping sacks. Tuomas came up behind and jumped on the runners. He almost lost his balance, but gripped the back and bent his knees, crouching low so Maiken could hear him.

"You need to get Paavo," he said. "Over there."

Maiken tugged on a rope attached to the reindeer's harness and waved her right arm at the same time. The animal immediately turned left, away from the movement. Within minutes, the sleigh had pulled up next to Paavo. Tuomas stepped off and helped Aslak lift him inside.

"I'll keep an eye on him," Maiken promised. She felt Paavo's forehead. "You're on fire. You need to stay warm. But don't let your mind fool you into thinking you're too hot; you'll start taking your layers off."

"Get under the blanket," Tuomas said.

"I'm fine," Paavo snapped. "I just went a little dizzy."

"You are not fine," said Henrik. "Do as you're told. Stay there and rest."

That finally silenced Paavo and he slumped back against the sleeping sacks in defeat. Everyone knew: if a village leader or mage commanded something, it was always best to obey.

"Take this," Henrik said as he handed Maiken the flask. "Make sure he drinks it."

"All of it?"

"Yes. He seems to be the worst of them all today. I'll make some more later for the other youngsters."

He placed a crooked hand on Tuomas's shoulder and steered him away to speak privately.

"The shrine is close," he said. "We need to go there now."

"Mihka has it too," Tuomas said. "He's started coughing. Are they going to be alright?"

"I hope so. They're both strong," Henrik replied.

"But?"

"There is no but. We just manage it as best we can, and they fight it as hard as they can."

Henrik walked to the sleigh and leaned over the side to speak with Maiken.

"Go ahead of us," he said. "We'll meet you further along the route."

"Can you catch up?" she asked.

"Yes, even if it's tonight at the camp," Henrik assured. "This is important."

Maiken nodded in agreement. There was no way they could halt the whole herd; the reindeer would keep going until after dark, and the people had no choice but to follow.

Tuomas placed his jerky pouch into the sleigh beside Paavo, so he would have food if he wanted any. Then he covered him with a blanket and tucked it around his chin. Paavo half-heartedly slapped his hands away.

"Stop babying me," he said.

"Stop acting tough," Thomas shot back.

Paavo glared, but his eyes were hazy and unfocused, and belied how weak he really was. He managed a small smile before he started coughing again.

"Watch out for the boy," he muttered.

Tuomas frowned. "What?"

A muscle twitched in Paavo's cheek. When he exhaled, Tuomas heard the crackle of liquid in his lungs.

"The little boy…" Paavo said again. His words fell over each other in a frail garble.

"Hush, now," Maiken said gently.

"He's hallucinating," Henrik said. "Give him water as well as that tea. And try to get him eating. Let him sleep if he needs to, but make sure he can breathe."

Tuomas stepped away, barely able to hide his alarm. Elin had said something about a boy too.

When he looked up, she was coming towards them, her skis under one arm. She presented them to Henrik with a nod of respect.

"Take these," she insisted. "I can ride in a sleigh."

"Thank you, girl," said Henrik.

Tuomas wanted to question her, but Henrik had already started tying the skis onto his shoes; he was eager to go. He threw an expectant glance at Tuomas, so he did the same. He could speak to her when they got back.

Elin jumped into a nearby sleigh and threw them a wave of farewell as the herd moved on. Mihka had also given up walking and joined Sisu in another sleigh, wrapped in so many furs, he looked like a reindeer himself. He caught Tuomas's eye and hurriedly wiped a line of blood from his chin.

Chapter Seven

Without a word, Henrik and Tuomas began their hike. Tuomas knew roughly where the shrine was, but he had never been to it before, so he let Henrik lead the way. He was immediately thankful for the skis – walking on such powdery snow without them could be gruelling.

"We take our cues from the reindeer," Paavo had once said to him when he was younger. *"You see how their hooves splay out and stop them from sinking? We don't have hooves, so we make them from wood. But our hooves are long too, so we can slide!"*

It wasn't long before they reached the shrine: a huge boulder deposited in the middle of the empty tundra. By itself, it looked unremarkable, but it was the only type of its kind: different from everything else around it. That made it powerful. Offerings from the previous migration lay all over its surface: antlers, bone carvings, pieces of woven material, all encrusted with ice and frozen in place.

Henrik brushed some snow off a natural seat in the boulder and sat down with a groan. Whilst he nursed his knees, Tuomas set to work spinning a protective circle. He had learned from past mistakes to not take any chances, but it was especially true at somewhere like this, where nature itself allowed the Worlds to touch.

He swept a hand around the entire shrine, feeling the *taika* lay itself down into the snow as an invisible yet impenetrable barrier. When it was secure, he built a small fire and joined Henrik on the seat. As soon as he touched it, he shuddered. The rock took his weight as he knew it would, yet it also felt as thin as reindeer skin, as though just beneath it, the space between the realms was pressing in upon itself.

He knew Henrik had felt it as well, because the old mage threw him a knowing glance. He untied his drum from his belt and held it above the flame, getting it ready for the work ahead. Tuomas did the same. When the skin was taught, they laid the instruments across their laps.

Henrik's new drum was smaller than his old one, and the skin was pale in comparison, with the alder juice ink of the symbols still a vivid red. But when he struck it, it let out a fine sound which reverberated through Tuomas's bones.

"Are you ready, boy?" Henrik asked.

Tuomas nodded.

"We'll make an offering. Cut some of your hair."

Both of them drew knives and sheared off a lock. Henrik rolled the strands in his palm until his white ones were peppered with Tuomas's blonde ones, then cast them onto the rock.

"Know our intention," Henrik continued. "We will ask for the Sun Spirit."

"Alright," Tuomas said. "I'm ready."

"Are you sure?"

"Yes. Let's go."

Henrik offered him a gentle smile, then raised his hammer. Tuomas did the same, and in unison, they brought the antlers down.

Tuomas closed his eyes as the rhythm began, reaching deep, sweeping him up and away. It felt like so long since he had heard this beautiful, simple sound. It was the music of the things beneath the skin, of nature's heartbeat, rising and falling with every strike.

He sensed his *taika* growing: the lingonberry taste, the sight of lazy evening light dappling a pool, the golden glow of an endless day and the smell of wild flowers on a sweet southern breeze. He started to chant. He didn't try to form words – there was no need for them, just like in the World Above. He wasn't capturing a thing, but becoming that thing.

His souls slackened inside him. He didn't fight it, just carried on chanting, holding the intention in his mind; gently, as though it were alive.

His body rocked back and forth as he separated from it. The cold disappeared; the rock beneath him melted like thawing ice. And then he was floating in nothingness, surrounded by it, wrapped in its invisible embrace.

For a long moment, there was nothing. He couldn't sense Henrik anywhere. He reminded himself not to panic; he focused on the drumbeats, clutched the intention to his chest. His heart slowed to match the rhythm.

Then he felt a presence drawing close to him. He recognised heat first, which grew into light and a stream of waving gold.

I see you, the Sun Spirit said. *I hear you calling for me, my son.*

We need your help, he said. He let the words become formless in his mind, and they sounded older than the body below him. He spoke with the part of him which did not belong to the humans.

Why are the children and young adults sick? he asked. *How can we help them? Does it have something to do with the stars falling?*

The Sun Spirit swelled and blanketed him in her light.

You cannot fight this with remedies, she said. *Many mages before you have tried, and all they have achieved is the knowledge to ease the pain.*

Isn't it physical? It's not a cold or influenza?

No. But neither is it mental. If it were those things, I would lift it away and let it be healed. There is no strength of body for me to give; no madness of mind to chase away. This is something more… a different breed of plague.

Tuomas reached out towards her. *What is it?*

It is a soul plague. Beings have brought it to the people.

Dread filled him. He recalled the feel of the knife, the smell, one blinded eye…

A being? It's another wicked mage? Or a demon? Has Kari come back? Please tell me he hasn't come back…

He has not returned. He is elsewhere, the Sun Spirit whispered.

Is he still in the World Below? Please, I need to know.

Yes, and there he will remain. Do not worry. He will never touch you again.

Relief melted around him. He allowed himself to drift through her warmth as it enfolded him like an embrace.

If it's not Kari or another like him, he said, *then what is it?*

Something older. Much older, replied the Golden One. *It is the work of creatures from the void between the Worlds, rising every generation to take the young. And with them is something of flesh and blood, but yet not. Something once living… perhaps still living… perhaps not still living…*

Her words brought back a memory of being on the ice, engulfed by the mist, hearing the slippery sound behind him. He tried to see into her meanings, to find a face to put with the noise, but nothing came. It tugged at some deep part of him, buried just out of reach.

The beings are called draugars, said the Sun Spirit. *You have dealt with them before, but you have forgotten it. They are wicked things. You must avoid the mist at all costs; if you touch it, they will be alerted to your presence and come for you.*

Tuomas froze in the air.

That's what the noise was on the Mustafjord, he realised. *And why Lumi tried to stop me from coming back. Why? What do they want from me?*

Your taika. You are a Spirit, my dear. There is nothing else like you in the World Between. Beware them.

I don't understand.

There is one who will.

A face appeared in Tuomas's mind. He watched it take shape, spinning out of the yellow light as though it were threads being woven into a pattern. There was a coat with sleeves of white reindeer fur; two long sandy braids; a scar stretching from left to right across the throat.

Lilja: the wandering mage who wanders no more, the Golden One said. *She will have the answers. Seek her out. Bring forth the secret she has locked deep inside, and you will know.*

He stared at Lilja. Even though he knew she was only an image, he felt as though he could reach out and touch her.

The Sun Spirit drew closer and enclosed him even tighter in her delicious warmth. It was a perfect feeling; sheer bliss. He basked in it like a child, never wanting to let it go.

But he knew he had to. His body was tugging at him, anchoring him to the World Between, back down in that place of gravity and hard edges.

He bid her thanks and farewell, and started to descend. But as soon as he was out of her sight, a huge silvery bulk suddenly rose before him.

He wasn't blinded as he had been when he'd seen the Sun Spirit. This wasn't as bright as her. In his mind's eye, he sensed a tall, thin woman; much like his mother, and yet the opposite to her. The flaming golden hair was dark and thin; her face was pockmarked with craters and mountains larger than any in the World Between; her fingers extended like spider legs and shadows fell upon her so harshly that she seemed hollow.

He shuddered. He knew who this was.

Silver One, he said.

I have not seen you in a long time, Red Fox One, said the Moon Spirit. Her voice was colder than ice; colder even than Lumi. He felt night closing around him; the dampness of holes in the earth; the crisp smell of incoming rain. She surrounded him with it, blocking them both off from everything else.

My sister and daughter kept you away from me when you were in the World Above, she continued. *How I longed to see you. You were always welcome with me, dear little one. You always are.*

Tuomas was filled with fright. He hadn't intended to see anyone but the Sun Spirit. He needed to get back, but as he gently tested the boundaries around him, he realised she wasn't going to release him.

He would have to tread with care. She was arguably the most dangerous and prideful Spirit of them all. He saw Lumi in her, and yet even his sister seemed like a gentle snowfall in the face of the blizzard of energy before him. This was the greatest winter Spirit: the eye which peered down upon the World Between through the Long Dark, forever watching and judging as she blinked from full to new. For as bright as she was, she was an entity of pure darkness.

Why did you not come to me? the Moon Spirit whispered. *You are my son. I raised you, my beautiful boy.*

If we are asking questions, I have one for you, he said, hating how scared he sounded. *Why did you switch me with her?*

The White Fox One? came the snide reply. *That vain and angry little girl? Who was she compared to you, my sweet? Who was she, who could do nothing but remind me of coldness and gloom? And then there you were, so beautiful, so perfect... everything which should have been mine. You were mine, dear thing. I may not have borne you, but I raised you. You came into yourself by my doing. You owe all you are to me.*

Tuomas hesitated. Her words lit a fury in him like fire – how could she bear to speak so cruelly of her own daughter? He pictured Lumi in her ethereal grace; her faultless dances and the care with which she cradled a soul. As revered as she was, no matter how harsh she could be, she hadn't deserved such abandonment.

The Moon Spirit sensed his anger. She floated closer and wrapped herself around him. There was no physical touch, yet he still felt it and recoiled.

Where is the Golden One? he asked. *Where is Lumi?*

The Moon Spirit scoffed. *You still call her by that ridiculous human name? There is no need for names among our kind, my dear. You know that.*

Tuomas stood his ground. *Where are they?*

Somewhere far away. I did not wish for our reunion to be disturbed, replied the Silver One. *I will not be kept from you. Not now you are aware, once again, of who you truly are. And where you truly belong.*

She pressed him against her. Despite himself, he let out a whimper. It was nothing like the feeling of the Sun Spirit holding him. It was hard and oppressive; not a gesture of love, but of ownership.

I do not want the White Fox One. I never did. I want you, she whispered inside his mind. *Come back to me. Return to the World Above and let me be your mother again, my dear Red Fox One. Be with me as you were always meant to be.*

He stayed deathly still. The grip around him was loose, but he also knew it could crush him like a fly. He had thought that nothing could be more terrifying than a furious Lumi running at him, on the night he'd first spoken with her, but that was quashed in an instant. The Moon Spirit was so much stronger than her daughter; deeper, darker, colder…

Tuomas steeled himself and pulled away from her.

I have… a life in the World Between, he said cautiously. *I have a brother, friends…*

Who will soon die, the Moon Spirit sneered. *And others after them will die, forever coming back, over and over again until the end of time. Such is the way of life-souls, dear. But not for you. You are a Spirit; you are not like them. You can never be like them.*

But I am, he insisted. *I need to find Lilja… I have to help them. I have to go. Please let me go. They need me.*

Like your precious humans needed you when you first left me? she retorted. *And what of me? Did you not think I needed you, that night when you leapt from my grasp and allowed yourself to take the form of a screaming baby? I thought you had learned your lesson!*

She drew close again, but Tuomas backed away so she couldn't grab him again.

Why do you shrink from me? she demanded. *Are you afraid?*

Yes, he replied. *I can't remember what happened to make me leave, but I did it for a reason. And I'm living a new life now for a reason.*

This is your home! cried the Moon Spirit. *I am your mother!*

A blaze of green suddenly broke through the barrier and shot between the two of them. It swirled around Tuomas in a massive flaming wall, and he saw Lumi hovering before him, her tail shooting red auroras in all directions.

No, you are not, Silver One! she snarled. *You are no-one's mother but mine, and he is the Son of the Sun! How dare you try to influence him like this! Did you think I would not notice?*

The Moon pulsed with furious light. *Stay out of this, White Fox One!*

She tried to force her way forward, but Lumi whisked Tuomas further back.

He will return to the World Above when it is his time, Lumi snapped. *I will hold his life-soul far from you. He shall be with his true mother again, and you must content yourself with me!*

She flung a jet of green at the Moon Spirit. Tuomas heard it split the air like lightning. The Moon Spirit threw her own light straight back and it hit Lumi so hard, she cartwheeled through the night.

Lumi! Tuomas shouted.

She leapt in front of him again. His vision exploded. All around, he saw swathes of colour, shot through with silver. The Moon Spirit seized Lumi in an iron grip and they wrapped around each other, trying to get purchase.

Tuomas, go! Lumi shrieked.

Then everything went black and he wrenched his eyes open.

Chapter Eight

In an instant, he became heavier, shrank back to a single form, felt icy air drawing deep into his lungs. Henrik was bending over him, tea-breath blowing in his face. Tuomas quickly rolled over to get away from it, and realised with a jolt that he was lying in the snow. He must have tipped off the seat while in trance.

"What did you see?" Henrik asked.

"Just give me a moment," Tuomas mumbled.

His entire body shook. He struggled to focus, but still saw only Lumi's Lights. He peered up at the sky and noticed a furious aurora. Beside it was the Moon Spirit, half her face in shadow. He felt the pressure of their fight on his chest.

"Keep away…" Tuomas breathed. "I'm needed here…"

"What are you talking about, boy?"

Tuomas held his hands to his face. The flesh felt separate from himself, as though he was on the outside looking in.

"You came back too fast," Henrik was saying. "Sit up carefully. Come on, now."

He grasped Tuomas's shoulders and set him against the shrine. Tuomas groaned as the blood rushed to his head. The surroundings spun around him as though they were made from water. Worried he would fall straight through the ground, he snatched hold of Henrik.

The Lights raged overhead, and then, in an instant, the night was still and silent once again. A faint waft of green trailed through the darkness.

"Lumi?" he called. "Lumi!"

"Focus on me," Henrik instructed. "It's over. You're safe."

"Where's Lumi?" Tuomas panted. With every breath, lucidity slowly returned, but he still didn't move. His legs felt a thousand miles away.

He rubbed the bleariness out of his eyes and searched the sky. The single tendril of the aurora lingered for a moment, as though to let him know she was safe. As soon as he saw it, she disappeared, and the pressure slowly ebbed away.

Tuomas let out a shaky sigh. "I'm fine."

"Good," said Henrik. "Now, tell me what you saw. Did you see the Sun Spirit?"

"Yes," Tuomas replied. He noticed the strained expression on Henrik's face and frowned. "What's wrong?"

Henrik sighed sharply. "I... I couldn't connect with the Spirits. Not one of them."

Tuomas pulled himself to his feet and immediately wobbled. He grabbed hold of the shrine to keep his balance.

"What do you mean?"

"It was like something was blocking me," Henrik said. "I could barely enter the trance without being pulled back to my body."

Tuomas swallowed. "Was it something I did? Was my *taika* out of control again? I didn't block you, did I?"

To his surprise, Henrik smirked. "No. Your *taika* was miraculous. When I realised I wasn't going anywhere, I watched you. It was beautiful."

A smile broke across Tuomas's lips. That was the greatest compliment Henrik had ever given him. After months of the old mage chastising him about control and practising the craft correctly, this was the praise he'd wanted to hear.

As quickly as it came, however, Henrik was back to his original question.

"I need you to tell me what you saw. What did the Golden One say to you?"

Tuomas let go of the boulder and kicked snow over the fire to end the work. Then he picked up his drum. His eyes lingered over the image of the Great Bear Spirit in the centre.

"She said it's not a physical illness like you thought. It's a soul plague. We need to find Lilja – apparently she knows something about it which can help us."

A shadow passed over Henrik's face.

"A soul plague, you say? But what does she have to do with it?

"I don't know," Tuomas replied. "Henrik… while I was up there, the Moon Spirit came and ambushed me. She wants me back… she tried to trap me. But Lumi fought her off…"

"You're talking too fast, calm down." Henrik stood directly in front of him so he couldn't look away. "The Moon Spirit cannot take you back. You know that, don't you?"

"No!" cried Tuomas. "If she did it before, she can do it again!"

"Not when you're in a human body. She doesn't handle souls, so she doesn't even have the same power as her daughter: to take a life-soul away. And remember, when she succeeded last time, you were none the wiser. You're stronger now. Nothing will drive you back to her unless you choose it, do you understand?"

Tuomas glanced at the silvery eye in the sky. He could feel it watching him.

"She can't do anything unless I give her permission to?" he whispered.

"No," said Henrik, with an assuredness which immediately made him feel better.

"So I shouldn't be afraid."

"I didn't say that. We should fear and respect all Spirits. Especially her."

There was a dark edge to his words, but he turned away from Tuomas and broke the magical circle around the shrine.

"Come now," he said. "Let's go back. We've been here for long enough."

Tuomas inspected the sky again. The evening was upon them, though it was still only afternoon – day and night would not be equal for another couple of months. But the brief spell of daylight was long gone: a sign that spring was arriving, even if spring itself was still frozen.

He closed his eyes and forced himself to breathe deeply. The Silver One had simply caught him off guard, and if she tried again, he had seen how vehemently Lumi had defended him. Both she and the Sun Spirit had kept him safe for an entire month in the World Above. Everything would be fine.

When he had collected himself, he and Henrik thanked the Spirits, strapped their drums to their belts, inserted their shoes into the skis, and began heading back. The snow seemed to glow in the blue half-light, before it faded into a haze at the flat horizon.

They didn't need to worry about going far. The reindeer were visible in the distance: a dark smudge against the white land. Soon they would be stopping for the night and the herders would erect their tents. Tuomas guessed that by the time he and Henrik caught up with them, it would be time for food and bed anyway.

After almost a mile of walking in silence, Henrik cleared his throat.

"You know, boy… I'm concerned about Lilja being involved in this."

His voice was tight, as though he had been mulling over the words for some time and mentally testing to see if they sounded right.

"Why do you say that?" Tuomas asked, even though he already knew the answer.

"Well, there's everything that's happened. She was like a wolf, growling and attacking Paavo –"

"She wasn't herself then. You know that. Kari had her under his control."

"But she's such a strange one," Henrik insisted. "Her and her brother both, even before you went looking for them."

"She had her reasons," said Tuomas. "I know her. I've spent time with her."

"As have I," Henrik replied, somewhat snappishly. "She came to Akerfjorden before. She was even on the migration years ago, back when your poor mother was pregnant with you. I traded with her for some fish hooks. Then she delivered you."

"I know. But you haven't lived with her like I have. It's different." Tuomas glanced at him. "Do you not want me to be her apprentice now?"

"Don't be childish."

"I'm not being childish. I'm asking a question."

"You're being insolent," Henrik said. "But you're a man now, you can choose to do what you want."

"You're the one who said I was still a boy. And you told me to ask her," Tuomas argued.

Henrik crossly brushed him off. "But with all this going on; a soul plague… You know my opinion of her. Too powerful. No good will come of it."

"I've heard that before, Henrik."

"Need I remind you of what happened? How do we know she hasn't followed in her brother's footsteps? Done something wicked?"

"How do we know she has? You're jumping to conclusions. I didn't trust her last time. I'm not making the same mistake now."

"It's not a mistake if it's well founded."

Tuomas looked straight at Henrik. "I know you don't like her, but she would never do something like that. *Never*. Are you saying all this because you mean it, or because you're jealous?"

"Mind your tongue! What would I have to be jealous about?" Henrik snapped. "To have no family? No home? No village to care for and act as a mage should?"

"To be touched by the Great Bear Spirit?" Tuomas retorted. "Or maybe you're afraid of her?"

His words seemed to cut through to the old mage, because he turned away. But before he did, his eyes changed, and Tuomas noticed it as though he'd slapped him.

"Are you afraid of me, too?"

Henrik cleared his throat and shot him the quickest of glances.

"By the Spirits, Henrik," Tuomas breathed. "Don't be afraid of me. I'm still just me."

"Let's not talk about her anymore," said Henrik, softer now.

Tuomas wanted to press him, but he let it lie. A tangle of unease grew in his stomach like a hairball. Henrik was scared. Everyone was. The only one who wasn't treating him any differently was Elin.

She was on the journey with you, he reasoned. *She knows what happened; she saw it. She knows you.*

But that didn't help. All the others, most of whom he'd been around his entire life, should have known him too.

He set his attention on the herd in the distance. It had stopped moving now; with every step they took, the dark mass grew larger. The tents glowed from the fires within them, but Tuomas knew that was no guarantee that anyone would still be awake. He could tell from the position of the stars how long he and Henrik had been gone.

The tundra dipped into a gentle slope and the two of them leaned forward, letting the skis carry them smoothly down. The tents were up and fires spread a welcoming orange over the land

"Anyway," Tuomas said, "the Sun Spirit told me it's caused by something older than a mage."

"Then what is it?" Henrik asked quietly.

Tuomas kept his eyes on the camp.

"She said something about creatures from the void between the Worlds," he said. "She called them draugars."

Henrik's eyes widened. "Impossible. Those are things of fireside tales."

"It's what she said," Tuomas insisted. "And she mentioned something alive, yet not alive... I didn't really understand. I suppose I'll just have to ask Lilja."

Chapter Nine

It was a restless evening. As soon as they arrived at the camp, Tuomas and Henrik shared a quick meal of dried char, then he left the old mage in bed while he prepared to leave. He went to the sleighs and pulled aside a small one filled with spare tent poles and tarp. It was a perfect size for a small journey, so he emptied the contents into a neighbouring one. When it was cleared, he raided the food sacks and dug out some smoked reindeer and ptarmigan strips. When he was sure he had all he would need, he drew a tarp over the top and went to his tent.

Elin lay on one side of the fire, and Paavo on the other, snoring softly. They had laid out Tuomas's sleeping sack too and left it ready for him.

He crept closer to get a better look at Paavo. His skin was still pale and tiny blood vessels were visible underneath it, but he had thankfully lost the blue in his lips. Tuomas wiped a few specks of blood off his chin and sat back on his haunches. He had never seen Paavo so thin. It was as though the muscle had simply dropped off him in a matter of days.

In his sleep, Paavo let out a weak cough, then rolled over and curled himself closer to the fire. The movement made him seem so small, like a child somehow trapped in a larger body.

Anger wrenched through Tuomas as he imagined the souls within Paavo, struck with illness, struggling to stay together inside their host. He was still young – only twenty-five years old. He should be looking for a nice girl, planning his own family, not struggling to breathe like a fish pulled from a lake.

"What's the matter?"

He jumped in fright and almost fell over into the tarp wall. Across the hearth, Elin had awoken and propped herself up on her elbows.

"Sorry," she mouthed. "Do you want to go outside? Talk?"

Tuomas shook his head and crawled to her, being careful where he laid his feet so he didn't make any noise.

"I need to speak to Lilja," he whispered. "I'm going tomorrow. I'll catch up with the herd later."

"Why Lilja?" Elin asked through a yawn. "Does she know why all the kids are sick?"

"Apparently."

"Alright. I'll see you in the morning."

Tuomas caught her meaning immediately. "You're not coming."

She shot him a pointed look. "Watch me."

"It's just for a couple of days. They'll have left Poro by now, I'm only going to be a few miles to the west," he argued. "There's no point in you coming."

"But I want to," she replied, "so I'm going to."

With that, she laid back down in her sleeping sack.

Tuomas looked at her incredulously. "You're impossible."

She didn't reply, so he got to his feet and gave her a gentle kick in the side. "Nobody falls asleep that fast."

"Then shut up so I can," she muttered.

Tuomas rolled his eyes and settled into his own sack, throwing another log on the fire as he did. Orange sparks flew into the air and disappeared through the smoke hole. He watched them soar, like miniature Sun beams, and mingle with the stars, before his eyes closed and he drifted away with them.

The last thing he heard was a faint cough from Elin.

They rose early, long before dawn had broken the horizon, and immediately set to work. After breakfast, Tuomas and Elin helped strike the camp, unravelling the tarp from around the tent poles and folding it all down to fit neatly into the sleighs. Everyone knew their jobs, honed from generations' worth of experience, and all were ready to move on before the reindeer had even finished foraging.

Paavo stumbled his way forward. Aslak and Anssi ran over and each pulled an arm across their shoulders to steady him.

"I can get there myself," Paavo insisted.

"I'm sure you can, but we're helping anyway," replied Anssi.

They didn't let go of Paavo until he was in a sleigh and covered with blankets. Paavo angrily waved Aslak away, but then curled over and coughed so hard, he retched.

Tuomas watched as the other youngsters made their way to the convoy. His breath caught in his throat. So many of them were struggling to walk. Practically every child was wrapped in all the layers which could be found, and some of the teenagers and young adults were as ashen as a corpse. Their lips had turned pale and their eyes were so bruised, they looked as though they had aged overnight. All were coughing.

Anxiety pressed on his chest. They had covered a fair distance from Akerfjorden now, but they still needed to get over the mountains and then down again to the coast. How were they going to manage?

An even darker thought passed his mind. How many were going to survive?

He went to the sleigh he had set aside the night before and threw his sleeping sack inside. Henrik, Maiken, Sisu and Mihka hovered nearby.

"This is twice in the same winter you're heading out to find Lilja," Sisu remarked.

"Well, at least this time, Mihka's awake," Tuomas replied with a small smile.

Mihka narrowed his eyes at him, trying to hold back a cough. His face was almost as white as his hair.

The sight was painful. Only a night had passed since he'd been able to hike beside Tuomas, and now he could barely stand. Sisu put an arm around him; Mihka melted into the embrace and clutched at his father's side like a child. He didn't bother trying to hide it: he was scared.

Maiken stepped forward so she could whisper to Tuomas.

"Before you go, isn't there anything you can do for them?" she asked.

"Henrik can keep giving them the tea," Tuomas said as steadily as he could manage. "It will take the edge off –"

"No, not like that," Maiken said. "I mean *you*. Can you do anything?"

Tuomas swallowed anxiously. "I don't think so."

Her face fell. "But you're –"

"Still just a mage," he cut in. "Maiken, please don't think I'm any different. I'm still figuring out how it all works myself. I can't just snap my fingers and everyone will be healed."

"Isn't the Sun Spirit the one responsible for healing?" she pressed. "If you're her son, then maybe you'll have the power to fix it."

"And maybe I don't," Tuomas replied. "I don't know what I can do. The best way I can help people right now is speak to Lilja and see what she knows."

Maiken looked at him searchingly, but she could tell from his firm expression that he meant it.

"You're right," she said. "I just hope she does know something. And that we're the only village who have been struck with... whatever this illness is."

Tuomas offered her a small smile and lowered his head in respect. To his surprise, she did the same, followed by Sisu.

Tuomas swallowed. It was usually everyone else who bowed to the leaders, not the other way around. And he'd only seen them bend that deeply when the Lights appeared.

He bit his lip. Not just with the Lights, but when a Spirit was among them.

He waited in uncomfortable silence until they straightened up.

"I won't be long," he promised.

"We," Elin called, walking over with her own sleeping sack. She removed her bow from her shoulder in mid-stride and tossed everything into the sleigh beside Tuomas's belongings.

"Yes, we," Tuomas conceded.

He spotted a nearby reindeer bearing his earmark and pointed it out to her. A bell hung on a length of fabric around its neck: a sign that it had been trained to pull. Elin grabbed a lasso, threw it, and it flew perfectly over the animal's head.

She reeled the reindeer close, dragged it to the sleigh and hitched it up to the poles. It was a male – taking a female would have put unnecessary strain on her and the unborn calf. It snorted and pawed at the snow, but soon calmed, and Elin pulled some lichen out of a sack to feed it from her hand.

Tuomas noticed Mihka pouting at Elin, but ignored him.

"We'll meet you further along the route," he said. He clambered into the sleigh, elbowing a tent pole out of the way as he sat down. Henrik approached and laid a hand on his arm.

"I'll do my best to keep the sickness under control," he said, "but get back here as soon as you can."

"What if you reach the mountains before we do?" Tuomas asked. "There's no way we'll catch up with you."

"Don't try to. Stay with the Poro herd when you reach them," said Sisu. "If we all make haste, nobody will be waiting too long. We'll just camp at the coast until we're together."

Tuomas nodded. It wasn't the best plan, but nothing would be perfect in these circumstances.

Henrik tapped his hand to get his attention again.

"Don't mind what happened last night, boy," he said in a whisper. "I'm just… concerned about not being able to connect with the Spirits."

"So you're not afraid of me?"

"No."

He said it too quickly. Tuomas sighed, but still nodded.

"Thank you," he muttered.

"Go in peace."

"Stay in peace."

Elin jumped in beside him and pulled her mittens back on. It was then that Tuomas noticed they were made from white fur – she had sewed them from the hare's pelt which Lilja had given her a few months ago.

She took the rope and gave it a snap. The reindeer grumbled, unwilling to leave the herd, but Tuomas waved his arms to mimic an eagle and that finally made it move. The sleigh jolted forward. He kept his attention fixed on the tundra so he couldn't see the convoy shrinking behind him – it was too much like the last time he had left Akerfjorden.

Before long, they were alone in the endless white. The miles were lost; the path was broken only by knee-high shrubs and spindly trees bending under the weight of snow. In the distance, the edge of the forest loomed, the topmost branches feathered by frost. And along the horizon, he could see the first peaks of the mountains: a great stone wall separating them from the islands on the other side.

The sky transformed a crisp pink and baby blue. The moisture in the air glittered, turned to ice where it hung. The temperature dropped and Tuomas's lashes began to freeze. He blinked rapidly, trying to clear the crystals, and held his hands over his eyes to thaw them out.

Elin wrapped an extra shawl around her shoulders. Then she fetched her bow and plucked the string with one finger to check it was still taught. It was a wonderful piece of craftmanship, made from ash wood and carved with a dazzling collection of patterns.

"Are you getting hungry?" she asked.

"A little. We'll stop soon," Tuomas replied. "Thank you for coming with me."

"Don't worry about it. It's nice to spend some proper time with you for once."

Tuomas smirked. "And I haven't even asked you to dance."

"You can dance with your sister, not me. Not unless it's midsummer or something." She threw a glance at him. "Do you think you'll go back and see her again?"

Tuomas went to say yes, but then he paused. The previous night's events were still fresh in his mind.

"I hope so. The last time I saw her, she was pretty angry."

"At you?"

"No, thank the Spirits."

Elin let out a low whistle. "Good. If it was at you, you're lucky she didn't strike you."

"She wouldn't do that," Tuomas said. "I hope."

"I did try to stand up for her, you know," said Elin. "When you went away, I tried to explain, but nobody wanted to listen. I think they just want to forget she was here."

"I thought something like that might have happened," Tuomas admitted. "It's safe if she's up in the sky. Well, as long as nobody insults her. But I suppose everyone's learned the hard way not to do that now."

"I suppose it's easier to bury things you don't want to remember," Elin mused. "Hey, what did Henrik mean before? He's afraid of you?"

Tuomas cast his eyes down.

"I hoped you hadn't heard that. He says he's not, but he is. Everyone is. Now they know… who I am."

Elin snorted. "What do they think you're going to do? Start striking anyone who doesn't please you? Or are they forgetting that you saved all their ancestors' skins in your previous life?"

Tuomas shuddered at her choice of words. It reminded him horribly of the Moon Spirit.

"I'm not sure what they think anymore."

He gazed up at the sky. Purple clouds had started to drift across it in thin wispy streams. Even though he wasn't going into trance, he could almost feel his souls swirling inside him. He focused on them, imagining one so much brighter than the other. How could they both be together and yet so different?

Elin cleared her throat to break the silence.

"Actually," she mused, "I know your *taika* is strong, but what are you the Spirit *of?* Lumi's the Spirit of the Lights: the White Fox One. So, what does that make you?"

"The Red Fox One," Tuomas said.

Elin blinked in surprise. "That's your Spirit title?"

"Yes. Lilja told me, the last time I saw her."

"Well, Lumi could make auroras and run really fast. Do you think you can do that?"

"No," said Tuomas, "I'm still just a human as well, remember. And there can't be two Spirits for the same thing. Even if it was possible for me to do half the things Lumi could, the Lights aren't what I'm in charge of. I just... know that."

The words sounded so strange, but he focused on them, rolling them around in his mouth as though tasting a new food. This was exactly what he'd needed to think about and hadn't had the time.

He glanced at his hands. They were hidden inside his mittens, but he imagined them, frostbitten and calloused, and wondered how it would feel to fling *taika* from them like Lumi did. To be so in control and at one with the element of his soul... it was like something out of a fireside tale.

But then, he remembered with a smirk, was he himself not a fireside tale? That was what the Great Mage had been for so long. And now he walked among the people again, in the body of a confused boy who didn't even know what his power was, except for getting into trouble.

Elin softly pressed her elbow against his ribs.

"Hey," she said, "doesn't this remind you of when we were going to the Northern Edge of the World?"

Tuomas smiled, grateful for the distraction.

"You told me you were scared of falling off the edge."

"No, I wasn't!" she protested. "I was scared of that when I was younger, but not now."

"*I'd* be scared if you still were," he joked. "What kind of crazy person would I be with?"

"Shut up," Elin snapped, but her eyes shone with silent laughter.

She suddenly tensed. Before Tuomas could even ask what was wrong, she lurched forward and coughed. It was a horrible dry hacking sound.

Tuomas's heart raced with worry.

"Are you alright?"

"Yes," she choked out.

Tuomas grabbed her shoulders and forced her to look at him. He pulled a mitten off with his teeth to feel her forehead.

"You're warm."

"Well, it makes for a nice change out here."

"I'm serious," Tuomas said.

Elin sighed, then took his wrists and made him let go of her.

"Don't worry about it. I'll be fine. It doesn't hurt – just feels like a little tickle at the back of my throat."

"That's what Paavo said at first."

He slid his mitten back on and urged the reindeer to go faster. The sooner they got to Lilja, the sooner all this would be fixed. If she knew what was causing the plague, then she must also be able to stop it. She was certainly powerful enough.

"Elin, you need to tell me if it gets worse," he said. "Don't try to be tough like Paavo. Fight it as hard as you can, but don't lie to me about how you're feeling, either."

"Alright, alright," she replied. "But you need to stop worrying about me. I've had worse than this."

"No, you haven't." The words were out of his mouth before he could stop them. "Henrik and I didn't tell anybody because we didn't want a panic. But this isn't a cold, or anything like that. It's your *souls* which are sick."

Elin's eyes went wide. "What? How can that be?"

"I'm not sure," said Tuomas. "But we're going to find out."

Elin coughed again. Tuomas slapped her between the shoulders, but she waved him off and settled back against the sleeping sacks.

Her head resting on them reminded Tuomas of the night before last. He turned to her again and shook her to get her attention.

"Elin?" he asked. "When you had that nightmare, what happened? You said something about a boy."

She frowned. "What does that have to do with anything?"

"Paavo said something about a little boy too, after he collapsed," said Tuomas. "I just think it's a bit strange for you both to mention it. What did you see?"

Elin rubbed her temples with two fingers and let out a soft groan.

"Uh… there was a boy, only a kid, maybe four or five. He was standing on a frozen lake. And there was mist too, like what happened on the Mustafjord; and something in the mist, but I couldn't see what it was."

"And then what happened?"

"I can't remember. I just felt really scared."

Tuomas silenced. Simply hearing about it made his blood run cold. There was something wrong. Terribly wrong.

They carried on until the Sun Spirit reached her highest point in the sky. A few lonely trees had somehow taken root away from their brethren in the forest, and Tuomas pulled the sleigh to a halt, tying the reindeer's harness around a thick branch. Then he and Elin threw down some skins and built a small fire. Tuomas retrieved a couple of bones from a sack and placed them in the flames to cook the marrow inside.

He had no sooner let go of them, however, when Elin raised her bow and let an arrow fly.

There was a garbled cry from somewhere in the snow. She trudged over to it and pulled up a ptarmigan, snapping its neck with a quick twist. Then she grasped it by its feathery legs and returned to the fire.

"Good shot," Tuomas remarked.

"Thanks," said Elin as she pulled the arrow free. "See? I'm still in good shape."

She thanked the Spirits and the soul of the ptarmigan for its sacrifice, sat opposite him and began plucking. By the time she had finished and stripped it to the skin, the bones were ready. Tuomas knocked them out of the fire and tossed half to Elin, before taking his smallest knife and driving it down the length of one bone lengthways. It split cleanly in two, exposing the pink marrow inside. He prised it out and slipped it into his mouth.

Elin hastily gutted the ptarmigan and wrapped its meat in a length of fabric. She tucked it amongst the tent tarp to save for dinner, and stuffed the white feathers into a hide bag. It was a rule of the Northlands: if a life was taken, be it animal or plant, none of it went to waste. To do so was disrespectful not only to the deceased, but to the Spirits who watched over all.

After they had eaten, the two of them carried on, following the Sun Spirit as she arched towards the horizon.

They went in relative silence, happy in the others' company. Every now and then, Elin would cough and sweep up some snow from the side of the sleigh, putting it into her mouth to melt and cool her throat. Before long, however, she had fallen asleep, and Tuomas let her rest.

The blue sky transformed into a magnificent mix of red and gold. He squinted in the low light, but kept his eyes straight ahead. He fished a torch out of the back of the sleigh, wedged it between his legs and struck a flint so the top caught. The fire brought a welcome glowing circle around them as day faded away, and the land descended once more into early darkness.

If there had been no noise before, now it disappeared completely. There were no birds calling or flying; no trace of a wandering wolverine. Any movement was dulled by the powdery snow. Even the wind stopped blowing. Time stretched on without end.

When he was younger, these were the moments which Tuomas had struggled with on the migration. Infinite nothingness, never changing, always feeling like they weren't moving at all. He had lost count of the amount of times Paavo had to juggle keeping him entertained and herding the reindeer onward. But his brother had never lost patience with him.

Then he saw what he'd been waiting for: a large mass of moving bodies and swaying antlers, flanked by people holding torches.

He smiled with relief and gave the rope a snap. The reindeer immediately sped up and trotted towards the new herd. Tuomas raised his torch in greeting.

A middle-aged man came forward. His face was covered by a scarf, but Tuomas noticed the hat above it was made from white reindeer fur: the material only worn by mages. A drum hung on a thong around his chest.

"Hello, Enska."

The man peered at him in astonishment. "Tuomas?"

"Yes, it's me. And Elin."

The mention of her name stirred Elin from her slumber. Noticing Enska, she grinned, her body tensing as she struggled to hold back a cough.

Tuomas manoeuvred his reindeer to walk alongside the others. Enska kept pace with the sleigh and wrenched his scarf down to reveal his face.

"It's good to see you again," he said, then turned and shouted over his shoulder. "Lilja! You have visitors!"

At the edge of the herd, a lone woman stopped dead. She wore a coat of reindeer fur – the sleeves pure white – and two long braided pigtails trailed down her front, their sandy strands laced with ice. A drum bounced against her hip, bound to her belt on a strip of leather.

As the sleigh drew parallel with her, she looked at Tuomas. The torch's light flickered in her icy eyes.

"I thought I wasn't going to run into you again until we reached the coast," she said.

"Nice to see you too, Lilja," Tuomas replied. Then he threw a glance at Enska. "How did you know I came to see her?"

At that moment, a cough sounded from somewhere on the other side of the herd. Lilja looked away. One hand strayed to her drum – Tuomas noticed it was shaking.

"Because our children have the sickness too."

Chapter Ten

Lilja didn't speak a word while they pitched camp for the night. Tuomas kept glancing at her, but she wouldn't look back, busing herself with scattering lichen for the reindeer to eat. The snow was frozen solid and they couldn't shovel through it with their hooves to the moss underneath.

Several familiar faces came over to greet the guests, headed by the small group of village leaders. But the courtesies were short, because everyone knew they needed to get the tents built. Slumbers were never long on the migration and every moment of rest went a long way.

As in Akerfjorden, however, Tuomas noticed those who did approach also threw him wary glances. He smiled widely, trying to show them that he was still the boy they remembered, but they hurried off.

"Don't let it bother you," Elin whispered.

"Did you see the way they looked at me?" he replied, equally quiet.

Elin gave him a gentle pat on the back, then coughed into her elbow. Her breath came short and strained.

"Don't worry about me," she said before Tuomas could fuss over her. "Come on, let's get the shelter up."

"I'll help you," Enska called over.

They dragged the poles from the sleigh and arranged them in a conical shape. Tuomas bent down so Elin could clamber onto his back and secure them at the top. Then, together with Enska, they rolled out the tarp and wrapped it around the skeleton. Like all tarps, it was made from reindeer hides stitched together with sinew, but it had worn thin in places and some of the seams had started to come undone from use.

"How long have you been walking?" he asked Enska.

"Two days," the mage replied. "There was no point leaving sooner. We're further north than Akerfjorden, after all. To be honest, we decided to leave a little later for the children's sake. All of them are ill – there's not a single healthy one. Some of the older ones are sick too. We were hoping an extra's day's rest would help them fight it off, but they actually seem to have gotten worse."

Tuomas tied the last knot to keep the tarp anchored to the poles.

"It's the same with us," he said. "My brother's twenty-five and he collapsed yesterday. Have you heard anything from Einfjall?"

"No, but I'd guess they're having the same problems."

"Have you been giving them nettle and angelica tea? That's what Henrik recommended. It takes the edge off the cough."

"Is that going to make a difference?" Enska asked sceptically.

"It's the best we can do for now," said Tuomas. "Henrik's lived through this illness before; everyone else has forgotten it. We should trust that."

Enska blinked in surprise. "Henrik's had the sickness?"

"A long time ago. He's the last one alive from the last time it struck. He said it only targets the young ones; older people are immune."

"Tuomas, I can tell this isn't a normal cold. No cold attacks only youngsters and not the elderly. Does Henrik know anything else about it?"

"No, but I do," Tuomas said quietly. He walked with Enska towards the sleighs so nobody could overhear, and whispered everything that the Sun Spirit had told him. Enska's eyes widened, but he nodded.

"Soul-plague," he repeated, horrified. "That actually makes a lot of sense. Even more so when you combine it with… well… what's inside the mist."

"Draugars," Tuomas finished.

"You know about them?"

"Not really. I just know the name. I was told Lilja was the one to speak to about it."

Enska's face darkened. Tuomas had never seen him look so serious.

"I understand, but be careful," he warned. "This is not an easy subject."

"I know, but –"

"No," Enska cut him off firmly. "I'm not talking about the draugars or the sickness here. I'm talking about Lilja."

Tuomas frowned. "What about her?"

"That's up to her to explain. It's not my place," replied Enska. "You and I both know she's anything but weak, but… she's also not as strong as she makes out. She has her own darkness, deeper than what you think you know. So please take care. I'm asking you this not as a fellow mage, but as her father. I mean it."

Without another word, Enska took the skins from the sleigh and laid them inside the tent to serve as a carpet. Then he waved to get Lilja's attention. Her face was unreadable, lips pressed so tightly together that they were almost invisible in the gloom.

Realising she wasn't going to come over, Tuomas made his way towards her. She watched his every step like a wary animal.

"I need to talk to you," he said.

"Well, I didn't think you'd come out here just to turn back again."

The gruffness came as no surprise, but in spite of it, Tuomas noticed her eyes were glazed, as though she was struggling to keep tears at bay. He hadn't been sure of what he had expected to find when he reached her, but it wasn't this.

"You know what's going on, don't you?" he asked, keeping his voice low.

A muscle twitched in Lilja's jaw. She glanced around to make sure nobody was within earshot, then leaned close to him.

"Listen, I need to ask you something. How did you know I had anything to do with it?"

"I went into a trance and spoke with the Sun Spirit," Tuomas explained. "She said to come looking for you."

Lilja's brows slanted into a frown. "Wait. You spoke with the Sun Spirit? You managed to do that?"

"Yes…" Tuomas said slowly. "What's the matter?"

"Because I can't connect with *any* of the Spirits. Neither can my father," said Lilja.

Tuomas's eyes widened. "Henrik couldn't, either. What does that mean?"

"I don't know," she admitted.

"But you *do* know about the sickness?"

"In a manner of speaking."

"The Sun Spirit told me it's a soul plague. She said it's being caused by something not alive, but not dead either."

Lilja turned her head away and a shudder passed through her body. At her sides, her fingers curled into tense fists.

Tuomas regarded her cagily. He knew Henrik was wrong, that she hadn't done anything wicked; but the way she held herself reminded him of when he had first met her. When she was carrying the heavy truth about Kari just below the surface.

She let out a sharp exhale and her shoulders slumped.

"Fine. I'll fetch you later, when everyone's asleep," she whispered. "Just you."

"Why not Elin?" asked Tuomas.

"Because I said so," Lilja snapped.

She strode off, ducked into her tent and pulled the flap firmly shut behind her.

To keep himself occupied, Tuomas offered to do all he could to help with preparing dinner, but everyone insisted he and Elin rest. He didn't argue; it was a custom among their people to always be hospitable to travellers. Indeed, when the two of them had come to Poro earlier that winter, Enska had immediately taken them in.

But he couldn't help but notice the shower of quick glances; the way the young children stepped closer to their parents before coughing overtook them. The heaviness of their eyes was everywhere, like a current invisible in the breadth of the sea, but there nonetheless, tugging at all it touched.

He perched on the edge of his sleigh and stared into the darkness. He recalled when he had met these people, Lumi beside him in her human form. It didn't matter that he didn't have snowy skin, pointed ears or a fox tail. They had stared at her then in the same way they stared at him now.

In an instant, he remembered the cynical truth of Lilja's words from what seemed like a lifetime ago.

"People find out you're linked to the Bear and you can kiss a normal life goodbye."

He sat next to Elin as everybody tucked into the evening meal. She had given over the ptarmigan as a gift, and it was received warmly, Enska heaping his portion with dried lingonberries. Lilja came out for a few meagre mouthfuls, then immediately went back to her tent without a word. Nobody seemed shocked by it – Tuomas supposed her old habits of keeping to herself hadn't worn off.

When dinner was finished and the fire cleared, he crawled into the shelter, followed closely by Elin. She lay awake coughing for several minutes, but finally her breathing became laboured as slumber dragged her under. The sound was awful, like a pair of hands were clasped around her throat.

Tuomas didn't dare close his eyes for fear of falling asleep. He stared at the fire; then at the smoke hole; then began counting the fibres of fur on his sleeping sack – anything to keep his attention. Eventually, he grabbed a needle and sinew thread and started sewing the gaps in the hide.

After what felt like an age, a shadow appeared on the tarp. Lilja pulled back the flap, a torch in her hand. She threw a glance at Elin to check she was asleep, then jerked her head, motioning for him to follow her.

Tuomas tied on his shoes and crept outside. Lilja strode to the edge of the camp, in the opposite direction to the slumbering herd. Several pairs of skis were sticking out of the snow. She knocked a couple down, slid them onto her feet and tossed another pair to him.

"Where are we going?" he asked.

"Not far."

Grasping the torch and a ski pole in one hand, she walked off, following the path of churned show made by hundreds of reindeer hooves. Tuomas hurried to keep pace with her.

"Are we going back to Poro?" he asked in surprise.

"Not quite." Lilja glanced at him. "I heard you ran off to the World Above?"

"Just for a little while."

"So now you've walked in all three of the Worlds. Impressive."

Tuomas widened his strides to prevent himself from falling behind. He'd never known her move so fast. There was an agitation to her gait, as though she wanted nothing more than to turn back the way they'd come and not take another step. And yet she forced herself onward, to get it over with as quickly as she could.

"How have you been?" he asked. "I noticed you made yourself a new drum."

"What's a mage without one?" she replied. "It didn't take too long. Father helped me."

"Are you working with him now?"

"Yes, but he's still the Poro mage. He did originally offer the position to me, but I told him not to push it. I think it's enough that I'm home without expecting too much."

Tuomas glanced at her drum. It was hard to see the details in the darkness, but whenever she moved her left leg, it swung into the flickering torchlight and the skin glowed orange. It was roughly the same size as her old one, with the central symbol of the Great Bear Spirit. He recognised other pictures which she had recreated: herself as a child with the Bear appearing in her breath; a little boy on a frozen lake; the day she had assisted in Tuomas's birth. Around the edges, she had painted a new series of interlocking spirals and waving lines, and a small smile crossed his face. Those were the Lights – a silent yet powerful reference to the time spent with Lumi.

"How long have you not been able to go into trance?" he asked.

"Just before the migration started," Lilja said. "You say it's the same with Henrik?"

"Yes. But not me."

"I wonder why that is."

Her words dripped with sarcasm. Tuomas leaned forward to catch her eye.

"What do you mean?"

"Use your brain. Have you noticed you're the only youngster who isn't coughing? And the only mage who can still connect with the Spirits?" Lilja cocked an eyebrow at him. "Work it out, Son of the Sun. You're a Spirit yourself. Of course it's not going to affect you."

Tuomas's brows rose. That made perfect sense. His *taika* was powerful; it would be no surprise if his souls were also strong enough to repel the sickness.

They dropped into single file to ascend a hill, struggling to manoeuvre their skis up the slope. When they reached the top, Tuomas bent his knees and went to slide down, but Lilja threw one of her poles across his body to stop him.

"No further," she said. Her voice was strained.

Tuomas frowned. "What's the matter?"

She didn't look at him. Her eyes were fixed straight ahead. Even in the low light, they shone with unshed tears.

Tuomas peered at the landscape below. The ground was cut by a giant lake, its icy top glimmering under the silvery glow of the Moon Spirit. A thick mist hung across it, just like at the Mustafjord.

He shuddered. Even compared to the quietness of the tundra, this was completely different. There was something not right here… something lurking and inhuman. Even the Spirit of the Lake seemed to have fled from it.

He spoke quietly, scared to break the silence.

"What is this place?"

"The Nordjarvi. This is where the mist first appeared," Lilja replied. "And… where my son died."

Chapter Eleven

Tuomas dug his poles into the snow to keep himself from falling over.

"You have a son?" he gasped.

"*Had* a son," Lilja corrected.

She wiped her eyes on her sleeve and looked straight at him.

"I've brought you here in confidence. I want it kept that way. Do you understand?"

She didn't blink. All the blood was drained from her cheeks. Tuomas had never seen her like this, not even when Kari had come up in conversation. It was as though cracks had appeared in her quiet strength, and the slightest breath of wind would blow away whatever remained.

He was so shocked; he simply gave a wooden nod.

Lilja held his eyes for a moment longer, then turned away. She stared at the lake, a million emotions fleeting across her face. On her ski poles, her hands trembled.

Tuomas swallowed anxiously. "I never knew you were a mother."

"My father is the only one still living who does. Apart from you, now," she replied.

"Well… was it the sickness?"

"No, it was long before all this started. Ten years ago, back when I was still wandering with Kari."

She kicked her feet out of the skis and knelt in the snow. Tuomas followed suit. It was bitingly cold, but Lilja barely seemed to notice.

"We were travelling around the north to do trade and healing. The last winter had been a harsh one; we needed to go among the people more than usual. And…well, things happened while we were there. And nine months later, I had a baby."

Her expression softened as she looked back into her memories.

"Aki was his name. He was born just after the end of the Long Dark. We raised him together, Kari and I. We taught him about the Spirits, how to look after himself, how to build fires and make crafts. He was a quick learner. And he had such powerful *taika*… he used to watch us as we drummed, and I always thought he could see through it as easily as I could. Kari said to me once, 'he's going to make an incredible mage one day, Lilja. He will be great.'"

Tuomas shuffled and his eyes shifted to her neck. The light was low, but he could see the line of pink scar tissue stretching across her windpipe. It was somewhat disconcerting to hear her speak of Kari like this, after everything he'd done, after all the pain he'd put both of them through. An image of her brother formed in Tuomas's mind and he quickly forced it away.

Lilja stroked her drum and carried on speaking.

"Kari was like a father to him. His real father wasn't with us, after all. It was just the three of us."

"Didn't you marry?" Tuomas asked.

"No. It just happened one night. Nothing else came of it."

"Then… who was Aki's father?"

"That doesn't matter," Lilja said tersely. "Kari and I were good enough to him. We were all he needed."

She paused for a moment, still staring out over the Nordjarvi.

"One day… at this time of year, to be exact… we were on our way to Poro to do some trading, before they all left for the migration. And I wanted my father to meet his grandson. But it got late, so we set up camp here, on the lakeshore. Poro isn't very far; we would have reached it the next morning. We did some ice-fishing, caught some char, then we went to bed.

"And in my dreams, I knew something was wrong. I could sense something I hadn't before. There were *things* in the lake, and they knew we were there. And they resented us."

She looked at Tuomas. "Have you ever heard of draugars?"

He swallowed. "The Sun Spirit mentioned them."

"They're monsters. They hate everything living, anything which can draw breath, because they can't. Especially children, because they have the most life left to live. And even more so if the child has strong *taika*. They feed off youth and power; the younger you are, the more they crave you. And the greater your *taika*, the greater the danger becomes. If they sense someone like that, they strike."

"That's why they keep coming back," Tuomas realised. "Henrik told me the mist returns once every generation and makes the youngsters sick."

"I know," said Lilja sadly. "Making mist is a way they ensnare their prey. You get lost in it and then it chokes you, from the soul outward. That's how they survive: they devour the souls first; stop them from passing on, and then, if they can, they'll go after the body as well. A few weeks ago, there were three children playing down there on the ice. My father heard a commotion, so he ran up to this hill to see. By the time he got here, it was too late."

Tuomas's blood ran cold. He recalled the three souls which had been ripped out of Lumi's grasp. They had to be from the children Lilja spoke of.

"Lilja," he said, "the Sun Spirit told me to be careful. That they would come after my *taika* if they could."

Lilja looked at him hard. "I can see that. You need to listen to her. These things are dangerous. I know that better than anyone else."

"What are they? Demons?"

"No. But neither are they people or animals."

"Then… are they alive?"

"I'm not sure what you would call them. They exist in the cracks between the Worlds; neither of one or the other. They can move through waters as mages can learn how to walk through fire. It doesn't matter how far away you go from one lake or river. If they want you, they will follow you to another."

Tuomas shook his head. "How can you know so much about them? Henrik said he's the last one still alive who remembers the last time."

"Why do you think I started visiting the World Below in the first place?" Lilja answered. "The Earth Spirits know more about them than I do. I've lost count of how many times I went to the Northern Edge of the World; how often I jumped down there, all so I could learn about draugars from them. But nothing they told me could reverse what happened."

She paused, biting back tears, then collected herself and carried on. Her eyes hardened with every word.

"The night we were camping here, I woke up, and draugars had come into the tent. I don't know how many; it felt like hundreds. They were holding us down, me and Kari, we couldn't move. But they weren't there for us. I screamed for

Aki, but I already knew they had him outside. I could hear them luring him away towards the water.

"Somehow, Kari managed to get his drum. He hit it and sent out a shockwave; all the draugars went flying off us. We ran out... I could see Aki by the ice-fishing hole, surrounded by them. They'd sensed his *taika*. They had him by the hands and feet, whispering to him, trying to make him come with them..."

She screwed her eyes shut, but forced herself to go on.

"We couldn't get to him in time. They dragged him through the hole."

Tuomas stared at her in horror. Tears rolled down her face and she gasped back a sob before it could overwhelm her.

"But that wasn't the worst thing," she said. "I refused to leave the camp. I couldn't get his voice out of my head. I was determined to make the wicked things suffer for what they'd done. So, while Kari was out hunting one day, I sat by the ice and started to drum. I challenged the draugars to come to me, to either return Aki or... to take me as well."

"You wanted to die?" Tuomas breathed.

"At that point, I would have welcomed it," Lilja admitted. "You see, draugars will only make a deal if they feel the exchange is equal. You need to offer something worth just as much as what they've already taken. But, in my heart, I knew they wouldn't take me in his place. Why would they? It didn't matter that I had strong *taika* – Aki's had the potential to be just as strong, and I was older; there was less life to give.

"So I used the whole thing as cover for another plan. If I couldn't make a deal, I'd have revenge. Behind me, I lit a fire and laid a torch in it. I felt one of them coming towards me. When it got close enough, I put down my drum, grabbed the torch, and shoved the burning end into its face."

Her lip quivered. "But then I actually looked at it… and it wasn't a draugar at all. It was my Aki."

Tuomas's pulse raced with shock.

"Was he… still alive?"

"Before or after I burned him?" Lilja said. Her dry tone told him she didn't expect an answer.

She pointed to a spot on the bank, not far from the ice.

"He just lay there, screaming, asking me why I'd hurt him so much," she said, her voice cracking. "I tried to apologise, to try and help him – I was so desperate, I started rubbing snow over the blisters to take the heat out of them. It didn't do anything. And then mist started pouring out of him… and the draugars came back, beat me down, dragged him away again. That was the last time I ever saw him. My beautiful little boy."

She sniffed hard. Her eyes looked as though a thin fabric had stretched across them, delicate as a moth's wing but stronger than stone.

Tuomas watched her carefully. His tongue felt too large for his mouth; he didn't want to speak in case the wrong words came tumbling out. But he could tell from Lilja's face that there was more to the story, and as he recalled Elin's nightmare, he had an inkling of what it was.

He glanced at the tendrils of mist curling over the lake.

"It's not just the draugars in there, is it?" he asked.

Lilja shook her head. "He's allied with them. Do you know what happens when the illness infects a child? They see him in their dreams. He sends the draugars into their minds. I've heard them crying about a little boy in the night and nobody knows what it means, except me and Enska."

She let out a shuddering breath.

"Those three children who died first… he came for them on his birthday. He died on his fifth birthday; you see. Well, the day I hit him with the torch would have been his birthday. And now it's five years again since that day. His little lifetime repeated."

Tuomas fidgeted, not sure what to do. He never would have expected such a tale as this. Now he thought about it, this was the most he had ever heard her talk about anything. He could see the strain in her face: an unending pain, silent and secret, which she had carried for years.

He shuffled closer and placed a hand on her shoulder. She tensed at his touch, but didn't shove him away.

"I'm so sorry," he whispered. "I don't know what else I can say."

"You don't need to say anything," she replied tightly. "It's my burden to bear."

"Then why did you bring me here?"

She hesitated. "Because the Sun Spirit obviously wants me to tell you the truth. Well, there you have it. Aki and the draugars are causing the illness. He's brought it on the youngsters to make us all feel powerless as mages. And to get revenge on me, for my negligence."

"You didn't neglect him," Tuomas insisted. "It's not your fault the draugars took him away."

"You're sure about that, are you?" Lilja shot him a cold look. "I should have sensed them before we camped here. I should have run faster, to get him away from that hole. And I should have looked before I threw a torch in his face!"

She drove her fist into the snow with alarming strength. Tuomas got to his feet and took a step back.

But the fury melted out of her as quickly as it had come, and she slumped over herself, clutching her drum feebly, as a child might hold a toy for comfort.

"There's so much I should have done. This sickness – this soul plague – it's all my fault," she said in a tiny voice. "If you ever have children, you'll understand. You do everything in your power to keep them safe. Well, that's what you *should* do. You shouldn't fail them."

She wiped at her eyes again. "I failed Aki. And now everyone's children are suffering for it."

Tuomas tentatively laid his hand on her shoulder again. "We can figure out a way to stop this. That's why you told me the truth, right?"

"We can't stop it," said Lilja sorrowfully. "I've tried. I've lost count of how many times I've drummed for him, but the draugars have him too tightly for me to break through. And now something's stopped us from even being able to get into trance. It's like the World Above has been cut off."

"But I can still go into trance," Tuomas said. "Let me try. I might be able to do something –"

"No!" she snapped with sudden forcefulness.

Tuomas was taken aback. "Why?"

"Because this is a problem I've helped to cause. I should be the one who fixes it. I don't care if anything happens to me."

"I'm the only one who can speak with the Spirits right now," insisted Tuomas. "I don't know why that is, but if I can connect with them, maybe I can connect with Aki. I could break through the draugars and make him stop."

"I don't want you doing anything of the sort."

"Why? It's better than all the kids being sick. What if they die?"

"Nobody has died yet. I still have time to figure something out."

Tuomas bit his tongue. The children on the lake had died. Henrik had admitted more deaths would come. But he knew better than to throw that information in Lilja's face.

"Isn't it worth the chance?" he asked instead. "Don't you trust me?"

"Of course I do! But what if something goes wrong? You've already admitted the draugars will come after you, given half the chance. What if you get hurt?"

Lilja grasped his hand. She wavered for a long moment, as though gathering up the courage to say something. When she eventually did speak, her words stunned him.

"I care about you, Tuomas. I don't extend that courtesy to many people. I won't have you getting hurt, like I had Aki hurt."

She stared at him, not letting go.

"I want you to promise me that you won't try to fix this by yourself. If there is a way, I will find it. This is not your problem."

Tuomas wanted to argue – of course it was his problem. It was everyone's problem; every child's, every parent, everyone who had to watch the plague spreading to their own loved ones. But he could see the desperation in her face, and relented.

He'd come looking for her because he had believed she would know what to do. Now he had to trust that she could follow through.

"Alright," he said. "What should I tell Henrik? I told him you might have the answers."

Lilja got to her feet, still keeping hold of his hand. "You can tell him I have information from the Earth Spirits and I'm working on a way to stop it. But not a mention of Aki to anybody."

"Not even Elin?"

"Absolutely not," she said firmly. "I mean it, Tuomas. If I'd wanted Elin to know, I would have brought her here tonight. This stays between us and Enska. Promise me."

He nodded. "I promise."

"And no connecting with Aki."

"Alright, I promise that, too."

The smallest smile of gratitude crossed Lilja's face.

"Good," she said, finally letting go of his hand. "Thank you."

Tuomas went to speak again, but she was already fitting her skis onto her feet, consciously turning away from the lake as she worked.

"Come on," she said. "We'd better get back."

Tuomas tied his own skis into position. "Are you alright?"

"As best I can be," she replied. "I will be alright, though. I will figure out a way to get him away from those monsters and lay him to rest. Or... whatever I can do."

He wanted to offer her more comfort; to tell her it wasn't her fault, or that she had done all she could to save her son, but he knew she wouldn't listen. She was too convinced of her own guilt, and no amount of pity would break down her wall of stubbornness. He only hoped that when the time came for her to attempt anything, she felt she could call on him for help.

They left the hill in silence, the Nordjarvi and its cloud of mist disappearing into the night.

# Chapter Twelve

She lay in the dark, the night open and silent around her. This was further from the edge of the World Above than she had ever been. It was a labyrinthine vortex of spinning stars, where everything was still and the familiar was too far away to even comprehend.

The struggle with her mother had left her weak. She had never felt like this, either up here or in the World Between. It was similar to when Tuomas had pulled her out of the sky, and her earthly form had started to melt. But at least then, he had been with her. Now, she was alone. He couldn't see her, and even if he could, he wouldn't be able to help.

All around her came the cries of the souls. They were looking for her. When the Moon had flung her away, it had left them stranded, and she sensed their panic as though it were her own. She tried to call out to them, to assure them she was still there, but she wasn't sure if they heard her.

She listened hard and focused on them to feebly pull herself closer. The stars spun as night passed over the World Between, shifting the labyrinth, disorientating her. With no visual cues to guide her, she had to rely purely on the souls, following their voices and the soft pulses of their energy.

Eventually, she noticed a faint sliver of paleness: Moonlight on snow. There it was: the skin between the Worlds. Even from here, she could see it rippling under the strain of itself; the tear which Tuomas had left hung like the edges of a broken spiderweb.

White Fox One!

She looked around for the voice. It was the Spirit of Passage, but she couldn't figure out where it was coming from.

How far are you from me, Carrying One? she asked.

I am close. Let me help you. You are weak.

A few moments later, the Spirit appeared underneath her. She let herself rest and it pulled her closer to the skin, then laid her in the sky where she usually danced. She spread her Lights wide, but too thin to be seen by any in the World Between.

Immediately, she was swarmed by the souls as they pushed themselves back into her aurora. They waved around like pollen on a breeze. She swept her tail a little to help them and the faintest wave of green rippled around her.

She had only been gone for a day and night this time. It must have been so painful for them when she was ripped from the World Above during the Long Dark. They would have been floating in this endless emptiness with nothing to hold them together, no way to dance and look down on their loved ones. Despite the fear she instilled in life, everything changed after death, when the souls clung to her as an anchor in the dark. Without her Lights, they were lost.

The Spirit of Passage swam in front of her in the form of a wispy cloud.

Are you harmed? he asked.

No, she replied, throwing a glance at the Moon Spirit. She had not battled against her mother like that for so long. Not since the last time her brother was in the World Above, before he was the boy called Tuomas, and the Silver One had tried to snatch him away from under the Sun Spirit's gaze.

Good, said the Spirit of Passage. *I am afraid I must leave you now, White Fox One. The Horse-Riding One summons me.*

She extended her aurora so it mingled with the cloud for a moment.

Thank you, Carrying One, she said, then watched as he dissolved into the air as though he had never been there. He swept down, through the skin, and gathered the soul of a runt wolf pup from a forest cave.

Suddenly, the Moon Spirit drew close to her. She spun around and threw out a warning. Both their powers pushed against one another.

Keep away, Silver One, she snapped.

I do not see you stopping me, the Moon Spirit countered. *Are you still so weak that you cannot even hold me back? That is what happens when you try to best one stronger than yourself.*

A silvery glow shone down upon the Northlands. It reflected off the flank of the mountains and made the peaks look like sharpened knives.

Then why do you provoke me? she snarled. The air shook and her Lights tinted an angry red.

Because I enjoy it, was the cold reply. *I enjoy regarding you, with your anger and your pride, and how little I must do to draw it out of you. You might try to keep him from me, fight me off, but it is like tiny hailstones upon a giant lake, White Fox One.*

And yet he knows you cannot take him, Silver One, she said triumphantly. *Your sly words were in vain. I hardly care that you never wanted me.*

Yet you do care that I wanted him, the Moon Spirit shot back. *You care about him. You care… like a human. It is most unbecoming of you. You even still cling to that foolish human name he gave you. What was it again? Lumi?*

She recoiled as though struck. When Tuomas spoke it, whether with breath or the invisible language of Spirits, it held a kindness and appreciation that had come to define her just as much as her title. But in the clutches of her mother, it became something sharp and unnatural, like a corrupted wound. It pulled at her, trying to tear her down, but she refused to let herself be beaten. No matter that it was a name which had almost killed her. It was hers, and now, in her own World, nobody owned it but her.

You cannot use that against me, she said firmly. *It is a part of me.*

And at what cost to yourself? the Moon Spirit sniggered. *Look at you. Accepting a name like a greedy human child devouring honey in the summer. Revelling in that restrictive body he put you in, and then daring to still behave as though you are the coldest being in all the Worlds. It is a farce, foolish White Fox One. You are so terrified to let them see your weakness.*

They have seen me at my weakest, she snapped, *which is more than you have.*

The Moon Spirit pressed harder over her. *Of course. They have seen your ultimate weakness. They have seen how you can love.*

The word took shape as a warmth which spread through her mind, but she also felt the malice behind it, spat out like a dart.

She pushed back against her mother and swept her tail until the aurora filled the sky. It danced in thick green waves which twisted and curled around each other, no pattern the same as the last.

Do you not think it ironic, Silver One, she said coolly, *that although Spirits are supposed to be formless and emotionless, emotion is exactly how we channel our power?*

At that, the Moon Spirit retreated a little. Her pockmarked face darkened with rage.

I love my brother, she continued. *That has only served to make me stronger in a way you will never know. Because you never loved me. You never even loved him. You only loved the idea of him, and he knows that now. He will not allow you to take him again.*

We shall see about that.

No, we will not. You cannot have him. He does not want you.

That is only you and my Golden sister infecting him against me. He has no memory of what it was to be my son; he admitted that to me himself. How can he know to avoid me unless by your doing, you selfish little spark?

He knows, she snapped. *He felt it. And he is not your son.*

She poured every ounce of her power into her words and the aurora transformed into writhing fire. As soon as she let it out, she sensed that the joust was over. She had endured her mother's abuse for so long, she knew it would return soon enough, as it always did. But now, she had nothing else to say. She would not let this moment of pride be taken away.

She ran higher into the sky. The stars shot past her; the World Between became so small, she could see the entire breadth of the Northlands in every direction. The mountains looked like pebbles, the lakes like raindrops, the trees like specks of dust. All so small and fragile, yet in its own way, stronger than anything Above or Below.

She let herself remember the feeling of running on top of the snow, the wind blowing in her hair, her tail brushing the ground so a miniature trail of Lights formed behind her.

Yes. As small and as fragile as a snowflake, but stronger... so much stronger.

Tuomas only managed a short slumber. He tossed and turned, then lay on his back and stared blankly out of the smoke hole.

The weight of Lilja's revelation hung heavy on his chest like a stone. He tried to imagine her with a baby in her arms, teaching it to speak, telling it fireside tales, playing with it out on the tundra as it stumbled after her.

No, not it. *Him*. Aki. Her son.

He had felt terrible when he thought he'd lost Paavo earlier that winter. What must she have felt to actually *see* the loss, witness it be dragged away from her not once, but twice? A little life which she had made and raised, gone forever? And now, to know he was back and dealing all this pain...

A soft spluttering across the hearth caught his attention. Elin twisted in her sleeping sack, waking for just long enough to cough. After she had settled, Tuomas crept over and felt her forehead. It was clammy; her black fringe was limp and clung to her skin.

His throat tightened with worry. She was strong, but she couldn't fool him.

He looked through the smoke hole. The flickering fire beside him made the sky appear even darker than normal, but when he squinted, he could see a tiny flash of green against the blackness. Lumi was there. She was alright.

It wasn't much, but it brought a small measure of relief. At least someone he cared for was safe in the middle of so much uncertainty.

He stayed awake until he heard the villagers stirring in the neighbouring tents. Soon, everyone was up and started to strike the camp. Tuomas pulled the tarp off the frame of poles and packed everything into the sleigh. Then he went to Elin, grabbed her bow out of her hand and tossed it in beside the reindeer skins.

"Hey!" she protested.

"You're not walking today," he said. "Get inside and keep warm."

"I'm fine," Elin snapped, but then she coughed, spitting phlegm over her shoulder. Tuomas seized his chance; he grabbed hold of her and bundled her into the belly of the sleigh. She glared at him, but he shot her a warning look and she reluctantly covered her legs with a blanket.

Another fit of coughing sounded behind them. Tuomas noticed a girl, perhaps a year younger than him, had fallen onto her hands and knees. She struggled to breathe, every inhale as though stones were lodged in her throat. Tears streamed involuntarily from her eyes. Her parents huddled around her, holding back her hair in case she vomited.

His heart fluttered. Everywhere, it was all he could hear. Even over the clicking of hundreds of reindeer knees and the crunch of footprints, there was coughing and wheezing. It filled the empty Northlands and pressed down upon them like a cloud. As with the Akerfjorden group, there were practically no children or young people left on their feet.

Tuomas walked over to the girl and knelt in front of her. She and her parents looked at him with huge eyes.

"It's alright," he said, hoping he sounded more confident than he felt. "What's your name?"

The girl let out a rattling breath. "Eevi."

"Can I check your temperature?"

When she nodded, Tuomas touched her forehead. She was even warmer than Elin and the skin around her eyes was veined and swollen. She looked as though she was going to faint.

"Put her in my sleigh," he said to her parents. "She needs to save her energy."

Eevi's father nodded and swept her up as though she weighed no more than a feather. He tucked her in beside Elin, who quickly shared the blanket and put an arm around her.

"Thank you," her mother said tightly. "I… yes, thank you."

She lowered her gaze and hurried past him. Tuomas watched her go with a sigh. Elin caught his eyes and offered a small smile of comfort.

As the herd moved out, he fell back to keep pace beside her in the sleigh.

"I was only trying to help," he whispered.

He looked at the front of the herd, where Lilja was walking alone, shoulders hunched and with a hat hiding her face. She raised a hand to her cheek, and even though he couldn't see, Tuomas could tell that she was wiping away tears.

Chapter Thirteen

They walked for three days, barely stopping, taking turns to rest. Every now and then, they came across a patch of grazing uncovered by melting snow, and the reindeer would grind to a halt, eager to fill their bellies. Each time granted a blissful few hours' break.

With every day that passed, the nights became a little shorter and the tundra more rugged. The mountains grew closer, until the Sun Spirit was completely blotted out by their massive flanks. One afternoon, they found themselves on the edge of a lake, a circle of clear blue water in the middle from where the ice had already started to thaw.

Tuomas knew just from looking at it that walking across was a bad idea. The surface didn't need to be very thick to take one person's weight, but that of an entire village and several hundred reindeer would spell disaster. They needed to go around.

Lilja ran to Enska and whispered something. He nodded, then held up a hand to tell everyone to stop, and called the leaders over.

Tuomas and Elin shared a glance, but before either could speak, one of the leaders raised his voice and addressed everyone.

"We can't stop for ice-fishing," he said. "It's not strong enough. We'll carry on."

There were several grumbles from the convoy. They had brought some food from the winter camp, but the promise of fresh char right in front of them was tempting. Even Tuomas's stomach rumbled at the thought of it. But he looked at Lilja, and she stared right back at him, the knowledge hanging heavy and silent between them. There might not be any mist on the lake, but it was a body of water nonetheless. It wasn't just thin ice which was dangerous here.

The herders spread out along the lakeshore to prevent the reindeer from dispersing. The animals tossed their heads in agitation, but slowly funnelled along the bank. It took a long time, but soon they were all on the other side, and the sleighs followed.

Tuomas walked beside his reindeer, holding it by the harness. Every few feet, he glanced behind to make sure the runners were clear of the ice. The path they were using was precariously thin and peppered with scree which had tumbled down the mountain slopes.

"Do you want me to get out? Would that be easier?" Elin asked.

"No, stay there," Tuomas said.

He guided the sleigh around a particularly vicious rock, then tapped the reindeer on the flank to urge it onward.

"Tuomas?"

He kept his eyes on the trail. "What?"

"Can you see that?"

He looked at Elin. She was pointing at the lake, her bleary eyes fixed on something.

He followed her hand and froze. A faint white vapour was gathering over the circle of meltwater. Under it, deep beneath the surface, he could just make out a figure floating face-up.

He looked at Lilja in alarm. She hadn't seen it, but Enska had. His eyes were huge.

"Move," he said to Lilja. "Now. Now!"

"What is it?" she asked, but before she could do anything, Enska grabbed her, bundled her over his shoulder as if she was a child, and ran.

The other villagers gasped as they noticed the mist. Several of the older ones made the sign of the hand to ward off evil.

"It's just like at the Nordjarvi!" a woman near Tuomas cried.

He couldn't move; his eyes fixed onto the silhouette under the water. No features were visible, but he could tell it was human; small, a coat billowing around it. It wasn't moving.

Then he caught sight of something else. All around the figure, the water was churning, as though a massive shoal of fish was surrounding it. But they were too large to be any fish found in such a lake.

The mist swept towards the banks and wound around Tuomas's ankles.

That was the fright he needed. He slapped his reindeer on its hind leg. It immediately bolted and he clung to the harness. Elin and Eevi yelped as the sleigh bounced over the uneven ground.

The path widened and the lake fell behind them. Tuomas picked up speed and didn't stop until he'd reached the safety of the herd. The other villagers followed, and then their worried mutterings rose into screams.

Tuomas looked over his shoulder.

The fish shoal was spilling out of the hole. The mist broke up here and there as their bodies slithered through it. They were moving unnervingly fast: as fast as Tuomas himself could sprint in summer when there was no snow to impede him. And he had been right: they weren't fish at all. They were human-sized, with arms and legs. A slithering sound filled the air.

His heart filled with dread. Draugars. And they were coming straight for the convoy.

Straight for *him*.

Everyone ran. Children started coughing even worse than before; in Tuomas's sleigh, Eevi clutched at her throat as though trying to prise something away from it. Horrified shrieks filled Tuomas's ears.

He struggled to get purchase on the snow. It was fresh and powdery here, undisturbed from a recent fall: the worst kind to move across quickly. Even those on skis could barely manage, and the sleighs, weighted down with people and supplies, were still far too slow. The creatures would catch up to them in no time, and then... Tuomas didn't know what would happen. Would they kill them all? Take the children, like they had at the Nordjarvi?

He suddenly recalled Lilja's observation when she had taken him there.

"Have you noticed you're the only youngster who isn't coughing? You're a Spirit yourself. Of course it's not going to affect you."

He stopped and rested a hand on his drum. Henrik had held off the creatures at the Mustafjord, but Tuomas was stronger. Much stronger.

Elin twisted in the sleigh.

"What are you doing?" she shouted through a cough. "Come on!"

Tuomas ignored her. He turned on his heel and bounded back towards the lake.

Elin screamed his name. The villagers bringing up the rear tried to reach out and grab him, but Tuomas evaded them until the entire convoy was behind him.

The draugars were approaching fast. Tuomas pulled his drum and hammer off his belt and took a deep breath. His heart juddered; he felt summer warmth on his back and smelled sweet flowers. *Taika* sang through his body like electricity.

He fixed his eyes on the snow between him and the draugars, swept his hand across it, then hit the drum.

A barrier soared towards the sky. It was denser than Henrik's; clung more tightly to everything it pressed against, until it became like a sheet of ice thick enough to support a whole herd. When the mist hit it, it swept back on itself and the draugars stopped dead on the other side. They let out a terrible gasping sound, like what a man might make as he drowned.

Tuomas stared at them in horror. He wasn't sure what he had imagined them to look like, but these things were straight out of a nightmare. They were barely more than sagging slimy skin draped over bones. Holes had rotted through the flesh in places, the edges puckered as though they had lain underwater for countless years. Although they had arms and legs, there was nothing human about them. Their movements were shuddery, like the muscles had stiffened and locked; muddy webbing spanned their long fingers and sharp red eyes rolled in gaunt sockets.

One leapt towards him. Tuomas kept his hammer on the drumskin and unleashed another wave of energy to hold the boundary. The draugar lashed out in fury. The air vibrated with each strike, but the shield held.

Tuomas stared into its eyes. There was a hunger in them; a hatred for the breath in his lungs and the blood in his veins. And for something more…

The draugar snapped its teeth, and Tuomas felt it, plucking against his power like a fish hook. He stumbled backwards in alarm. It was tasting his *taika*.

Mage, it snarled inside his head. *There you are, Son of the Sun...*

Tuomas recoiled, but forced himself not to break eye contact. They couldn't reach him behind the barrier. No matter how many there were, he was stronger than them all, and he knew it.

And so did they. The one at the front let out a screech, then flung itself away. The others followed suit, and as one massive animal, they slithered over each other and rolled towards the lake. They dived back into the hole, the mist dragging behind them, and as quickly as they had come, they disappeared into the depths.

Tuomas didn't dare move. He panted hard, his chest constricted from fright.

Footsteps crunched in the snow, then Enska and Lilja appeared in front of him.

"Are you alright?" Enska asked.

Tuomas nodded. He looked back at the convoy. The reindeer had spooked and several people were trying to round them up before they could disperse. Others stood still beside the sleighs. The screams had been replaced once again with coughs and painful wheezes.

Certain they were safe, Tuomas lowered his drum and tied it back onto his belt.

"Do you have any idea how dangerous that was?" Enska hissed. "What if they'd gotten to you first?"

"Well, they didn't," Tuomas replied. "And I knew they wouldn't."

Lilja kept her eyes on him for a moment, then approached the barrier. She extended a hand and tapped it, gently, so it wouldn't break. She sniffed back a sob.

"Why did you stop me?" she asked, barely above a whisper.

Enska closed his eyes despondently. He let go of Tuomas and walked over to her.

"It was for the best," he said.

His expression softened and he cupped her face in his hands. Tears spilled down Lilja's cheeks, but she still didn't break; she straightened her shoulders and stared straight ahead, as though Enska wasn't even there. Then she turned to Tuomas, her lip trembling.

"Did you see him?"

Tuomas's stomach tightened. "I... don't know. There was something in the water, but I don't know if it was him."

Lilja glared at Enska. "See? I could have gotten to him!"

"No, you couldn't. You saw how many there were," he insisted gently. "Lilja, listen to me. We can't do anything for him now. We need to carry on."

"What if they come after us?" Tuomas asked.

"They won't. They need to stay near water to survive. This is the last lake on the route; the further we get from it, the safer we'll be."

"Well... can't we at least give Lilja some time?"

Enska's mouth twisted with pity. "The children can't wait, and neither can the mountains. We need to get across them before the snow becomes unstable. We can't risk the females dropping the calves."

Lilja nodded. Despite her own pain, she knew he was right. She allowed her father to embrace her, and when she drew away, she pulled the sadness back inside herself. Tuomas could see it leaving her face: her lip stopped quivering and her eyes took on a flat cast. In no time at all, she looked the same as she always had.

Tuomas regarded her. Even now, she was so controlled; nobody would have any reason to think she was connected to what had just happened. It was alarmingly natural: the mask she had worn for so long simply slotted into place.

When he was sure she was ready, Enska squeezed her hands and led the way back towards the convoy.

"Thank you for stopping them," Lilja whispered to Tuomas.

He offered her a small smile, hoping she could take some comfort from it, but she didn't look at him; she kept her eyes firmly on the snow. Tuomas watched her in his peripheral vision. For as painful as this was, how much more did it hurt her to keep silent, so no-one would suspect anything?

Never mind that she had rebuffed him at the Nordjarvi, or the fright he had gotten when he last went into trance. He had to figure out a way to help her connect with Aki.

They caught up with the herd and walked on, leaving the lake and the protective shield behind.

Chapter Fourteen

When the lake passed out of sight, small peaks rose on either side of the convoy, trees clinging stubbornly to the rocky flanks. The ground began to slope upwards as they entered the gateway to the mountains. It wouldn't be long now before they reached the pass: the most treacherous part of the journey.

No matter where Tuomas looked, he saw danger. This was the place of avalanches and impatient Spirits; wolves could be hiding anywhere and trolls slept under the ground. No lichen or heather grew. What appeared to be flat snow could only be a thin cover over a huge crevasse. When he was a child, a man from Akerfjorden had accidentally tumbled down one – his scream had lasted for so long, Tuomas thought he'd never stop falling.

The land was unforgiving at the best of times, but here, even the soundest knowledge would be tested.

They didn't stop to pitch camp when the night drew in. The leaders reminded everyone that there was a migration stop a short distance into the mountains: a permanent cluster of turfed huts, built by the ancestors and maintained every year. This was the only place with such measures. Too many people had lost their lives to take chances with hide tents alone.

Heeding the leaders' words, the herders pressed on. It wasn't just for the sake of reaching the stop, either; everyone was very aware of the need to get away from the lake.

Tuomas lit a torch, fetched his skis to make the ascent easier, and walked beside Elin in the sleigh. Eevi was asleep with her head against Elin's chest. A trickle of blood had run out of her mouth and stained her scarf. Elin wiped it away with shaking hands, then hid her face in her white hare mittens, trying to keep warm – but Tuomas suspected it was so he wouldn't see her weakness so clearly. The skin around her eyes had darkened and she could barely manage three breaths before coughing.

"Why don't you try to sleep as well?" he asked.

"I can sleep when we get to the stop," she replied.

"Elin, you look like you're going to faint. Your body needs the rest. You don't want to end up like Paavo."

"Well, unlike Paavo, I'm sitting down, so no need to worry."

She was arguing for the sake of it. He could tell by her tone.

Tuomas swallowed nervously. What if she fought so hard, she wore herself out? Nobody had died yet, but a terrible feeling told him that there would be fewer children with them by the time they reached Anaar.

That made him think of Paavo. The Akerfjorden herd would have moved through the pass already and set up camp at the coast. He prayed to all the Spirits that they had made it unharmed and Henrik was able to care for everyone. Had Einfjall joined them yet? How many of their youngsters were sick too?

Feeling eyes on him, he glanced up and noticed a group of women staring. They didn't stop when he looked at them. He shuffled uncomfortably as they started muttering among themselves. He heard his name, then the words "Son of the Sun."

He clenched his teeth together so hard, his jaw ached.

"I'll be back," he said to Elin, and skied ahead to get away from them.

It didn't take him long to find Lilja. She was alone at the front of the herd, not speaking to anyone, her attention fixed straight ahead. She didn't even break it when he drew alongside her.

"Are you alright?" he asked.

"As much as I can be," she replied. "How are you?"

"Fine. I just… they're talking about me."

"What do you expect me to do about it?"

"Nothing," Tuomas said. "I just needed a break from hearing it."

"You don't have to give me an excuse for why you came up here. Your company is one I don't actually mind."

"Well, that's a relief. You were stuck with me for long enough."

Lilja cocked one eyebrow in agreement. She dug both ski poles into the snow to help manoeuvre herself over a half-exposed rock

"Was this what it was like for you?" Tuomas asked. "When they found out you were saved by the Great Bear Spirit?"

The tiniest of smirks passed Lilja's lips. He couldn't tell if it was in response to his question or that she was happy for a distraction.

"It *started* like this," she admitted. "Mutterings, glances… then they started hounding me, asking me for everything. That was when I got tired of it. Thankfully, they're keeping away from me now – I think they've finally realised I didn't appreciate it."

"Do you think they'll start doing that to me?"

"Who knows? The question you should be asking is, what are you going to do about it?"

"What can I do? I can't help who I am."

"And there's the rub," Lilja said, with a strange kind of wicked triumph. "We can't win, can we? Why do you think I preferred to be away from it all?"

Tuomas looked at her. "Lilja, do you know why the Bear saved you?"

She was quiet for a long moment. "No. But I don't think it's important."

"Why? It hardly ever intervenes like that. There must be something about you which it saw was worth saving."

"What, are you saying I'm special? The same kind of special which meant you got stuck with the Great Mage's life-soul?" she asked sarcastically. "Everyone knows I'm strange, but the only reason I am is because of the shape of the Bear appearing in my breath in the first place. I told you, Kari was the mage-in-training, not me. I was a nobody."

"Maybe you were never a nobody though," said Tuomas. "There's nothing special about my *body*. I look the same as everyone else. It's only since the whole ordeal with Lumi that things have changed."

Lilja pondered that for a moment, then gave a conceding nod.

"You say some wise things on occasion, you know. But I think it's best not to dwell on *why* things happened. You got that soul, and the Great Bear saved me. If anything is going to come of it, we'll see it happen in time."

She pushed back her hat to scratch an itch on her scalp, then spoke again.

"That's the first I've heard you talk about the Spirit of the Lights."

Tuomas sighed. "I miss her."

A darkness spread over Lilja's eyes. "I know. It's never easy, is it? When a sibling leaves you."

He hesitated. "Isn't it… difficult for you? How can you still love him, even after all he did?"

"The same way you can love Lumi even though she attacked your best friend."

Tuomas shook his head. "Lumi did something bad and then redeemed herself. It's different."

"Is it?" Lilja said tightly. "You only saw Kari as he was… *after*. And I will never defend him for what he did, to you, to me… But no matter what he became, he was still my brother. My companion."

Tuomas fell silent. Even after Kari betrayed her, she had climbed the Einfjall mountain to give him some semblance of funeral rites. He had never known such a powerful loyalty.

"You're stronger than me," he admitted. "I could never forgive someone for that."

"I didn't say I forgave him," Lilja said. "There's a fine line between forgiveness and acceptance."

"I know," he said. "That's why I haven't really spoken about Lumi. Henrik and the Akerfjorden leaders told me not to. They didn't like how at ease I was with it."

"They're just not used to it, so that makes them scared. It's different for you and me. We were with her for longer. You got to know her best of all."

"But they saw how she saved us. Why can't they remember that, and not just be scared of her?"

"You were brought up to respect the Lights too," Lilja reminded him. "When you first saw her in human form, you were terrified – I remember the look on your face. You can't just forget that fear. And she's still a Spirit; she's not human. She's neither light nor dark. If you had no real exposure to that, could you honestly accept it so easily?"

Her words sent a shiver down his spine. In his mind's eye, Lumi's face twisted into one darker; her curtain of green Lights became straight and silver. He remembered the crushing embrace around his souls, the seductive voice flowing through his head.

No, he told himself. *She can't take you. She never will.*

A faint glow suddenly streaked across the snow. Everyone exclaimed in horror.

Tuomas immediately saw why. The stars were showering out of the sky. They fell gently, as though they were passing through water rather than air, and in an instant, the night was as bright as day.

"Not again," Tuomas gasped.

"What is that?" someone cried. "Why are they doing that?"

"It's a sign!"

"Something terrible is coming!"

"We don't know that," Enska said loudly, but even he couldn't keep his voice from wobbling. Lilja's eyes grew so wide, Tuomas could see her entire iris.

Then, just like the previous time, the final sparkling trails faded and the darkness was still once again.

Everyone froze, not daring to speak above a whisper. They bowed their heads and made the sign of the hand to ward off evil. Tuomas wasn't sure it would do anything, but before he could even speak, a gust of freezing wind hit him. He put a hand on his head so his hat wouldn't be whisked away.

He looked over his shoulder. An oppressive cloud was hanging heavy over the distant eastern horizon.

"That's not good," he muttered.

They couldn't run in their skis, but Tuomas and Lilja quickened their pace at once. Behind them came the collective sounds of everybody else doing the same, and the herders began to call to the reindeer, urging them to move faster.

"We're not far from the stop," said Lilja.

Tuomas read between her lines at once. If they didn't make it to the huts before the storm reached them, they could be battling through a whiteout – the last thing they needed at any time, but especially when half the village was ill.

The cloud encroached on them, growing and darkening until it blotted out the stars. The wind became bitter; it whipped up the loose snow and hurled it in all directions. It stung Tuomas's cheeks like needles and he tugged his scarf right up to his eyes to shield himself. The reindeer were unfazed – the flurry didn't even penetrate their thick coats – but they moved as swiftly as they could.

Mercifully, once the initial onslaught blew itself out, the wind moved behind the herd. After trying to move against it, everybody took advantage of it pushing from the back. Those on skis powered ahead; the reindeer broke into a trot. The cloud was above them now, and in the distance, snow began to fall. The wind caught it and turned it into a raging blizzard.

Tuomas had outrun one of these on the migration only once before. He had been younger; riding in a sleigh after annoying Paavo too much. All he'd had to do was sit there and let the others pave the way to safety.

Not this time.

He crested a small hill, and his heart raced with relief. Straight ahead were several squat huts, as low to the ground as they could be, roofs covered with several inches of snow.

Lilja saw them too. She slid down the slope with such speed, her braids flew out behind her. Enska followed with the village leaders. Tuomas worked to keep pace with them, quietly praying to the Spirit of the Winter Winds to keep the storm at bay until they were safe.

The first heavy snowflakes were falling by the time they reached the huts. Tuomas unlaced his skis and ran to a smaller hut where he knew a reserve of firewood would be kept. He loaded his arms with as many logs as he could carry, then hurried to each shelter, throwing as much as could be spared into the fire pits.

Icy wind battered him and snow blew in all directions. With every passing moment, visibility became worse and worse. Tuomas took a length of leather from his belt and tied it around his head so his hat wouldn't be swept off. The reindeer huddled together in a giant group to wait it out. Those hitched up to the sleighs were freed so they could join them, and the strongest men quickly covered the bellies with tarps. Everyone else grabbed food, sleeping sacks, and the children.

Tuomas hoisted a coughing toddler into his arms, then noticed a man run past carrying Elin, still wrapped in the blanket from the sleigh. Relieved she was safe, he followed them towards the nearest hut. The snow blew hard into his face and almost knocked him over.

"It's scary," the little boy whimpered.

"Don't worry," Tuomas said as cheerfully as he could. "The Wind Spirits are just having a game, that's all. They're seeing who can make the strongest wind."

"They're all winning," the boy muttered.

Tuomas leapt through the door and slammed it shut behind him. He peered through the gloom to see who he was sharing with.

His eyes found Elin first. Enska was kneeling next to her, coaxing a fire into life in the dusty hearth. Eevi was there too, along with her parents, who quickly introduced themselves as Frode and Ritva. Lilja had pressed herself into the furthest corner like a mouse, knees drawn up to her chest. The only other person was the man who had brought Elin inside.

Tuomas frowned. He wasn't sure if he recognised him. The man seemed to realise though, and if he was offended, he didn't show it.

"Stellan," he said. "We met briefly when you came to Poro."

Tuomas remembered at once: he was the one who had let him and Elin into the village. It seemed like an eternity ago now.

He smiled in greeting. "I'm sorry. Nice to see you again."

"Likewise. I just wish it was under better conditions than this," said Stellan.

The toddler in Tuomas's arms spluttered. Enska noticed and picked him up, then laid him across his lap so he could feel the growing heat from the flames.

"Hey, Tarvo," he said. "You're being so brave."

Tarvo coughed feebly.

"The Wind Spirits are winning… The little boy's winning…" he breathed. "Can you ask him to stop? Please?"

Tuomas threw a worried glance at Enska. In the corner, Lilja screwed her eyes shut.

"Hush, now," Enska whispered.

Tuomas sank down the wall until he was sitting next to Stellan, then loosened the cord around his hat and pulled it off. The snow caked to his clothes began to melt. As the fire gathered strength, the interior of the hut swam into view. It was a similar size to the ones at Akerfjorden: about twelve feet wide, with a smoke hole in the roof. The floor was laid with overlapping birch twigs, all arranged in the same direction.

Around the hearth were a series of flat stones to contain the logs. The walls, made from various layers of compacted turf, were supported by curving wooden beams; the branches had been sheared off to leave makeshift hooks for hanging clothes and food.

The entire place smelled stale; it had been six months since the herders had last passed through, and it showed. Some of the earth in the roof had crumbled and fallen away; the old reindeer hides on the floor stank of damp. But none of that mattered. The shelter was secure and it would be warm soon enough. It was all they needed to wait out the storm.

The fire flared into life and Enska placed a pot on the hearth, filled with snow. As soon as it melted, he dipped some wooden cups inside and passed them around.

"Thank you," Tuomas gasped as he took a mouthful.

"You look as though you can't wait for tea," Enska smiled. He threw dried angelica and nettle into the pot and left them to simmer while he helped Tarvo to drink.

The wind howled between the huts. A flurry of snow forced itself through the smoke hole and swept the fire into a frenzy. Enska leaned back until it subsided so no flying sparks could catch on his clothes.

"Don't worry," he said, noticing the concern on Ritva's face. "Our people have been making this journey since the very first reindeer walked the Northlands. Things will turn out fine."

"Why were those stars falling?" Frode asked anxiously. "I've never seen anything like that."

"Stars fall every night," Enska replied.

Frode shook his head. "But not like that. Not all at once. You know that, Enska, don't pretend it's nothing. It happened a few days ago, too. Something's wrong."

"We have no reason to believe anything's wrong," Enska insisted. "And I also know that it's important not to jump to conclusions. The truth is always deeper than what we may first think. Nothing bad has happened because of it so far; it's not connected to the mist or the illness, that much I do know."

His voice was kind, but firm, and Frode could do nothing but nod. Tuomas took comfort from it too. Neither Lilja nor the Sun Spirit had said it had anything to do with the plague. But then what was it?

"You're a mage for a reason," Frode said. "I'll trust your word. Everything will be fine."

"Sure, it will," said Stellan. "You're forgetting something else: we've got the Son of the Sun on our side. Can't you just… blow the storm away or something?"

Tuomas's expression dropped. In the shadows, Lilja raised her eyes to look at him.

"Hey, it was just a joke," Stellan said quickly.

Tuomas knew it wasn't, but he didn't say anything. He could tell Ritva was staring at him and kept his gaze pointedly on the fire, watching as the herbs steeped into tea. But she didn't stop, only cleared her throat to get his attention.

"How did you stop those things?" she asked. "What were they? What did they want?"

"They were draugars," Enska answered. "They're the ones causing the sickness. We're doing what we can to figure out how to fix it, don't worry."

"How can we *not* worry?" Ritva insisted. "How did you stop them?"

"I put out a protective barrier," Tuomas replied, still not looking at her. "It's something all mages do."

"Then… do you know something from the World Above? There were so many rumours that you ran away there."

"I didn't run away. It was a visit."

Her eyes widened. "Well, what was it like? What did the Spirits tell you?"

"I don't think Tuomas wants to talk about it, Ritva," Lilja said. Her voice was polite, but belied a gentle warning.

"But, with all due respect, maybe he should," Frode replied. "Maybe the answer to the sickness is up there. It's so difficult to see the youngsters suffering like this. We've already lost our Niko."

He caressed Eevi's face and wiped away the sweat which had gathered on her cheeks. Every breath bubbled and cracked, as though her lungs were full of water.

Tuomas swallowed so hard, his throat hurt. Niko had to be one of the children who'd died on the Nordjarvi.

He threw a searching glance at Lilja and she looked straight back in confirmation. Her face was as composed as ever, but in the firelight, he could see her eyes blazing as she bit back tears. Enska noticed her struggling too, and took her hand in his. Tuomas observed how flippantly he seemed to do it, to not draw attention to her.

The sight brought a tiny smile to Tuomas's face. Enska truly was one of the kindest people he'd ever known. Despite everything that had happened with Lilja, he remained her loving father, always there to help and comfort her.

"We will find a cure for this sickness," said Enska gently. "I know it's difficult to not worry, Frode. Especially after Niko and his friends. But we're trying as hard as we can. And once we get to the coast, we can make all the youngsters more comfortable, and then work with the other mages."

Ritva stifled a sob. "I can hardly bear it. It's so awful! What have they done to deserve this?" She turned her eyes on Tuomas. "Can't you do something?"

That caught Tuomas off guard and his words tumbled over each other.

"I've only been training since last summer. Enska and Lilja and Henrik and Aino are all more skilled…"

"But you're the Son of the Sun!" Ritva insisted. "Surely you can do something! *Please* do something!"

Eevi coughed and specks of blood appeared on her chin.

Ritva's sorrow broke her. She collapsed into Frode's arms; her cries barely stifled by his coat. Tuomas looked at Enska and Lilja again, and noticed his own helplessness reflected in their eyes.

This must surely be the worst pain for a mage, he thought. To see such suffering, and have no way to stop it. Not even the ability to reach the Spirits for help.

Chapter Fifteen

Tuomas couldn't move. His wrists were above his head, tied together and hooked over a rock. A demonic stink filled his nose, and something else: warped *taika*, twisted in a way it never should be. It pressed on him like a physical weight and made him feel sick. The air was so cold, every inhale stung his lungs.

Kari appeared. He untied Tuomas's belt and coat, then sliced his tunic open until his torso was exposed to the elements.

"Help me!" Tuomas cried. "Somebody, please!"

Kari smiled at him.

"Time to see what the *taika* in that beating heart tastes like."

"Help!" Tuomas screamed as the blade stabbed down on his chest. "Lumi!"

But she didn't come. Pain fired through his skin. The sharpened flint inched its way through muscle and bone, deeper than ever before. And then Kari was standing over him, clutching a bloody heart…

He woke with a start.

He was in the hut. Not on the mountain, not a prisoner: safe and surrounded by his companions. Elin was right next to him, a grimace pinching her features. Beads of sweat had broken out on her forehead and left her fringe jumbled at every angle.

The blizzard was still raging; through the smoke hole, he saw no stars. But he could tell time had passed by the fire: it was smaller, and the shadows on the ceiling had grown longer as the flames dipped closer to the embers.

He sat up and buried his face in his hands. Tears welled and he let them fall. Terror still raced in his blood – the smell and pain lingered like phantoms.

"Get a hold of yourself," he snarled under his breath. "He's not coming back. You know he's not…"

"Who are you talking to?"

He lowered his hands. Elin's eyes were open. Despite everything, they still shone with her usual determination.

"Nobody," he said, too quickly.

Elin wriggled a hand out of her sleeping sack and touched his arm. Even though she was lying right next to the hearth, her palm was freezing cold.

"Kari?" she asked.

Tuomas sighed. There was no point in lying to her. She had been up on the mountain too.

"I know it's stupid," he said. "The Great Bear Spirit took him away; when I spoke with the Sun Spirit, she said he can't hurt me anymore. But…"

"It's alright," Elin assured him. "It's not stupid. I understand."

"I'm still scared of him."

"I don't blame you for that. But he's gone. This was just a nightmare."

"But what if it isn't?" he whispered. "Dreams happen when the life-soul wanders… what if mine is going to where he is?"

"That's not what's happening, and you know it," she replied steadily. "Life-souls don't leave the World Between unless the body-soul dies."

That was true. He made himself listen to her words, let them remind him that he was truly safe. Kari would never come back for him. The Spirits wouldn't allow it. All this was just the aftermath of surviving the trauma.

He sat in silence for a few moments and allowed himself to breathe. When he felt under control, he looked back at Elin. She hadn't taken her eyes off him. Even in the low light, he could see how bloodshot they were; how much her face had paled. Her cheeks were gaunt and tiny blood vessels marbled her clammy flesh.

"How are you feeling?" he asked.

"I'm fine."

Tuomas couldn't suppress a bemused chuckle. "Liar."

Elin didn't look away. "Where's my bow?"

"In the sleigh, I think."

"I want it."

"In the morning," he promised. "It's still storming out there. Don't worry, you don't need it right now."

"I know I don't need it," she shot back, "but I want it. It's… like your drum, I suppose. I made it with my father. It helps."

Tuomas gave her a gentle smile. "I understand. But believe me, you're going to be alright. I'm going to do something about this."

She covered her mouth with the edge of her sleeping sack and coughed.

"Like what? How can you fix sick souls? Has anyone ever done that before?"

"I don't know," Tuomas admitted. "But I promise, nobody's going to have to do it again, because we'll figure out a way to fix it. We just need to get to the coast. It will be safer when we're all together. Then I'll sit down with all the mages and we'll…"

He let his words trail off. What *would* they do? How could they hope to progress when Lilja had forbidden him from speaking about Aki?

Elin yawned. Tuomas took her hand and tucked it into her sack.

"Go back to sleep," he said.

"I'm not sleepy," she protested.

"Yes, you are."

"No, I'm not…"

Her eyelids fluttered closed. Tuomas watched as her breathing slowed, and soon she was silent save for the rattling in her lungs. She curled herself close to the embers, in a way that horribly reminded him of Paavo.

He glanced around the shelter. Despite the cramped and smelly environment, nobody else had stirred. Stellan was in the corner; Ritva and Frode had Eevi between them, sandwiching her with their bodies to keep her warm. Enska was opposite, one arm draped over Lilja's back.

Tuomas knew he needed to sleep too. As soon as the storm was over, they would be carrying on. So he laid down, grabbed his hat to use as a pillow, and forced himself not to think about Kari.

A sudden crunch sounded behind him.

He listened hard. The crunch came again, cutting through the howling wind. Tuomas frowned and raised himself up on one elbow to hear better. It almost sounded like feet.

He shrugged it off. It was probably just a reindeer wandering about. Then an awful thought crossed his mind. What if it was a wolf?

Don't be stupid, he told himself. *Greylegs won't come out in weather like this.*

He closed his eyes and extended one hand towards the fire to feel its warmth. His fingers landed so close to it; the embers almost touched the ends.

Red Fox One...

He sat bolt upright. The voice had been inside his head, just like how it was in the World Above.

He threw a glance at Lilja to see if she had heard it too, but she didn't move a muscle.

Then it came again: the same crunch, closer this time.

To his relief, it wasn't the Moon Spirit; he could tell that much. But it wasn't Lumi either, or the Sun Spirit. It felt deeper than any of them.

Glad he hadn't bothered to take off his shoes, Tuomas pulled on his coat and bound it with his belt. Then he crept to the door, rested one hand against it, and unsheathed his longest knife with the other. He didn't care that instinct told him there would be no wolves; he wasn't taking any chances.

He took a deep breath, then shoved the door open and stumbled out into the night. He shut it quickly so the cold couldn't wake the others.

The blizzard had lessened a little, but it was still nowhere near safe enough to travel through. Snow had banked up against the walls of the huts. Most of them weren't even visible from where he stood.

He would have to be careful. If he lost sight of where he had come from, there was no way he'd find his way back. He considered returning and waking someone, but then he spotted movement close by, followed by more crunching.

He held his knife out warily. On the chance it was a wolf, it would be able to smell him; it could pounce at any moment.

The silhouette grew larger in the swirling whiteness, morphing into a giant shapeless bulk. Then it came straight at him and swam into view.

Tuomas yelped and fell onto his backside.

It was a bear.

Its fur rippled like grass in the wind and its nose twitched as it padded closer on four huge paws. Tuomas caught a glimpse of the claws, longer than his eating knife, and his stomach flipped in terror. A single swipe and he would be dead before he hit the ground.

What was this thing doing here? Bears were supposed to be hibernating until spring was well underway. Had it attacked the reindeer? Had it broken into the other huts? They never would have heard the screaming in this weather.

The bear halted barely three feet away and looked straight at him with its small black eyes. It was pure white, as though it was made from snow. He could feel its hot breath on his face.

He didn't dare blink, and the bear didn't move.

He remembered how close he was to the hut. He opened his mouth to call for Lilja. There might be a chance she'd hear him, or Enska or Frode. Anybody…

The eyes suddenly began to twist and swirl, and he saw the stars reflected in them. He frowned – there were no stars out tonight.

Then the voice came again, echoing in his head.

I summon you tonight, Son of the Sun. I summon you only.

The voice was soft; not quite a woman's or a man's, shifting and formless. Every word rang with incredible power.

Tuomas's mouth fell open. He raised his hand, the knife falling from his grasp, and reached towards the bear's muzzle.

His fingers brushed fur which stuck to his skin and came away like snowflakes... and then he was falling yet rising, spinning around himself. He felt the summer warmth and caught the fleeting taste of lingonberry as his *taika* engulphed him. His life-soul flew upwards; there was a distant thud as his body collapsed onto the ground.

The bear grew, each hair splitting into a thousand stars, until a gigantic being stood with him, not quite in focus – in the strange purgatory, he wasn't sure if it was because he was too close or too far away. There was no light, yet it glittered and shone.

Then, around it, a river of green and blue fluttered through the darkness. It pulled with it the voices of a million souls; and at its head, Lumi floated as effortlessly as a feather on the wind.

Tuomas gasped with happiness.

Lumi! he cried. *You're alright!*

Of course I am, she replied. Her white tail swept the sky and she drew closer so he could feel her: a cool and piercing presence, edged with whirling snowflakes and freezing fire.

Did the Moon Spirit hurt you? he asked. *I saw you in the sky, but you looked faint...*

I was weakened, but not harmed, she said. *She is stronger than me, after all.*

Thank you for defending me. I didn't think she'd let me go.

You defended yourself as much as I did. But that is not why we are here, Tuomas.

With that, she moved back so the Great Bear Spirit was in full view. Tuomas bowed low in respect. He sensed the power radiating off it: beyond comprehension, as though the vibration of everything which had ever existed was condensed into a single form.

Tuomas Sun-Soul, it said.

Tuomas didn't move for a long time. There was a gravity to the Bear's tone which he hadn't heard when he had previously connected with it. It pressed on his heart and made him gasp for breath.

What do you want with me? he asked, as respectfully as he could.

Much, replied the Bear.

It swam around him, small and huge, ever moving. The stars and vapours which formed its shape sparkled in a thousand different ways. Tuomas felt like a tiny ant beside it; as miniscule as a leaf in the middle of a vast forest. If he had been standing, he would have been driven to his knees. All of life and reality seemed to be looking at him through those unblinking black eyes.

Firstly, the Bear continued, *I know you have seen the stars falling. Do you know why?*

No, Tuomas answered. *You know I don't.*

A paw swirled through his mind and drew out the memory of when he had pulled away from Lumi. He could feel her grip on his wrists as though it were only yesterday. Then he felt himself bring his magic forward, push it against her until she was forced to let go; and as he tumbled towards the Mustafjord, something ripped open.

Do you see? said the Bear. *Balance must always exist between the World Above and the World Below, to keep the Word Between balanced in turn. It gives stability to life and death, to light and darkness, and to all the Spirits who dwell Above and Below. But now, it is compromised. When you unleashed your taika on your sister – equal powers used against each other in a way they should not have been – you tore the boundary. Now the skin which separates the World Between and World Above is frayed. A hole lies open like a wound.*

Tuomas hung still in the air, struck dumb with shock. He looked at Lumi and the graveness surrounding her was all the confirmation he needed. It welled like a sadness within her: a perfect snowflake on the verge of thawing into rain.

It is as much my fault as yours, she said. *I held on, even though I knew you would pull harder. I was only trying to protect you.*

From the draugars, Tuomas nodded. *I know they want me. I should have listened to you.*

Yes, you should, Lumi agreed with a hint of anger, *but now the damage is done.*

Is it bad?

No, but enough to weaken the boundary.

That's why the mages can't speak to the Spirits. They're cut off from the World Above, Tuomas realised.

Yes, said Lumi. *The only one still able to enter here is you.*

Because I'm a Spirit, he finished. He turned to the Great Bear in panic. *Can't you repair it?*

The Bear fixed him with its penetrating stare. Each hair on its ethereal body sparkled with colours he had never even seen.

I maintain the balance, nothing more. The Worlds are not on a collision course yet, but they will be if you abuse them again. If you, or any being with power, cross physically between the Above and Between again, the tear will rupture further. Terribly.

I understand, Tuomas said in a small voice. *Can I fix it?*

While it is your responsibility, a more pressing one draws me to you tonight. I have summoned you, and for you to understand, I must remind you of your past. Are you prepared to take this knowledge, Son of the Sun?

Tuomas hesitated. The severity in the Bear's words was so strong, he wanted nothing more than to escape this encounter, wake up once again in the hut and have Elin convince him it was only a dream.

You wouldn't have come to me if this wasn't important, would you? he said quietly.

The Bear didn't answer. There was no need to.

Tuomas threw a glance at Lumi. She looked back steadily, and gave him the tiniest of nods.

I trust you both, and I will listen, he said. *Tell me.*

I will not tell you, the Bear said. *I will show you.*

In a heartbeat, Tuomas suddenly found himself alone in the middle of the tundra. There wasn't a single landmark in sight, and the Spirits had disappeared. The horizon and sky blended together seamlessly, both as white as the other, without even a line of footprints to break the monotony. The only difference was beneath him: he was standing in the middle of a frozen lake.

Despite the lack of detail, he vaguely recognised it. It was the Northern Edge of the World. He had sat here with Lilja, while Elin and Sigurd had watched, not too long ago…

No, it was earlier than that. He sensed that it was long before the mist had arrived; before anyone he knew was even born, or their parents.

He inspected himself. He was younger than he was now – no more than ten. A drum swung at his belt, but it wasn't his current one. It was larger, with different symbols; some of them had been painted so small, he couldn't make out what they were. Either side of the Bear's head in the centre were two foxes, one beneath the Sun Spirit and the other beneath the Moon Spirit.

But the greatest change of all was on his head: two furry ears protruded from his hair and rose into a sharp point, just like Lumi in her human form. He looked behind him and noticed a tail sweeping under his coat. However, it wasn't white. It was red.

He untied his drum and took the antler hammer in his hand. The spectral body seemed to move on its own; he had no control.

He struck up a beat and raised his voice in a chant. The power in it shook him – it was his own *taika*, with the feeling of the Sun Spirit in summer and the sweet scent of flowers – and yet more concentrated than he had ever experienced. He drove it into the lake, so deep, he almost lost his grip on it. It split the dark, broke through the skin between the Worlds, and a jet of light shot out of the ice.

The force was so strong, it blew him onto his back. But when he looked at it, a hole had opened where he had stood, and a herd of ghostly white reindeer were spilling from it, running in all directions until the empty landscape swallowed them.

One of the Earth Spirits rose out of the ice. Its body was woven from lichen and flowering heather, plump lingonberries cascaded down its front.

What have you done, Red Fox One? it whispered.

Tuomas blinked, and when he opened his eyes, the surroundings had changed. Now he was on the frozen Mustafjord. And he was no longer a child, but a fully-grown man: his body felt heavier, more muscular, and he was as tall as Paavo. He wore a coat of white reindeer fur: the sign of a mage. It was paler and purer than any mage pelt he had ever seen, as though the fur was made from miniature icicles.

On the bank a mile away, there was no sign of Akerfjorden. All he saw were thick trees extending down to the water, their canopies rendered completely white by heavy snow. Akerfjorden didn't exist yet, but behind him, a crowd of people walked, spluttering children in their parents' arms. He had led them out of the north, looking for a new place to call home, somewhere the Moon Spirit's gaze wouldn't be as strong upon him.

And now they were almost there. So close…

Mist suddenly spilled across the surface and the ice cracked underneath him. Something snatched at his ankles.

He barely had time to scream before the freezing water closed over his head. The crowd screamed and ran forward to help, but it was too late. The hole at the surface shrunk as he was pulled down. All around, draugars grabbed at his clothes and skin. They tore his coat off with their slimy hands and scratched his chest so deeply, he felt claws against his breastbone.

Taika! So much taika! they hissed, teeth flashing in the gloom. *Give it to us, Son of the Sun! Give it! Be ours!*

The fjord filled his lungs. He tried to fight them off, but there were too many of them, and they were too strong. Blood turned the green water red. He was drowning…

The aurora pulsed over the ice, then shot through the crack after him. The Lights swarmed in all directions and beat the draugars away. A spectral fox face hovered before him in the water.

It is too late, he said, in the language of the Spirits which he had never forgotten. *I am a dead man. You cannot save me, sister.*

I cannot save your life, came the reply, *but I will save your soul. I would save you a thousand times.*

One of the Lights plunged into his chest. The draugars screeched in anger, but the white fox bolted back to the surface, a single glowing life-soul streaming in her wake. It was brighter than any other, like a droplet of pure Sunlight. And the Great Mage hung dead in the water, slowly sinking into the black abyss, the Spirit of Passage following him to collect the body-soul which was left.

Tuomas blinked again.

It was over. He was hanging in the trance, himself again, Lumi and the Great Bear Spirit spinning their glow around him. Even though he wasn't in his body and couldn't cry, a sob flowed through his mind like the echo in a giant cave. No number of fireside stories could measure up to what he had just witnessed.

Lumi watched him warily and flowed closer so she could touch him. For the briefest of moments, she transformed into the snowy girl who had travelled with him across the tundra.

Are you alright? she asked.

I think so, Tuomas breathed.

So now you understand, said the Great Bear Spirit. *When you first leapt from the World Above and were reborn in a human body, you sought refuge in the World Below. To reach a place as far from the Moon Spirit as possible, you opened a gateway: the only place where there can be physical passage between the Worlds.*

The Northern Edge of the World, Tuomas said.

Yes, the Bear confirmed. *The Earth Spirits gifted you, as the Great Mage, a herd of magical white reindeer. They helped you to survive; you brought them with you when you went among the people. Then you headed south to Akerfjorden in an attempt to find solace further from the Silver One's reach. But you never made it.*

So I saved you – pulled out your life-soul as you drowned, said Lumi. *Your people's legends about me were correct in that sense.*

The fright pressed in around Tuomas. He couldn't shake the sensation of the Mustafjord choking him; the hands pulling at him, trying to reach his heart.

There were draugars there, he said, his voice trembling. *He didn't – I didn't – just fall through the ice, like in the stories. They pulled me under. How were they there?*

The Bear drew closer, trailing stardust in its wake.

The waters of the Worlds are the womb of life. When you opened that gateway to the World Below, you also allowed the waters to seep into the gaps between where the Worlds meet. The draugars came forward for the first time out of that darkness.

Tuomas was so horrified, he thought he might fall out of the sky. Lumi noticed and quickly wrapped him in her Lights to keep him anchored.

I unleashed the draugars? he breathed.

Your actions did. It is part of the web which you inadvertently spun, said the Bear gently. *There is no fault that I place upon you, Son of the Sun, but you must understand the situation. Draugars by themselves are powerless. To spread the illness which claims young lives, to let their poisonous mist emerge from the waters, they require a channel: a living being of strong taika.*

Like Aki, said Tuomas. *Lumi, he was who we heard, when he pulled the souls away from you, wasn't he? You said it was something you hoped you'd never see again.*

And yet I always do, she said darkly. *But that boy they have now is merely the latest.*

What do you mean?

For every generation that they return, they require another mage, the Bear explained. *They will drain the power from them; trap them beyond time so they cannot age nor die. There were other mages who fell prey to them before Lilja's son – so many, should you line them up shoulder to shoulder, they would reach beyond the horizon. The draugars use them as a lure for as long as they can, and then will search for another, forever hungry for the strongest taika.*

It paused to look straight at him.

That is why they pulled you under the ice, Son of the Sun. They wanted you. They will want you until the end of time, and with every generation, children will sicken while they search for you.

Can I stop them? Tuomas asked. *You wouldn't tell me this if I couldn't, somehow.*

And now we come to the task I give you, said the Bear. *There is only one way to stop them. Go to the Northern Edge and cross into the World Below. The Earth Spirits will help you to draw the draugars out so I can restrain them, as I did with Kari.*

Tuomas shivered as he saw Kari's face in his mind, but the Bear noticed his discomfort and swept the image away.

Won't that rip the Worlds more? he asked.

Only if you pass between here and the World Between, said Lumi. *This skin is always more delicate than the other, because here is formless. The World Below is not – for the most part.*

The Bear stared at him with its bottomless gaze. *Will you do as I have instructed?*

It wasn't a request. Tuomas threw a glance at Lumi, took a deep breath, and then said, *Yes*.

Something jolted him far below. Both the Bear and Lumi disappeared into darkness. He spun away, back down towards the earth. Hands were grabbing at his body, pulling him out of the trance. He opened his eyes, but his limbs were dead and his flesh felt like cold meat.

He was bundled into someone's arms, then the wind disappeared and the air became warm. He dropped onto a reindeer skin and lay on his back. This body was his, but he was somewhere else; still too far away…

A face appeared in front of him, very close, shouting.

"What were you doing, you idiot? Do you want to get frostbite again? Want to lose the rest of your fingers? Stupid boy!"

His chin lolled, arms lying useless at his sides. If he concentrated, he was able to twitch his fingers, but not much else.

He forced himself to look at the face. Slowly, details swam into place: two long sandy plaits, a woman's features, blue eyes, a scar across her neck.

"Lilja?" he managed to blurt. He sounded as though he was drunk.

"Yes, it's me," she snapped. "What were you thinking? It's a good thing you decided to stop by the door, or we might never have found you!"

"Ease off him, Lilja," said another voice – a man… Tuomas vaguely recognised it as Enska. "He's groggy. You pulled him out of the trance too quick."

"Well, tough. I'd rather him come out of it like this than have frozen himself to death," she replied angrily.

Tuomas noticed other people standing around him, further away, against the walls of the hut. He supposed it was Stellan, Ritva and Frode. Their faces were etched with worry. He heard mutterings about whether he had come down with the sickness too. He tried to shake his head, but everything swam before his eyes, so he stopped.

"What's he done?" he heard Elin asking. He couldn't see her anywhere; he guessed she was still lying by the hearth. "Where is he? Tuomas?"

"He's right here," Enska said. "Don't worry, he's not hurt."

"He's a lucky fool," Lilja snarled.

Tuomas breathed deeply, filling his lungs with air, and immediately began to feel better. Then he let it all out in a massive sigh.

There was a collective gasp of shock. Even Lilja moved away from him.

He frowned. "What's the matter?"

"Look," Lilja whispered, pointing at the air in front of him.

Tuomas blinked hard and made himself concentrate. His breath had misted in the cold, but the cloud was twisting around itself, until it formed the shape of a bear's head, nose turned skyward. Then, as quickly as it had come, it disappeared into nothing.

Lilja was back at his side in a heartbeat.

"You saw it again?" she asked, notably quieter.

Tuomas nodded, still focusing on getting his limbs to work.

"What did it say? No, tell me later. We need to get you warm."

"I'm fine," Tuomas said.

The sound of his own voice startled him. It was no longer slurred, and with every breath, he could feel the cold draining out of him, as though he had just drunk fire itself. He looked at his hands in alarm, and found the flesh pink and healthy, not chilled at all.

Lilja pulled off his hat and felt his forehead. Her eyes widened.

"You *are* fine," she said in amazement. "You're actually warm. In a good way."

"How is that possible?" Frode asked. "How long was he outside?"

"I don't know," Tuomas admitted. "But I'm not cold. Honestly."

"Get by the fire anyway," Lilja said. She didn't even wait for him to protest and bundled him closer to the hearth.

He clutched at her sleeve. "Lilja, listen…"

"You can barely keep your eyes open. Get some sleep. We'll talk in the morning."

"No… Lilja, please listen to me."

She glared at him. "I said, get some sleep."

She left him and went to Enska, the two of them drawing close together and speaking in hushed voices. Frode and Ritva threw Tuomas a distressed look before they settled back down with Eevi.

Elin grasped Tuomas's wrist.

"What happened?" she asked.

He turned over to face her. "The Great Bear Spirit came to me."

Elin blinked in alarm. "Well, what did it say?"

"Hey," Lilja snapped. "Sleep. Both of you."

Realising they weren't going to get any peace, Tuomas gave Elin a small shrug and they lay down on the skins. But even though he closed his eyes, he was still wide awake. He couldn't stop replaying the encounter in his mind.

He shuddered, remembering swirling nothingness and dancing Lights.

Lumi, he thought, *I wish you were here*.

Chapter Sixteen

Stellan rammed his shoulder against the door. Snow had piled up against it and wedged it shut during the night. Once the gap was wide enough, Tuomas shimmied outside with a shovel and began clearing a path as best he could.

He looked around at an alarmingly quiet landscape. Overhead, the sky was pale and clear of any cloud, transforming an icy blue as the dawn lingered below the horizon. The snow was up to his knees; in places, it had banked so high, it was almost touching the sloping roofs of the huts.

Now the storm had blown away, he could see the last of the mountains, standing like great monsters off to his left. Three jagged peaks, carved by generations of wind and ice, reached so high, he wouldn't have been surprised if they could pierce straight through to the World Above.

He shuddered. He thought of the tear between the Worlds, the gateway he had opened at the Northern Edge, the feeling of the draugars dragging him into the fjord…

He looked at the way they had come, and his heart sank. The snow rose higher than the tallest man. Even if they'd wanted to go back, now it was impossible. The only way across was to climb, and go through the pass. Tuomas could just make it out from here: a narrow slit through the flank of the foremost mountain. The rock on either side of it was sheer, as though it had been cleaved straight with a giant knife. All through his childhood, it had reminded him of the Mustafjord, like the entire landform had been somehow lifted and recreated in the air.

He took stock of the reindeer. The females were desperate to get to the coast now. Their bellies bulged and they bellowed in agitation. It wouldn't be long before it was time to drop their calves, and to do it anywhere but the summer grounds was dangerous. On Anaar and its neighbouring islands, there were no land predators; no wolves or wolverines lurking in the shadows. And there, the three villages would be together, able to support and protect each other at last.

He sighed sharply. The only chance he would have to reach the Northern Edge now was to continue to the coast and then rebound back on himself, the long way. But even so, his sleigh was taken and his own energy was drained from the long migration. There was no choice but to carry on.

Enska emerged and whispered thanks to the Spirit of the Winter Winds. If the blizzard hadn't dissipated so quickly, they might have been trapped here for days.

"Come on, everybody," he said. "We need to move quickly and get through the pass before it gets more dangerous. If we hurry, we'll be at the coast tomorrow evening."

After a laborious morning, everyone managed to get out of the shelters and helped arrange things for moving on. The Sun Spirit had risen by the time all was done, and her glow transformed the land gold and blue. The reindeer were fed from the lichen sacks; the sleighs dug out and stripped of their tarp coverings. Firewood was fetched and piled into the backs, and when there was nothing more to do, the youngsters were finally allowed to leave the shelters.

Many of them were too weak to walk even a few steps. Tuomas looked on as children were carried in their fathers' arms, concealed by blankets, with only their pallid faces exposed. Their lips were chapped, their eyes bruised and dark. Some had a little blood at the corners of their mouths. The air filled with a horrid rattle as they snatched breaths from the thin air.

Then Elin appeared. Her eyes were hard with determination, fixed on the nearest sleigh. But she barely managed to two strides in the loose snow before her knees wobbled and she tumbled over.

Tuomas took a step forward, but Stellan reached her first and swept her into his arms. She kicked feebly.

"I'm fine. I just lost my balance," she protested.

"Let me help anyway," Stellan said, and carried her the rest of the way.

The sight hurt Tuomas more than he had been expecting. The sickness had spread through her so fast – she had only started coughing a week ago. There was no way she could shoot an arrow now, no way she could even stand for longer than a few heartbeats.

He fetched the bow from the sleigh she had been in the day before, handed it to her, then turned away so she wouldn't see the fear on his face.

When everyone was accounted for, they moved out. The herders let the reindeer go first, so their legs could flatten the snow and leave a path, but it was still difficult. Several times, they needed to stop and hurriedly dig out a sleigh when the runners became stuck. But they didn't give in. They had to keep going. Even the animals moved faster, as though sensing the lost time.

The bulk of the mountains grew more enormous. A few resilient trees and shrubs had managed to take root at their base, but they were soon lost as the height overpowered them. Not even halfway up the massive flanks, there wasn't a single branch left to be seen.

After several miles, the ascent truly began. It was gentle at first and Tuomas barely felt as though they were moving at all. But then he would look up, and see the peaks rising before them, dwarfing the herd in their colossal shadow. The earlier climb after the lake was nothing compared to this.

His legs burned with the effort. He loosened his belt slightly to give himself more room to move inside his coat, and dug his ski poles deeper into the snow. Nobody had bothered wearing skis for this section, but the poles provided a wonderful extra grip.

The Sun Spirit shone down from above; he could swear he felt a caress of heat in her rays. That brought a small smile to his face. Despite the ice and frozen skies, spring was definitely here. It would have already reached Anaar, and after the silence of winter, the sound of running water would be filling the air. It wouldn't be long now before all this snow was gone completely, and all the Northlands would turn green, and he could wander the wilderness to gather cloudberries and mushrooms…

His heart jolted at the thought. The shadow of the Great Bear Spirit's words loomed back over him like a shadow. He couldn't escape it, and it brought a fresh wave of terror. What was he supposed to do?

He looked around for Lilja and was relieved when he saw her coming towards him, her strides long and awkward in the powdery snow.

"Alright, then. Tell me what happened," she said.

Tuomas glanced around to make sure nobody else could hear them.

"The Great Bear Spirit came to me," he whispered.

"I know, I saw," Lilja said. "But that doesn't explain why you decided to go outside in a blizzard. With no mittens on."

"I heard a noise. I thought it might have been greylegs."

"Even greylegs aren't stupid enough to go out in weather like that."

"Well, it doesn't really matter, does it? The point is, I went out, and the Bear was there. It pulled me into a trance. Lumi was there, too."

Lilja threw a sideways glance at him. "So now you're not just the only one who can connect with the Spirits. You're doing it without even trying."

Tuomas went to defend himself, but then realised by the half-smirk on her face that she was being sarcastic.

"I'm sorry I snapped at you last night," she added. "I only did because... I care. And at least one of us can connect with them. One is better than none."

Tuomas hesitated, touched by her honesty. If he'd been speaking to Henrik, he doubted the exchange would have been so civil. But he couldn't dwell on it; the anxiety of the situation forced all other thoughts from his mind.

He moved closer to her and lowered his voice.

"That's exactly the point. The reason why nobody else can go into trance is because I've torn the boundary to the World Above. It's why the stars are falling."

Lilja turned to look at him fully, unable to hide the alarm on her face.

"Why in the name of all the Spirits did you do that?" she snapped.

"I didn't mean to!" he insisted. "It was an accident; I pulled away from Lumi too hard when I came back from the World Above. I... lost control."

Lilja snorted. "You don't have the best record for control, do you?"

Tuomas winced. "It was an accident..."

"I heard you the first time. Did it say anything else?"

"Yes," he admitted, and relayed the entire experience as quietly as he could. When he was finished, Lilja's eyes were completely round and all the blood had drained from her cheeks.

"*You* unleashed the draugars?" she breathed. "And they killed you?"

Tuomas looked at her warily. He couldn't tell if she was going to hug him or hit him.

"I'm scared, Lilja," he said. "The Bear told me I need to draw them out – I think it wants me to use myself as bait in the World Below, but I can still feel them, trying to rip out my heart…"

"Ssh!" Lilja hissed, but she slipped her poles into one hand so she could rest a hand on his shoulder. Even through her layers, he felt her shaking.

"Are you mad at me?" he asked.

She shook her head. "I'm sure the Bear will have your back."

Her voice was tight. Tuomas pressed his lips together sullenly.

"All this because I'm the Son of the Sun," he spat. "It's so unfair! I didn't ask for any of this!"

"But you've got it nevertheless," Lilja countered. "Life isn't fair. There's no point complaining about something you can't change."

She let go of him and gave him a soft smack with one of her poles.

"We'll try to make some sense of it all once we're at the coast. You can't go to the Northern Edge until we get there, anyway. And I'll do my best to help you, if I can. You're not in this alone. But in the meantime, let's keep this between us. Everyone's frightened enough right now."

Tuomas fell silent. Something about how she spoke made him remember the day they had left Akerfjorden, when Henrik had given him back the drum. Now he knew who he was, the old mage had warned him to be prepared.

"You're not in this alone, either," he said. "I want to help you figure out how to reach Aki."

"I told you," Lilja snapped, "that's my problem to solve. And you promised me you wouldn't say anything to anybody."

"I won't. I haven't –"

"You also promised me you wouldn't get involved. Should I not have told you about him? Can't you understand? I don't want to talk about him. It's too painful."

"Don't you trust me?"

"I do, but I want you to stay out of this."

"We have to do something," he argued. "Think about it, alright? If I can connect with the Spirits, I might be able to connect with him, too. Maybe we can find a way to save him before the Great Bear –"

"Tuomas," Lilja said, "leave it."

He knew better than to argue. He had spoken his piece, now the best thing to do was let Lilja consider it.

It would be difficult for her to accept help after living as she had. For so long, she'd relied on nobody, save for herself and the two people who had, in their own ways, abandoned her. She reminded him of the Northlands itself: both beautiful and harsh, moulded by the very essence of what surrounded her. Even her eyes were like ice, warning away everybody so they wouldn't fall through the surface and be drowned.

Lilja cleared her throat, bringing him back into the present.

"Are you cold?" she asked.

Tuomas went to say no out of habit, but then paused when he realised he genuinely wasn't. He was just comfortable. Even the exposed skin on his face was warm.

Lilja noticed his hesitation. "I'll take that as a no, then."

"How?" Tuomas asked. "It's freezing. And last night…"

"I think it's another result of you accepting who you are," she replied.

"What do you mean? I've got the Sun in my blood, or something? Then how could I get frostbite?"

"No, you fool. You might not be able to sense it, but I can. Your *taika* is growing. It's stronger than any I've ever felt." Lilja looked straight at him, her eyes shining. "It's shielding you from the elements. Like how Lumi was always unharmed no matter how harsh the winter got."

Tuomas nodded to himself. She raised a good point.

"Well, it would be nice to be able to walk on the snow like she could," he said. "It would make climbing this mountain a lot easier!"

Lilja smirked.

"Actually, since you knew what my Spirit title was, do you know what I'm the Spirit of?" he asked.

"No. You'll have to figure that out," she replied. "Remember, the Red Fox One came out of the World Above and into a human body generations ago. Whatever he's in charge of, nobody's seen it. And if they have, it's been forgotten."

Tuomas bit back a stab of disappointment. Ever since Elin had raised the question, he'd hoped that Lilja might be able to answer it. He absently touched his head and imagined the pointy fox ears which had sat there in his vision.

They carried on in silence for a while. His drum banged against his hip with every step. Tuomas laid a hand on it in comfort. It suddenly reminded him of what Henrik had said about his lessons.

He spoke up before he could convince himself it was a bad idea.

"Can I ask you something?"

She gave him a wary look. "What?"

"I was speaking with Henrik, before we started on the migration. I asked if I could be his apprentice again, so I could learn how to control my *taika* better. But he said I should actually talk to you about it."

Lilja was so stunned, she stopped walking. Tuomas paused too and dug his feet into the snow at an angle so he wouldn't slide backwards.

"You want *me* to teach you?" she repeated in amazement.

Tuomas watched her face, not sure if she was insulted or not.

"Yes. If you wouldn't mind."

"And Henrik told you to ask me? I thought he didn't like me."

"He doesn't, really," Tuomas admitted begrudgingly. "But I stood up for you. And I think he's right. He told me that I need help enhancing my *taika* and learning to keep it under control. You're one of the most powerful mages in the Northlands. You'd be better at it than him."

He jerked his head to encourage her to start walking again. Realising that nearby people were beginning to look at them, Lilja quickly complied.

"That's praise, I must say," she muttered, still taken aback. "I'm not sure how great a teacher I'll make, but… feeling your *taika*, I don't think you really need to be taught much."

"That's what Henrik said."

"Well, he's right."

"So, what do you think?" Tuomas asked. "Forget teacher. How about as a mentor? As a friend?"

Lilja didn't answer straightaway. Her eyes roved over the snow, as though searching the churn of hoofprints for what to say.

"I don't think I've ever really had a *friend* before," she said, more to herself than him. But ultimately her shoulders slumped, and she gave a conceding nod. "Alright. I suppose I can try."

Tuomas smiled at her in thanks. Then the two of them quietened and continued up the slope.

Chapter Seventeen

As the day wore on, the route became steeper than ever as it twisted and wound around smaller peaks. Tuomas had to kick his shoes into the snow to get purchase. The reindeer, usually fanning out, narrowed their formation until they were only walking five abreast. The sleighs slotted in with them as best they could. Soon, all conversations ceased, and the only sound drifting through the air was the occasional cough. Even the snow dulled the reindeers' hooves until silence reigned.

When Tuomas looked over his shoulder, he saw they had left the tundra far behind. It extended below, stretching on for miles. The huts where they had sheltered were mere specks against the vast whiteness. Anything further than that was obscured by the horizon, melting in so perfectly to the sky, he couldn't quite say where one ended and the other began.

The air grew thinner. The wind howled eerily through the mountains. It blew into his face and he struggled to breathe. He pulled his scarf over his mouth to make it easier, but it offered little relief.

After climbing another mile away from the ground, the route slowly levelled out as they emerged into the pass. It cleaved its way through the rocks in a giant sweeping path. The blizzard had hit up here too. Enormous rocks lay hidden beneath fresh snow, but a layer of ice had formed over the top of it, making it slightly easier to walk on.

Tuomas was glad for that. This place was treacherous. The less time they spent in here, the better. Even the reindeer seemed to sense it: they could have moved out again, but they stayed together.

The sides of the pass loomed above like a gaping maw. Huge slabs of snow hung precariously over their ridges. Tuomas eyed them nervously.

There were tales of the things which lived up here. Stories were often told around the fires: of beings which didn't take kindly to trespassers, who would send bad weather and avalanches down on those who refused to acknowledge them. Even the largest boulders, eroded into strange shapes, were said to be trolls: evil man-eating giants who hadn't escaped the Sun Spirit's rays in time, and now stood petrified in stone. Indeed, every single spring and autumn, Tuomas could remember the migration leaving an offering after travelling through, to keep the entities appeased. So far, it seemed to have worked.

A wave of coughing broke out. He recognised it as coming from Eevi.

Stellan approached the sleigh carrying her. Tuomas watched anxiously and leaned over to whisper to Lilja.

"Is she alright?"

She narrowed her eyes, trying to see.

"I don't know. But I don't want to go over there. We need to walk carefully."

Tuomas nodded in agreement. The crust of ice was still underfoot. It wouldn't be dangerous if they fell through it, but it would certainly cause a hindrance.

Stellan bent to scoop up some snow and pressed it firmly into a ball. Then he handed it to Eevi, trying to get her to put it in her mouth. It wasn't as good as water, but if she let it melt on her tongue, it would do.

More coughing came from nearby. Elin.

Tuomas dropped back until her sleigh caught up with him. She was sitting against the sleeping sacks with a blanket wrapped around her. Only her eyes were visible, peering out from a gap in the fabric, heavy and red with exhaustion. She clutched her bow between her knees.

He rummaged in the food pouch at his belt. There were some strips of reindeer jerky and a couple of salmon cakes inside it. He removed the cakes, reasoning that they would be easier to eat, and passed them to her. She took them with a shaky hand and pulled the blanket down a little to show him a grateful smile.

"Thank you," she mouthed.

Tuomas motioned to his own face, urging her to cover herself again. She didn't argue and did as he said.

Eevi started coughing again, harder this time. The sound was horrible. Stellan hurried to the reindeer pulling the sleigh and grabbed its harness, forcing it to stop.

Tuomas skied over and almost balked at the sight. Eevi was only a little younger than him, but she was so ravaged, she looked like an old woman. Her entire face was whiter than the snow; even her lips had completely lost their colour and turned blue. Blood dribbled down her chin.

Panic mounted in Tuomas's chest and he waved frantically at Lilja.

"Where's her parents?" he hissed to Stellan.

"Over there. I'll get them," he replied, and hurried off.

Lilja skidded past him and came to rest beside the sleigh.

"Tuomas, get in there with her. Keep her warm," she ordered, pulling her mittens off as she spoke.

He immediately climbed into the sleigh's belly. Lilja wrenched a reindeer skin out of the back. Tuomas gathered Eevi in his arms and pressed himself against her, trying to lend her as much body heat as he could. Lilja laid the skin over them, fur side down. At that moment, Ritva and Frode arrived, their faces tight with worry. Ritva leapt into the sleigh to help.

"Keep her warm," Lilja said again. "Make sure she can breathe."

Eevi coughed again, bringing up more blood. It stained Tuomas's sleeves bright red.

Then he almost screamed. Mist began to pool out of the girl's mouth. It wrapped around her throat like living ropes.

Ritva tried to bat it away, but it slipped through her fingers. She cried out with fright and pulled Eevi close, rubbing her arms, desperate to get heat into them.

"Help her!" Frode shouted at Lilja.

"I am," she insisted, eyes wide as she tried to think. She started trembling.

All the time, the mist continued curling, spreading over Eevi's face and worming into her eyes.

"Make it stop!" she gasped. "Please! Mother!"

"*Enska!*" Frode bellowed. "Enska, where are you?"

His yells echoed around the pass and bounced back from all directions. The reindeer sensed the panic and quickened their pace. A few herders hurried to keep up with them, but most ran to the sleigh to see what the matter was. When they saw Eevi, a gasp of horror flew into the air.

Tuomas looked at Lilja. He could hear her muttering under her breath.

"Please don't… Aki… please stop…"

Enska shouldered his way through the crowd. He tried to prise the misty tendrils away too, quickly realised it wasn't working. Then he held a finger under Eevi's nose.

He leaned across Tuomas, pulled her out of the sleigh and laid her on her back in the snow. He latched his mouth onto hers and blew hard until her chest rose.

Eevi lurched forward and coughed again. Enska sprung away, narrowly missing a spray of blood. Ritva and Frode watched with bated breath.

"Mother…" Eevi wheezed as her eyes glazed over. The mist drew tighter around her neck until it pressed like a noose against the skin. She drew in a feeble gasp, bubbling deep in her lungs, and then fell silent.

Nobody moved or spoke for a long moment. Ritva jumped out of the sleigh and tapped Eevi on the cheek. When there was no response, she started shaking her harder and harder. The girl still didn't move.

"Eevi?" she shrieked. "Eevi! Baby, wake up! *Wake up!*"

Frode fell backwards into the snow, his face blank. Ritva began screaming. The sound filled the entire pass and tore through Tuomas like a physical wound. He had never heard a noise like it.

Lilja was frozen in shock. Eevi's eyes were still open, gazing blankly into nothing. All the light had gone out of them, like ice had formed across their surface.

Tuomas tried to stand, but his legs refused to work and he tumbled over the edge of the sleigh. He landed at Lilja's feet. She snatched his coat and bundled him upright, but didn't let go, as though the entire World would crash around her if she did.

Frode crawled to Ritva and put his arms around her. She was rocking back and forth in distress, cradling her daughter to her chest, as if Eevi wasn't a teenager, but the infant she had once nursed.

Enska approached Lilja and Tuomas. He laid one hand on his drum for comfort and bit his lip hard to keep his emotions in check. His face was speckled with tiny flecks of blood.

"There's our first," he muttered. "I fear it won't be the last."

Lilja didn't look at him. She still had hold of Tuomas's coat, and as she squeezed it, her knuckles turned white.

"What do we do now?" Tuomas asked. He had never seen anyone die in the mountains before.

"We'll take her with us," said Enska. "I can't do funerary rites here, and we need to get through this place as quickly as possible. We'll wrap her up and carry her in the sleigh, then bury her when we get to Anaar."

Tuomas's alarm must have showed on his face.

"But what about the others?" he whispered. "The other children, their parents… they'll know there's a dead body with us. And the sickness caused it."

"There's nothing we can do about that," Enska insisted.

Tuomas looked past Lilja to where Elin's sleigh had stopped. She was peering at him through her blankets. Even from here, he could tell she knew what had happened. Everybody did. Ritva's screams were unmistakable.

Then came another noise, somewhere above, rising over all others. A crack.

Tuomas glanced at Lilja. She was still staring at the ground, face hollow with guilt. He quickly shook her to get her attention.

"Did you hear that?"

She blinked hard. "What?"

"There's something up there…"

He had barely finished speaking when it came again, louder. This time, Enska and a few others seemed to hear it too, because they all turned to look up at the sides of the pass. Right on cue, a huge chunk of snow fell from one of the ridges and crashed down on the path behind them. Then, as quickly as it happened, all was quiet again.

"We need to get out of here," Enska said.

He hadn't even raised his voice, but at once, the herders began to move, running ahead and ushering the reindeer to go faster.

Tuomas chanced a glance at the ridges. No more snow had come loose, but they couldn't risk staying here. The onset of the spring thaw, coupled with the blizzard, had left the place unstable. It could collapse at any moment, and all it would take was one slide in the wrong direction.

The Spirits and monsters of the mountains had been awoken. Tuomas felt them rumbling under his feet; they were angry a death had occurred in their domain.

Another crack came, louder than the ones before. He froze, hardly daring to look.

The screaming started: a noise of sheer panic. Everybody ran; even the reindeer stampeded, their eyes rolling crazily.

The last of the snow slipped from the ridges in a great slab. It quickly gathered momentum as it flowed down the mountainside, roaring like a thousand demons. It grew into a giant cloud and flew through the pass, straight at them.

Tuomas abandoned his ski poles and fled. He slipped on the hard ice crust, barely keeping his balance. Terror raged in his blood as the avalanche swelled behind him, rising a hundred feet into the air.

It was coming faster than any of them could run. Soon it would be upon them.

Lilja sprinted alongside him. She was clutching her drum against her chest, so tight, he thought her fingers might tear through the skin.

An insane idea suddenly shot through his mind.

He had laid down a protective barrier at the lake, but drums could unleash restraints and shockwaves if the mage struck them with enough *taika*. He had seen it done; managed it himself once before, when he'd faced Kari on the Mustafjord.

There was no time to warm his drum or spin a circle. He would just have to take his chances.

He ripped it from his belt, stopped running, then turned and faced the avalanche.

Lilja noticed and came at him.

"What are you doing?" she shrieked.

Tuomas didn't listen to her – he could barely hear her over the deafening noise. She wouldn't reach him in time.

He planted his feet and raised the antler hammer high in the air. He closed his eyes, drew up all his power, let it race through his muscles until they felt as though they were on fire. It was almost enough to lift him off the ground…

He called to all the Spirits, to the mountains, to the Great Bear. Then he let out a bellowing chant and hit the drum as hard as he could.

The avalanche caved in two, a line splitting it cleanly down the middle. The blast almost knocked him over. Walls of raging snow formed on either side, held at bay by sheer will.

He carried on chanting, as loud as his lungs could bear, pushing his *taika* outwards. The snow curved around him, flowing past the herders and reindeer like two thundering rivers split at a confluence. Everyone stopped running and looked around in wonder.

The force of it drove Tuomas to his knees, but he kept drumming, snatching breaths as quickly as he could to maintain the chant. He wasn't singing to the avalanche; he *was* the avalanche, and it would move where he decided.

It rushed down the pass, boulders and snow tumbling over each other, powder shooting towards the sky, until it finally began to slow. After what seemed like an eternity, he sensed the last of it draw to a halt, and all was still.

He collapsed onto his side. His chest burned with *taika*; it felt as though he had been trampled by every single reindeer in the herd. Groaning with exhaustion, he raised his head to check if anyone was hurt.

An amazing sight greeted him. The settled avalanche had formed two massive white flanks along the pass, tapering out like arrowheads. In the untouched space between them, the animals and people were huddled together, looking shaken but definitely alive. They hadn't even lost a single sleigh.

Lilja ran over and threw herself down next to him. For a moment, she couldn't even speak.

"What… how…? How did you do that?"

"Shockwave. I just focused," Tuomas breathed. "I just…"

She suddenly pulled him into a hug. Enska appeared behind her, his mouth hanging open.

"I've never seen anything like that," he said, visibly shaken. "Ever…"

Tuomas managed a small smile. Even he could barely believe it had worked. He lay limp in Lilja's arms and stared up at the sky. The Sun Spirit shone down upon him.

"Thank you…" he muttered, then his eyes rolled back in his head and he lost consciousness.

Chapter Eighteen

The convoy headed along the pass as quickly as they could, taking advantage of the clear sky to keep moving until they lost all light. They sheltered behind a rock face to build the camp, but nobody slept well. The memory of the avalanche was still too close for comfort.

Tuomas didn't wake until the next morning. As soon as the sky began to lighten with the approaching dawn, the herders packed the tents and carried on, over the last crest.

At the top, they were met with a glorious view. The route started sloping down the far side of the mountains, back towards the smooth tundra, darkened here and there by the figures of birch trees. In the distance, a blue sea sparkled like diamonds, the welcoming summer islands rearing from its water.

It was strange to see after months of whiteness. Spring was well on its way here: colour splashed across the landscape, and in places, patches of grass and heather had broken through the snow. And not far from the coast, a massive crowd of reindeer was visible: the Einfjall and Akerfjorden herds.

The sight gave everyone new energy. They descended the slope, moving carefully to avoid triggering any more avalanches. But when the snow became solid underfoot, the reindeer ran the rest of the way until they were back on the flat. The herders let them, too relieved to be going down after climbing for so long.

With no more room in the sleighs due to the sick children, those who walked took turns riding on the runners. Everyone stayed clear of the small sleigh though, which hung behind at the tail end of the formation. It was the one Tuomas and Elin had arrived in. Now, it carried Eevi's body, wrapped in a single blanket for modesty. The rest of the layers had been taken from her and given to the other youngsters in a desperate bid to keep them warm.

Akerfjorden and Einfjall must have noticed them approaching, because their herds drew to a halt and waited for Poro to catch up. After almost a full day of walking, they met. The reindeer hurried to the exposed grazing and tore mouthfuls of moss from the rock. After walking constantly for almost two weeks, they had finally found plentiful food.

Leaders and mages from the three villages swarmed together. Tuomas's heart swelled to see them again. It felt like years since he'd last spoken with someone from Akerfjorden. He waited for Lilja to join them, but she kept her distance and hurried away, leaving Enska alone to represent Poro. Henrik shot a suspicious glare at her.

Aino, the Einfjall mage, noticed Tuomas and dropped into a low bow. A teenager at her back quickly did the same. Tuomas fought the urge to cringe.

"It's good to see you," said Aino. "You managed to put the Spirit of the Lights back, then."

"In the end," Tuomas admitted. "Thank you so much for everything. We never would have managed it without your help."

"And the wicked mage is gone."

"Yes. That too."

Aino noticed his discomfort and quickly changed the subject, ushering the teenager forward. She was a few years older than him, short and stocky like Lilja, with a head of thick red hair which hung loose around her face.

"This is my apprentice, Niina," Aino said. "I'm sorry you didn't get a chance to meet her when you stayed with us. Niina, this is the Son of the Sun."

"Tuomas," he said quietly.

Niina immediately lowered her head. "It's an honour to meet you."

"And you," he replied, "but please, call me Tuomas. I insist."

He threw a pointed glance at Aino, Maiken, and the other leaders; then let it rest. Everyone looked too exhausted to get into this topic now.

"How was the journey?" Anssi asked. "Uneventful, I hope?"

"Hardly," Enska replied. "I suppose I don't have to ask whether the sickness has struck you as well?"

Aino and Henrik nodded.

"Any losses?"

"Unfortunately, yes," said Maiken softly. "Two from Einfjall and one from Akerfjorden."

Tuomas held a hand to his mouth. "Who?"

"Jaana. Hekla and Jorn's little girl," Sisu said. "Hekla's got it too."

Tuomas looked away sadly. He remembered Jaana being born six years ago; the way she had sat entranced by Aslak's scary story at the start of the migration. She had once wandered into Tuomas's tent and claimed Paavo's cooking was better than her mother's. As for Hekla, she was the same age as Paavo: only twenty-five.

The emotions on his face must have been easy to read, because Sisu approached and laid a comforting hand on his shoulder. His eyes were heavy – from tiredness or sadness, Tuomas couldn't tell.

"Your brother's fine," Sisu assured. "So is Mihka."

"Are they any better?" Tuomas asked, though he already knew the answer.

Sisu pressed his lips together grimly. "They're holding on."

"Can I see them?"

"Last I checked, they were both sleeping. Leave them be for now; they didn't rest easy on the way here."

"Are they still drinking the tea?"

"We ran out of herbs," Niina said in a wretched voice.

"I've got a few left," Enska volunteered. "Not many, but enough for anyone who's really suffering. I'll brew them when we stop."

"Well, we may as well stop here," suggested Anssi. "The coast is just there; we can cross to Anaar first thing tomorrow. Everyone needs to rest."

Tuomas nodded in agreement. No migration was easy, but this one had to be the most gruelling any generation would have faced. Everywhere he looked, he saw fatigued faces; people dragged their feet and leaned on each other for support. They had all lost weight, and even those who weren't ill had felt the effects of caring for their loved ones. Tuomas had never seen them so dejected.

"We'll set up camp, then, before we lose the light," said Maiken. "Let's go and tell them to stop."

She and the other leaders headed towards the front of the herd, where it would be easier to draw attention. Grateful for the opportunity to be alone, Tuomas left Enska to retrieve the nettle and angelica and wandered over to the unpacked sleighs. He rummaged in a sealskin pouch until he found a tiny piece of jerky and half-heartedly chewed it.

He drew in a deep breath and relished the briny smell on the air. Even though they were in the north, it felt a little warmer with the sea so near. He glanced at the glittering water, the shores of Anaar tantalising close on the other side. Journey's end was in sight, mere miles away, and tomorrow, they would be there.

It was almost over.

That thought brought the weight of everything crashing down as though a blizzard had engulfed him. It pulled at him from every angle and refused to let him go. In a flash, he remembered the draugars snarling at him through the shield; Lilja's face when she spoke about Aki; the sound of Elin's cough mixing with Eevi and Tarvo and Mihka and Paavo...

And then there was the Great Bear Spirit. He could still feel the sensation of it brushing against him: the touch of a million stars and all the mysteries which held them together.

That was the heaviest of all. He let out a whimper and covered his head with his hands.

He heard footsteps crunching through the snow. It was staggered, hobbling, and he recognised it without even needing to look up.

"Hello, boy," Henrik said. His voice was weary, truly showing his age.

Tuomas turned to him. Over his shoulder, the tents were going up and the soft orange glow of fires reflected off the snow. It was not a moment too soon. The daylight was quickly fading even though it was only mid-afternoon, and the first stars were already beginning to appear, flanked by the silvery face of the Moon Spirit. By the time the last tarp was tied, night would be upon them.

The air was filled with coughing. Tuomas's eyes fleeted over Eevi's corpse and he bit his lip to keep himself from crying. He could still hear her mother's scream echoing in his head.

"We're here now. No need to worry about panic on the migration," he said. "Henrik, the people aren't stupid. They'll have figured out it's not just a cold by now. We need to be honest with them. They need to know it's a soul plague."

Henrik shuffled. "I have been getting questions about that. I thought it best to leave it until all the villages were together." He ran a hand over his drum for comfort. "I'll speak with the other mages and leaders again tonight. Then maybe we can tell everyone tomorrow, when we get to Anaar."

"Fine," Tuomas said.

Henrik quickly changed the subject. "I hope Lilja told you how we're supposed to stop this sickness. And don't say it has anything to do with draugars."

"It does. I saw them."

"I doubt that."

"Henrik," Tuomas said firmly, "*I saw them*. We went past a lake and they all came slithering out of the water. The only reason nobody got hurt was because I put up a shield."

Henrik opened his mouth, then closed it again and shook his head, as though trying to shake something off.

"Well, then… are the Poro children having nightmares, too? About a little boy? What does she know of that?"

Tuomas gathered the hem of his coat in his hand and twisted it.

"It's just a way they're tormenting the kids," he said quickly. "She's spoken with the Earth Spirits about it. I'm going to go to the Northern Edge as soon as I can and stop the draugars with their help."

Tuomas went to walk away, but Henrik blocked his path and grasped his elbow so he couldn't leave.

"That's all you have to say?" He leaned closer to whisper. "What does she have to do with it?"

Tuomas stepped back. "Nothing!"

"Are you sure? Who's the boy?"

"Of course I'm sure! She'd never hurt anyone! Please, Henrik, leave me alone now!"

Tuomas wrenched himself free and stormed off through the maze of tents. He was so furious, he didn't look where he was going, and ran straight into someone.

He cried out in shock and flew backwards into the snow.

A man turned around, regarding him with annoyance. But as soon as Tuomas saw him, all the anger flew away. He carried an ash-wood bow across his back, and his face was weather-worn, framed by deep black hair cut into a fringe across his brow. It was the exact same shade and style as Elin's.

Tuomas scrambled to his feet.

"Sigurd?"

The man's eyes brightened.

"Tuomas! Oh, it's so good to see you!" he said, in a deep voice which could rival Henrik's. "Where have you been? We looked out for you when we joined with Akerfjorden."

"It's a long story," Tuomas admitted. "Is Elin back with you? Where's Alda?"

"I'm right here," said a woman, shoving past Sigurd and throwing her arms around Tuomas. The force of the hug almost knocked the breath from his lungs, but it brought a wonderful comfort to feel her and catch the familiar smell of herbs on her clothes.

In an instant, he was back in his sleeping sack in their hut, fresh from escaping Kari on the mountain. She had been there every time he had woken from the fever dreams, caring for him and wrapping bandages around his frostbitten hands. It hadn't been for very long, but in that time, she had arguably become the closest to a human mother he'd ever known.

When she finally let go of him, she moved her hands to his face.

"You seem well, Tuomas," she smiled fondly. "Are you not sick?"

"No," he replied. "I think I'm the only one left who isn't."

"Lucky boy. Make sure you keep taking care of yourself. Whatever you're doing is working."

"Don't be silly," said Sigurd. "He's the Son of the Sun. That's why he's not sick."

Tuomas squirmed with unease, but Sigurd didn't notice.

"The things we've heard… You went to the World Above? And on the way here, you flung up a shield –"

"Any mage can do that," Tuomas insisted.

Sigurd looked straight at him. "You split an avalanche."

Tuomas closed his eyes. "Yes, fine, I did."

"You saved everyone. All the reindeer, too. And those creatures… what were they? All the Poro people have been talking about it –"

"Sigurd," Tuomas said, "do you mind if we don't talk about this right now? The Son of the Sun thing is all I've heard for weeks."

Sigurd frowned, but gave a gentle shrug. "Sure." he said. "Your migration doesn't sound much easier than ours. There have been some terrible storms near Einfjall in the past month. The snow's come so thick, it's completely blocked off the north."

"Can you still get to the Northern Edge?" Tuomas asked anxiously.

"We couldn't have even gotten to the shrine on the mountain, let alone the Northern Edge," replied Sigurd. "It's a good thing you and Lilja went to see the Earth Spirits when you did. If we went now, there's no way we'd be able to reach the lake."

Tuomas's heart sank like a stone. What was he supposed to do now?

"Speaking of Lilja," Sigurd continued, "is she here? We heard she'd gone back to Poro. I was hoping to speak to her, say sorry for telling her to leave."

"She's…" Tuomas turned around to point her out, but she was nowhere to be seen. "She's somewhere."

"Typical," said Alda. "Don't worry, Sigurd. You'll find her soon enough."

Tuomas glanced over her shoulder at the nearest hut.

"Are you staying in there?"

"Yes. Why?"

"Is Elin with you? I didn't see where she was taken."

Sigurd nodded. "Enska and Aino brought her to us earlier. She's asleep."

There was a darkness to his words. Tuomas could only imagine how hard it must be for the two of them. The last time they had seen their daughter, she had left Einfjall with him, almost two months ago. And now she returned to them at death's door, a shadow of her former self.

"I'm sorry," he said. It was all he could think of.

"Why are you sorry?" asked Alda. "It's not your fault."

But Tuomas could only shake his head. He was sorry for everything. For not sending Elin straight back to them after

Lumi was returned to the sky; for not being able to stop her getting ill; for too much for him to even name.

Yet, despite it all, he saw from their eyes that the joy of seeing her again outweighed their worry. And that hurt him more than anything he could have said.

Sigurd motioned towards the tent.

"Do you want to come in and see her?"

Tuomas stepped back. "No, not if she's sleeping. Tell her I'll visit tomorrow."

"Can we offer you any dinner? You can eat with us?"

"No, thank you. Honestly. I think I need some time alone."

Alda nodded in understanding. "Fair enough. We won't keep you." She pulled him in for another hug. "Take care of yourself, Tuomas. We'll see you in the morning."

They disappeared into the tent. Tuomas thought he heard a weak cough from inside before the flap fell down. He grimaced at the sound. It was probably just Elin turning over in her sleep, but unable to hear it a second time, he walked away.

Chapter Nineteen

Tuomas stayed out of the way until the last tent had been raised. He wandered across the plain, relishing the open space after the uneasy claustrophobia of the mountain pass. What little light there was reflected off the snow and sea, turning everything a faint blue-grey. He imagined the inky sky overhead as the ancient skull of the Great Bear Spirit, and all the stars looked down upon him in earnest.

He inspected it closely. If he squinted enough, would he see the tear that he'd caused in the World Above?

He lowered his head and gave himself a faint slap on the cheek.

"Stop it," he muttered. "It's going to be fine."

He stared at the ground to distract himself. For the first time since the snows had fallen in the autumn, there was something other than white to see. Their details were lost in the darkness, but he still marvelled at the patches of heather and grass. At long last, life was returning. He pulled his mittens off to touch it, but was immediately nosed out of the way by a hungry reindeer.

He chuckled to himself, then fetched the last sack of lichen and threw down what was left. There was no point carrying it over to Anaar, and the animals would need all the strength they could get. Tomorrow, they would swim across the water between here and the island.

The reindeer nibbled at the lichen; some even took it from his hands. When the females came closer, he scratched their necks and silently congratulated them on making it this far.

They truly were amazing creatures. They survived further north than any other, through the coldest winters and the most bitter blizzards. In summer, they tolerated the clouds of mosquitoes which spawned from the lakes. They were faultless, adapted perfectly for this harsh life. They were a source of everything: food, clothing, transport, milk... there was nothing they couldn't give. Without them, the people would never have survived in the Northlands.

When the sack was empty, he tossed it away, stroked the nearest reindeer around the ears, and wandered back into the camp. Nobody was left outside except him. Usually, a small group would take turns keeping watch for wolves, but they had left the territories behind long ago.

It was the largest collection of tents Tuomas had ever seen: three times the size of the typical Akerfjorden one. Each shelter was lit up from within by fires, and he could see the silhouettes of their occupants against the tarps, tucking into an early evening meal. Tuomas was glad they hadn't decided to hold a communal feast. Everyone was far too tired – it could wait until they reached the island.

He heard coughing from practically every tent, as well as the occasional worried sob as parents wept into their clothes. He recognised the sewn hide pattern on one and gently tapped a pole near the flap.

"Who is it?" Sisu asked.

"It's Tuomas," he replied.

"Oh. Come in."

Tuomas pulled the flap aside and leaned through. Sisu was sitting on the opposite side of the fire, the bone beads on his tunic shining in the flickering light. Some of the threads had broken, so the pattern hardly resembled the waves of the Mustafjord anymore.

Tuomas's eyes went to the figure next to him. Mihka was curled up in his sleeping sack with one hand on his father's lap. His eyes were closed and his mouth lolled open; Sisu had done his best to clean him, but tiny smears of blood were still visible around his lips. Even his white hair looked dead. The only way Tuomas could tell he was still alive was by the rise and fall of his chest.

"How is he?" he asked in an undertone.

Sisu regarded Mihka and gently stroked his head. "He's fighting. Brave boy."

"Can he still walk?"

"Yes, but I've told him not to if he can help it. I didn't want him to suffer any more this winter."

"Neither did I," Tuomas admitted.

He reached to the back of his belt and pulled off the small sealskin pouch. He didn't need to open it to feel the fox carving and imagine the strands of snowy hair.

He bit his lip, but the tears came anyway. They dripped onto his coat and caught on the brown fur like rain.

Sisu looked up in alarm. "What's the matter?"

Tuomas shook his head. "I've been so selfish. Mihka was right, I've hardly spent any time with him. I got his life-soul back and then I ran off because I was scared. And now, when I want to be with him, he's…"

He screwed his eyes closed and took a deep breath, trying to get himself under control.

Sisu crawled around the fire so he was kneeling in front of Tuomas, and clutched his arms in his two large hands.

"Look at me," he said.

Tuomas did, but his cheeks burned with shame.

"I will be forever grateful for what you did for him," Sisu whispered. "He's all I have left. I know he's never helped himself, but I love him so much, and I owe everything to you. And I can't even begin to imagine what you had to go through to bring him back to me. You can cry, Tuomas. Cry all you need to."

Tuomas squeezed the pouch so hard, the bone cut into his stumpy fingers. He remembered whittling it in Lilja's tent, back before he knew anything, when all that mattered was waking Mihka. It was all so much more now. He wanted to tell Sisu, to open his mouth and let all his anxieties pour out, but he restrained himself; only sniffed and wiped his nose on his sleeve.

"Thank you," he said.

Sisu didn't let go of his arm. "Are you alright? Why don't you stay awhile and get warm? Have you eaten?"

"I'm warm enough," Tuomas said. "Can you tell me where Paavo is, please?"

"He's in with Henrik," replied Sisu. "The last tent on the right, I think. Do you want me to come with you?"

Tuomas shook his head. "No, stay with Mihka. He needs you."

As though he'd heard his own name, Mihka spluttered and twisted around in his sleeping sack so he was closer to the fire. A fresh line of blood trickled out of his mouth.

Sisu immediately returned to his side. Tuomas let the flap fall back into place and walked away until he spotted Henrik's tent. He heard coughing from inside.

The sound tore his heart, but it also lent a wave of relief. Paavo was awake.

He tapped the frame to let Henrik know he was there, then let himself in. The shelter still stank of Henrik's tea. It made Tuomas's eyes water, but he was glad for that. It would disguise the fact that he'd been crying. Even with Sisu's kind words, he couldn't let Paavo see how distressed he was.

"You took your time," Henrik noted, but not nastily.

"I needed to be alone."

Tuomas looked past him to where Paavo was lying. As well as his sleeping sack, he was wrapped in blankets and covered with Henrik's own coat. The layers disguised him in a mound of fur and fabric, but Tuomas knew that beneath them, his brother's once-strong body would be as skinny as a sapling.

Paavo peered at Tuomas with bleary bloodshot eyes.

"Where have you been?" he asked, but coughed loudly before he could finish.

The sight shook Tuomas to the core. He turned back to Henrik and laid a hand on the old mage's shoulder.

"I'm sorry," he said. "Thank you so much for looking after him while I was gone."

Henrik held his eyes for a moment, then nodded and patted his wrist gently.

"We're all family here, boy. You know that."

He grasped one of the poles and used it to haul himself to his feet. His knees clicked as he moved and he let out a loud groan.

"Have some time with him," he said. "I need to speak with Aino and Enska anyway. We need to figure out an alternative for when the herbs run out."

Tuomas helped him hobble his way outside, then closed the flap behind him. As soon as Henrik was gone, he manoeuvred his way to Paavo's side and checked his temperature. It was still alarmingly hot. His forehead was soaked with sweat; it had seeped into his hair and turned the blonde strands dim and greasy. He smelled terrible.

"Where have you been?" Paavo asked again.

Tuomas did his best to offer a small smile. "Elin and I went to find Lilja. Remember?"

"Not really…"

"Well, it doesn't matter. I'm back now. You'll have to put up with me again."

"Spirits, help me," Paavo smirked. "Sorry I won't be able to cook for a while."

Tuomas snorted. "*That's* what you're worried about?"

Paavo managed a weak shrug. "On the other hand, I did tell you not to go running off again, or I'd stop feeding you."

"You'll thank me for it later," said Tuomas.

He twisted around to the hearth, where a pot of tea was bubbling in the flames. Tuomas grabbed a cup and half-filled it. He curled his hand around the back of Paavo's head and raised him so he could drink.

Paavo grimaced. "Not that stuff again."

"It's good for you," Tuomas insisted. As soon as he spoke, however, he bit his tongue. The best thing the tea could do was alleviate the symptoms, but it would never be the cure. And he was no closer to discovering that than when he and Henrik had visited the shrine.

Paavo managed a few meagre mouthfuls, then gagged and coughed violently. A mixture of tea and blood splattered his front.

It wasn't the first time Tuomas had seen it, but it suddenly broke something inside him. His tears returned with the force of a wave, spilling down his cheeks before he could stop them. He laid his body across Paavo's and hugged him. Through the layers, his bones felt as brittle as twigs.

"Don't give up," he begged. "Please! I need you to fight this! Lilja and me… we'll fix everything, we'll make it better!"

"I'm not going anywhere," Paavo replied. "It's going to take more than this to end me."

For some reason, his steadfastness hurt Tuomas even more. He didn't dare let go, in case Paavo would somehow slip away from him. With every breath, he could hear the crackling in his lungs. His whole chest vibrated from it. Tuomas could almost picture the horrible mist writhing under his ribs, growing stronger, entwining around his souls until the time it would burst out of his mouth and choke him.

"Promise me," he cried. "Please."

Paavo wormed both his arms free and crossed them over Tuomas's back.

"I promise."

Chapter Twenty

By the time Henrik returned, Paavo had fallen into a fitful sleep. Tuomas accepted a cup of tea and drank it slowly, letting his mind wander so he wouldn't taste it as much. The two of them ate a piece of salted reindeer flank, then Henrik threw another log on the fire and laid down.

"Best get some rest, boy," he said. "It will be a hard day tomorrow."

Tuomas nodded, but then paused. "I haven't got my sack. I must have left it in one of the sleighs."

"Well, go and get it, then," said Henrik. He wriggled around on the reindeer skins so there would be room for Tuomas and closed his eyes.

Tuomas stepped back outside. It was truly night now – the temperature had plummeted, but even though he was aware of it, it didn't chill him. He felt as though he could have taken off his coat and easily carried on with no ill effect.

He walked to the sleighs at the edge of the camp. Another was a short distance from the others: the small one which he and Elin had taken to find Poro. Inside were four dark shapes. They were wrapped in old blankets, but their shape was unmistakable. They were the bodies of the children.

The mages had laid down a protective circle to keep evil out, though Tuomas couldn't help but feel the effect was lost. Evil had gotten into the poor youngsters while they were still alive. It had already claimed their souls. This ritual was more for the comfort of the living than the dead.

He let his feet carry him to the circle. He raised a hand and held it to the barrier, and sure enough, it repelled him like the clearest sheet of ice. The bodies wouldn't be buried until the crossing was done. They would be taken across the water with everything else, and then, when the migration was finally over, they could be buried at the shrine on Anaar. To let them lie in the middle of nowhere, with nothing to mark them, would be discourteous to their souls.

Then he noticed Lilja sitting by herself on the other side of the circle, staring into the dark distance. She was barely visible, far outside the glow of any fire. Only her silhouette against the white snow showed she was there.

He approached slowly so as not to startle her, but even when he was close enough to touch her, she still didn't move.

"Are you alright?" he asked.

She turned around. Her eyes were still as wide as they had been in the mountain pass. It made him uncomfortable – she was the only one who hadn't looked at him differently, even from the very beginning.

He went to leave, but she caught his wrist and silently invited him to sit with her. She had taken an old reindeer skin from the sleighs: the only barrier between her and the snow. As he settled at her side, he caught the damp smell of it and grimaced.

"Please stop staring," he said.

She averted her eyes. "I'm sorry. I'm just still a little shocked."

"About Eevi and the others? I noticed you ran away before anyone could speak to you."

"That was…" She broke off and quickly changed the subject. "About the avalanche, as well. How did you manage to do that?"

Tuomas shrugged. "I just tried to make a big shockwave."

"No mage has ever had the power to do something like that," said Lilja. "I suppose I shouldn't be surprised. You are the Son of the Sun, after all. But it's something else to actually *see* it."

Tuomas shuffled uncomfortably. "Does it change the way you see *me?*"

She shook her head. "Of course not. I'm just shaken, that's all. Don't mind me."

"It's changed things for everyone else." He ran his fingers through the snow between his legs, pushed it into a mound, then flattened it with his palm. "They were treating me strangely before, but now… they're looking straight through me. It's like I'm not even human."

"Well, that's half right," Lilja mused. "You're a Spirit in human form. Not really one thing or the other."

"I hate it," Tuomas snarled. "I don't understand why it had to be me."

Lilja glanced at him, then tentatively laid a hand on his arm.

"Well, if it's any consolation, I don't know what it's like to be the Son of the Sun, but I know what it's like to be alone." She let out a long sigh. "Even with Kari and my little boy, I was alone. They never saw the Bear like I did."

She shifted her hand across his shoulder until her fingers hovered over his breastbone. There, under the layers of coats and tunics, was the scar from when her brother had tried to cut out his heart.

"Does that ever hurt?" she asked.

Tuomas shook his head. "No. Does the one on your throat hurt?"

"No. Not since Kari died." Lilja let go of him and hugged her knees to her chest. "You know, when you met me, I didn't know what to think about him. He was the only one who stayed with me when I left Poro. He raised Aki, tried to get him away from those draugars. And then... I found him that morning, making a demon, and he set it on me when I refused to help him..."

She held a hand to her neck.

"Calling the Spirits to seal him in that cairn was the only thing I could have done. I loved him and I hated him," she said. "I suppose that extends to practically everyone I've ever known. Except Enska. And you."

Tuomas blinked in shock. "Why?"

"Because you've never been superfluous."

"What does that mean?"

"You've never hounded me or asked me to do stupid things. You're genuine. When you came looking for me, it was for something bigger than yourself. I haven't seen that all too often. It made for a nice change."

Lilja cleared her throat awkwardly. "And maybe because of who you are. As much a Spirit as you are a human. Spirits have always been better company to me."

Tuomas smirked. He could tell how difficult it was for her to pay a compliment like that. But he couldn't deny how much it meant to him, for reasons Lilja hadn't even said.

"Why are you out here by yourself?" he asked.

She shot him a wry look.

"Well, fair enough. I know you prefer it," he said.

"I thought it would be better for me to stay out of the way," she admitted. "I couldn't bear the idea of seeing all those children and their parents. And the three villages coming together like this... It's not really my idea of a good time."

She twirled the end of one of her braids between her fingers. Tuomas glanced at her, trying to choose his words carefully.

"Have you ever thought that maybe it wouldn't be so awkward if you did join in?"

Lilja snorted. "Easier said than done. I'm sure you're beginning to understand why."

"But people have been asking for you," Tuomas insisted. "Sigurd and Alda were wondering how you were."

"You can tell them I'm fine," replied Lilja.

"Sigurd was saying he wanted to apologise for turning you away. When I was sick. Do you remember?"

"Like yesterday. It's fine. Let's not talk about it. That whole ordeal isn't my fondest memory."

Lilja let her braid fall and turned back to him. "Anyway, didn't you say you were going to the Northern Edge?"

Tuomas threw up his arms in defeat. "I can't. Sigurd told me the way is blocked. Too much snow."

Lilja rolled her eyes. "Of course it is."

"What am I going to do?" asked Tuomas.

"The only thing you can," she answered. "Come to Anaar. Help your fellow mages and keep an eye on your friends. Once everyone's there and settled, hopefully the thaw will have spread a little and cleared the route. Unless you blasted through the snowbanks with your *taika*."

"You think I could do that?"

"You're asking *me* what *you're* capable of? I'm not the one who split an avalanche."

"I don't know what I'm capable of," Tuomas said in a tiny voice.

Lilja gave him a sympathetic look. "Well, when things feel out of control, the best thing to do is control whatever you can. So… about being your mentor. I told you I couldn't teach you anything. I can't hold a torch to your power."

"Then why not teach me how to do smaller things?" asked Tuomas. Even if it was something as miniscule as mixing a new tea, he would have been grateful for the distraction.

"Like what?"

"Like…" He thought quickly. "Like walking through fire. Can you do that?"

Lilja raised an eyebrow. "Yes, I can."

She laced her fingers together and cracked her knuckles. "Alright, I suppose there's no point in sitting here and moping all night. Get some wood. I'll show you how to do it."

Tuomas jumped into action. He headed to the sleighs and peeled back a tarp until he found a supply of logs. He loaded them into his arms, careful to take thin ones with the papery bark still clinging to the edge. When he couldn't carry any more, he and Lilja walked further from the camp so they wouldn't disturb anyone.

He kicked away the snow to expose bare rock and arranged the wood in a criss-cross pattern so the air could get in. Then he struck a flint over the bark and it caught at once, spreading first to the smaller twigs before reaching the logs. While he nursed it into life, Lilja took the remaining wood and built another fire several metres away. Before long, both were burning strongly.

"Get your drum," Lilja said, "and go stand over there."

Tuomas obeyed. He untied his drum from his belt, held it close to the fire to prepare it, and spun a circle around himself.

"Nice to see you remembered to do that this time," Lilja noted. "There's no good way to explain this. You just need to drum, and chant, and picture the place you want to go. Then when you feel ready, step into the fire."

Tuomas hesitated, nervously eyeing the flames. He could feel their heat reaching him already, and he wasn't even close.

"Won't I get burned?" he asked.

"Only if you believe you will," said Lilja. "Watch. I'll show you first."

She laid down her own circle, warmed her drum, then steadily struck it with the hammer. A chant poured out of her mouth: jumping and ululating in a staccato rhythm. Tuomas heard the flickering of the flame within it, captured perfectly in song. He felt Lilja's *taika* growing, like a mounting pressure in the air; her voice became deeper until she sounded nothing like herself.

Once again, he was awed by her power. It spoke of the empty tundra and open sky, the first flowers in spring, crisp lake waters and the milky scent of new-born calves…

Then, with a confidence which made his hair stand on end, she walked into the fire. It flew up around her, licking hungrily at the fur on her coat.

Tuomas cried out in fright. He started running towards her, hands outstretched to push her to safety. But then he realised the flames were snapping at nothing but thin air. She was gone.

Mere seconds later, she appeared behind him, in the fire he had built. She stepped into the snow, red ashes dripping off her like water. She quickly brushed them away so they wouldn't singe her clothes, then opened her eyes and looked at him with a smirk.

"See? Easy."

Tuomas gaped at her. "How long have you been able to do that?"

"A few years. Long enough." She nudged him with her drum. "Your turn."

Fear bit at his insides as he looked at the fire. Every part of him screamed to keep away from it. And, suddenly at the forefront of his mind, he saw Kari appearing just as she had then, murder in his eyes, reaching towards him…

His breath became shallow with panic. Lilja noticed and put her hands on his face, forcing him to look at her.

"He isn't here," she said softly.

There was such assurance in her eyes, it chased the worry back down to where he could control it. She wouldn't let anything happen to him. And he had faced worse things than a tiny fire. Even if he did get burned a little, it would probably hurt less than enduring the frostbite which almost cost him two fingers.

He nodded to let her know he was ready. She stepped away to give him room, then he gritted his teeth and began drumming.

He listened to the beat, letting his arm do what it wanted, striking out a tune which would capture the fire. When he felt it in his bones, he started chanting. First, he released a stream of simple sound and allowed it to move and change as needed, echoing the drum, leaping and diving like a living thing. With every breath, he felt warmth growing within him; summer light on water, ripe lingonberry and the subtle fragrance of heather.

The *taika* swelled and his souls began to loosen inside him. He didn't fight it, just carried on chanting and beating, rising higher…

He moved towards the fire. The heat instantly shot through his leg and he recoiled with a yelp.

"Don't stop," Lilja said, somewhere close yet far away. "Keep going. You're the Son of the Sun, remember… harness that!"

Her words struck him deep and cut through the spinning sounds. Of course he was the Son of the Sun. He bore the Golden One's power, entwined with his own *taika*, lending him a strength unheard of among mages. No temperature was too hot. No flames could harm him.

He suddenly remembered hanging before his celestial mother, cocooned in her warmth, and it hadn't hurt. At first, he was blinded, but then he had been able to look at her, as none other could.

He held onto that feeling and wove it into his chant like the strands of a braid. He spun it around himself, lifting it, letting it flow and pulse and breathe. The drum vibrated in his hands, the symbols leapt from its skin and danced with him as he pictured that other fire; as he strode forward, first one foot, then the other.

He opened his eyes. The last note cut off abruptly as he looked around, stunned. Lilja was standing almost thirty feet away, highlighted only by the flickering flames beside her.

He stared at his drum, then at the fire.

"I did it," he said in amazement. "I did it!"

Lilja walked over to him. Her eyes shone with pride.

"Well done," she said. "It took me a lot longer than that to get the hang of it."

Tuomas beamed at her. "Thank you so much for teaching me that!"

"Well, it seems to have put a smile back on your face, at least," she said, and elbowed him fondly. "There isn't really anything else I can say to instruct you in this. Keep practising if you want, but I'm going to get some sleep. We've got a long day tomorrow. And I really do need some time to myself now. No offence."

"None taken," Tuomas said.

Lilja headed back towards the tents, tying her drum onto her belt in mid-stride.

Overhead, the Moon Spirit stared at him, her pale light growing as she turned her face towards the Northlands. Beside her, in the distance, a faint green glow appeared. As Tuomas watched, it grew brighter and spread through the night. He imagined movement within its depths: a dancing white fox, sweeping the sky with her tail.

He knelt beside the fire and stared into its flickering depths. There were flames in the sky tonight, as well as down here.

A sudden idea came to him. If he had walked through it unburned, and his *taika* was starting to shield him from the elements…

He pulled back his sleeve so his forearm was exposed, closed his eyes, and moved his hand towards the smouldering logs. His skin prickled, protesting the heat, but he held his nerve. Then, as quickly as it had come, the pain disappeared and he was left with only a comfortable stroking sensation along his flesh.

He inched his eyes open and gasped with delight.

His entire hand was in the fire. It was waving under his palm and between his fingers like water. His *taika* encased him like a glove, protecting him, creating a barrier between his body and the flame. It was a part of his power over which he had no control; it was deeper than instinct, beyond anything physical, as though his life-soul itself had spread out across his skin.

He pulled his hand free and inspected it. There wasn't a single mark or blister; his skin wasn't even reddened.

An elated laugh burst from his lips. He turned around, hoping Lilja was still there, but she had disappeared inside. He could see her silhouette sitting opposite Enska in his tent.

"Did you see that?" he cried to the aurora.

Lumi didn't reply; there was no sound from her at all. But he could have sworn the Lights danced a little faster.

He ran back to the camp, taking the long way around to avoid going close to the bodies, and went straight to a sleigh which was still heaped with supplies. After a few moments of rummaging, he found what he was looking for: a pouch of peeled alder bark.

He returned to the fire and bent close to it so he could see what he was doing. Then he drew a knife from his belt and chopped the bark as finely as he could upon a stone. Finally, he spat on it and used a finger to mix it all together until it formed a dark red paste.

He dipped the knife's point into it, laid the drum over his lap, and began drawing directly onto the skin. He worked with care, so the tip wouldn't puncture it. Close to the symbol of the Great Bear Spirit in the centre, he sketched a series of spirals and lines. Every now and then, he paused to look up at the Lights and copied their swirling formations. He brought the lines into a point, and from there, dragged out the shape of a running fox with the aurora bursting from its tail.

He glanced towards Enska's tent. Lilja had similar patterns to this on her drum – he remembered seeing them when she took him to the Nordjarvi. Recalling that moment, of how she had entrusted him with her darkest secret, brought a new wave of respect. They had only known each other for this one winter, yet already they had saved each other numerous times.

He dipped the knife into the alder bark juice again and drew in an empty spot of skin close to the edge. After a few calculated strokes, the image of a woman appeared, the Great Bear's head hovering over her.

He grinned at his handiwork. Now he would have his sister and his mentor with him always, here on his drum.

Chapter Twenty-One

The sight was wondrous to behold. There her brother sat, his hand in the flames as she could extend her own into the Lights. The orange tongues surrounded him and yet he was unburned. He cried out in excitement, his eyes turned to the sky, and she spun on the spot so he could see her.

It had barely been two weeks since he had left the World Above, but she already missed him so much. How could it have been that she managed fifteen years like this, watching from afar as his human body grew and matured around his sparkling soul? Even when she had walked beside him in that single form, how had she found the strength to keep the truth secret?

No matter who he was or what form he took, he shone. Finally, he was looking inside himself and seeing what she had known since the beginning of time. It grew like fire, danced within him: her opposite equal.

Her entire aurora blazed with every colour imaginable. She was no longer annoyed at him for pulling away from her, or even for tearing the skin between the Worlds. It was small enough; after his task was repeated, he could repair that with a flick of his wrist. And she would help him.

He finished painting his drum and blew on the skin so the alder mixture would dry quicker. Then he held it close to the fire to tighten it again, took his hammer and started to strike out a rhythm. It started soft, barely audible, then became soft and flowing. It was the sound of the Lights themselves, and he didn't try to make it anything else. She felt the rhythm mixing with his *taika*, forming a link between the two of them which stretched beyond the Worlds. Tuomas let the rhythm do what it wanted, and she watched it ease his souls apart. One of them remained in his body, to keep him breathing and drumming, while the other one soared upwards until he was floating in the blissful dark.

She reached out to him with a touch lighter than snowflakes. He felt her and smiled.

Lumi! he cried. *Did you see! Tell me you saw that! I walked through the fire, then put my hand straight into it, and I wasn't even burned!*

I know, she replied, the Lights brightening with her pride. She moved her tail and swept them into a moving cloak.

He held onto her and spun around so fast, the stars were transformed into a whirlpool of white. Then he paused and looked at her anxiously.

The Moon Spirit isn't here, is she? he asked quietly.

No, she assured him. *And I will not let her come near you.*

Thank you, he said. *Lumi, listen… I wanted to ask you something. When I put my hand in the fire just now, it didn't hurt at all. I've been getting more used to the cold too, but the fire felt different. Why is that? Does it have something to do with my power?*

Something? she repeated. *It has everything to do with it. Have you not realised yet what you are the Spirit of?*

He stared at her, first in confusion, then in alarm.

Fire? he gasped.

She smiled again. *Yes, Red Fox One. You are the Spirit of the Flames. I thought you might have figured that out by now.*

I didn't… Why didn't you tell me?

Because with every day that passes, you come into your power more and more. If you had tried to put your hand in a fire just a few weeks ago, it would have burned you, just as being out in a blizzard would have frozen you. You have already suffered frostbite; you were not always immune to the elements. But now, the Spirit in you is growing.

She held him tightly to her. *Tuomas, if only you could see what I see. The light of your soul, it is so bright. It is like the Sun Spirit upon the earth.*

Tuomas grinned. There was no physical body before her; no face or mouth, but she felt his excitement coursing through the air like electricity.

So, can I control fire? he asked. *Like you can control the aurora?*

In his words, she sensed how much he had been amazed and terrified of her ability to shoot the Lights from her hands.

You must control your taika before you attempt it, she warned. *You are still in a human body. Take it slowly.*

Slowly, he repeated. *But I can do it?*

In time, with practise, I see no reason why not, she said. *But that should not be your first concern now.*

As she spoke, Tuomas glanced back at the World Below. She followed his gaze, past the coast and further into the tundra, where Einfjall sat in the middle of the freezing whiteness. The mountain behind it was banked with snow which had blown in on the blizzards. And to the north, it lay so thick that it looked as though several avalanches had fallen on top of each other. The Northern Edge of the World was hardly visible at all.

She felt Tuomas's heart sink.

How am I supposed to get through that? he asked miserably. *Could I split it, like I did with the avalanche?*

Perhaps, she said. *You need to go there.*

I know. And I will. But... He paused and looked at her. *If I corner the draugars, will that free everyone they've trapped?*

Her Lights pulsed at the thought. To be able to rescue all those poor lost souls, let them come to her at last…

I do not know, she admitted.

She sensed the fear racing through him and pulled him close; colder than ice and softer than a feather.

His thoughts raced. *Well, is there any way I can save them before I do anything? Get them away from the draugars and set them free?*

I wish I could tell you there was, but I do not know.

They spun together through the shifting colours. The World Below tipped underneath them. Gravity had no meaning; only the sky, stretching on forever, surrounded by starlight.

Lumi, Tuomas said, *do you know anything about Aki at all? Why would he ally with the draugars? Lilja said it was to hurt her and make us all useless…*

She looked straight at him. *Do you truly think any mage would voluntarily ally with those creatures? Even the demon-mage would have known better than that.*

The mention of Kari sent a shudder through Tuomas, but he pushed it away and clutched tightly at her.

Are you saying he didn't go willingly?

Of course I am, she replied. *He was all of five years old. Why would you ever assume he would have chosen to leave his mother and uncle?*

Tuomas stiffened in alarm. *Lilja thinks it's to hurt her. To make all the mages feel powerless…*

He is not the one who sends the sickness, she insisted. *The draugars are; they are only using him. How can you not see that? None of the mages they took ever went willingly. They were children. They were all so young.*

He hesitated for a moment, hovering awkwardly in the air as his emotions swam about him in a current.

Lumi, he said, *is Aki's father with you in the Lights?*

She waved around him. *No. He is still alive. And within your midst.*

He's here? Tuomas blurted. *I mean… in one of those tents, down there?*

Yes.

Who is it? he asked. *Please, tell me.*

I do not know who it is, she admitted. *I have watched you, my brother, every night of your life. But only you. And while I know every single soul I care for, I only come to know them after the Spirit of Passage brings them to me. Those who are still living… I do not know. The only one who can tell you is Lilja.*

Tuomas sank despondently. *She won't tell me.*

Does the father truly matter? she asked. *No father will stop the draugars, or bring Aki back, or any of the others.*

I know, but something just doesn't feel right about all this.

Well, you can do nothing about anything at the moment. You should go back, catch your rest while you can.

I don't want to, Tuomas said. His soul sparkled so brightly, it reflected in her Lights like the dawn upon a sheet of ice. *I want to stay here for a while… just a little while. Everything's so different down there now. And I miss you, Lumi. This place is home just as much as Akerfjorden is; you're my sister as much as Paavo is my brother. Let me stay with you again.*

There was such earnest longing in his voice, she might have fallen apart from it were she not already unbound. She twirled around him and sent out a new stream of the aurora. It cascaded through the sky and spread so wide, even the stars were lost among its waving green glow.

I miss you, too, she replied, with the softness that only he could bring to her silent voice. *There are nights when I almost wish I was with you down there again, running through the snow. But for now… one dance.*

Tuomas smiled. *Perfect.*

They spun through the darkness. First, she was an orb, then a white fox, and finally the girl he remembered, but never completely solid. It was as though she were made of light itself, of air given shape, bound together by pure energy. The night sang of power and joy, and she found herself wishing it was somehow still the Long Dark, when one night – one dance – could last for more than an entire month.

Tuomas woke with a jolt, unable to remember when he had even fallen asleep. The last thing he could recall was running through the sky with Lumi. But now he was in a tent, covered with skins and blankets, and through bleary eyes, he saw movement across the fire as people pulled on their clothes.

Someone booted him softly in the ribs.

"Come on, let's get moving."

He recognised the voice immediately. "Sigurd?"

"Yes, it's me. I found you half-asleep all by yourself out there. You ought to be careful; you don't want to get frostbite again."

A tiny smirk formed at the corner of Tuomas's mouth.

"I don't think I need to worry about that anymore."

"Well, you should know better than to tempt fate," Sigurd shot back. "Now, come on. We need to go."

Tuomas sat up. Sigurd and Alda were already tying their sealskin shoes closed and pulling on hats. In a sleeping sack beside them was Elin, still dressed in her warm clothes. The only difference was her hair: Alda must have untied her braid the night before to brush it out.

Tuomas stared. He'd never seen Elin with her hair down before. Even as she lay there, it framed her face, and its black shine made her look whiter than the snow.

He shuffled over and helped Alda lift her while Sigurd pulled the sleeping sack from around her legs. She groaned at the movement and her head fell back onto Tuomas's shoulder. She squinted up at him.

"I'm fine," she said.

Tuomas couldn't help smiling, though it came out as more of a grimace.

"Liar."

"I can walk. Just watch me."

She pushed him off and got to her feet before anyone could stop her. But she had barely taken her own weight before she staggered and snatched hold of one of the tent poles.

Sigurd leapt after her and caught her by the elbows.

"Hey, take it easy," he snapped. "Sit down."

"I'm fine!" she protested.

"Elin," Tuomas said. "You're not fine. Please stop."

With a shuddering sigh, she relented, and allowed herself to be lowered back onto the skins. Alda quickly combed through her hair with her fingers, then wove it into a braid with practised ease. As her mother worked, Elin reached for her bow and cradled it against her chest. Finally, Sigurd carried her outside.

Tuomas helped to pull the tent down, folding the tarp as small as it could go and binding the poles together in bundles. Then everything was packed away, taking up as little space as possible. Most of the sleighs and shelters were being left behind on the shore. There was no way they could be carried across the water, and turfed huts lay in wait on the islands themselves, more than suitable for the summer which lay ahead. The tents were only for travelling – they would keep until the autumn, when the time came to return to the winter camps. The only sleighs coming to the coast were those carrying the children. To try and save as much space as possible, the youngsters were laid in groups of three, tucked close together to keep warm.

When he was done, Tuomas hurried over to Lilja and Enska, who were busy striking their own tent. Lilja looked so harassed; she hadn't even stopped put her hair into its braids.

"I have something to tell you," he said.

"Can it wait?" she asked as she pulled down two poles at once.

He wanted to say, no, it couldn't. He wanted to tell her that he had discovered his Spirit power; that he had put his hand in the fire; marked her on his drum. More than anything, he wanted to tell her about Aki. But the moment he opened his mouth, no sound came out. This wasn't the time. There was too much to do.

"Tell me when we get to the island," Lilja said.

Tuomas nodded in assent and headed towards the Akerfjorden sleighs. Then Henrik approached with a scowl on his face.

"You didn't come back last night," he said.

"I know. I was speaking with Lilja. She's agreed to be my mentor. And then I was drumming. I'm the only one who can still connect, aren't I?"

"Mm," muttered Henrik. "All the same, Paavo was asking after you."

"How is he?" Tuomas asked.

In reply, Henrik tossed his head in the direction of the furthest sleigh. Aslak was hitching a reindeer to the poles at the front, and Paavo was inside, cocooned in layers. Two other young adults were next to him – Tuomas immediately recognised one of them as Hekla: Jaana's mother. She looked a little better than Paavo, but dark circles had still formed under her eyes and there was a line of blood below her lips. Beneath the illness, her face was frozen with grief.

Tuomas gathered a quick breakfast of salmon cakes and stuffed one into his mouth before taking the others to the sleigh. He handed them out, giving the largest to Paavo.

"Running off again last night," his brother wheezed.

"No, just staying outside," Tuomas replied. "Can I get any of you anything?"

The three of them shook their heads. Tuomas quickly checked their temperatures and heartbeats. They were all horribly warm; their clammy skin stuck to his palm when he touched them. Their breaths came short and hurried, chests heaving as they worked to fill their lungs.

At the head of the herd, the village leaders let out a shout. It rang through the crisp air and the reindeer immediately began moving. The herders still on their feet walked beside the sleighs or slid forward on their skis.

Aslak gave the animal at the front of Paavo's sleigh a quick smack on the rump. It jolted forward and Tuomas jumped onto the runners. He fixed his eyes on the sea and watched the fractured light dance across its surface. The shadow of Anaar turned dark blue in the growing dawn, the thin pine trees laced with ice crystals. He had never been so glad to see it.

The miles fell away, and before long, they arrived at the shore. The sea ice had melted with the Sun Spirit's returning heat, and now only a few stubborn chunks still floated here and there. The waves lapped against the shingle, drawing in and out in a ghostly whisper.

Everyone worked together to fetch the boats which had been stored nearby from last autumn. After being checked for any damage, they were pushed into the water.

"Take the sick ones first," Aino called so everyone could hear.

Everyone hurried to lift the youngsters out of the sleighs. They were carried over and laid at the backs of the boats, so the herders could sit in the middle to row. Tuomas helped Aslak move Paavo into one, then joined the crowd of people behind the herd. He watched as Elin and Mihka were brought forward, both coughing so much, Sigurd and Sisu almost dropped them. Once they were settled, the first wave of vessels began rowing away.

When they reached the halfway point of the channel, Maiken clapped her hands.

"Now!" she shouted.

As one, everybody behind the herd spread into a living wall, hands outstretched, and walked forward. The effect was instant: the reindeer, sensing the corral, pressed together and stumbled down towards the shore. The females went first in a surge of white water; only their heads and antlers rose above the surface. After a few had taken the plunge, the others followed until all of them were swimming in a great line that kicked towards Anaar. The island lent them new strength – they were so close now. Just half a mile more, and they would be at their destination, able to give birth in peace.

It was an incredible sight. Tuomas had never known so many reindeer driven into the channel at once. He fancied that if he was quick enough, he could walk from one side to the other just along their backs.

The last boats were readied. Tuomas helped Henrik step over the edge and Stellan fetched some oars. In the vessel beside them, Sisu was already sitting with Mihka splayed across his lap. His breath came in snatched gasps and he clutched at his father in desperation.

Tuomas hurried over to check he was alright.

"Nice to see you, idiot," he said, trying to keep his voice light-hearted.

Mihka looked at him with tired eyes, and despite everything, stuck out his tongue.

"I'll be up and kicking in no time," he rasped, then lurched forward and coughed so hard, blood sprayed over Sisu's coat. Sisu didn't bother wiping it away, just pulled Mihka closer and hushed him like a babe.

Lilja and Enska appeared on the other side of the boat. Their faces were grave.

"Sisu," Enska said carefully, "I hate to tell you this, but the bodies need to come in here with us. There's no more room in the other boats."

Sisu's cheeks paled. "Really?"

"I'm afraid so."

Tuomas glanced back at the boat he was sharing with Henrik and Stellan, but it was already packed to the brim with reindeer skins and sleeping sacks. The other vessels were equally full. There wasn't even enough room for Sisu and Mihka to squeeze in beside the rowers.

Henrik overheard the conversation and waved to get their attention.

"They should travel with the mages," he insisted. "Sisu, listen. Aino and Niina have already gone, and they can't fit in here with Tuomas and me. You'll have to. Ours are the last two boats."

Sisu pressed his lips together sullenly, but shuffled further towards the back of the boat and turned his face away.

Without another word, Enska and Lilja started placing the bodies into the prow. They were still wrapped in the blankets, but there was no mistaking what they were.

Tuomas threw a glance at Lilja. She was deliberately not looking at them, yet behind her stoic mask, he saw guilt eating away at her. In an instant, he understood why she had been so stressed that morning. She must have insisted the children travel with her. Maybe it was her own silent way of punishing herself, or doing some small service to the grieving parents, without having to tell them why.

His heart broke for her. She had done everything she could to save her son, and yet death still came. But not for her. It came for those she should be able to protect, laughing in her face, belittling all her powers of healing and help.

"Tuomas!" Stellan called. "It's time to go!"

Tuomas tried one last time to catch Lilja's eye, but she had drawn deeply into herself. So he turned to his boat and shoved it with his shoulder until he felt the keel leave the ground. Then he jumped in, sat beside Stellan, and the two of them began rowing.

As they approached the swimming reindeer, Henrik watched the animals carefully from the front. All it would take was for one of them to get tired and turn back, and then the others could follow. Every now and then, he would clap his hands loudly and shout to urge them to keep going. The sudden noise worked: the reindeer moved away from it, heading straight for the further shore. The first ones had already reached the island and were staggering onto the shingle.

Tuomas couldn't see it, but he recognised the noise of hooves. He was facing the way they had come, too focused on keeping his rowing at the same pace as Stellan. The Sun Spirit broke the horizon on his left and transformed the mountainsides a stunning pale pink. The summits looked so far away now; he could barely believe he had been up there mere days ago.

There was a sudden clunk on the other side of the boat. Stellan let out an alarmed cry.

"What is it?" Tuomas asked.

"I hit something!" Stellan replied and raised his oar to check it.

"Probably just a fish," Henrik barked from the prow. "Keep going. We're almost there."

Stellan didn't put his oar back though, and glanced nervously at Tuomas.

"It didn't feel like a fish. It was bigger than that."

"A rock, then," said Henrik. "Lucky we didn't go over it. It would have put a hole straight through us. Come on, now! We'll fall behind."

Tuomas shrugged in defeat. Stellan took the hint and the two of them plunged their oars deep into the grey water. They were so close now. The promise of rest at the summer camps was too much to resist.

"Hey!" someone cried from a nearby boat. "Over there! Can you see that?"

"What is that?"

"Henrik?" Tuomas called over his shoulder. "What do you see?"

The old mage didn't reply. Groaning in frustration, Tuomas threw down his oar and stood up. He rocked gently with the swells to keep his balance.

He froze.

There was a boy in the water. An oversized coat fanned around him, hiding the rest of his body, so he just seemed like a floating head.

Tuomas looked straight at Lilja. She had seen it too, and unmistakable recognition was on her face.

"Can I play?" the boy said. His voice bubbled and cracked, as though he hadn't used his lungs in years.

"Aki…" Lilja breathed.

Aki opened his eyes, revealing horrid white globes.

A blanket of mist sprung out from him, twisting and curling over itself. The water churned like a bubbling spring and a mass of dripping bodies leapt from the depths, all slimy skin and mouths of pointed teeth. Tiny red eyes gleamed; webbed hands flailing, stringy green reeds clung to a wiry skeletal frame.

Enska shouted, "Draugars!"

Chapter Twenty-Two

Panic erupted. The reindeer bellowed and desperately tried to escape, but the draugars jumped onto their backs and wrenched at their antlers. The people in the nearest boats swung their oars to smack them away.

Tuomas knelt down so he wouldn't fall. He remembered the way they had appeared in the water by the foothills; heard Lilja's warning in his memory:

"It doesn't matter how far away you go from one lake or river. If they want you, they will follow you to another."

"Things of fireside stories, huh?" he snapped at Henrik. "I told you I saw them!"

Henrik was too stunned to even respond. Tuomas snatched his drum off his belt and went to hit out a shield like he had at the lake, but hesitated. The draugars were among the people and reindeer now; there was no clear line to draw the barrier. Some carried on terrorising the herd, but others made straight for the boats, slithering across the surface like horrid crabs.

Tuomas panicked. He brought the hammer down on his drum and pushed his *taika* out as fast as he could.

A shockwave swept across the channel and sent the draugars flying away from the animals. He struck it again, frantic, hardly lifting before hitting the next beat. There was no time to chant, no time to think. He pressed his *taika* towards the reindeer, encouraging the herd to keep swimming. He imagined two great walls forming on either side of them, like the split avalanche, creating a safe path for them to follow.

"Help me!" he gasped at the other mages.

At once, he heard more drumming, sensed their *taika* entwining with his own. He recognised it by feel, without even having to look. First came Aino; then Enska; then Henrik. And finally, Lilja. His souls swam with it: a pulsating mixture of scents, temperatures, tastes, memories… it was all around him, pressing on his chest, filling his nose until he could barely breathe. His balance spun and he almost tumbled over.

He forced himself to focus on his own magic. First, he caught the sharpness of lingonberry, then the Sun Spirit's warmth on his back, and held onto it like an anchor. He couldn't let himself get swept away in everyone else's power.

Lilja's *taika* was the weakest he had ever known it. He risked a glance at her, but her eyes were fixed on Aki. Her face was wet with tears and she made no move to stop them. Her hands were trembling on her drum, so much, she risked dropping the hammer. Aki himself wasn't moving, but even over the frothing waves, Tuomas could still see the burn scars extending down his cheeks.

"Keep rowing!" he said to Stellan. "Hurry!"

Stellan grabbed both oars and thrust them over the side. Tuomas returned his attention to his drum, his eyes darting in all directions. The draugars were everywhere. The air was filled with the sound of their slimy skin slipping through the water. Tuomas heard them inside his head: hundreds of whispers all building atop others until it formed a mass of white noise. It battered his senses; together with the pulsing *taika*, he was shocked he didn't pass out from it. The other mages were struggling too – Henrik groaned and collapsed against the mound of sleeping sacks.

The reindeer powered forward and, at last, made it to the shore. They immediately bolted onto the island, desperate for shelter.

The draugars hissed, then they all dived under the surface, dragging Aki with them.

Everyone stopped drumming. Tuomas looked around, but there was no sign of them. Beneath the sheet of mist, the water was as still and grey as it had been moments ago. The last two boats floated in complete silence.

The villagers who had reached Anaar huddled together with fright. They muttered apprehensively to each other, but nobody dared raise their voices too loudly. Some made the sign of the hand while others dragged the ill youngsters away from the channel. Aino laid Paavo on a large flat rock, then she and Niina ran to the shore.

"Where did they go?" she called.

"I don't know!" Anssi shouted back. "Do you see them?"

"No!" Enska replied. "Is anybody hurt?"

"No, we're all fine!"

"Lay down a protective circle! We're coming!"

Lilja ignored everyone. She was leaping from one side of the boat to the other, frantically peering into the water. Enska quickly hauled her back.

"What were those things?" Sisu demanded over another attack of coughing from Mihka.

"We ran into them on the way; I'll explain later," Enska said. He set Lilja down and snatched an oar.

Henrik kept tight hold of his drum. Tuomas glanced at him anxiously, to check he was alright, but Henrik waved him off.

"Come on, boy, they're gone," he said. His normally deep voice trembled with shock.

Stellan started rowing again, using both his and Tuomas's oars. But Tuomas's eyes moved back to the water. Something didn't feel right. Why had the draugars only harassed the reindeer and then disappeared?

They must have known that all the youngsters were in one place; sensed it through the spreading sickness. And they would have known the convoy needed to cross the channel to reach the summer islands. All they needed to do was wait, and then, when everyone was contained in the boats, sweep in to claim what they were was after.

What they were after...

Tuomas's eyes widened. When the children on the Nordjarvi had vanished, the draugars hadn't just taken their souls. The bodies had vanished too. And now, four bodies were stranded in the middle of the sea, alone.

Along with him.

His blood ran cold with realisation.

"Sisu, Enska!" he yelled. "It's a trap!"

The entire channel exploded. Water flew skywards and rained down with the force of a storm. It soaked Tuomas, salt stinging his eyes; he could barely see, but he heard the draugars underneath the boats like thunder. Now the reindeer were gone, they had more room to move. The surface heaved with their bodies; the attack renewed with more vigour than ever.

On the beach, the herders drew out their bows. Sigurd and Alda stood as close to the waves as they dared and unleashed a relentless shower of arrows onto the draugars. Every time one hit, the creatures shrieked in pain, but it only seemed to make them angrier.

One flung itself onto Tuomas's chest and knocked him to the bottom of the boat. His drum flew from his hands. He gasped, winded; the draugar was the size of a grown man and it pinned his wrists either side of his head.

Memories flooded him, of Kari holding him down, bringing the knife close, salivating at the thought of cutting out his heart and eating it…

Stellan and Henrik snatched the draugar off him. It kicked and squirmed like a wild animal, trying to take a bite out of Henrik's arm. He narrowly avoided its jaws and tossed it into the water.

Tuomas staggered upright, shaking with fright. Another wave of arrows showered around him and a sudden cry made him freeze. Over in Lilja's boat, several draugars had crawled inside and were slithering over the dead children. She tried to ward them off, but they grabbed a body each and leapt away with a splash.

Aki was back too, spreading the cloak of mist all around them. It writhed like a living thing. And through it, Tuomas watched in horror as he began pulling Mihka into the channel. Mihka shrieked, trying to claw his way free, but he was too weak. Aki wrapped his pale arms around him and held him fast.

Tuomas grabbed his drum, but the hammer was missing – he realised with a stab of horror that it must have fallen overboard.

Another draugar vaulted into the boat and landed on Tuomas's back. It snatched a handful of his hair and wrenched his head up, then ran its slippery fingers over his shoulders and down his chest.

Here you are, Son of the Sun! it rasped. *We have you! Give it to us! Come with us!*

"Help!" Tuomas cried. "Get it off me!"

Stellan swung an oar at it, but the creature leapt aside and over Tuomas, then took his legs and started to drag him towards the water. Tuomas grabbed the side of the boat and held on so tightly, the ends of his fingernails bent back. Stellan quickly seized his wrists, but the draugar was relentless. They both pulled him so strongly, the joints of his spine cracked.

"Will you play with me?" Aki rasped at Mihka in the other boat. Putrid water spilled out of his mouth. "Please? Will you be my friend?"

Sisu let out an incomprehensible shout and leapt straight at Aki. As he lunged, he drew a knife and slashed it across Aki's arm.

Lilja shrieked, but Enska pinned her before she could move. The draugars all squealed in panic, as though they were one enormous creature. Sisu tackled Aki and the two of them crashed under the surface with a splash.

Immediately, the draugars withdrew. The one clinging to Tuomas let go of him and dived. Their dreadful drowning voices vanished, leaving only a cutting silence.

"Father!" Mihka screamed. "Father, come back! *Father!*"

He crawled to the edge of the boat, but Enska snatched him and pulled him to safety. As soon as he let go of her, Lilja dived over the side.

"No!" cried Enska.

"Hold!" Sigurd snapped. Everyone on the beach lowered their bows.

Henrik and Stellan watched in horror as Lilja faded into the gloom. Tuomas trembled, not even daring to blink. A faint trail of bubbles popped where she had disappeared.

He held a hand to his mouth. Had her heavy layers pulled her down? Had the draugars seized her too?

When he could hardly stand it any longer, she burst back to the surface.

"He's gone!" she cried. "They're all gone!"

Mihka screamed: a terrible sound, as though his heart had been torn in two. He beat his fists against Enska's chest, but he had no strength and collapsed, gasping for breath.

Lilja floated still in the water. Ignoring his own concern, Tuomas flung his drum down, stripped out of his coat and jumped in.

He paused as he landed, getting his bearings, listening in case there was still any draugars lurking about. But there was nothing. Lilja was right: they had all vanished.

The mist swarmed around him; when he breathed it in, he tasted it, heavy with decay and *taika*. But it wasn't the *taika* of any mage who had drummed with him just now. It was so simple, like a child's drawing in the snow. He saw bright colours; smelled woodsmoke; heard happy laughter ringing across the tundra. Then a smile as warm adult arms beckoned for an embrace. Lilja's arms.

Aki's *taika*. She had been right; it was strong. Just as strong as her own.

Tuomas swam through the mist until he was treading water in front of her. She didn't react, so he grabbed her shoulders to get her attention.

"They're all gone…" she breathed. "He took them all away…"

"Lilja," Tuomas said. "We need to go."

She looked at him. Her face was vacant with shock and pain. Tuomas didn't wait; he took her hand and started dragging her towards the shore. The two of them crawled wretchedly onto the shingle.

Seeing that it was safe, the villagers ran forward to help. Enska and Stellan rowed closer and everyone dragged the boats free of the waves. As soon as he was within wading distance, Enska leapt out, landing in waist-deep water, and splashed his way to Lilja. He eased her to her feet and she staggered against him, barely able to take her own weight.

"Come on," he whispered. "This isn't where you want to be right now."

"He took them all," Lilja said again, her voice hollow. "Why did he take them? They were innocent…"

"Lilja!" Enska snapped. He shook her firmly. "Stop it! This isn't your fault! Now, come with me."

He wrapped his coat around her and ushered her up the beach.

Now the danger was over, the air filled with horrified cries. First Tuomas recognised Mihka; then Hekla; and finally, the same one he'd heard in the pass: Ritva.

He looked back at the misty water, imagining Eevi and Jaana sinking to the bottom, down to the space between Worlds… Was Sisu still alive, fighting against the monsters, or had he already drowned?

A shiver ran through him and he was tempted to dive after them as Lilja had, but he knew it was too late.

He helped Henrik out of the boat, snatched his drum from where he had thrown it and checked it for damage. It was a little wet and the skin had loosened, but there were no holes and the paintings hadn't bled. He tied it back onto his belt.

"I lost the hammer," he muttered.

"Better you lost that than the drum," Henrik replied.

"Tuomas!" Aino called. "Where are you? Tuomas!"

"Here!" he shouted.

He spotted her at the other end of the beach. She waved him over desperately.

Tuomas's stomach twisted into a knot. She was standing by the flat rock where Paavo had been placed.

Paavo.

Fear lent him new speed. He sprinted over, sending pebbles flying. Paavo was paler than snow, blood smeared around his mouth. Tendons stood out in his neck like ropes. His eyes were roving and unfocused.

"His heartbeat's jumping," Aino whispered, but there was no mistaking the darkness in her voice.

Tuomas stared at her. "No."

She shook her head gently.

"No!" Tuomas snapped. He laced his fingers around his brother's. "Paavo? Squeeze my hand if you can hear me."

Paavo's breath crackled, then mist poured from between his lips and began to wrap around him.

Tuomas shrieked. He tried to claw the tendrils away but they slipped straight through his grasp. Remembering what Enska had done with Eevi, he leant over Paavo, checked to make sure his mouth was clear, then blew hard into his lungs. He tasted blood, but he kept going, pinching Paavo's nose shut so no air could escape.

Paavo stiffened beneath him, and Tuomas hurriedly drew back so he could cough. Blood flew from his lips and splattered down Tuomas's front.

"*Henrik!*" Tuomas shouted. "Henrik, please... Paavo, look at me!"

Paavo spluttered something unintelligible. His eyes rolled back, exposing the whites, bloodshot and sickly.

Aino pressed her fingers to his wrist. Tuomas noticed and slapped her away.

"No, you don't need to do that!" he barked. "He's not dead! Paavo, come on! Say something!"

He swept at the mist so savagely, his nails left marks down Paavo's skin. Then he snatched his arms and shook him as hard as he could. Tears blurred his vision.

"Paavo! Don't you dare leave me! You promised me!"

Paavo coughed one last time. Then he let out a long sigh, and was still. The mist around his throat floated into the empty air.

Chapter Twenty-Three

The next three days passed in a haze. Every dawn brought new pain. The only ones who didn't seem fazed were the reindeer, who had no sooner recovered from their fright when they began helping themselves to the rich lichen underfoot. The giant herd spread out across the island and the villagers left them to do as they wanted. The Spirit of Motherhood flew through on a warming southern wind. A few of the females started to drop their calves and Anaar was filled with the bleating of young deer. Within a few hours of being born, they were on their feet and following their mothers around.

From his seat on a slab of exposed rock, Tuomas watched one of his own suckle her baby. She was used to him, but still kept her distance behind the trees, and Tuomas made no move to approach her.

Even up here, near the cliffs, he heard the sound of weeping. It carried on the wind no matter where he went. Part of him wanted to be with everyone in their shared grief, but he couldn't bear to face them and see his own hurt looking back at him.

Never had he felt so sad, so alone. He'd been very young when Paavo swept in to act as his parent. Paavo had raised him, dressed him, cooked his meals, tucked him into his sleeping sack and told him scary stories. Here and at the Mustafjord, they had lain together in the same shelter, shared their food, learned how to live.

To have all that suddenly ripped away was indescribable. He couldn't help but remember the fear from just a few months ago, when Kari had tricked him with an illusion, pretending his brother had been killed and skinned. When Tuomas had returned to Akerfjorden to find Paavo safe and sound, he felt as though his heart might have exploded. Now, a part of that same heart had died with him.

The Sun Spirit was beginning to appear in the east. As her rays hit the island, the snow sparkled as though the stars had sprinkled the ground with their dust. It was earlier than when she had risen at the start of the migration, but Tuomas hardly noticed. For the first time in his life, the gradual return of the light left no effect upon him at all. A dark cloud had swept in and obscured her from reaching him.

He hadn't even found the strength to speak to Lilja. He had barely seen her since the incident at the beach; she'd kept to herself in the hut she and Enska had claimed. Every time he noticed her, her features were pinched and her eyes held a peculiar fusion of numbness and furious sorrow. She looked how he felt, and that hurt more than he had expected it to.

Behind him, the snow crunched with footsteps. He could tell it wasn't a reindeer, but he still didn't turn around. The smallest movement was an effort.

"Tuomas?" a voice said – a woman. Alda. "You need to come down to the village."

"Why?" he asked. "The funerals aren't until later."

She slid a hand onto his shoulder and gently squeezed.

"The mages want to speak to everyone before that."

"How did you know where I was?"

"I saw you leave this morning. I followed your tracks."

Tuomas didn't look at her. "How's Elin?"

Alda's breath caught and she swallowed hard.

"She's… well, she's Elin. She fighting it. I've told her to rest; Sigurd's looking after her at the moment."

She moved so she was standing in front of him. "Tuomas, I hate to ask you this… I know you'll hate me for asking… but is she going to die?"

Tuomas's throat tightened. He bit his lip and gripped the hem of his tunic with such vigour, it almost tore.

"Are you asking me as a mage," he asked, "or as the Son of the Sun?"

Alda's guilty expression betrayed her. He hauled himself off the rock and stormed back down the route she had taken. Alda raced after him.

"Tuomas!" she cried. "Please, I'm sorry! I didn't mean…"

"I don't know!" he said, wheeling around to let her see his face. His eyes blazed with grief and fear. "That's the answer. I don't know *anything* right now. Alda… if only you knew… you have no idea what I'm having to deal with, and I don't just mean Paavo! This whole thing, Spirit in human form, the Great Mage reborn… I'm still me, and everybody seems to have forgotten that! Don't you see the way people look at me? The way *you're* looking at me?"

The outburst left him breathless. He clutched at a nearby tree to hold himself up, then angrily smacked snow off the low-hanging branches.

"That was why I went to the World Above in the first place: I knew it wouldn't be as it was before. I should have stayed there… things would have been so much better if I'd just stayed –"

Alda sprang forward and pulled him into her arms. The embrace happened so fast, Tuomas couldn't bear to push her away. She rested her chin on the top of his head and rocked him gently back and forth until he relaxed.

"I'm sorry," she said again. "That was unfair of me. I'm just frightened… but I know you are as well."

Tuomas screwed his eyes shut, but tears still escaped.

"I don't know what I can do…"

"Hush. It's alright," she whispered. "It will be fine. We all have to believe that."

Tuomas let out a sob, then drew away from her to collect himself. She stood back until his shoulders had stopped shaking, then took his hand tenderly and eased him down the path of footprints.

They descended through the forest in a gentle slope, placing their shoes carefully to avoid slipping on the snow. It had started to melt in places, only to re-freeze and leave treacherous patches of black ice. They held onto the trees as they passed, and eventually emerged into the village.

It was practically identical to the Akerfjorden camp at the Mustafjord: a collection of turfed huts all arranged around a central large fire pit. The roofs touched the ground in places and insects had eaten through some of the walls, but people had tried to keep themselves busy by patching holes and repairing doors. Practically every shelter rang with coughs.

The sound shook Tuomas to his souls. In every snatched breath, he heard Paavo; saw his face.

How many more dead faces would he have to see before this was over? He imagined an entire generation wiped out, their lungs filled with blood and stinking water, mist choking their lives away…

He bit his lip to stop himself from crying again and walked over to the crag at the edge of the settlement. Henrik, Aino, Niina, Enska and Lilja were already standing atop it, where they could see everybody gathered below. They all looked at Tuomas as he approached, except Lilja. Her eyes were fixed straight ahead, over the heads and roofs; and when he stepped up to her level, he could see why. In the distance was the beach, and the sea, with a faint cloud of mist still lying over the water like a blanket.

Henrik held up one hand for silence.

"We have something to tell you," he said, his deep voice carrying easily through the air. "We've been working very hard – as hard as we can on a migration – to manage the sickness. But now we're all together; the mages have been able to convene. And… the illness is a soul plague. It appears in the mist and spreads to the youngsters, because they have the most life left to live."

The entire crowd muttered. Tuomas noticed many people making the sign of the hand against evil. He was almost tempted to do it himself.

"Did those monsters have anything to do with it?" an Einfjall man asked from the front.

"Yes, Dagen," said Enska. "They are called draugars."

A few of the older people cried out in recognition.

"But those are just stories we were told as children!" one woman insisted. "The young ones probably don't even know a thing about them!"

"Then what about the little boy?" another asked. "What does he have to do with anything?"

As inconspicuously as he could, Tuomas glanced at Lilja. Her face was unreadable, perfectly hiding every emotion, but she put her hands behind her back and dug her fingers together hard.

"A child already taken by them," Enska said simply. "I want you all to know that we're working to find a cure. This will not destroy us. When our ancestors took their first steps into the Northlands, they laid down a legacy of overcoming adversity. We are that legacy. That same power runs in our blood. Since the beginning of time, we have survived the storms. We have survived the Long Dark. We have survived lean hunts and bad calf seasons. We will survive this, too."

Despite the worry permeating everyone's thoughts, Enska's words raised a small cheer. Even Tuomas felt uplifted by them. He knew the mages were doing all they could; every night since the attack in the channel, he had heard them chanting around the fires, trying desperately to connect with the Spirits for help. But each time, they were left disappointed.

Because of him.

As dusk spread a lilac cast over the land, the mages led the way to the Anaar shrine. Enska went first with Lilja; then Aino and Niina. Lastly, Henrik and Tuomas brought up the rear, and everyone else followed.

The three head mages wore their full ceremonial headdresses: Enska's antlers were black against the fading light; Aino's traditional Einfjall fringe was hidden behind a string of reindeer teeth; and Henrik had strapped two sides of a jawbone across his scalp. All six of them had smeared their faces with ash from the central fire pit, drawn as the circular symbols of death and rebirth. With every step, they intoned a long mournful chant, the sounds all blending into each other to signify the never-ending cycle of life. Six flaming torches were carried between them: one for each of the dead.

Tuomas did his best to stay calm. This wasn't the first funeral he had attended, but it was the first at Henrik's side. He had to hold himself together for everyone else's benefit; play the part he had so desperately craved twelve months ago. The ash made his cheeks itch, but he ignored it.

For the most part, the ritual would be a token one. Only Paavo had a body to be buried. The day before, Tuomas and Henrik had sewn him into a shroud made of birch bark. As the Akerfjorden mages, it was their responsibility to tend to him. When his entire figure was covered, they had fetched alder bark, mixed it to paste and painted symbols all over the shroud. They gave Paavo images of reindeer, so he would still have his portion of the herd; a bow and arrow for plentiful hunting; a tent for warm shelter on the cold routes to the other Worlds.

Tuomas wished it was that simple. Had he died any other way; all those promises would be waiting for him, up there among the dances of Lumi's Lights. But in the grasp of Aki's *taika*, he could be anywhere. That was the most harrowing thing of all: the souls may not rest, couldn't come and go to check on their loved ones still living. And nobody would ever know.

The shrine was a large circular pond in the middle of the island, in which sat a beautifully-smoothed boulder. Pink crystals in the stone caught the light and reflected it like a million diamonds. Numerous shed antlers were scattered along its bank, along with strands of hair, strips of clothing, bone needles and beads... too many offerings to count. Some of them were recent, placed there only a few days ago by mages and villagers alike.

Tuomas noticed one which made his heart jolt: an arrow pierced with a length of long black hair. Sigurd and Alda had left it for Elin.

He, Lilja and Niina spun a circle between them, walking around the shrine and beating their drums. Tuomas had substituted his missing hammer with a small antler. He could fashion a proper head for it later, but it meant he had to concentrate on not hitting the skin too hard with the exposed root.

He and the others continued the chant, letting it evolve into a prayer for the Spirits. When the circle was complete, they all laid something of value on the ground: tools, fish hooks, pieces of embroidery, heather gathered from around the island. Lilja deposited one of her intricately decorated cooking utensils. Tuomas could barely imagine how long it must have taken her to carve such detail into the bone, but she gave it over anyway with a bow so deep, her braids touched the earth.

When it came to his turn, Tuomas swept his hand around his belt and fetched the small pouch containing the lock of Mihka's white hair. It didn't matter that his friend was still alive; Sisu had cut it from his head for Tuomas to take with him on his journey. Now he could return it.

He removed the little bone which he had whittled into the shape of Lumi's fox head, slipped it inside his tunic, then placed the pouch at the edge of the pond. The water itself shone with a thin layer of ice, not frozen all the way through. In the low light of the torches, it looked like a hole which could stretch straight into the World Below.

When the offerings were laid, the funerals began. Everyone gathered, heads bowed and eyes red from crying. Ritva and Frode stood wrapped in each other's arms, not even trying to put on a brave face. Mihka watched the proceedings blankly, staring a thousand miles into the distance. Despite his weakness, he had insisted on walking to the shrine himself. Maiken came behind him to put a comforting hand on his shoulder, but he didn't even blink. All he'd ever had was his father, and now that wonderful strong elder was gone.

Tuomas tried to block out the sound of Paavo being lowered into a shallow grave; the piling of stones on top to mark his place. The mages stood in a line, all beating their drums in unison, calling out for the Spirit of Passage, the Spirit of Death, the Spirit of the Lights. They chanted to the Spirits who presided over the rocks and trees, the island they stood on, the air they breathed; asking them to watch over the dead.

Tuomas could feel them all hovering nearby, invisible yet powerful, close enough to touch him if they wanted. He knew the others could feel it too, vibrating against their *taika*, but he didn't open his eyes to check. He carried on drumming until the Sun Spirit's last ray disappeared into the west.

He imagined Lumi standing before him.

I know they'll have been ripped away from you, he said silently to her, *but if you can, please watch over them.*

In his mind, she extended a hand, then vanished into nothingness.

When the first stars began to shine, people retreated into the forests. Those from Akerfjorden led the way, knowing the island's trails better than anyone. Mihka stumbled on the thawing snow, but Anssi caught him at the last second and swept him into his arms. Lilja snatched her drum and went in the opposite direction to everyone else.

Tuomas went to follow her, but thin fingers closed around his wrist and stopped him. He turned around to see Henrik, eyes heavy and face drawn. The grey ash had worked into all the lines in his cheeks and made him look like a gnarled tree. He seemed so much older, as though he had aged ten years overnight.

"Stay here," he said.

"Why?" Tuomas asked stiffly. "I want to go."

"I need to tell you something. For my own piece of mind, if nothing else."

His tone struck Tuomas. He had never heard Henrik sound so fragile, not even when he'd told him about surviving the illness as a young man.

He allowed the old mage to lead him to the edge of the shrine and they sat on a fallen tree. The light of the six torches cast just enough to see by, and Henrik rested his drum in his lap. It was barely two months since it had been made; the symbols on the skin were bold and the lines still crisp, though Tuomas could tell they had been painted by a shaky hand.

"Look here," Henrik said, pointing to one of the pictures near the edge.

Tuomas did. It showed a young girl standing on a frozen lake.

"That's not on your old one," he frowned with a glance at his own drum.

"No, it's not," agreed Henrik. "I only painted it on this one last night. It was something I'd made myself forget, and did not want to remember. Until I saw… the draugars." He took a deep breath. "Again."

Tuomas was so startled, he almost dropped the drum.

"Again?" he repeated. "You knew all along, they were real? Why did you deny it? Why did you try to shoot me down when I told you?"

"That is why I need to tell you now," Henrik said. "I didn't want to acknowledge they existed. It was too painful. And so long ago."

Tuomas went to speak, but then a thought fleeted through his mind and he stared again at the painting on Henrik's drum. His heart flipped inside his chest. Lilja had the same symbol on hers.

"Her name was Runa," Henrk said as he ran a fingertip tenderly across the red lines. "She was my younger cousin: the Akerfjorden apprentice mage before me. She was powerful – she was only fourteen, but even at that age, she showed such promise. But a few years before the last illness came, she was enticed away by the draugars. They beckoned her onto the Mustafjord and took her.

"So, I stepped into her place as the mage in training. I wasn't as strong as her, but it was better than nothing. And when it came time for my mage test, it wasn't too unlike your own, boy. I went into the north. I travelled to the Northern Edge of the World and sought answers from the Earth Spirits. I hoped they might be able to tell me how I could save Runa, but all they told me was that the creatures will only accept an equal sacrifice. I had nothing to give – my own *taika* was hardly like hers, and I was older; almost twenty at that point. Nothing I could offer was enough. And then, when the mist appeared with the illness, the draugars used her power to spread it and sicken the youngsters. Just like how they're using that little boy now."

Tuomas nodded slowly. "The Great Bear Spirit spoke to me in the mountains. It told me there were others before him."

Henrik eyed him. "The Bear spoke to you? Like it spoke to Lilja?"

Tuomas swallowed. "Yes," he said. "That's why you've never trusted her, isn't it? She's powerful, like Runa."

"And look where it got Runa," Henrik finished. "That brings me to something I want to ask *you*. I might be old and stubborn, but I'm not stupid. The Sun Spirit instructed you to seek Lilja out. You told me she spoke to the Earth Spirits, too. She knew about the draugars."

He turned to face Tuomas directly.

"Who is the boy?"

Tuomas's pulse sped up. He gripped his drum hard and gave a tiny shake of his head.

"I can't tell anyone," he said. "I promised."

"You can tell me," Henrik pressed. "He had the patterns of Poro embroidered on his coat. What is he to her?"

"Henrik," Tuomas said firmly, "please, do not try to force this out of me."

Henrik's brows lowered and he went to argue, but Tuomas looked straight at him until he realised it was futile. So he simply nodded and let out a sharp breath.

"Thank you for being honest with me," Tuomas said. "I appreciate it."

"I wish I could say the same to you," Henrik snapped.

"I won't tell you, because it's not my place. It's Lilja's decision to make, not mine."

Henrik huffed disdainfully. Tuomas stood up and extended a hand to help Henrik to his feet. Then the two of them walked back towards the village in silence.

Overhead, hidden by the trees, the stars streamed down.

Chapter Twenty-Four

By the time Tuomas and Henrik reached the huts, a feast in honour of the dead was well underway. Everyone was there except Lilja, who made herself scarce in the forest, but nobody worried about going after her.

They sat on skin-covered logs around the fire pit in the centre of the village, sharing out bowls of stew and fresh flatbreads, roasted ptarmigan and mashed lingonberries. Even the sick youngsters were there, still wrapped in their blankets, chewing softly on some cooked bone marrow. Sigurd balanced Elin on his lap as though she was no more than a toddler, and helped her eat by lifting tiny pieces of salmon cake to her mouth.

It all reminded Tuomas of the meal held on the first night of the migration. That seemed like it had happened in another lifetime. Now the journey was over and six were dead, not including the three Poro children who were taken before. Never mind that the reindeer had all made it with no casualties or lost calves. It hardly seemed like something to celebrate.

He thought back to one night in Akerfjorden when he was younger, and an old woman had died in her sleep. After the mourning and singing at the funeral, he had quizzed Paavo about the whole affair. It was the first time he'd ever seen a body, and a strange morbid fascination filled his five-year-old mind.

"Why do we put them in the ground? And why don't we cover them up again?"

"We do. We use stones."

"But why not the soil?"

"Because if they were covered in soil, the souls couldn't get out. If we leave gaps like this, they can leave, and go on to their next place. And it lets nature in, so all the Spirits can say goodbye too, and take the body back."

Tuomas hadn't really understood at the time, but as he got older, he began to see how the dead lived on, in their own way, as invisible as the Spirits which guarded them. And now he was becoming a mage and had visited the formless World Above, he saw it clear as day. Hadn't he himself been so at home up there, where body and time had no meaning? It was welcoming, wonderful. If that was what it was like to be free, there was nothing to be scared of.

But that still didn't lessen the loss he felt now, as one of those left behind. The dead had it easy. Living on afterwards was much harder.

And these souls would never know that freedom. They were trapped somewhere beyond any reach, even that of Lumi. They were helpless, gone forever, never to be seen again.

Sigurd stood up, cradling Elin in his arms, and carried her away from the fire. Tuomas watched as they passed. She was still awake, but her face was drawn. She would be asleep within moments.

Unable to eat any more, he shuffled over to the corner where Mihka was sitting. He had chosen a spot slightly back from the others and was resting his shoulders against a tree, the firelight only just reaching him.

Tuomas perched on the log beside him.

"Are you alright?" he asked.

"No," Mihka said.

Tuomas cast his eyes down. "I'm so sorry."

Mihka coughed into his elbow, then turned his face away to wipe at his tears. Tuomas went to touch his arm in comfort, but he shuffled back as though burned.

"I know how you feel," Tuomas said gently. "We can get through this together."

Mihka snorted. "Liar. You don't know how this feels."

"Yes, I do," he insisted. "Paavo's gone, too. And my parents."

"That doesn't count," said Mihka coldly. "You could bury him. And you never even knew your parents before they died."

Tuomas stared at him, stung.

"How can you say that? I only came over here to try and help."

"Well, I don't need that kind of help," Mihka replied, still not looking at him. "Anyway, what do you care? You've hardly spoken to me since you got back from your little adventure. I see how it is."

People were starting to stare at them, but Tuomas didn't pay any attention. He was too busy struggling to keep his composure.

"How *what* is?" he snapped. "I came to see you! I looked out for you!"

"After I told you so. I had to point it out to you, how you weren't there, how you were acting so differently!"

"I had a lot on my mind, Mihka! Alright? If *you'd* bothered to speak to *me*, rather than listen to all the Son of the Sun stuff, you'd have noticed that!"

"Oh, I noticed it," growled Mihka. "I also noticed how you rushed over to pull Lilja to safety, but not me. Not my father."

277

Tuomas flung his hands up in exasperation. "You were still in the other boat! And why do you think Lilja jumped in the water in the first place, if not to go after Sisu? You're being stupid."

"Yes, that's me, isn't it?" Mihka said. "Stupid. Idiot. The one who can't do anything right. The one who gets his own soul ripped away by... who is she again? Your *sister?* You're not even human."

Tuomas's knuckles went white on the log.

"Yes, I am!"

"Then why aren't you sick, huh?"

Mihka whipped his head around. Tuomas was stunned at the hatred on his face. He had never seen his friend look at anyone like that.

"Go away. Leave me alone," he snarled.

Tuomas narrowed his eyes. "Gladly."

He got to his feet and strode away into the forest. He walked at first, and then he ran, as though by gathering speed, he could escape the darkness in his mind. But it caught up with him soon enough and brought him to his knees, alone on the beach.

He stayed there, bent double on the shingle, and wept. He hadn't cried so hard in his entire life. The sobs wracked his whole body and tore at him from the inside out. He wrapped his arms around himself and rocked back and forth, listening to the waves as they sucked at the pebbles.

When he had eventually exhausted himself, he sat down and let himself be still, relieved that nobody had followed him. He stared out to sea, at the mist which hung faintly over the shifting waves. The tendrils couldn't reach him, but he scurried away all the same, until he was right at the back of the beach near the boats.

He remembered he still had the ceremonial ash on his face. Not willing to risk going to the water, he gathered a wet handful of snow from nearby and scrubbed at his cheeks until they felt clean. It wasn't much, but it took some of the weight away.

Overhead, the Lights were dancing. They were very faint; if he hadn't looked up, he might not have even noticed them. But as he watched, they grew brighter, until great curtains were flowing through the entire sky in a haze of green, blue and purple. They moved as though caught in a silent wind, or flowing through a skyward ocean, ethereal and perfect.

He spun a quick circle, retrieved his drum and started to hit it gently. He needed to hear Lumi's voice, to take some comfort from her. Perhaps even pretend that down here was simply a bad dream, and the real lucidity lay up there, miles away from anything solid or painful.

It took him longer to enter the trance than usual; his body felt heavy, pulling him to the earth as though it were made of stone rather than flesh. But he fought against it until he was free, and called out for her.

But before she could answer, another light swam into his vision. It was cold and piercing: liquid silver in the sky.

I sense your sorrow, my dear, said the Moon Spirit in a voice like chilled honey.

I did not ask for you, Silver One, he said bitterly.

And yet here I am, she replied. *Never mind the White Fox One. Did you not spend enough time with her that night to know how much you miss the World Above? Do you not long terribly for it, to come home?*

He tried to twist away from her, but she drew close and caressed him.

I have come to help you, she whispered in his head. *Look at those around you. Your neighbours fear you. Your friend hates you. Your brother is dead...*

Stop it, will you? Tuomas snapped.

Life has no meaning anymore, does it? the Moon Spirit continued. *This silly, short, human life... it was never meant for one such as you. What should you care for those left, all wallowing in their own shortcomings? They have no choice, but you do. You need not live it a moment longer. Would you not want that? To be free, forever?*

With you? he finished.

She swirled around him, never letting go for a second. It felt like wet grass stroking against him; icicles working down to his bones. She had him like a fish on a line, drawing closer, and the more he twitched, the harder she pulled.

Come home, my sweet thing, she insisted. *Do not let the voices of others poison your own opinion of me. I may be a winter Spirit, but so is your sister, and I see how much you care for her. Extend that to me, my son. Come, be mine again.*

Her voice wormed towards his souls. It would be so much easier to take her up on the offer. To leave it all behind for what he had always meant to be...

But then he thought of Henrik's revelation at the shrine, and his conversation with Lumi, and the expression on Lilja's face when she saw her little boy floating in the water. He remembered how desperately she had dived after him and surfaced with nothing but her own guilt...

The Sun Spirit's warning rang in his memory:

Beware her. No matter what she says to you, do not allow her to ensnare you again.

No, he said.

The Moon Spirit bristled. *You do not mean that, my son…*

I am not your son, he said, so powerfully, his soul trembled with it. *I told you last time, and I mean it this time. Now, leave me alone, Silver One. I do not want your offer.*

She faced him directly.

If I cannot have you, Red Fox One, she said chillingly, *then no Spirit will.*

He looked straight back, then drew himself towards his body. He was falling backwards, spiralling through stars and cloud. He became aware of his muscles and lungs and heart, and opened his eyes.

The cold pebbles were under his cheek; he must have fallen over when he ascended into the trance. He looked at the sky, at the still-dancing Lights, the half-face of the Moon Spirit glaring at him through the green curtains. The stars had shifted position; he had been up there for longer than he'd realised.

It might not have been the intention he had set, but he knew what he needed to do.

He leapt to his feet and ran towards the camp. A few people were still at the fire pit; he noticed Sigurd and Alda nestled in each other's arms whilst Enska told a story. There was no sign of Lilja.

He bypassed them, sneaking through the shadows so nobody would see him. The huts were arranged close together here, in a glade formed by the trees, and only a little of the Moon Spirit's silvery light managed to filter through the evergreen branches.

A door suddenly creaked open and he winced.

"What are you doing?"

He looked over his shoulder. Elin was holding onto the low-hanging roof, her knees bent under the strain of carrying her own weight. The pale light fell on her face in all the wrong places and showed how thin she had become. She clutched her bow in one hand like a lifeline.

Tuomas hurried to her.

"I thought you would have been asleep by now."

"I'm not tired," she said, even as her eyes drooped.

"Liar."

"You're calling me that a lot. Please stop it."

"Elin, you're not well," Tuomas said. He grasped the tops of her arms, worried that she would plummet to the ground in front of him if he let go. "Stop pretending you're fine. I know you're not. You need to rest."

"All I've done on this migration is *rest*," she snarled. "Why do you look so shaken up? What's happened?"

"I just don't like seeing you like this," he replied quickly.

She didn't move. "Now who's the liar?"

Tuomas faltered. He hadn't expected her to see though him that easily.

"What's happened?" Elin asked again. "You can tell me. You know you can trust me."

He shook his head. "I need to speak to Lilja first. It's important. I'll talk to you about it tomorrow, alright?"

Elin held a hand to her mouth to stifle a cough, then wiped it on her tunic in an effort to hide the blood. The sight sent a shiver through him. He couldn't help but wonder how much longer she would be able to hang on.

"Is it to do with the soul plague?" she asked.

Tuomas nodded. "In a manner of speaking."

"Please stop keeping secrets from me…"

She let out a shuddering breath and Tuomas felt her wobble in his arms. Before she could protest, he turned her around and guided her back inside the hut. She didn't resist as he helped her sit down on the nearest reindeer skin. Then he helped her wriggle into her sleeping sack and tucked a blanket around her shoulders.

"Just try to get some rest," he said. "I'll speak to you about everything in the morning."

She coughed again. No blood came this time, but when she breathed in, her lungs crackled horribly.

A thought passed through his mind. He slipped a hand inside his tunic and drew out the little bone carving of the fox. He pressed it into her palm.

"Keep hold of that," he said. "I made it when I was going into the tundra with Lilja."

"Why are you giving it to me?"

"Maybe it will help, somehow. It helped me, in its way."

Elin nodded and held the carving against her chest. Tuomas offered her the best smile he could muster, then slipped out into the night. She took the hint and didn't follow him.

He crept through the forest until he reached the hut Enska and Lilja were staying in. It was one of the furthest from the fire pit, nestled against the base of a hillock, the turf roof blending seamlessly with the sloping earth. He crouched by the wall to listen, and sure enough, heard the soft tapping of a knife. Lilja was back.

Without even bothering to knock, he burst through the door. Lilja looked up in alarm, almost dropping the bone ladle she was carving. Like him, she'd wasted no time in washing the ashes off her face, but despite how hard she had scrubbed, he could still tell she had been crying.

"What's wrong?" she asked.

"I need you to come to the beach with me," Tuomas replied.

She eyed him suspiciously. "Why?"

"Just come with me."

Lilja didn't budge. "Why?"

He relented. "I want to see if there's a way to free Aki, and he's the only one who's close enough to the draugars to know. I have to try and reach him, and I need your help to do it."

Lilja pressed her lips together and slammed her knife down angrily. The force of it made Tuomas jump.

"I told you not to get involved," she snapped. "You promised me you wouldn't. Twice."

"I know, but things are different now. People are dead."

"I'm well aware of that, Tuomas. He couldn't just make me suffer – he had to let the draugars take the children. All those innocent children… *I* killed them."

"You didn't."

"I might as well have."

"No, you didn't," Tuomas said again, more firmly. "Listen to me. You did your best. That's all anyone could have asked for. Now, would you rather I help you with Aki or have the others pounding on that door? Henrik knows you have some kind of connection to him."

Lilja's face paled, then her brows shot down with fury. "How? Did you tell him?"

"He tried to make me, but I didn't breathe a word," Tuomas snapped back. "You know this isn't the first soul plague. Well, Aki isn't the first mage taken by them, either. They need a new mage for each time the mist comes back, and those they take don't age and don't die. Henrik lost his cousin the same way. He's in exactly the same boat as you. And you might think you hide it well, but not from someone who knows what to look for."

Lilja stared at him. She took hold of the knife handle and clutched it so hard, her knuckles cracked. Tuomas approached slowly, holding his hands out in an attempt to placate her.

"I'm only trying to help," he insisted. "And the migration's over now. We can't delay any longer. The draugars went after Sisu even though he's older; he didn't even have the sickness. The other kids are going to die too, and you know it. Elin is going to die."

Speaking those four words tore something inside him. He could barely fathom their meaning; the consequence they could bring. He knelt before Lilja and fixed her with a soft yet steady gaze.

"We have to do something before anyone else dies or the draugars come back. We can work together. I'm the only one who can connect, but maybe Aki will listen to you."

"Are you mad?" she snarled. "I was there when we were crossing the water. The drumming didn't work then. Every time I've drummed for him, it didn't work. Why should it work now? What makes you think he'll pay the slightest bit of attention to me?"

Tuomas held her eyes. "You're his mother. He came back to you at the Nordjarvi even after the draugars took him."

"Do I have to remind you again, what I did to him? You saw the state of his cheeks."

"Alright, do you remember the other day, when I said I had something to tell you? Well, I spoke to Lumi after you went to bed. She said that Aki would never have chosen to leave you. He's not allied with the draugars, he's their prisoner. They're just using him as a puppet, you see? That's why they retreated when Sisu cut him: his *taika* is their only link to keep the sickness going. He isn't doing this to hurt you. Lilja, please. We *must* try."

285

She looked at him and didn't move a muscle. Her face was unreadable; Tuomas couldn't tell if she was going to cry or slap him. Her free hand curled into a fist, and for the briefest moment, he thought he might have pushed her too far.

Eventually, she let out an explosive sigh and snatched her drum.

"Fine."

Chapter Twenty-Five

Tuomas led the way back to the spot he had fled to, snatching twigs and peeling birch off trees as he passed them. When they arrived on the beach, he arranged the kindling, quickly struck a flint and let a small fire spread across the wood. It was far enough away from the main gathering; nobody else would see. The only ones who might be watching were some curious reindeer.

Lilja's eyes moved nervously towards the sea. The mist was still floating there, thinner than before, but its presence was unmistakable. It drained the energy out of the air; tasted foul and felt cold against the skin even from a distance.

Tuomas stared at the fire. He rolled back his sleeve and held his hand as close to the logs as he dared.

"Lilja," he called. "Watch this."

She glanced over her shoulder. When he was sure she was looking, he moved his hand into the flames. Just like the last time, it didn't hurt at all.

Lilja rushed over and stared as the fire twisted around Tuomas's fingers. He spread them wide and then wiggled them, leaving them there for even longer. There was no danger and no pain. This was as much a part of him as his own soul.

He looked at her with a half-smile on his lips.

"I found out what Red Fox One means," he said.

Lilja nodded, not moving her eyes from his hand. When he removed it, she inspected the flesh, but there wasn't a burn in sight.

"Spirit of the Flames," she breathed. "Of course."

The two of them shared a grin, but then a shadow returned to Lilja's face as she recalled the reason the fire had been built in the first place. As soon as her own smile dropped, so did Tuomas's. The brief moment of not thinking was gone, and suddenly he was surrounded once again by poisonous mist, crackling coughs, the memory of Paavo's lifeless eyes and the Moon Spirit's cold beckoning...

He shivered and rolled his sleeve down. He felt a hundred times heavier, as though the beach had filled his every organ with its stones.

"I want you to know I'm not happy about this," Lilja said. She sounded how he felt.

"I'm sorry," said Tuomas. "I mean that."

"I can't believe I let you talk me into it."

"You can go back if you want. I can do it by myself."

"Not a chance," Lilja snapped. "I'm not letting you get hurt. Now, what did you have in mind? How are we supposed to reach Aki?"

Tuomas faltered. "I... I don't actually know." He thought quickly. "Can we combine our *taika,* like we did when we were crossing the channel? If I do the drumming, and call him out, then you can do the talking."

Lilja shrugged, but a glint of hope flickered in the depths of her icy eyes.

"I guess there's only one way to find out."

She threw herself down beside the fire and dangled her drum over it, balancing it on the end of one finger. Tuomas couldn't help but smirk at the offhand way she did it. It reminded him of the night when he'd met her, and Lumi demanded she put her back into the sky.

As she held it, he looked at the symbols. He had seen them on the way to the Nordjarvi, but once again marvelled at the time and complexity she'd taken to recreate them from memory. The level of detail didn't surprise him – he had realised during their travels together that everything Lilja touched was beautifully decorated. In places, the alder paint was so thin, he supposed she must have applied it with the tip of a needle.

His attention lingered on the image of the little boy in the middle of a frozen lake. It was practically identical to Henrik's.

She laid the drum over her legs and ran her palm across the surface, as though caressing a child. Then she glanced at the Lights, nervousness tangling into a knot behind her eyes. Tuomas didn't have to look twice at her to sense the whirlpool of emotions raging inside her. Fear, sorrow, guilt… and yet also strange excitement.

"You're looking forward to seeing him again, aren't you?" he asked.

Blood rose to Lilja's cheeks. "Uh… well…"

"It's alright," said Tuomas. "I understand. He's your son."

She looked straight at him, not blinking, and two tears dripped down her cheeks. Tuomas offered her the sincerest smile he could manage, then held his own drum to the fire to warm it. After a few seconds, he pulled it out, but jumped when Lilja suddenly reached over and took hold of his hand.

"Sigurd," she said.

Tuomas frowned. "What?"

"Sigurd," she said again. "He's Aki's father."

Tuomas almost dropped his drum in shock.

Elin's father? The kindly man who had taken both of them in, travelled with them to the Northern Edge of the World, helped rescued him from Kari's clutches?

Lilja watched him carefully, gauging his reaction. She wasn't joking.

"But…" Tuomas stammered, "but… that means Elin and Aki… they're half-siblings?"

"That's correct," said Lilja.

"Does Sigurd know?"

"No. I told you, the only ones who know are me, you and Enska."

"So, he never met Aki? Not even once?"

"Never." Lilja poked at the fire with a nearby piece of driftwood. "I wasn't proud of the fact that he was already a married man. So I kept it quiet. Like I said, Kari and I were enough to Aki. We were the ones who raised him."

With a jolt, Tuomas remembered the evening she had taken him to the Nordjarvi. She had forbidden him from telling anyone, even Elin, who she knew they could trust. It all made sense. Why would she have excluded Elin so blatantly if there was a risk of word getting back to Sigurd?

His heart raced.

"The Great Bear Spirit coming to you wasn't the only reason you stayed wandering for all those years, was it?" he asked. "It was so nobody would find out about this."

Lilja nodded sadly.

"So why did you tell *me?*"

She gave a gentle shrug. "I don't know. Maybe because I don't know what's going to happen now. Calling Aki, trying to connect with him, this whole business with the rip in the Worlds… Someone ought to know the truth. I'd rather it be you."

Tuomas swallowed anxiously. "But what about Sigurd? Aren't you going to tell him?"

"It's better this way," said Lilja. "Think about it. He has a wife and daughter. Their family is secure. They love each other. If I told them about this now, it would tear everything apart for the three of them. I won't do that. I'm the one who deserves to feel the shame, so I'll have it myself."

Tuomas's shock melted into an overwhelming sense of pity. He knew better than to pry into how or why the affair had happened, but the way Lilja spoke sent chills down his spine. She had borne her burden, practically alone, for ten years, simply to give one family a chance at happiness. And, most tragic of all, they would never know she'd done so.

He was reminded, in a strange way, of his relationship with Lumi. Son of the Sun and Daughter of the Moon, switched at birth, then separated by two Worlds. When they had been reunited, how long had Lumi held off telling him who they really were to each other?

He could remember her words as though it was yesterday:

"I was not sure it would be best for you. You had a life, a mission you needed to accomplish. I simply became ensnared in it when you summoned me."

He crawled over to Lilja and put his arms around her. She stiffened, not expecting the embrace, but then held him back and pressed her face into his shoulder.

"Thank you for not judging me," she whispered.

"I never will," said Thomas. "I promise."

That earned him a small snigger from Lilja. She pushed him away gently and motioned to the drums in their laps.

"Well, speaking of promises about to be *broken*," she said, "let's do this, and then hopefully we can go home."

Her nonchalance didn't fool Tuomas for a moment, but he didn't say anything. It was just her last line of defence against the torrent of emotion which was about to hit her.

He took his position beside her and they drew a circle around themselves. Already, he could feel their *taika* weaving together like the strands of a braid, to keep out all the evil which might be lurking nearby.

Then they struck up a rhythm. They were different at first, but then settled into one, followed by their chants; voices dipping and rising, using muscles that mere speaking could not find. In Lilja, Tuomas heard a sound he'd never sensed before: all her longing and sadness, as she held the image of her little boy in her mind.

He felt her souls fluttering, like a bird with a broken wing; as hard as she tried, she couldn't rise high enough. Tuomas latched onto her and pulled both of them away from their bodies, up into the beyond, where there were no boundaries. She held him tightly and they broke through.

His summery *taika* twisted with hers: warm light on the tundra; lingonberries and spring flowers. Then a landscape began to fall into view: first banks of powdery snow, followed by a grey sky and a plane of flat frozen water.

He recognised it at once. They were on the Nordjarvi – or a version of it from long ago. And in front of them was a five-year-old boy with hair like his mother's, wide-eyed and smiling, running around with a small antler held to his head. He looked so similar to Lilja, with the same upturned nose and ice-blue eyes. There was hardly anything of Sigurd in him at all – if she hadn't told Tuomas about his parentage, he never would have even guessed.

But more than anything, it struck him how eerily different Aki was. His clothes were dry; his skin was plump and his laughter rang through the air like a bell. It was like watching the complete opposite to what had appeared in the channel. He was so *alive*.

Lilja stifled a sob.

Aki? she said.

He turned to look at her and dropped the antler.

Mama? he asked, taking a tentative step towards them. *What took you so long?*

Lilja choked. *I… I thought… Have you been waiting for me?*

I've been so lonely! Aki cried, stamping his feet. *I miss you! I want to come home!*

For a long moment, Lilja was unable to speak. She clung so strongly to Tuomas, he wasn't sure where her power ended and his own began. In that crushing grip, he felt all her years of darkness; all the lingering uncertainty as she drummed for an answer which never came.

I want nothing more than for you to be home with me, she cried. *I love you so much, baby.*

Where's Uncle Kari? Aki asked. Then he looked straight at Tuomas. *Who's that?*

This is a very good friend of mine, said Lilja. *He's a mage too, just like you. He's the reason why I can talk to you now. His name is Tuomas.*

Aki suddenly smiled. *I'm going to be the best mage ever, aren't I, Mama? Uncle Kari said so! He said I was going to be amazing!*

Yes, that's right, Lilja cried, not bothering to hide her tears. *You would have been wonderful.*

Behind Aki, the ice of the Nordjarvi sparkled in the pale light. He picked up the antler again and swept it around himself, pretending to beat an invisible drum.

Bam, bam, bam! See, Mama? I'm going to hit you with a shockwave – wham! Amazing!

He giggled so hard, he lost his footing and slipped over. As he landed, blood smeared across the ice and Tuomas felt Lilja tense at the sight. It was coming from a large gash down his forearm from when Sisu had attacked him.

Aki stumbled upright and took a step closer. Tuomas instinctively shied away, nervousness getting the better of him, but Lilja held tight and refused to let him back off. This moment was too much for her to give up.

You're already amazing, Tuomas said. *I can sense how much power you have.*

That's because my Mama is touched by the Great Bear Spirit, Aki said proudly. *Did you know that?*

I did, smiled Tuomas.

And then when I was sleeping in her tummy, she gave the power to me as well! Aki clapped his hands gleefully. *Are you going to carry on teaching me, Mama? Is that why you've come? Can we make a shockwave? Or can you tell me a story? Tell me about the mage who skinned people to wear them like a coat! No... no, the one about the Great Mage who came down from the sky!*

A lump rose in Tuomas's throat. Lumi had been right. He was truly just a child.

I need to ask you a question first, baby, Lilja said carefully. *Did you send... something... out to the other children?*

Aki squirmed. *Am I in trouble?*

No, no, she said. *I just need you to tell me, alright?*

Aki clasped his ears, as though trying to tear them from his head. *They don't want me to tell you.*

Who, baby?

Neither of them had to guess what he meant, but Tuomas realised what Lilja was doing. She needed to know about the draugars from his own lips.

They say I'll be in trouble if I tell you, said Aki, still pulling at his ears.

No, you won't, Lilja insisted. *I'm your Mama, I'm the only one who can say you're in trouble, aren't I?*

Yes...

So, tell me. Come on. It will be alright.

Aki sank down onto his knees and crawled towards them. The movement was hampered by his baggy coat, which hid his torso, making him look like the floating head which had appeared in the channel. The sight sent a shiver of alarm through Tuomas before he could stop it.

Aki glanced at him. *Why is he scared of me, Mama?*

Where their bodies sat on the beach, Lilja dug her elbow into Tuomas's side.

I'm not, he said quickly. *I promise, Aki. I'm not scared of you. Are you going to be a good boy and tell us what happened?*

Aki stopped crawling and dropped himself onto his backside. The shimmering Nordjarvi framed him like a halo.

I'm lonely, he said sadly. *I'm so lonely, Mama! They said they were my friends, but they weren't, not really! They said they loved me because I was going to be the best mage ever, and that if I went with them, I'd be even better, but then they pulled me into the hole, and I tried to come back, and...*

He broke off and started to cry. Water spilled out of his mouth.

Tuomas felt Lilja trembling beside him. She had been bracing herself to have to hear that last part, when she'd thrust a burning torch into his face. For her sake, he was relieved it hadn't come.

But what did you want? he asked. *Why did you make the other children sick?*

I was lonely! Aki yelled. *I never had any friends with Mama and Uncle Kari, and it was my birthday! I wanted friends! And they said they could get me some; I just needed to give them my power, and they would bring more friends than I could ever play with!*

He covered his face with his hands and wept so loudly, his voice echoed all around.

They took me, Mama! They wouldn't let me come back to you, and now they're making me do bad things! They just wanted my power, so they could take people away and eat them up! I couldn't stop them! And then, when that man in the boat cut me, they pulled him down too because they can't do it without me!

He snivelled pitifully. *I'm sorry, Mama. I love you. I love Uncle Kari too. I just wanted friends...*

Lilja whimpered. Tuomas moved closer to her and pressed his *taika* against hers in comfort. He could tell she wanted nothing more than to run to Aki and enfold him in her arms, but the trance held her back. There was nothing physical here; nothing to hold.

See? You didn't kill him, he whispered. *They're just using him.*

He's still my little boy, she cried. *Aki? It's alright. I'm not angry with you at all. Thank you for telling me the truth. Now, I need you to tell me one more thing. How do we get you away from them?*

Aki kept his face buried in his sleeve. *I want to come home!*

I know. We'll get you home. You just need to tell us how we can do that.

Aki wiped his tears on his coat and looked up.

Tuomas jumped. His eyes had turned completely white.

Aki? Lilja said carefully. *Baby, it's alright, I'm here. Stay with me.*

But Aki shook his head. The movement was juddering and unnatural, like he was using muscles atrophied from years of lying under the ice. Mist started to creep around his ankles.

I can't, he said, water dribbling down his front.

Aki, Lilja said again, *I know you can hear me. Listen to me. We're going to work this out. We will get you away…*

They say I belong with them, Aki rasped. *They say I'm their best mage, they are my friends, and they have brought me new friends… I belong down there, with them, they say.*

No, you don't! Lilja cried, unable to keep the panic out of her voice. *You belong with me!*

They won't let me come home…

Aki twisted around to peer towards the sky, but his eyes rolled in his head and Tuomas wasn't sure if he could see anymore. The air became thick. It reminded Tuomas of the night he and Lilja had gone to the Nordjarvi, and he'd sensed something terribly wrong.

Aki, what have the draugars done with the souls? he asked, trying a different tack. *There's nine of them. Niko, Inga, Eevi, Paavo…*

They're down here, said Aki. With every word, his voice grew more distorted. *Down here, with me. With us. They will always be with us.*

He shuddered. *They're saying you're trying to take me away. And the souls… you'll take them away, too. But the souls*

297

*belong to them. I belong to them. So do all the other mages…
Elvind, Joni, Annika, Runa… We belong to them.*

Lilja reached towards him. *No, no, baby. Don't listen.
We're going to help you.*

Aki snapped his head back so he was looking straight at
Tuomas.

You will belong to them, he said, *Son of the Sun.*

Behind him, the Nordjarvi exploded. Mist flew into the
sky; Draugars snatched Aki by the legs and dragged him
through the hole in the ice. Lilja screamed and tried to grab him,
but he was gone before she could even touch his fingers.

Tuomas struck his drum as hard as he could. The note
sent out a shockwave, flinging the creatures away, and at the
same time slammed him back down into his body. He felt Lilja
land next to him, breathless, crying in horror.

Then Tuomas opened his eyes, and saw why.

They were on the beach again, side by side as they had
been before, the fire burning at their feet. But the draugars were
still there, leering out of the dark sea, teeth bared, and coming
straight towards them.

Chapter Twenty-Six

Tuomas screamed. The draugars lunged forward from the misty water, webby hands outstretched. He flung his arms up in an attempt to shield his face.

But nothing happened.

He peered over his elbow tentatively, and let out a gasp of relief. The circle he and Lilja had cast was still in place. The draugars had all stopped outside it, snapping angrily at the air, their long nails raking against it. They were only a few feet away, but Tuomas had never been so happy to have laid down a barrier in his life.

"We've got to get out of this," Lilja muttered as the draugars surrounded them. The creatures swept over the top of the dome until the two of them were completely encased by slippery bodies.

Tuomas eyed the tiny area of exposed shingle left between them and the edge of the circle.

"How long will it hold?" he asked.

"Not long enough. Maybe if we make a shockwave…"

The draugar nearest to Tuomas leered at him, pulling its bloated lips right back to expose rows of crooked teeth. He stared through the thin shell of air. It suddenly stopped snapping and looked straight at him. Its red eyes shone, as though hot embers were burning behind them.

Son of the Sun, it snarled inside his head.

Tuomas recoiled in fright. It started clawing again, water dripping from its mouth like a rabid animal. Panic flared through him and he kicked out at it – and broke the circle.

The draugars immediately swarmed both of them. Wet hands seized their limbs and tugged at their hair. Tuomas tried to throw them off but they quickly overpowered him.

"Stupid boy!" Lilja shouted.

"I'm sorry! I didn't think!" he cried.

The mist forced itself down his throat and made him retch. He could taste the undercurrent of Aki's magic, but now it was drowned out by the smell of rotting flesh; the pull of complete nothingness from the void between Worlds.

The breath was forced from his lungs as one of the draugars straddled him. It ripped his drum away and threw it aside.

Taika! it grinned horribly, then tore his tunic down the middle, exposing the pink scar on his breastbone. He threw a punch, but the draugar snatched his wrists and pinned them above his head with one hand.

"No!" he screamed.

Lilja managed to get an arm free and pulled a knife from her belt. She swung at the draugar and managed to gouge its leg, but another pounced on her and she was quickly restrained again. The one on top of Tuomas barely reacted to the wound. It drew itself over him until its hollow nose socket was inches from his face. Its nails appeared on his skin.

Taika, he heard it whispering. *Taika, so much taika! Give it to us! Come with us!*

He screamed again. The creature above him had transformed into Kari, coming in for the kill…

An arrow shot over his head.

The draugar on his chest flew backwards with an awful screech. Before Tuomas could even look to see what had happened, someone leapt onto the shingle beside him, swinging a bow around like a club, and smacked the rest of the creatures away.

Tuomas could hardly believe his eyes.

It was Elin. He would recognise that long black braid anywhere.

She wrenched another arrow from a quiver on her back, nocked it and shot it between the shoulder blades of the draugar atop Lilja. It collapsed, lifeless. Taking advantage of the confusion, Lilja kicked the others off and grabbed her drum. Tuomas did the same and they both slammed the hammers down. A shockwave blew and sent the draugars cartwheeling back towards the water.

Elin bent double as the blast hit her, just managing to stay on her feet. She started staggering towards Tuomas, but the adrenaline flooded out of her and she crashed to her knees. She dropped her bow and coughed, spraying the shingle with blood.

"What are you doing here?" Lilja asked, too stunned to move.

"I'm sorry," Elin spluttered. "I followed you…"

The draugars hesitated at the shore, then suddenly spun around and headed straight for Elin. They snatched handfuls of her clothes, held her arms behind her back, and dragged her into the sea.

Tuomas bolted after her, but the draugars were too quick for him. A wave closed over Elin's head, and in a heartbeat, all of them were gone.

Tuomas flung his drum aside and went to jump into the water, but a single beat rang out and his feet stopped still. His legs snapped together and he toppled onto his front.

"Lilja, let me go!" he roared.

"No, it's a trap! If you go after her, they'll take you, too!"

"*Let go!*"

He thrashed about and tried to crawl forwards with his hands, but Lilja hit her drum again to restrain him even harder. Pressure crashed down on his arms and left him as immobile as a fish caught in a net.

"Elin!" he shouted. No answer came except the crackle of the fire and the rhythmic hiss of waves on stones.

After several dreadful seconds, Lilja lifted her hammer from the drumskin. The pressure around Tuomas's body instantly vanished. He lay there trembling, too shaken to even cry.

"How could you do that?" he breathed. "I could have reached her!"

"And *they* would have reached *you*," she replied carefully as she knelt beside him. "I couldn't let that happen."

"You chose me over her?" Tuomas cried.

Lilja looked straight at him, her eyes rimmed with tears.

"I've already lost someone to those monsters. I will not lose another. And certainly not the Son of the Sun."

Anger rose inside Tuomas like a bubbling spring.

"There it is," he snarled. "Save the *Son of the Sun*. The special one. The Spirit in human form. That's all I am, isn't it? Of course, you could afford to lose Elin, but not me! Nobody else is important or worth saving, are they?"

Lilja gasped as though he had slapped her. Then her brows shot down and she hauled him to his feet. She held him by the front of his tunic and thrust her face forward.

"How dare you," she hissed. "I sacrificed everything for that girl and her family. But yes, Tuomas, this time I chose you!"

She threw him away so hard, he fell over again. Then she stormed to the back of the beach and tried to control her sobs.

Guilt twisted Tuomas's gut. He knew he'd hurt her, but he couldn't bring himself to apologise. His own pain was too overwhelming. It turned his muscles into stone and his bones felt as brittle as twigs. He wanted to crumble under the weight of himself, but his body betrayed him, trapping him in one single form.

He slammed his fist on the shingle. Grit flew in all directions. He kept hitting until his wrist hurt and beads of blood laced his knuckles.

He noticed Elin's bow nearby, the ground red from her own blood. He picked it up and all the fight drained from him, leaving only hollowness. He stared at the curved ash limbs in disbelief.

She had been so worried about him, she had followed, despite how weak she was? Had she been crouching in the bushes behind the beach the whole time? What had she heard?

Time seemed to slow down. He heard the clamour of approaching voices and feet, and when he turned around, he noticed a crowd of people spilling out of the trees. Many were panting; they must have come running when they heard the commotion. Every face was a knot of fright.

Enska quickly took in the scene and ran to Lilja. She fell into her father's arms with a whimper. She pressed her face against his shoulder, tears streaming down her cheeks, then her eyes flickered to Sigurd. He and Alda had seen the bloody shingle.

"Where's Elin?" Alda cried. "She wasn't in the hut… why's her bow here?"

Sigurd stumbled towards Tuomas and snatched the bow out of his hands.

"What were you doing?" he demanded. "You didn't take her with you, did you?"

Tuomas shook his head.

"Did she come after you?" Sigurd pressed. "Where is she? Tuomas, answer me!"

Lilja pulled herself free from Enska's grasp and quickly wiped her tears away so Sigurd wouldn't see them.

"The draugars were here. They took her. Like Sisu."

Sigurd stared at her. The moment hung between them, drawn out into eternity.

Alda let out a terrible cry and her legs crumpled beneath her. Sigurd flew to her side. Lilja watched in silence, her expression completely broken.

In the crowd, those from Einfjall covered their mouths; some began to cry. Their neighbours pulled them close to comfort them, making the sign of the hand, turning away from the evil still hanging in the air. At the front, Aino staggered forward and grabbed hold of Tuomas. Her eyes blazed with tears.

"What happened?" she demanded. "What were they doing here? Did you summon them?"

"No," Tuomas said tersely. "I tried to stop them…"

A log tumbled in the fire and sent sparks shooting into the night.

Enska took off his coat and wrapped it around Lilja's shoulders. The sudden weight made her stumble; she fell forward onto her hands and knees with a cry. She clutched her drum close. Through her trembling fingers, Tuomas saw the painted image of Aki on the lake.

"What can we do?" Sigurd asked frantically. "We have to do something!"

Aino looked over Tuomas's shoulder at the sea.

"Was she still alive? We could go after her, get her back?"

Tuomas suddenly froze. His mind raced; a thousand thoughts tumbled over each other. In an instant, he saw all the wary looks thrown his way; felt Lilja's restraint around his legs; heard Mihka's accusing words mix with Alda's cries. He remembered the avalanche and the night he had held his hand in the flames as easily as if it were water.

His rage returned, stronger than ever, until it felt as though an inferno was roaring throughout his entire body. He glanced at the fire and an idea sparked like a lightning strike.

The Great Bear had said that the Earth Spirits would help him draw the draugars out so they could be trapped. But before that, could he manage to bring back those who had been taken?

He wriggled out of Aino's arms and picked up his antler hammer.

Lilja spun around to look at him.

"What are you doing?"

Before anyone could react, Tuomas grabbed his drum, beat it furiously and ran towards the fire. There was no fear, no trace of it at all. Determination and anger coursed in his blood. His *taika* swelled around him, denser and more powerful than he had felt in weeks.

Lilja leapt to her feet and bolted after him.

"Stop!" she shouted. "Where are you going?"

He ignored her. He couldn't tell her – she would follow him. He filled his head with thoughts of a single huge mountain;

a cluster of turfed huts; Elin's face when he had first met her. Then he screwed his eyes shut and leapt into the flames.

They surrounded him and swept him away. The heat pulled him apart and pushed him back together again. He spun and twisted around himself, hanging in empty air, sparks and ashes flying into his hair and down his neck like snowflakes. Then he took another step forward and his shoes met solid rock.

He swept the embers off his clothes and looked around. It had worked. He was no longer on Anaar. He was standing in the central fire pit at Einfjall.

Chapter Twenty-Seven

There was a surprised gasp as people leapt away from the fire. Bowls of sautéed reindeer flew in all directions. Tuomas jumped out of the smouldering logs and tripped over one of the benches, falling flat into the snow.

A pair of hands closed around the tops of his arms and pulled him upright. He looked into an old face criss-crossed with almost as many lines as Henrik's. Several other people hovered around him in disbelief. They were the caretakers: those who had stayed behind to maintain the winter camp while everyone else took the herd to the coast.

The man holding him didn't let go.

"What is this?" he asked. "Who are you?"

"My name's Tuomas. I was here during the Long Dark. I stayed with Sigurd and Alda."

Recognition flashed across the man's face. He glanced at Tuomas's hands and his eyes immediately latched onto the frostbitten stumps. He stepped away in awe and lowered his head.

"Son of the Sun," he gasped.

Tuomas gritted his teeth. "Please. I don't have time for this. Elin's in danger."

The mention of Elin's name snapped them all to attention.

"Elin? What's happened to her?" asked one of the women.

"No time to explain," said Tuomas as he tied his drum back onto his belt. "I need to borrow some skis from you. It's urgent."

"Where are you going?"

"The Northern Edge."

A nervous mutter flew around the group.

"You can't go that way," a woman protested. "The snow's too thick."

"Which is why I need skis."

"No, you don't understand. You won't be able to reach it even with skis. If you need to speak to the Spirits, you're more than welcome to use our shrine, up on the mountain."

Tuomas swallowed and turned his eyes to the huge peak towering over the village. The mere sight of it brought forth a stab of panic. The last time he had been up there, Kari had almost murdered him.

"No, thank you," he said tightly.

Another woman dashed over. "Wait a moment! Why's your tunic torn? And where's your coat? Aren't you freezing?"

"Not really," said Tuomas. "Please, the longer I stay here, the less chance I have of helping Elin. I'll dig through the snowdrifts if I have to, but I am going. So will you kindly lend me some skis now?"

He tried to keep calm, but the words came out exactly how he felt: impatient and angry. The caretakers immediately sprang into action and fetched a pair of skis and poles from one of the huts. A woman came forward with a leather bag and thrust it into his arms before he could object.

"It's a day's journey," she said. "Please, take some food with you."

Tuomas gave her a grateful smile, then bent to strap the skis onto his shoes.

"I'm sorry for being rude," he said. "And for interrupting your dinner."

"It's fine," said one of the men. "Are you sure you know what you're doing? It's so dark out there... what if you hit a rock and break your ankle?"

In answer, Tuomas picked up one of the flaming torches from beside the fire pit. Seeing that he wasn't going to talk him out of it, the man sighed in defeat.

"Wait," he said, and shrugged out of his coat. He held it out and stood on the end of one ski so Tuomas couldn't move. Tuomas accepted it with a small smile and the man took the torch while he pulled it on and fastened his belt around it.

"Thank you," he said. "Thank you all."

The man lowered his head in respect.

"Go in peace, Son of the Sun."

Tuomas fought off a grimace and returned the gesture.

"Stay in peace," he replied, then he set out of the village, using the skis to glide down the small slope which the huts rested upon.

He set his eyes on the North Star and thrust forward. In places, the land slanted at a gentle angle, allowing him to coast and pick up speed. The torch barely granted enough light to see by, but he let his eyes grow accustomed to the darkness and kept his attention on the horizon.

Soon, Einfjall disappeared behind him and he emerged into the remote tundra. Sigurd hadn't been lying: the entire desolate plain was still buried under thick snow. Hoar frost had spread across the surface and it crunched as his skis slid over it. It was frozen enough to take his weight, but he still moved with care, in case it gave way.

Overhead, the Lights glowed even brighter than before. Lumi was as close to the boundary as she dared get. Tuomas heard her voice in his head as clearly as if she was standing beside him.

What are you doing?

What do you think I'm doing? he snapped.

You cannot bring them back! I beg you, just help the Great Bear to trap the creatures and stop this from ever happening again!

I will! Tuomas replied. *But first, I'm going to save them. All of them. Enough is enough.*

Do you think you are the first to try that? And all of them failed! Henrik, Lilja...

They weren't me.

He pushed forwards stubbornly over the crest of a hillock.

Tuomas, listen to me! Lumi shouted.

I'm bringing them back, he said. *My mind is made up. The Earth Spirits can help me. They're closer to the draugars than you are.*

They cannot help! Why will you not stop and listen to me?

Tuomas glared up at her.

Because I won't leave Elin to those things! Or Paavo or Sisu or any of them! And you've seen how much Lilja has suffered. She needs her son back. I will find a way. You can't stop me.

Suddenly, the Lights raged. The entire sky roared and a green jet shot towards him, knocking him to the ground. The torch flew from his grasp and skittered across the ice. The aurora pressed on his chest, holding him down with unbelievable power. He could barely breathe. Every hair stood on end and his heart raced inside his chest.

The Lights slowly morphed into the form of a girl with white hair and blazing eyes. Her pointed fox ears were flat against her head. She wasn't there, not completely; she was still in the World Above, but her strength reached through the skin like a storm.

I cannot stop you? she snarled, snatching his throat in one hand. *How dare you speak like that to me!*

Tuomas glared at her. *I'm just as strong as you and we both know it. I'm not afraid of you, Lumi.*

Well, maybe you should be afraid, she said. *Maybe I should make you afraid again, so you cower before me like you once did!*

Is that what you want? I thought you said I was your equal!

No equal of mine dares to insult me!

What are you going to do, then? Turn my hair white? Rip my soul away to teach me a lesson?

The words were out before he could stop them.

Lumi's furious expression lapsed, first into shock, then hurt, and then back again to rage. Her hand tightened around his throat, making him gasp for air. Tuomas clutched at her wrist but his fingers passed straight through her, as though she was nothing more than smoke.

What kind of Spirit do you call yourself? Lumi hissed coldly. *I never should have taken you to the World Above!*

She leapt off him and disappeared back into the sky as quickly as she had come. The Lights swept the stars, coating the Northlands in an angry flare of red, before blinking out altogether.

Tuomas lay there for a moment, getting his breath back.

Lumi? he called. *Lumi, please, I'm sorry...*

She didn't respond. There wasn't even the faintest flash to show she had heard him.

He stood up, locking his skis together so he wouldn't slip. Pain and grief dug into him like needles. He had lost Paavo and Elin, fallen out with Mihka, alienated Lilja and now Lumi…

He wiped away his tears. Lumi might have disappeared, but the Moon Spirit was still there, shining her silvery face down onto the tundra. He didn't want to give her the satisfaction of watching him cry.

In sullen silence, he snatched his ski poles and torch from where they had fallen and carried on into the north.

As Tuomas travelled, the snow became deeper. A chill came off the fresh powder and crept up his legs. He was aware of it, but it didn't cause him discomfort, so he carried on. He didn't even stop to eat his flatbread. The miles fell behind him, though he felt as though he was barely moving. Everywhere he looked was the same: flat whiteness and dark sky. No trees grew and the few shrubs which might have taken root were buried.

The sky lightened and the Sun Spirit peered over the horizon to his right. As soon as it was bright enough to see, he discarded the torch. Ahead, the snow built into a massive mound, and although its slope appeared gentle, Tuomas could tell there was no way he would be able to climb it. Thick ice had coated the surface; grip would be non-existent.

He drew to a halt in front of it. It reared fifteen feet high, rendered a faint blue by the low angle of the light. He touched it with his fingertips, then stuck his ski poles into the snow and untied his drum.

He took a deep breath and focused. His *taika* pulsed, not just with power, but with pain and anger. It flickered like a flame and every beat of his heart hurt. The lingonberries tasted sour; the heat of the Sun Spirit further away than normal. It was so dense; he almost lost his balance. But he forced himself to stand his ground, and beat the drum.

A shockwave blasted through the snowbank. Powder flew into the sky and left a thin channel in the centre. It wasn't enough, so Tuomas hit out at it again, pushing further and harder. This time, he broke all the way to the other side and the entire mound parted down the middle.

He struggled to breathe. His muscles screamed from the effort. He was tempted to sit down and recover, but shook his head before he could succumb. The longer he waited, the more time slipped by since Elin had been dragged away. And she had to be still alive. He refused to let himself think she wasn't.

He pushed on and slid between the walls of snow. Eventually, he made it through and the ground gradually dipped towards a giant lake. It was still far in the distance, but he could tell it was larger than the Nordjarvi and almost as wide as the tip of the Mustafjord.

Relief sang in his blood. There was snow on the frozen surface, but nothing too thick, and no mist. The worst was over.

By the time he reached it, the Sun Spirit was at her highest in the sky and turned the landscape into a palette of lilac and gold. He tested the ice, making sure it would take his weight, then slipped out of his skis and left them at the edge. He walked towards the centre, where a perfectly circular hole opened onto a pool of water darker than night. The edges were smooth and shining, made not by any blade, but by *taika*.

His *taika*.

He knelt beside it and ran his hand around the hole. He couldn't believe he had done this: opened the only physical gateway between Worlds. For countless generations, it had lain here unchanging, and all because of him.

He sat down, drew a circle around himself and began to chant. He followed it with a steady beat, letting warmth gather in his belly, spreading out his *taika*, pushing it deep into the ice.

After several long moments, a light appeared in the hole, bringing with it a sound like a waterfall crashing over rocks. It grew and grew, until it hit the edges, and Tuomas leapt back as the herd of spectral reindeer burst onto the surface. They ran straight out from the gateway in all directions, galloping through him as though he wasn't even there.

He hugged his drum to his chest and jumped through.

Like last time, he didn't hit the water; he simply fell. Air tore past his face, whistling in his ears. The surroundings lost their coldness and became damper, milder. He inched his eyes open and found himself plummeting towards an identical lake, the trees around its shores ablaze with leaves of red and gold.

He landed in a boat positioned directly underneath him. He forgot to brace himself and cried out in pain. The entire vessel jolted as he hit it and the front flipped up, but didn't tip over.

Amazed he hadn't broken a bone, he looked around. He was alone; there wasn't a single Spirit in sight, but he could still sense them in the air. And simply being on the lake made him uneasy. It was glassy and perfect now, but he didn't want to risk the draugars sensing him. At least, not yet.

He fetched an oar from the bottom of the boat and hurriedly rowed to the nearest bank. As soon as the keel scraped the ground, he stumbled out. Then he slid his antler hammer into his belt, picked up his drum and walked away with it hanging in his hand. He felt safe, but wanted to be able to hit it if he needed to.

Under his feet, the ground was soft and spongy, softened by several inches of leaf litter and rotting pinecones. Mushrooms sprouted from the carved tree trunks here and there, their pales heads fanned out to expose the filigree underneath. He touched them as he passed and watched them spring back when he let go.

The World Below was the opposite of the World Between. If spring was approaching up there, then autumn would be coming here. And as it had been day when he left, now it was twilight.

As he headed into the forest, the occasional white reindeer raised its head to watch him, black eyes unblinking, antlers more glorious than any borne by their kin in the other World. He paused to look at them. These were the children of the ones he had been gifted a long time ago, with their magical milk and pelts paler than the purest snow. He remembered his vision on the Mustafjord, when he had worn a coat made from their fur.

He carried on and followed a faint path which wound its way through the ancient trees. Eventually, he arrived at the place he had been looking for: a gaping cave mouth. On the stony wall either side of it were two flaming torches. He made his way inside, descending far away from the light, deep into the earth.

It didn't take long for him to start worrying he had taken a wrong turn. The last time he was here, one of the Earth Spirits had met them on the shore of the lake and brought them into the cave, to a giant cavern decorated with paintings and carvings. He'd never been here alone before. What if he got lost and never found his way out?

The tunnel suddenly branched into two before him. A ghostly light was emanating from the nearest one. Tuomas stared at it with interest. It was bright and yet pale, as though it wasn't being cast by anything at all, but was rather its own entity.

Curiosity got the better of him. Maybe the Earth Spirits had sent it to show him which way to go.

He headed towards it. The stone walls grew tight around him, and he worried he might get stuck if he went much further. But then they suddenly opened like a flower and he stepped out into a massive expanse.

His feet sank into a powdery substance. At first, he thought it was snow, but when he bent to touch it, he was alarmed to find it was something else. Not snow, not sand… yet the colour of ash, every ridge and crest bound in shades of grey.

The sky overhead was complete black. In fact, the more he looked at it, the less sure he was that it even was a sky. There were no stars, no clouds… it was darker than anything he had ever seen. His body cast no shadows, as though the flat light was coming from every direction at the same time.

Not a single gust of wind blew; no noise was to be heard. Tuomas felt like the only living thing which had ever stood here, and it chilled him deeper than he ever thought possible.

In the distance, something caught his eye. He squinted at it, trying to make it out.

It was a river. Its waters wound around the desert like a serpent, somehow both black and white; opaque and also transparent, shimmering with light and yet dark with shadows. One moment it raged, and then it was calm, then somewhere in-between; currents lapping against the ashy banks as though alive.

He went to move towards it, but a hand came down on his shoulder and stopped him.

"Not a step further, Tuomas Sun-Soul."

He spun around and found himself face to face with an Earth Spirit. Its entire form was made of overlapping autumnal leaves, from skin and hair to clothes and shoes. Seeds and nuts hung across its front like buttons; a crown of mushrooms grew out of its scalp in a perfect circle.

"What is that?" he asked.

"That is the Night River," said the Spirit. "The border of the Deathlands."

An involuntary shudder passed through Tuomas's body.

"Why did you bring me here?" he asked, scared to even speak loudly.

"You came here yourself," the Spirit replied. "You came looking for death. This is the only place in the World Below where you may find it."

Tuomas fought back a flare of panic.

"Is Elin here? Or Paavo?"

"No," said the Spirit. "None of those taken by the draugars are here. They are outside the grasp of the White Fox One, and also of the Horse-Riding One."

Tuomas frowned. He had heard Lumi speak that title before. Then he remembered Henrik's words when Aslak had told the story around the fire, and realisation settled on his chest like a spreading frost.

"The Spirit of Death," he said.

"There is no need to be afraid," said the Earth Spirit, "if you do not walk any closer. You must be dead to enter that domain, and you are very much alive, Red Fox One."

At that moment, a horrible thought crossed Tuomas's mind.

"Is that where Kari is?" he asked.

His companion nodded. "Yes."

"Then he's trapped there?"

"The Horse-Riding One released his life-soul, to go on and give new life to another. But his body-soul will remain there."

Despite all the evil Kari had spread, Tuomas couldn't hold back a wrench of sympathy. He knew that was the way things were done: the two souls would be separated after death. But in practically all cases he was aware of, the body-soul went to the World Above, to Lumi, to dance in the Lights and be reunited with its ancestors. Kari would not have that. He would be down here forever, alone. When it was time for Enska and Lilja to die, they would never be reunited.

"He made his choice," said the Spirit. "If he had behaved differently, then things would also have been different."

"I know," said Tuomas. "That's where the Great Bear Spirit will trap the draugars too, isn't it?"

"Yes. Is that why you have come? I know it set you a charge."

"That's not the only reason. Lilja said you know the most about draugars. Her and Henrik both came here looking for answers. So have I."

The Spirit regarded him. Then it slid its leafy hand down his arm and pulled him back towards the cave mouth.

"Such topics are best left for more mutual ground," it said.

Tuomas didn't resist as it led him out of the ashen desert. He wanted to get as far away from that terrifying river as he could.

As they left, the light dimmed, until there was nothing but silence and raging water.

Chapter Twenty-Eight

Eventually, they emerged back into the forest. The only light came from the torches scattered about the trees; the grey sky had turned dark and the clouds edged with fading gold. Tuomas could see a veil of rain across the faraway hills, which reminded him eerily of Lumi's aurora. It wouldn't be long before it turned to snow, and as summer descended upon the World Above, this one would be locked in winter.

"I need your help," Tuomas said. "I want to free the souls that have been taken, before I trap the draugars. Can I do that? Aki as well? And Elin and Sisu, they were taken while still alive, just like those three Poro kids on the Nordjarvi –"

"Please stop rambling," the Spirit said.

Tuomas took a deep breath. "Please. I know Henrik and Lilja came and tried to pull back their loved ones –"

"It is not possible. If it were, it would have been done."

"But why? All because the draugars won't take anything unless it's an equal exchange?"

"Precisely," said the Spirit. "For as powerful as her son is, and had the potential to be, Lilja was still stronger than him when she stood where you stand now. Still, they would not have taken her in his place."

"Because she was older," Tuomas finished. "It was the same with Henrik. He was older than Runa. But I'm more powerful than either of them. Everyone's been forcing the Son of the Sun matter down my throat enough; I might as well embrace it completely."

319

"In these circumstances, that is most unwise," the Spirit warned.

"I don't care!" Tuomas snapped impatiently. "I need my brother back! Mihka needs his father; Lilja needs her son! And Elin…"

His voice broke as he spoke her name. He held a hand to his mouth and struggled not to cry. His knees wobbled and he knelt on the ground.

"*Please*. I've never begged for anything. I will give you whatever you demand. All my reindeer, my tools, my blood, *anything*. Just help me bring them back."

A breeze whistled by and rustled the Spirit's leafy body. Some of the edges peeled back to expose the empty air beneath the shape they formed. More leaves fell from the canopy like golden snowflakes.

The Spirit extended a hand to Tuomas and touched his cheek.

"Your power must be used to draw the creatures out so they can be restrained. Nothing more," it said gently. "You cannot save the souls. I am sorry."

Tuomas shook his head. "No, that can't be."

"I am afraid it is," the Spirit said.

"But I need to save Elin… and Paavo…"

"You cannot. They are gone."

The rain reached them and cascaded through the branches. It soaked Tuomas immediately, plastering his hair against his scalp, running down his face and mixing with his tears. He clutched his drum to his chest, sank onto the floor and wept like a child.

"I came here so you could help me!" he cried. "Please! There has to be a way!"

"The Great Bear has already given you your way," the Spirit replied, its voice unchanging. "Now you must follow it. Come with my brethren to the lake, tempt out the draugars, summon the Great Bear and let their reign of terror end."

Tuomas stayed still. He wanted nothing more than for the damp ground to swallow him and let him lie in the dark forever. He didn't want to move or think. Every flash in his mind was as painful as if boulders had been dropped on top of him. It was colder than frostbite; sharper than even Kari's blade. It hurt in a place so deep within him, he could barely comprehend where it was.

Then he froze. His eyes roved over the fallen leaves, slotting the pieces together in his mind.

"Wait…" he whispered. "It's an equal exchange they want, right?"

"That is correct," said the Spirit.

Tuomas nodded to himself, one hand going to his drum.

"Then what about a *greater* exchange?"

The Spirit looked at him suspiciously. "What are you talking about?"

Tuomas sat up.

"They took Elin to try and draw me out," he said. "I know they want me more than anyone else. If I give them what they want, I could bargain for the others. Couldn't I?"

For the first time, a semblance of panic flashed across the Spirit's face.

"You would sacrifice yourself?"

Tuomas shrugged.

"Why not? There's no point in me sticking around now. I might as well do something good, for once."

"Think about what you are proposing!" the Spirit insisted, grasping his hands urgently. "You would give up not just your *taika*, but your soul! You would be trapped with them forever!"

"If my *taika* is that powerful, they can live off it forever. I don't care. It will stop them from having to spread the sickness if they can just rely on me."

"You must not! You are the Son of the Sun!"

Tuomas's frustration suddenly rose to the surface. He leapt to his feet and pushed the Spirit away.

"I don't care about that!" he exploded. "I don't care who I am, or what soul I got stuck with, or why that means I *should* do anything! You know what I should have done? I should have saved Elin! I should have saved all of them! They're all gone because of me!"

He shook his head coldly, then turned on his heel and sprinted back through the woods. He fixed his eyes on the lake. With every step, he hit the drum, letting his *taika* grow and twist as large as he could bear. He imagined it sweeping across the land like a beacon. It would be impossible to miss.

"No! Stop!" the Spirit shouted after him. Then its voice swelled, booming through the trees in a silent scream. *Stop him!*

The rain drove at Tuomas; long grass tangled about his feet as though trying to hold him back. He tore through them. The leaves swirled before him on the path, but he bent his head and ran on, beating them away.

He noticed movement on either side of him. A group of white reindeer were running there, antlers down. Among them were more Earth Spirits, some upon the animals' backs, others in the air or on the ground. They came closer, meaning to cut him off.

Tuomas thought quickly. He didn't break his stride for a moment, stepped up on a fallen log to give him lift, and leapt as high as he could. As his feet left the ground, he spun in the air and hit out a fast beat on his drum. With every strike, a circle formed around him. But this time, it was tainted; it felt heavier and tugged at his souls in a way he'd never experienced before. This wasn't to keep evil out, but to keep *everything* out.

The circle sealed as he landed. The reindeer and Spirits surrounded him in a perfect ring. Tuomas took a step forward, and those in front of him backed off. It had worked. They couldn't step inside his barrier.

But he was still trapped by them. He could see the lake just over the sea of antlers. In the darkness, it didn't even look like water; more like a massive hole cleaved straight through the ground.

More Earth Spirits appeared out of the trees, in the branches, standing among the ghostly herd. They pressed against the boundary and tried to reach him.

"Tuomas Sun-Soul!" one of them cried. "Please, do not do this!"

But Tuomas shook his head.

"Let me pass."

"We cannot!" another of the Spirits replied. "Stop what you are doing! You must not sacrifice yourself!"

Tuomas didn't listen. He brought the hammer onto his drum and sent a line of power straight through to the lake. Then he pushed and the reindeer suddenly parted down the middle, just like the avalanche. Without wasting a moment, he ran between them.

The lake came closer and closer. He closed his eyes, drawing up the memory of those slimy pale limbs, the protruding bones, the snapping teeth.

You want me? he thought. *Come and get me.*

"Tuomas!" the Spirits shouted after him. "Stop!"

He jumped into the boat and pushed off from the bank. As soon as the prow cut through the water, tendrils of mist began to creep across the surface. He let it entwine around him, making sure it had sensed him, then leapt overboard.

Every single muscle in his body contracted; it felt as though he was being stabbed with a thousand knives. Paavo had once warned him that if he was ever to fall into cold water, the temperature would kill him faster than drowning, and he had never believed it more than now. It took all his self-control to not gasp in pain.

He held his drum tightly as he descended. The protective circle stayed all around him like a bubble. He kept it strong, in case the Earth Spirits somehow reached him and tried to pull him out. The light drew further away, until it was so small, it looked like a faraway star, and he hung suspended in an endless dark. But it wasn't like the World Above. The pressure made his throat want to burst. His *taika* screamed in protest, but he pushed it back under control.

He realised he must be at the edge of the void between the Worlds. Ignoring the pain, he flipped onto his front and kicked deeper. He could hold his breath for a little over a minute: more than enough time to act.

He didn't have to wait long before a pair of red eyes appeared out of the gloom. Then more came, surrounding him, white teeth clicking together eerily.

Their voices slithered around his head like a thousand worms.

So much taika…
 All this taika…
All this youth…
And it comes to us willingly…
We knew it would.

Tuomas raised his drum before him.

You know who I am, he said, in the silent, powerful words of a mage.

The draugars hissed excitedly. Stringy green fronds trailed behind them like scraps of clothing.

Son of the Sun! they snarled in unison. *We knew you would come! We saw how you looked at that girl! We knew!*

I've come to bargain with you, Tuomas replied as steadily as he could. *Where's the little boy who you stole away five years ago?*

One of the draugars swept the perimeter of his circle, gnashing its teeth.

We did not steal! it growled at him. *He came to us… just like you…*

You sensed his magic, and lured him away from his mother and uncle, Tuomas snapped back. *You called to him from Lake Nordjarvi and told him a pack of lies, so he wouldn't know any better than to go with you! And you've been taking advantage of his power ever since!*

The creatures sneered horribly. The loose skin around their eyes wrinkled as they moved.

He belongs to us, they said. *All of the little mages belong to us, and so do the souls they have brought to us, down here in the depths!*

They pushed closer, pressing their bodies against the circle. Tuomas quickly sent out another surge of *taika* to keep them at bay. He spun in the water, trying to watch all of them, in case one managed to somehow break through and sneak up behind him.

His lungs were starting to ache. He needed to act fast.

Here is my bargain, he said. *Release Aki and all the people you've taken with him, including the girl you stole last night. Let them be free, and promise to never go after them again. Do this, and you can have me instead. Just like you've always wanted.*

A wave of anticipation swept over the draugars. Tuomas couldn't even see how many there were anymore; they extended too far into the darkness for him to count them. They glided about like a school of disgusting fish, forming clouds of sliver bubbles; some glanced at him hungrily and pointed their webby fingers. The slippery sound of them filled his ears.

At last! they whispered, forming an eerie chorus which cut through the lake like a knife.

So much taika…

The taika from the Son of the Sun…

Tuomas clapped a hand over his mouth to try and keep his breath.

All of them, he insisted. *Release Runa and all the others too.*

The creatures turned their eyes back to him. The movement was perfectly synchronised, as though they were one huge entity. It sent shivers down his spine, but he held his nerve.

All? they sniggered. *Can you bring forth the food you ate as a child, Son of the Sun?*

Tuomas's gorge rose. They had consumed all of them? There wasn't a single soul left from the previous plagues? The idea of it was so unnatural, it almost made him sick.

Then all those you took this time, he countered quickly. *Every single one.*

It is lucky our feasting has not yet begun, the draugars replied cruelly. *But it will soon! Oh, so soon! So much taika…*

Tuomas swallowed hard. Every fibre of his body was urging him to take a breath. The muddy darkness swirled around him; he felt death and decay touching his skin like a physical thing. The moment he let down his barrier, there would be no escape.

A strange calm descended upon him. It didn't matter that he would be stuck down here with them forever. Everyone else would be free, the children cured of the plague.

Once again, it was a small price to pay.

We accept your bargain, Son of the Sun, the nearest draugar hissed. *Your taika… your youth… your souls… for them.*

Tuomas nodded. *Deal.*

The draugars in front of him slowly parted, tendrils of mist slithering around them. In the middle of the cloud, Aki appeared, rubbing his eyes, as though he had just awoken from a long sleep.

They held him before Tuomas, just outside the circle, their long fingers clutched around his arms and legs. Then the others appeared, and Tuomas's heart leapt.

There, floating limp in the water, he could see the ghostly bodies of nine people; among them Paavo, Sisu, Eevi… and Elin. They looked like they were made from the mist itself: their flesh drifted and hair waved like smoke. He wasn't sure what was keeping their souls together, but it just needed to work for just a little longer.

Aki looked at Tuomas with his white corpse eyes.

I saw you yesterday, he said, twisting his coat nervously. *They said you were going to take me away.*

The need to inhale was almost unbearable, but Tuomas forced himself to ignore it. He lowered his hand so Aki could see all of his face.

I've come to take you back to your Mama, he said. *It's alright. They're going to let you go.*

The draugars snarled at his words, but Tuomas ignored them.

All you need to do is swim up there. He raised his arm towards the surface. *It's not far. And then the Earth Spirits will be able to help. Your Mama will be waiting for you.*

Aki hesitated. *You promise?*

Tuomas nodded as best he could. He glanced at Paavo, then Elin, committing their faces to memory.

I promise. But you need to go now, alright? And take your new friends with you.

The ache in his chest swelled. He coughed, unable to hold it in, and a jet of bubbles streamed out of his mouth.

Aki, go now! he cried.

Before the little boy could protest, the draugars flung him upwards, followed by the misty souls. Once he felt movement, Aki started to kick, and grew smaller and smaller as he ascended towards the faraway light. Tuomas watched, biting his lips to keep them together.

Aki reached the surface and thrust his hand into the air.

It was done. They were out. Safe.

Tuomas kept his eyes on Elin and Paavo, bid them a silent farewell, and let the last of the breath leave his lungs.

He sucked in icy water and immediately choked. Pressure crashed on his ribs, burning him, closing his throat. He thrashed about; mouth stretched wide in a scream of agony. The drum slipped from his grasp and drifted into the darkness.

At once, the circle collapsed. The draugars darted forwards and swarmed him, pulling at his clothes, his hair; slimy fingers pressing over his face. It felt like they were going to rip him apart.

And he was drowning.

He hadn't expected it to hurt so much. It made him cough, which in turn forced more water down his throat, and brought forth another bout of coughing…

Suddenly, he was the Great Mage again, under the ice of the Mustafjord. How much time would it take? How long would he be here, gasping, slowly dying?

He started to lose the feeling in his fingers. His kicking slowed. The draugars seized him tight and began nibbling his flesh. Their nails pressed on his chest and opened the old scar over his heart. He tasted his own blood in the water and his eyes rolled back in his head.

Tuomas braced himself, and waited for the end.

Chapter Twenty-Nine

She fled deep into the World Above, far away, so not even a trace of her Lights would be seen. She spun in the labyrinth of stars, fury tearing at her, pulling her in a hundred different directions. She felt the souls of the dead shudder around her as they sensed her uncontrollable rage. They knew she hadn't been this angry for centuries – this was even worse than when she had attacked the insolent boy at the beginning of the Long Night.

But Tuomas…

The nerve of it! To not only doubt her power, but to openly defy her! And to manipulate the equality she had given to him… it was disgusting! He was lucky she had only pinned him to the ground. When he had thrown that insolent comment in her face, it had taken all her strength to not do exactly what he'd suggested. It wouldn't have been the first time she had torn his soul out. Leaving him alone was the only thing she could have done to protect him.

He had struck her too deeply, disrespected her too much. If she returned now, she wasn't sure what she would do to him.

The Sun Spirit rose over the Northlands. Unable to cast her aurora, she decided to distract herself, and floated towards the tear in the skin. Once again, she shuddered as she inspected it. It seemed to have stabilised itself since Tuomas had opened it; no more stars had fallen and the cleft was no larger. She tried to draw the two edges together but they resisted each other and drew apart again.

A sudden wail flew past her like a wave. It was so strong; it sent her cartwheeling through the air.

When she stabilised herself, she realised it was coming from the Sun Spirit.

My son! she was shrieking. *No! No, my son!*

What is wrong, Golden One? cried the Spirit of the Winter Winds.

The Sun Spirit didn't answer. She twisted around herself in anguish and pushed vainly against the skin between the Worlds.

My son! Please, no!

She flung herself away from the tear and approached.

What has he done? she demanded.

The Sun Spirit looked at her.

The draugars have him! He gave himself to them! Oh, my boy, no!

The souls around her spun in alarm. Panic flared through her entire being; her tail stilled and she thought she might fall out of the sky. All her fury transformed into sheer terror.

She stared at the Northern Edge. Its icy surface shone in the afternoon light, the hole in the centre so small that it looked as though it had been pricked through fabric with a needle. She could just about see the trail of Tuomas's prints across the snow; his skis sticking upright on the lakeshore.

Her eyes rose to the cleft in the sky.

She didn't stop to think. In all her centuries of existence, never had she made a decision so quickly.

She gathered all her strength. Her aurora bloomed even though it was the middle of the day. Then she shot forward like an arrow and leapt across the rip. It pulled at her, trying to keep her in the World Above, but she let out an almighty cry and tore herself through.

Something ruptured around her. The edges of the hole flew in opposite directions and split the entire sky in two. A collective scream rebounded between the stars.

What are you doing? the Sun Spirit screamed. *White Fox One, stop!*

She didn't listen. The air became denser and she fell. It was still daylight; the Sun Spirit was high in the sky. Her Lights flickered, unable to find purchase, incapable of even moving. She needed the darkness… she shouldn't be here…

She focused harder than she ever had before and thought of the body Tuomas had given her. She drew herself together; made a chest and breathed into it. Legs and arms sprouted, and pointed ears; white hair burst forth from her head. She opened her eyes.

In a matter of moments, she had transformed from shapeless aurora into a physical girl. Then she came down hard on the ice.

Its firmness made her hiss. Everything was solid. It all felt heavy and constrained; the physical flesh was like a cage after floating free. The Sun Spirit's glow bore down on her like a weight and burned so deep, she cried out in agony. In the World Above, they could exist alongside each other, but not here.

The Spirits were screaming at her. She sensed them in her mind: all overlapping each other in a frantic chorus of dread and rage.

She looked up at the sky and gasped with horror. What had she done?

But her own panic was greater. She would deal with the rip later.

Biting her lip against the pain, she crawled as fast as she could towards the hole in the middle of the lake. She thrust her power towards it, wrenched open the gateway, and leapt through.

She fell again, through a haze of nothingness which then transformed into heavy rainclouds. The light disappeared and a wonderful rainy night surrounded her. She panted with relief and landed in a boat in the middle of the lake. The surface was hidden beneath a thick coat of mist.

Several Earth Spirits were dragging bodies onto the banks. They reached out their hands as soon as they saw her.

White Fox One! they called. *What are you doing here?*

She didn't answer; just threw herself into the water. Darkness surrounded her, but she burst through it. Her tail swept back and forth and transformed the lake into a flickering pool of green and blue. Then she saw a mass of slimy, swirling figures – and in the middle of them, a glow as bright as the Sun Spirit.

She flung her Lights at the draugars and struck them with the force of a tempest. The creatures shrieked and swam away, slithering over each other in a desperate attempt for shelter. They left Tuomas hanging in the water, surrounded by blood. She saw shallow bite marks all over him and a deep wound on his chest.

To her amazement, he was still alive.

She plunged her hand into him and drove deep until she found his souls. They were beginning to separate, their shine dimming by the second. A moment more and she would have been too late.

With a great push, she forced them back together. Then she wrenched herself free, seized his body and swam upwards. They broke the surface and she held his head above the water while she kicked towards the bank. As soon as they were within distance, the Earth Spirits ran over and pulled them both away from the lake.

She grabbed hold of a tree to steady herself. She could barely stand; she had never used so much energy so quickly before.

The Earth Spirits laid Tuomas beside the other bodies. They looked as though they were made of the mist, but with every moment, colour slowly returned to their cheeks. Life was coming back to them, bringing firm flesh and warm blood. They were all unconscious, but she could tell they were breathing.

She tapped Tuomas's face in an attempt to get him moving. No response came. Desperate, she held a hand on his chest to stem the blood. Rain soaked her, pulling her hair straight and making her ears droop. Every drop was like acid – even their faint touch was almost too much for her to bear.

One of the Earth Spirits approached and helped her press down on the wound. Blood spilled over its leafy fingers.

The draugars will come after him, she said. *Summon the Great Bear.*

Do you have any idea what you have done? the Earth Spirit asked in a trembling voice. *Did you not feel it? You tore the –*

Summon the Bear, she repeated firmly.

An awful slithering sounded from the water. Then a torrent of draugars burst through, their eyes furiously fixed on her. There were thousands: more of them than she had ever seen. The entire lake was filled with them. They slinked up the bank and came straight towards Tuomas.

She threw another stream of Lights and knocked them back several feet.

Not a step further! she shouted.

The draugars skidded to a halt. She couldn't help a surge of satisfaction when she saw they were afraid.

White Fox One! they shrieked. *The boy is ours now!*

I contest that! He is the Son of the Sun! He is far above any grasp such as yours, you disgusting, scavenging bottom-feeders!

She rose to her full height and swept her tail back and forth. With every movement, a miniature aurora flew through the air, its edge red with rage. In her human form, she was smaller than the draugars, but her presence was enough to stop them in their tracks.

The nearest draugar thrust its chin toward her.

He is ours! He came to us willingly! He gave us his taika!

And you have not taken his taika yet! she snarled. *His life-soul is still where it belongs, and that means it is still his own!*

The draugars didn't back off. They crawled as close as they dared, threat in their flaming eyes. She held up her hands and they glowed warningly.

The deal was made, they hissed. *An exchange greater than any human has ever offered, and it was accepted! By coming here, you have broken it, White Fox One! So we claim not only him, but all those he has tried to save! Every single one of them!*

She took a step forward.

You do not challenge me! Ever! she bellowed. *You know who I am, and I will crush you all!*

The draugars quietened, but they still gnashed their teeth at her. Their fear turned to disdain.

With all due respect, they drawled, *there are more of us than of you. You may be strong, White Fox One, but so are we.*

And you have a weakness unlike any other Spirit. You love him… like a human.

She heard more slithering behind her and spun around. To her horror, the huge crowd of draugars had crept through the trees and now encroached from all sides. She, Tuomas, the bodies and the Earth Spirits were trapped by a wall of monsters.

Her breath caught in her throat. Where was the Great Bear? They were all here, in prime position for it to trap them…

Why should we not drag you with us too? they said. Their eyes shone with slimy triumph. *The Son of the Sun, and the Daughter of the Moon. Ours, together, forever. Tell us, White Fox One, what does human love taste like as a Spirit?*

Dread wrenched deep inside her. This had been what Kari wanted to do, after he discovered who she was. These creatures were just like him. And just like him, she would strike them down. They would look upon her and be afraid, as all things should be.

She flung out her hands and threw up a circle of Lights. The aurora struck the ground and bloomed like green fire, but it was too late. The draugars shouldered their way through, hissing in pain, but not allowing it to hinder them. The Earth Spirits hurriedly surrounded Tuomas.

Stay away, or I will destroy you all! she thundered. *It might take me a hundred years, but not a single one of you will escape! I will not warn you again!*

You cannot win, White Fox One! the draugars cried. *We will have you both!*

In response, she shot a jet of Light around the circle. It was so powerful, every draugar at the front fell and didn't move.

A flicker of fear flashed around the crowd, but disappeared just as quickly, and they swarmed forward like a plague. She hurled out more auroras and tried to repel them, but they were soon upon her. The Earth Spirits tried to help, but one swipe from the draugars' arms smashed their thin leaf shells apart.

There was nothing left to do. She grabbed the two bodies nearest Tuomas – Aki and Elin – then threw out a second circle around the four of them. Closer to her, she was able to hold it easier, and she swept the freezing flames high over her head until they were completely encased. The amount of energy was so extreme, she dropped to her knees, but never once did she lower her hands.

She screamed. The sound tore through her like a knife; her lungs opened properly for the first time and her throat felt as though she had swallowed an icicle. She was too weak; too vulnerable from the daylight and the dive, and the leap across three Worlds in a matter of moments. Every part of her body hurt.

Her arms trembled. She couldn't hold the monsters off...

Something swept over her and blew the aurora away. She jumped up, ready to defend herself, but paused.

All of the draugars were floating limp in the air. Some were so high up; she couldn't see their faces. Even the rain had stopped still and hovered as though frozen. And above everything, the clouds had twisted into the unmistakable image of the Great Bear Spirit.

The Earth Spirits quickly reassembled themselves from nearby leaves and stared into the sky. More appeared from within the forest, some scaling the trees to see better.

The Bear turned its eyes to every single one of them. Then it looked straight at her. She almost buckled under its gaze; she had never known it so incensed.

It spoke, in a silent voice that still managed to rattle the ground underfoot.

Take them to the Deathlands.

The clouds broke apart. At once, the Earth Spirits reached out towards them and swept them down. As the cloud passed over the draugars, it ensnared them like flies in a spider's web. Soon the twisting vapours covered the entire forest and she couldn't even see her hand in front of her face. She crouched over Tuomas protectively and watched as the Earth Spirits forced the draugars into the cave.

When the last one had disappeared, the sky was left perfectly clear and dark. Even the torches around the trees had been extinguished in the fray. She flicked her tail and sent a gentle green glow into the night. A few reindeer peered from behind the carved trunks, their white coats ghostly under the aurora. The lake shone; the blanket of mist was gone, as though it had never been there.

Her ears pricked up in alarm as she looked around. The three she had grabbed: Tuomas, Elin and Aki, were still there, all the mist vanished from their bodies. But the others – Sisu, Eevi, Paavo – had vanished.

Tuomas was still bleeding from the gash in his chest, but it was beginning to slow down. She pressed on it again and her snowy hands stained red.

He shuddered beneath her; coughed and spewed half the lake out of his mouth. He gasped for air, then inched his eyes open. They were bloodshot and weary, but alive.

"Lumi?" he mumbled in disbelief.

Her anger flooded back. She thrust out a hand and sent his head flying onto the ground. The impact knocked him unconscious again.

Good. At least that way, he couldn't cause any more damage.

One of the Earth Spirits stepped out from the cave. As it approached, it drew leaves from the ground and swirled them around itself until they found places as skin, clothes and hair.

Where are the souls? she asked.

The Spirit lowered its head sorrowfully. *We could not hold them off. The draugars took them again before we could reach them.*

She stared at it, then at Tuomas. Her eyes lingered over his bruised and bloodied body. All his clothes were torn so badly, they barely covered him. Small pink crescents, dotted with the unmistakable dents of teeth marks, peppered every inch of his skin.

He did all this for nothing? she cried, unable to hide her anguish. *That is why he tried to sacrifice himself, is it not? To save them all?*

Yes, said the Earth Spirit. *I tried to stop him. He would not listen.*

Hardly surprising, she snarled. *Stupid fool! He had no idea what he was doing!*

He is not the only one guilty of that, White Fox One.

She looked over her shoulder. A shape was rising from the lake. It walked with purpose and grace; nothing like the slithery movements of the draugars, and its entire form was made of water. A thick body took shape, then powerful paws and eyes as bottomless as time. It held something solid in its mouth: a drum.

Immediately, the reindeer lowered their heads as it passed. The Great Bear regarded them with the gentleness of a parent. The Earth Spirit bowed too, and so did she. She kept her eyes on the ground until the Bear was standing directly over her.

It deposited the drum at Tuomas's side. The skin was slack and saturated with water, but amazingly, the symbols were intact.

Have you any idea of what you have done? it said.

I am sorry, she said meekly. *I just had to save him –*

And in that you have succeeded, replied the Bear, *but at such cost! You have torn the boundary between the Above and Between! And it is not a thin rip such as your brother made – it is the entire skin! That is why it took me so long to reach you when you summoned me here! You were with me when we warned him about abusing the power – you knew the danger and you still acted!*

She cowered. She had never known the Bear to shout. Its words were so sharp, it physically hurt her to hear them in her mind. It was the feeling of crushing disappointment, of ice cracking under itself.

I will repair it, she insisted. *When I come back, I promise I will undo what I have done!*

The Bear was silent. Only when she met its eyes did it answer her.

The tear is too great. You cannot come back.

She was so shocked; the Lights froze in the air and she fell over. The Bear didn't move. Every fur on its watery body shone, as though each one contained a trace of stardust.

You must be able to go back, she cried. *Take me with you!*

I am beyond all three Worlds. I am all three, everything in them, all that was and ever will be. Yes, I can pass between them: the only Spirit who can now. But I will not take you back to the World Above with me.

She dug her fingers into the earth in disbelief.

What? Why?

You have brought this upon yourself.

*But his soul – his Spirit – would have been lost forever!
I had to save him!*

Which I could also have done, replied the Bear. *He made a choice upon which I could have acted. You chose to act rashly, with no thought or consequence, just as you have before. But this time, it was not out of your wounded pride – no foolish human boy who dared not lower his head when he saw your display.*

It drew so close, its nose almost touched hers.

The Silver One was correct in one respect, White Fox One, it continued. *The human love you have learned is a strength, but it is also your greatest weakness.*

She sat so still, she thought she might turn to solid ice. The Earth Spirit beside her laid a hand on her arm, but she hardly felt it. Even the sharp physical touch suddenly seemed so far away.

The Bear stepped back a little, but didn't take its eyes off her.

I shall grant you the ability to shift between your forms, not to be bound only to this one. Girl, fox, aurora – all are yours, it said. Then it moved towards Tuomas, Elin and Aki. *I will take you all to Anaar. Do what you all must to recover.*

And then what would you have me do? she asked quietly.

Your brother should have completed the task I set him and not tried to outwit the draugars. I told him to do this because I have another he must complete: the very reason why he lives again in this body. Now, you will do it alongside him. Then you must both repair the boundary together, as both of you have contributed to it. And finally...

It paused and pressed its nose into Tuomas's chest. As soon as it touched him, light surrounded his body, and she watched as it settled around his head and hips. The wound over his heart closed into an enflamed line until he was left with his original scar, although notably larger than before. Then two pointed ears and a tail emerged, but unlike hers, they were not white. They were a stunning golden red.

After what he has done today, his power grows towards its peak. He is truly a Spirit in human form now. And yet, all things must come to an end. The choice of how will be his.

She ground her teeth.

More riddles? she said, unable to keep the impatience out of her words.

The Bear eyed her again.

It is what I am.

The moment the Sun Spirit set, the Great Bear Spirit whisked her and the three humans out of the gateway. They emerged into a World turned purple by the low light, but that wasn't what stunned her. Now her panic over her brother was gone, she could see the true extent of the tear in the sky. It was a great line which ran from north to south, split like a crack in an egg. Stardust rained from the edges in a waterfall of diamonds.

And she had done it.

She turned away and shuddered with guilt. She could feel the difference; in the air, the ground, everywhere. Each tree, rock, and ice crystal had changed. *Taika* surrounded her, leaking through the gash, unchecked and wild. She had never known anything so broken, and it was all her fault. All because she had been foolish enough to feel like a human.

The Bear took them high, just enough for her to feel the pull of the other realm. She deliberately didn't look at it. She didn't want to think about how close and yet so far she was from home – or see her mother's smug pockmarked face.

Please, look after the souls for me, she said quietly.

I promise you that, White Fox One, the Bear replied, in the first gentle tone she had heard all day.

Before long, the coast appeared below, the migration islands rising from the glistening water like a series of jagged teeth. Just like in the World Below, all the mist had vanished from the surface. On the largest island, Anaar, she noticed the reindeer roaming over the hills, their young calves staggering after them on the search for lichen. Smoke drifted from the tops of the huts. Only a few people lingered around the central fire pit. Everyone else was asleep. Even from the sky, she heard the sound of weeping.

The Bear descended onto the beach where she had watched the draugars drag Elin away. It deposited them on the shingle, then rose up again and disappeared into the darkness.

Still weakened from her ordeal, she crawled wretchedly into the trees. She found a patch of snow, laid down upon it, and closed her eyes.

Chapter Thirty

The pain was everywhere. It was in his chest, his throat, all the muscles in his body and over every inch of his flesh. Tuomas managed to drag a hand to the back of his head and felt a lump. His hair was wet. He opened his eyes and checked his fingers, but was relieved to find no blood.

He was lying on his side, his drum right next to him. Everything was hazy and blurred. The waves lapped around him, then drew away, hissing and whispering as they drained through the pebbles.

He frowned. Where was he? Why wasn't he under the water? How was he even breathing?

Wherever he was, the surroundings were different. There was something unhinged in the air, as though all the forces holding things in their place had shifted and come apart. It tasted strange; felt dense, like he was stuck in thick mud. It was wrong... so very wrong...

He suddenly became aware of a burning pain in his chest. He explored the edges of his torn tunic, then across his skin, and drew back with a yelp. There was no wound, but it felt as though there should be. He hadn't been that tender since Kari had stabbed him.

He looked around and noticed a blurry figure nearby. He saw fur trousers, a tunic embroidered with a mountain, a long black braid...

"Elin?" he groaned. Slowly but surely, she swam into focus.

Ignoring the aches, he flipped onto his front and crawled towards her. His hand came down on her shoulder and relief flooded him. She was real.

Her chest was moving. She was *alive*.

The haziness began to fade. Colours found their boundaries again and the shape of her face appeared. Her eyes were closed, but her skin was pink and solid – there wasn't a patch of grey on her at all. The mist was gone. He could even see a little muscle twitching in her neck.

"Elin?" he said again, and immediately winced. His voice rasped like an old man's, throat still in spasm from the amount of water it had sucked in. He clutched his ribs, trying to breathe through the pain.

Elin stirred, then coughed. But there was no rattle to it; no blood welled between her lips. In fact, she looked healthier than she had for weeks.

"Tuomas? Is that you?"

He managed a smile. "Yes. Are you alright?"

"Mmm."

Tuomas tore his eyes away from her to look around. The sound of running water was on the air, and the grunts of baby reindeer. There was no ice; no tundra. He recognised the beach: they were back at Anaar.

Then he glanced upward and froze. The entire sky looked like it was on fire, but not from Lumi's Lights. It was so horrifying, he cried out.

Elin forced herself into a sitting position. She saw the cascade of stardust too and gasped.

"Tuomas…" she breathed. "What is that?"

"I don't know," he rasped back.

"Tuomas!"

"What?"

345

He looked at her. Her eyes were huge. She motioned to his head.

"Your ears!"

He frowned and reached up to his hair. His fingers brushed something soft and furry. They ended in fleshy points, either side of his head. Then he looked behind him and yelped in alarm when he noticed the tail.

"What in the name of –?"

He tried to move the tail. Sure enough, it flicked from left to right and sent shingle flying. He turned his attention to the ears and they responded, too. He felt for his human ears, but they were gone; only the root of the fox ones lay in their place.

Elin went to stand and crashed down onto all fours. Tuomas hurried to help her, but she sharply turned away from him.

"Don't," she snapped.

"What's the matter?" he asked.

Then he noticed another figure, lying face-down a few feet away. Elin saw it too and stopped dead.

Tuomas crawled to the body and turned it over. Shock stung him. It was Aki, surrounded by the sodden folds of his coat. He looked just like he had in the trance with Lilja: in the body of a five-year-old child. And perfectly alive.

Tuomas pulled him into his lap and fished long strands of sandy hair out of his mouth. His cheeks were still scarred, but his flesh was pink and warm. Tuomas peeled back his eyelid, half-expecting to find a cloudy white globe, but there was nothing of the sort. Only his mother's brilliant blue.

"They let him go," Tuomas gasped. "But… wait… why am I here? I gave myself over to them."

He broke off, looking around the empty beach. "Where are the others? Where's Paavo?"

"Why didn't you tell me?" Elin asked tensely.

Her words crashed onto Tuomas like hailstones. He turned to face her. Her mouth was pressed into a thin line and her eyes flickered between him and Aki, blazing with tears.

"That's Lilja's son," she blurted. "All this time, she had a son. She told you, didn't she? Why didn't you tell me he was the one behind the plague?"

Tuomas's stomach flipped. "He wasn't... not really. And I promised Lilja I'd keep it secret."

"Did you know about her?" Elin demanded. "Her and... my father?"

"No. I swear. Not until last night."

Elin trembled, holding in sobs with all her strength. "I heard you talking about it. I was only behind that bush."

"I'm sorry. I thought you were in bed."

"You weren't even going to tell me, were you? Even if those things hadn't dragged me off!"

Tuomas reached towards her, but she scuttled away from him, her brows slanting in contempt.

That snapped something inside him.

"I don't know what I would have done, alright?" he barked, spitting out the words in a choked wheeze. "But you know what I *did* do? I tried to end the plague and save you! I went after you! I told the draugars they could take me instead of you!"

Elin stared at him, then reached into her tunic, withdrew something, and threw it. It hit him in the face and bounced onto the stones between them. It was the fox carving he had given her.

Before he could speak, there was the crunch of a footfall on the shingle and Aino appeared. She took one look at the state of them and yelled over her shoulder for help.

It didn't take long for a crowd of people to swarm out of the woods. Gasps of alarm flew through the air. Everyone started talking at the same time; Tuomas couldn't make out individual words. When they saw him, they exclaimed; some fell onto their knees. Tuomas tried to flatten his ears and hide the tail behind his legs.

Alda and Sigurd saw Elin and ran over so fast, they almost lost their footing. Elin scrambled upright and met them halfway. The three of them collapsed in a heap, crying and showering each other with kisses.

The mages shouldered their way to the front. Lilja's legs wobbled and Enska snatched her shoulders, but she shrugged him off and bolted towards Tuomas. She flung herself down in front of him, took a moment to touch his cheek tenderly, and pulled Aki from his lap. She ran her fingers across her son's hair, unable to believe he was real. Then she held him close and buried her face in his chest, sobs wracking her entire body.

Over Elin's head, Sigurd's gaze flickered to Lilja. His eyes widened and his cheeks grew paler than death. He covered his mouth with one hand, realisation written blatantly across his face.

Henrik strode past Lilja and snatched Tuomas's arm with surprising strength.

"What have you done, boy?" he hissed. "What in the name of all the Spirits have you done?"

The afternoon passed in a fog as Tuomas fought to stay lucid. But every now and then, fatigue would overcome him, every muscle screaming with pain, and restless slumber dragged him under. It reminded him horribly of the fever he had endured in

Einfjall, when hypothermia had gripped him and the skin of his iced fingers peeled away.

He was vaguely aware of being laid down, and staring up through a smoke hole, the Sun Spirit spinning overhead. Her glow pulled at him until his souls became loose and he floated towards her, spinning through the endlessness.

But this time, it felt different. Wrong. It was as though an invisible pressure was closing around him, filling the air with something awful and unnatural. Uncontrollable terror mounted inside him.

What is this? he yelled.

No reply came.

He jolted awake with a cry and sat up. Two faces snapped around to look at him.

It was Enska and Lilja. He realised he must be in their hut. Both their drums hung on knots in the wall beams, and the unmistakable smell of healing herbs shot up his nose with every breath. Tuomas's own drum hung beside theirs, the skin around the frame wrinkled from moisture.

"So, you're awake. At last," Enska said. He pulled his shoes on and glanced at Lilja. "I'll get the others. Do you want to take Aki somewhere? Henrik will ask questions."

Lilja looked at Aki, lying in her lap with his eyes closed. She'd changed him into some new, dry clothes – they obviously belonged to her or Enska because they swamped his little body.

She felt his temperature and shook her head.

"No, he's too cold. And if an old man can keep his own secrets for an entire lifetime, then surely he can keep mine."

Enska squeezed her shoulder in comfort. Then, without another word, he walked past Tuomas and disappeared through the door. A blast of cold night air flew in and made the flames in the hearth dance.

Tuomas stared after him nervously. Enska's voice held none of its usual warmth. In fact, he seemed livid.

"What others?" he asked Lilja.

"The mages," she replied. "We all need to talk to you."

Tuomas held a hand to his chest and coughed. His ribs were burning; it felt as though he had breathed in acid rather than water. Then he examined himself. He was wearing new clothes too: the tunic had no rip down the middle and was embroidered with Poro patterns, just like Aki's. His hands and arms were covered with bite marks. They weren't deep, but the sight of them sent a shiver through him. He could still feel the draugars pulling at him as the lake filled his lungs.

He touched his head. The ears were still there. He grasped the tip of one and dug his fingernail into it. He winced – yes, it was real. It was part of him.

"Why do I have these?" he asked.

"How should I know, Red Fox One?" Lilja replied.

Her tone startled him. She hadn't spoken to him like that since they had first met. Back when they were strangers.

Desperate to break down her defensiveness, he looked at Aki again. She cradled him like a baby, as though terrified he would slip away if she let go of him.

"The mist is gone off the sea," he said. "Please tell me the draugars are gone, too. Have the kids stopped coughing?"

Lilja nodded. "Yes."

Tuomas was so relieved, he fell back against the wall. He couldn't figure out how, but whatever he had done had worked. They were safe.

Then he thought of the moment he had woken on the beach. Anxiety returned like ice in his heart.

"Have... Sigurd or Elin been here?" he asked.

Lilja glared at him over the flames.

"No. Elin's sleeping off her ordeal. And anyway, why should either of them come?"

Tuomas nervously twisted his fingers into the fur of the sleeping sack. He chose his words with care.

"Lilja, Elin heard you telling me about him. And Sigurd saw you at the beach."

She tensed and swallowed a sob before it could overcome her.

"So, they know," she said quietly. Her voice broke with defeat. "I never thought it would happen this way. I didn't think it would happen at all."

Tuomas swallowed. "Are you angry with me?"

She didn't answer, so he tried a different tack.

"I'm so sorry for what I said to you. I was just –"

"I know you were upset."

"I did my best. I just didn't tell you where I was going because I knew you'd try to follow me. I didn't want you to get hurt. I tried to save him."

"Did you?" Lilja said coldly. "And while I'm personally overjoyed to have my baby back, did you stop for a moment to think about the consequences of whatever you did?"

She snatched the topmost log from the woodpile and hurled it at the fire. It bounced off a hearthstone and sent sparks flying.

Tuomas flinched. He had never seen her like this. None of her past frustrations with him came close to the fury which now blazed in her eyes. In a way, it scared him even more than when she had been under Kari's control.

"There's only one option open to me now," she said. "As soon as he's well enough, Aki and I are leaving."

Tuomas gasped. "No, please! Don't!"

"What else can I do?" she snapped. "Everything I worked for has been undone."

"So you're going to just run away?"

"You're a fine one to talk about running away."

Tuomas opened his mouth to argue, but her remark cut him too deeply and all that came out was a cough. Then the door swung open and Enska stepped back in, followed by Henrik, Aino, and Niina.

They settled around the fire. Their expressions were grave, unreadable; and bore down on Tuomas like a physical weight.

Henrik was the first to speak.

"You have some explaining to do, boy."

Tuomas squirmed. "I was only trying to help."

"Forget what you were *trying* to do. This is about what you *did* do." Henrik glared at him. "I thought I had prepared you better than this."

The disappointment in his old teacher's voice was more hurtful than if he had been struck.

"We all felt something happen yesterday," said Niina. "The sky's torn open."

Tuomas's breath turned to stone in his lungs. He shot a terrified glance at Lilja. She looked back evenly, silent knowledge hanging between the two of them. She was the only one who he had told about the tear, back in the mountains.

He shook his head. "I didn't do that. I didn't go anywhere near the World Above."

"Then how do you explain it?" Aino snapped. "You are the only one here with enough power to do something like that!"

"I didn't do it!" Tuomas cried. "I swear!"

"Who knows what you did?" Lilja said darkly.

"That's not all which is different," Enska added. He reached over and touched Tuomas's ears. "Your *taika* has changed. I can feel it coming off you. It's too strong... far too strong to be contained in a physical body. Frankly, I don't understand how you're still alive, Son of the Sun or not."

Tuomas's pulse hammered in his ears. He looked beseechingly at Lilja, but her face was as blank as a stone.

"Please," he said, on the verge of tears. "I don't understand. I didn't mean to hurt anyone! I just wanted to –"

Suddenly, it all came flooding back. He remembered choking on the cold water, then the jet of green coming towards him; staring up at Lumi in her human form. There had been no sign of Paavo, or Sisu, or any of the other dead. Only Elin and Aki, when he awoke on the shore.

The terrible truth dawned on him.

"She sacrificed them to save me," he breathed.

"What, boy?" Henrik barked.

Tuomas held his hands to his mouth, struggling to process it all.

Enska crawled closer to him. "You need to tell us everything. No excuses, no guesses. Everything."

Tears burst from Tuomas's eyes and flowed uncontrollably down his face. He didn't even have the energy to sob. He simply recounted everything that had happened since he left Einfjall: Lumi's furious warning in the tundra, the Great Bear Spirit's revelation that he was the one meant to trap the draugars in the World Below. And how he had wantonly defied it to save all who had been lost.

The only part he left out was the Deathlands across the ashy desert. Despite everything, he couldn't bear to mention that river of nightmares.

When he was done, the mages sat stunned, not uttering a word. Even Lilja looked shaken by the story.

After several long moments of uncomfortable silence, Aino finally spoke.

"So that's how you came back with Elin and... the boy," she said, glancing uneasily at Aki. Lilja manoeuvred him so he was more hidden in the shadows, her eyes like daggers. Aino noticed and looked back at Tuomas.

"But if they were the price set to you by the Great Bear Spirit," she continued, "you should have paid it. No option was ideal, but that was clearly the best of all of them, otherwise the Bear wouldn't have told you to do it."

"But the draugars are still gone," Niina said carefully. "The youngsters are all free."

"At the cost of the boundary between the Above and Between," Enska replied.

And all the others, Tuomas thought. After everything that he had done, all the hurt he had caused, he had still failed.

"But at least someone gets a happy ending," Henrik muttered, then raised his voice at Lilja. "Your son? He looks enough like you to be your son."

Tuomas glanced at everyone's faces. He could tell from their subdued reactions that Henrik had told them all about Runa.

"Yes," Lilja said quietly. "His name is Aki."

Henrik gave a snide nod. "And now you've got him back. Even though everything else is gone."

"Shut up," Lilja snapped.

Henrik was on his feet in an instant. "What did you say to me?"

Lilja held his eyes like an incensed wolf.

"You heard. Don't take your own insecurities out on me just because that stupid boy tried to play the hero."

Henrik's face turned red. "You do not speak for me! And that reminds me, since I'm sure you never married, who's the father?"

"That's enough, Henrik," Enska warned. "It's none of your business, so don't assume a thing."

Henrik wheeled on him. "You know as well, do you?"

"Stop it!" Tuomas shouted before the argument could escalate. "This is all my fault – be mad at me, not Lilja! Leave her and Aki out of this."

Sure enough, Henrik turned his anger away from Enska, but then threw it straight back at Tuomas.

"You're right, boy. This *is* all your fault. At least now you have the gall to admit to it."

Tuomas bent his head in shame. Even in his grief, he couldn't believe he had been so thoughtless. Hadn't Henrik warned him at the start of the migration that he needed to be careful? Yet he'd still let his anger get the better of him. It had been luck which led to him being unharmed by the blizzard, to splitting the avalanche, to helping the reindeer swim to Anaar. Once again, all reckless, risky uses of a *taika* he could barely control.

And now his luck had run dry. No matter that he had somehow escaped the abyss. It was *he* who would ultimately pay the price.

Fifteen years old was the age of manhood. Eight months ago, at midsummer, he had leapt on that idea with open arms. But as he sat there, under the judgmental and disappointed gazes of his fellow mages, he realised how much he was truly still a child.

Chapter Thirty-One

Night gave way to day, and then back to night again. Stars spun through the tiny gap of the smoke hole. Clouds swept in and emptied flurries of snow over Anaar.

Lilja and Enska cared for Tuomas, but it was always with an uncomfortable distance, and they never held his eyes for longer than was necessary. Lilja kept to herself at the back of the hut, hardly leaving Aki's side. He didn't wake up for more than a few moments at a time: just enough to swallow a cupful of water before falling back to sleep.

Tuomas heard Lilja telling her father she believed his body was still adjusting to being alive again. Even though it made sense, Tuomas couldn't repress a shudder at the concept. This little boy, who had inadvertently caused so much suffering, had come back from the dead. It was unheard of. But, then again, he supposed nothing could be said to be unheard of now. Nothing was simple anymore.

This is the price of growing up, he thought to himself. As a child, everything was just so. There was a place and time for all things, and those things never broke out of the boundaries laid around them. He'd clung onto that idea like an anchor. Life didn't have to change, if he didn't let it.

But then, gradually, the waves of his tranquil sea transformed, creeping up slowly until he couldn't even notice they were rising at all. And on the other side, as a new dawn bled across the rough water, he realised that it wasn't the sea which had changed. It was him. And there was no way back to what had once been.

On the third night, Tuomas fetched his drum and left the hut. He still didn't feel completely recovered – every movement was laborious and each breath tore at his lungs, but he knew he needed to go back to the shelter he had shared with Paavo. The longer he put it off, the harder it would be.

He trudged through the forest, keeping his eyes on the ground to make sure he didn't trip over any rocks. His tail smacked against the trees as though to remind him that it was there. In frustration, he tried to keep it still, but that only made it flick more irately from side to side.

He ran a hand along it. It protruded from just below the base of his spine, the waist of his trousers tied underneath it. The fur felt exactly like Lumi's: so fine and silky, it seemed as though it was air somehow given form. Each strand was a shiny coppery colour, but its beauty was lost on him. He reached up to his ears and tugged at them, half-hoping they might detach from his head if he pulled hard enough. He gave up when the pain became too great and smacked out at low-hanging branches with a snarl. He would have had just as much luck trying to pull off his arm.

Before long, he reached the main area of huts. The fire in the central pit was almost out; only a handful of red embers continued to smoulder at the bottom. Everyone was in bed. But a small part of him wondered if they somehow knew he was walking around, and were keeping their distance. It wouldn't surprise him. He deserved it.

His eyes lingered on the hut where Sigurd, Alda and Elin were staying. The door was securely closed. He hadn't seen them since that day at the beach – even Elin had stayed away. Tuomas told himself it was because she was still weak. Whether it was from the sickness or being dragged into the water, she had taken a terrible beating. But deep down, he couldn't forget the awful way she'd looked at him; the accusation and hurt.

He wondered if she'd told Sigurd what she'd heard. Sigurd had obviously made the connection when he saw Lilja and Aki together, but where did that leave the family? Lilja had worked so hard to protect them, and now it would all be for nothing.

He needed to speak to Elin. Tomorrow, he would come to the hut and try to explain.

Then he heard something: a hard scraping sound.

He frowned. Was somebody still awake?

He stole past the shelters and crept in the direction of the noise. It led him to the edge of the beach. A figure was dragging one of the boats towards the sea. A torch had been stuck into the shingle to give some light, and by the orange glow, Tuomas noticed a head of white hair.

He gasped.

"Mihka?"

The figure spun around. Tuomas jumped onto the pebbles and hurried over.

"What are you doing?" he asked.

When Mihka saw him, his face hardened into stone.

"I'm going," he replied.

Tuomas quickly took stock of the boat. It was packed for a long journey, with a sleeping sack, food, spare clothes, skis, hunting gear, and a small sled to pull it all in.

"Where?"

"What do you care? Anywhere's better than here."

"What? Why? What's the matter? You can't go, you've been sick!"

Mihka stepped towards him. His body was still horribly thin, but the colour had returned to his cheeks and the skin around his eyes was no longer bruised. It was a huge change from just a few days ago, yet the expression on his face was as though he was a completely different person.

"I came looking for Henrik a few nights back, to ask him for some herbs," Mihka said. "I followed him to Enska and Lilja's hut. All the other mages were going there, too – to speak with you. So I waited outside, and I heard *everything*."

Tuomas froze.

"You saved that kid and your new best friend, but the price was my father's soul," Mihka snarled.

"I had no control over that," Tuomas protested. "I tried to save all of them!"

"Shut up!"

Mihka shoved him hard. Tuomas fell onto his backside and stared up at his friend in alarm. Mihka's eyes were ablaze, wet with tears, hatred written across his entire face.

"Mihka…"

"No! I don't want to listen to you!"

"Please! I've been so stupid, and I'm sorry! I tried!"

"Well, it doesn't really matter, does it? My father's dead, and he is never coming back! And even if you managed to save him, you still would have doomed us all!"

Tuomas staggered to his feet. "Mihka, don't go. Please."

But Mihka narrowed his eyes.

"Don't come after me, Tuomas," he said. "I never want to see you again."

Without another word, he turned back to the boat and gave it one last shove. The water lifted it; he leapt inside, took up the oars, and started rowing away, towards the dark bulk of the mainland.

Tuomas ran to the edge of the waves, but didn't go any further. His entire body trembled with shame as he watched the boat become smaller. Soon, even Mihka's hair was only a faint white speck in the distance. And then, in a heartbeat, the darkness swallowed that too.

Tuomas stood rooted to the spot. His legs felt separate from himself, as though they were dead tree stumps upon which he was resting. They crashed underneath him; he sank to his knees and wept.

He noticed something in the shingle in front of him: paler than the greyness which surrounded it. Bone.

He picked it up. It was the carved fox head.

It was only a few inches long and weighed practically nothing, but he felt as though he was holding a boulder in his hand. He drew it back, to throw it as far as he could.

But then his eyes rose from the sea to the sky. The tear spilled across it in a line of piercing light. Even the stars seemed dimmed because of it. He was so small underneath it – he knew every Spirit in the World Above was staring at him through the gash.

He noticed the constellation of the Great Bear and lowered his hand.

He had never felt so terrible. He thought of Lilja's words after he'd woken up; how she intended to leave. Once again, she would cut off everything for the benefit of all others.

Was he not in a similar position? Those he loved were lost and hope was gone. She'd said to him, only a few weeks ago, that when things felt out of control, the best thing to do was control whatever one could.

He got to his feet. Even taking his own weight again was a physical effort. He pocketed the carving and headed towards the boats.

"Tuomas."

He stopped dead. That voice… it was clearer than a bell, purer than virgin snow.

He looked over his shoulder and his heart skipped.

"Lumi?"

She stood as still as an ice statue; in the same form he had once forced her into. She had the same arms and legs, her long pure white hair, her garment of starlight and ethereal piercing eyes. Pointed ears rose from her scalp and her bushy tail swept gently at her heels. Sparks of green and blue flew from the fur.

She walked towards him. Her feet were bare, and so light, the pebbles didn't even move as she stepped on them. Tuomas didn't move his eyes from her.

"How are you here?" he blurted.

"What are your intentions?" she countered.

Tuomas hesitated. He threw a fleeting glance at the nearest boat.

"I was… going to leave," he admitted. "It would be better for everyone."

"Is that not the same logic you applied to sacrificing yourself?" Lumi replied.

She stood between him and the boat, but not close enough to touch. The falling stardust from the rip made her skin glitter like frost crystals. She was solid, yet so delicate, he found himself wondering once again how she could be contained.

When she next spoke, some of the coldness lifted from her voice.

"You must not run. It will do no good to anyone. You and I, least of all."

"But look at what I've done," Tuomas cried, pointing at the sky.

For the first time since she had appeared, Lumi closed her eyes.

"You did not tear the Worlds," she said sullenly. "I did."

"What?"

"When I realised what you had done, I jumped across all three Worlds to reach you. I threw all my power behind it."

She looked at him again and explained everything that had happened since she had left him in the tundra. With every word, more blood drained from Tuomas's face. His initial relief at not causing the rip melted into sheer shock.

"*You* finished off the draugars?" he breathed. "And you trapped yourself here for me?"

"I had to take a physical form to reach the World Below," she explained. "It was a price I was willing to pay, however thoughtlessly I acted upon it."

"But it was daylight. Didn't that hurt you?"

"Of course it did," Lumi replied snappishly. "It is why I have been hiding in an old fox burrow for the past three days, so I could recover. But what does it matter? None of this would have happened if you had listened to me in the first place. Why did you insult me like that?"

Her ears twitched and the edges of her eyes turned red. Tuomas took a wary step back.

"I didn't want to listen," he admitted. "Lumi, I'm so sorry. I didn't mean to offend you."

Her tail twitched irately and sent a small aurora flickering over the shingle. Then she approached him and took his hands in hers. She was so gentle, he barely felt her.

"Your power is different," she observed. "Aki and Elin are not the only ones who died and came back to life in the lake. You have too, twice in the same body. That has never happened before in the histories of all the Worlds. You now hold the full strength of a Spirit inside you, Tuomas."

Tuomas swallowed nervously. "How am I going to be able to control it? It was hard enough before!"

"I will help you," said Lumi. "I once told you that I would save you a thousand times. Now we must work together to save everything. And if we succeed, we need only do it once."

Tuomas's breath shook. He didn't want to do a single thing more for anyone.

"I can't," he cried. "All I do is hurt people. And these things…" He pulled at his ears. "These are to show I'm really a Spirit in human form? Well, one thing's right about it being the Spirit of the Flames. Flames destroy everything they touch."

"If unchecked, yes, they do," Lumi said. "But contained – focused – they are the reason for life. Every piece of ash left behind is a chance for something new."

She dipped her head to catch his eye.

"I know you feel alone," she said softly, "but you never have been. I have always been with you, and I will continue to be with you. My brother."

Tuomas sniffled and wiped his nose on his sleeve. He squeezed her fingers as hard as he dared, worried that too much pressure would break her like ice on a thawing lake. But it didn't. She stayed as strong as ever, and just as it had in the World Below, a grip as powerful as a mountain took hold of him. But this time, he didn't pull away. He would never pull away from her again.

"My sister," he whispered.

The two of them stood hand in hand, watching the starry waterfall drift into the sea. Then they turned away from the open sky and walked back into the forest. All that was left to show they had been there was a tiny trail of green aurora, floating away like mist in the morning.

The drumbeats end…

The Night River

The Foxfires Trilogy
Book Three

Read on for an exclusive sneak peak!

Prologue

The stars twinkled and the Moon Spirit was bright, but despite the glow they cast over the snowy tundra, Mihka felt like he had never known a night so dark. Somehow it seemed even blacker than at the height of winter. The air was sharp around him; not from cold, but something else which ran deeper, through the very veins of the Northlands. It left him breathless, as though he'd climbed to a mountain summit where the oxygen thinned and he had to struggle to fill his lungs. He was no mage, but even he could sense the Worlds moving away from each other, like currents pulling water in different directions. Overhead, the sky was torn clean in two and the edges of the abyss waved like a spiderweb in the breeze.

The sight was terrifying, but he forced himself to concentrate. He had only fled Anaar the night before, but already the island was a dark blue speck in the distance behind him. He'd crossed the channel in a boat, then emptied it of his belongings and strapped them all into a small sled made from lightweight birch planks. Attaching it to his belt and slipping his shoes into a pair of skis, he had set off in the direction of Akerfjorden's winter camp. The only things which he hadn't tied to the sled were his bow and arrows. Those were slung across his shoulders, in case he came across a hare or ptarmigan.

He had decided to take the long way. Keeping to ground level meant he could stop at the Poro winter camp, rest and perhaps trade for some food if he failed to catch anything. Going through the mountain passes was a definite short cut, but with spring approaching, he didn't want to risk it. Spring was the most changeable and dangerous season of all. If he became trapped up there, alone, nobody would ever find him.

It wasn't even late in the evening, but the nights were still coming early. The hours of daylight wouldn't catch up for several more weeks. It was time to stop and pitch camp.

There was a forest in front of him, branches heaped with snow, their ends feathered by the glistening of ice crystals. Boulders peppered the ground here and there – he supposed they had broken off the nearby mountains in some long-ago avalanche and crashed down into the trees. Perfect. They would block a little of the wind.

Mihka stepped out of the skis and untied the eight long poles lashed to the top of the sled. He arranged two in front of the largest boulder, balancing them against each other in the air, then added the others until he had a skeletal cone structure. Finally he opened a length of reindeer-skin tarp and wrapped it around the whole thing to create a tent. It was smaller than a typical one, but it would do. He only needed room for his sleeping sack.

Usually he would have carried the poles in a sleigh, to make things easier. But for a sleigh, he needed a reindeer, and they were all still on Anaar. He wouldn't have been able to leave so quietly if he'd had to urge one of the animals across the channel.

Mihka thanked the Spirits and chopped a few branches off a nearby birch tree; then he ducked inside the shelter and woke a fire. It took a while; the wood was damp with snow, so he peeled the papery bark off for kindling and split the logs into smaller pieces with a knife. That gave the flames more purchase. Satisfied, he huddled close to warm his hands and tucked into some salted salmon cakes from his pack. They weren't much, but would keep him going until he reached Poro.

Unease bit at him. He'd never been out on his own before. Now, miles from his people, he realised how truly alone he was. It was an isolation he had brought on himself, but that didn't make it any easier.

The space opposite him was empty: just the shadows of flames flickering on a blank tarp wall. His father Sisu should be sitting there, as he always had.

But his father was dead. Gone forever. Mihka wasn't even sure if he would see him again in the other Worlds.

As he worked through the cakes, chewing them slowly to make them last longer, he held a hand to his chest. It was still hurting from the illness which had ravaged him. The plague had vanished from his lungs practically overnight, but at the back of his mouth, he remembered the taste of blood; heard the rattle of his own breath in his ears. All his ribs felt as though they had cracked like rotten twigs. And his head had been filled with images of a little boy with white eyes and scars down his cheeks…

The same little boy Tuomas had appeared with on the beach.

Mihka's anger swelled with the force of a spring tide. Having stopped walking, there was nothing to distract him from it. He kicked at the fire with a snarl and sent sparks shooting into the air. Tears prickled his eyes, but he hurriedly wiped them away. No matter that nobody would see them fall. He couldn't bear to cry. That would make it too real, too soon.

He touched his hair; pulled a few of the strands straight so he could see their whiteness in his peripheral vision. How could so much have happened in such a short space of time?

First, he'd been struck by the Spirit of the Lights and trapped in the World Above; then he'd come back and caught the soul plague; and now he was orphaned. All in a single winter.

And then there was Tuomas.

That brought a new wave of fury as his face floated in Mihka's mind. He had loved that face once: his best friend, with whom he'd grown up and laughed. Now there was only hatred. All they had shared, which drew them together, was severed like the rip in the sky above. It hadn't been a clean cut; it had been rising for a while, ever since Tuomas began to change. Now he wasn't even human anymore and the final straw had come not a day ago, when Mihka had overheard everything.

He thought of the red fox ears, the tail, the way Tuomas spoke of Spirits. *He* was the reason Mihka's father was dead, as well as all the others who had fallen sick. He might not have murdered them with his own hands, but he had still killed them.

And despite everything, Mihka couldn't stop thinking of how the entire nightmare had started. Tuomas had gone into the Northlands by himself, risked his own life in the Long Dark, just to save Mihka's soul. It had all been for him.

Mihka's hands curled into fists so tight, his knuckles went white. Would it be worth asking the Poro caretakers if he could stay in their village? There was nothing left for him in Akerfjorden now. He could separate his reindeer and integrate them with the Poro herd. Then he wouldn't have to see Tuomas again; wouldn't have to think about him, or anything, ever again.

He kicked the logs, harder this time. They spilled out of the pit he had made for them and sizzled as they hit the snow. Smoke instantly began to fill the tent.

"No!" Mihka gasped. He quickly snatched one of his ski poles and manoeuvred them all back into the centre. Then he flung the flap aside and stepped out to tie it open. Now he'd near to air the place before he could bed down for the night. Idiot.

He closed his eyes. That was what Tuomas used to call him, in an affectionate way. Deep down, he supposed there was some truth in it. He was an idiot, but he didn't know any other way to be. Playing around, cracking jokes and pranks… But there was no place for that now.

Above, close to the cleft in the sky, the Moon Spirit let out a pulse of silvery light.

A long, low groan suddenly floated through the boughs.

Mihka looked up in confusion. He was the only person around here for miles – Poro was still several days' walk away.

He pulled his bow off his shoulder and nocked an arrow to the string.

"Hello?" he called. "Is someone here?"

His fingers curled around the sinew bowstring, ready to draw. Was it a wolf? He'd never heard one make a noise like that, but their howls could be twisted by wind and distance into something eerie.

He thought quickly. He hadn't seen any tracks. Maybe he was hearing things.

The groan came again. It was closer this time, but he couldn't figure out the direction. And while it definitely wasn't a wolf, something about it didn't sound human either.

Mihka swallowed nervously. The sound swept through him as though he wasn't there; the trees seemed to present more of an obstacle than his body did. His bones chilled, and beneath his coat, the hairs on his arms stood on end.

His initial wariness gave way to fear. Not wasting a moment, he ducked behind the nearest tree.

He had barely pressed his back against it when a great bang came from the other side. Mihka's heart pounded. Moving carefully, he peered around the side of the trunk.

He bit his lip to stop himself from screaming.

The boulder he'd propped his tent against was moving. It uncurled like a huge snail; rock splintered and rose into the bulk of a giant creature.

As it stirred, it seemed to soften into something lifelike. Its skin turned a horrid green-grey colour, more stone than flesh. It stood fifteen feet tall, long-limbed and stocky, its torso covered by moss and fronds of ice. It snatched at a nearby tree for balance and sent the snow cascading from the crown in soft whumps. With its other hand, it reached to its hip and withdrew a vicious flint blade as long as Mihka's arm.

Terror rooted him to the spot. It was a troll.

He had heard of these things before, in the old fireside stories, but had never really taken them seriously. They hadn't been seen for generations. It was thought they had all died long ago.

The troll turned around and poked at the shelter with its knife. Then it snatched the tarp and tore the whole thing off the skeleton of poles. It grabbed the sleeping sack and shook it hard. When nothing fell out, it dropped it.

With a low grunt, it slowly turned around, black eyes shining in the exposed firelight. Mihka quickly ducked back behind the tree before it could spot him. His hands shook on his bow. Arrows would be useless against that creature. It would be like trying to shoot a mountain.

He heard the troll sniffing like a hungry beast. Then it came closer.

Mihka held his breath and closed his eyes.